# THE DEVIL'S EYE

## OX DEVERE

This is a work of fiction. Unless otherwise indicated, all the names, characters, businesses, places, events and incidents in this book are either the product of the author's imagination or used in a fictitious manner.

Copyright © 2024 by Ox Devere

All rights reserved.

ISBN: 979-8-9895424-2-0

No part of this book may be reproduced in any form or by any electronic or mechanical means, including information storage and retrieval systems, without written permission from the author, except for the use of brief quotations in a book review.

*For the victims of October 7th*

Hell is empty and all the devils are here.

WILLIAM SHAKESPEARE

# CHAPTER ONE

*1582*

**LONDON, ENGLAND**

Hell had emptied itself into the skies of London.

That night in March, the sun had set as always. The canopy of night had unfurled, smudges of cloud drifting across the starry black.

Then it had appeared, at first like bloody shreds in the darkness. Within an hour, the sky rippled with flame. Peasants and gentry, nobility and monarchy all lifted their eyes in terror. The inferno had opened, not below but above. As the bloody glow settled on thatch roof and stone alike, cries for divine mercy trickled upward into the night.

From his cottage along the Thames River, one middle-aged man had watched with fascination. Nothing in his astrological studies had prepared him for this.

Whether it was the explosion of the heavens or the wrath of God, the man could not tear his eyes away from the molten sky. Until the wee hours of the night, he wandered in and out of the cottage, roaming from his overstuffed library out onto the dank streets of Mortlake.

The queen would surely call on him to divine this celestial omen. The council of her court was versed in economics, law, and the dastardly stabs of politics, but in matters of great portent and mystical truth, it was solely to John Dee that she turned.

Yet John Dee had not seen this coming.

Nor did he see coming the mysterious stranger who appeared at his door the next day, a young Englishman with deep, earnest eyes who wore a monk's cowl pulled over his ears.

He introduced himself to John Dee with determined charm, and said, "My name is Edward Kelly. I understand you have need of a scryer."

## 1588

It was only Kelly who could see the angels. Dee never could. Nor could he hear them. They spoke through the scryer alone, and their instructions were always detailed.

John Dee stood over the table in his library, fingertips grazing the quill that lay beside the open notebook. He gazed down at the wax piece in the center, an intricately carved seal as wide as a man's hand. It was a work of precision, down to every tiny etching and geometric measurement.

The Sigillum Dei Aemeth.

It had been the archangels Michael and Uriel themselves who had pronounced it "the true Circle of His eternity, comprehending all virtue." Finally, it was ready.

The angels were always right.

Kelly stood across from Dee at the table, holding a velvet pouch in one hand. A nervous twitch tugged at the fleshy edge of his mouth as he pulled out a smooth crystal. It was nearly the size of a fig, and so transparent that it looked more like an enormous drop of water than a stone.

Dee couldn't help but stare at it. They had crossed the Holy Roman Empire for this. They had ventured into the pagan lands of the Ottomans. They had knelt in the mud and dug a hole with their own hands...and found the buried talisman that had been foretold.

It was the Devil's Eye.

Kelly looked at him, then settled down into a chair. "You've said your prayers."

It was less a question than a statement, since Dee always prayed fervently before their sessions. He was desperate to understand the universe of God, to master the cosmic realm, to conjure the power of the divine. It was only through the supernatural gifts of this most unlikely scoundrel, Edward Kelly, that he had finally begun to receive the knowledge of the angels.

Dee picked up his quill and sat across the table from his scryer, who placed the enormous crystal on the wax seal. He hunched over and put his face down, peering through the stone at the etchings below.

The silence pressed into Dee. It was unbearable. His hand was poised over the open notebook.

Then Kelly cried out. He shot to his feet, stumbling back from the table with a sick, strangling noise.

The Devil's Eye lay still on the wax seal, but now Kelly stared at it in wordless horror.

"What..." But Dee could hardly get out the words.

In all their work together, in all of the beautiful and terrible things that Kelly had seen in crystals and in glass, he had never reacted like this.

"What do you see?"

Kelly looked up, fear shining out from his eyes.

"It is not for me," he croaked. "This is not meant for me."

Dee frowned and leaned forward to look into the crystal.

"No!" shouted Kelly.

He lunged, but he was not in time to stop his companion. Dee's eye settled over the clear stone, gazing down onto the seal beneath it.

From the night that the skies of hell opened over London, John Dee had believed that one day he would behold the purest glory and fullest fury of all existence. It had been the blazing omen of this path he would seek.

This step had been one too far.

Dee reeled back. His face went ashen. A whooshing roar began in his ears, and he had to grip the back of his chair to keep himself from collapsing.

When he looked up, Kelly was standing at the table again, his expression stricken.

"It's not meant for me," gasped Dee.

"It's meant for neither of us." Kelly shoved the pouch down over the crystal. "It will be for another."

He drew the strings tight, and fastened the Devil's Eye in a velvet tomb.

## CHAPTER TWO

*Present Day*

**WASHINGTON, D.C.**

SHE HAD ONLY MEANT to take a dawdling trip to the restroom.

Then Ridley Samaras saw the baby grand piano sitting unattended in the far corner of the dining room. It had been an age since she had sat in front of a row of ivories. She glanced quickly over her shoulder. To her relief, she couldn't see her table from here.

The restaurant was about the finest one could get in Washington, D.C. The clientele reeked of distinguished power. Dozens of them were scattered about a room laden with white linen and sparkling crystal. She could hardly believe she had agreed to dinner here. Then she had caught glimpses of slivered beef carpaccio and the warm scent of chocolate soufflé, and thought maybe she did belong.

Ridley slipped through the tables until she reached the baby grand. Sliding onto the bench, she looked down at the keys and took a deep breath of contentment.

She had been on a few bad dates before, but never one that had swirled the drain of boredom as quickly as this one had. Rachmaninoff would have to fix this.

As she stretched her broad hands over the keyboard and started to play *Rhapsody on a Theme of Paganini*, diners began to glance her way. Their eyes often lingered.

At five-eleven, with broad shoulders and dark gull-wing brows, she looked like something of an Amazon. Her height she had gotten from an Icelandic mother. Her thick mahogany hair she had gotten from her Greek father. It was swept up now, as stylish as she could get it on her own. She was striking, but not beautiful. Tonight she'd worn a sleeveless silk indigo top tucked into a thick belt, and a gray skirt that made the most of what curves she had. She'd even accentuated her amber-brown eyes with mascara and eyeshadow.

*Wish it had been worth the effort.*

As much as Ridley wished she could lose herself in music, she could never be "off" in public. She was aware of the gazes of the diners, as well as the surprised stares of waist-coated servers.

*Who would kick out a customer playing Rachmaninoff in a fairly competent way?*

Her fingers were airy but certain, flowing and dancing across the ivory. She just lacked the soaring melody of the string section to really send it.

She was nearly through the piece when she noticed a familiar figure who had appeared at the end of the bar.

He was in his mid-fifties, with tightly cropped silver hair and a light black complexion of ambiguous background. It had often allowed him to blend well into Middle Eastern countries. His mid-section now matched his shoulders for thickness, but his eyes never changed. They read everything and everyone in the vicinity. They had settled on her with a bemused admiration.

Booker Douglas swirled a lowball glass of bourbon in one hand.

Ridley finished out the piece. She rose from the bench immediately, not wanting any more attention from the rest of the diners. Even so, they watched her stride across the restaurant to the bar.

"You just *never* call, do you?" she said, leaning her forearms on the counter beside him.

"This is usually the only kind of assignment I get to give myself anymore," said Booker. "You know how much joy it gives an old man to flex his operational muscles now and then?"

"It's a stalking kind of flex."

"I'd ask how the date's going, but, uh...Paganini?" He nodded at the piano, then raised a brow at her.

"Oh, yeah," she said, glancing in the direction of the table she'd abandoned. "Don't you think an editor who rock climbs and works in nonfiction should be interesting?"

He shrugged. "Is this an editor in pants or a skirt?"

Ridley gave a sly smile.

"*His* name is Aiden. Friend of a friend who raced me up the rock wall at the gym. We tied on the climb. Not so much in conversation," she said, straightening up, "but this checkup on my love life better not be why you're here."

He gave a steady shake of his head. "We're not talkin' here, though. This place has *white carpets*. In a *restaurant*."

"Aiden swung really big."

"You need anything from your table?"

Ridley slipped a phone out from the thick buckle of her belt. "I travel light for emergency extractions."

He finished off his bourbon and slid the empty glass across the bar. "Poor guy."

. . .

Thirty minutes later, they were strolling along the Signers' Memorial. The small pond nearby glinted in the darkness. Ridley held a paper cup that steamed with hot chocolate, her wool coat drawn tight against the early December cold.

"Have you heard of John Dee?" asked Booker.

"I think in a video game once."

"You regularly surprise me."

"You never leave the office anymore except to stalk down your own operatives. You could use a little more surprise."

"If you're begging me to hire a shrink for mandatory sessions, I'll do it. Don't tempt fate, or Booker Douglas."

"Okay, who is John Dee?" said Ridley.

"I was hoping you'd ask! The most interesting man in the world. Mathematician, alchemist, conjurer, and the personal astrologist of Queen Elizabeth I. She had such confidence in him that she wouldn't agree to a coronation date until he'd divined the best day and time for her ultimate power and success."

"So he did something right because she was pretty ultimate."

"However it worked, it worked. He also proposed the idea of a 'British Empire.' At that time, Spain ruled everything, including the New World of the Americas. They had the navy. They had the riches. No one in Britain thought they could seriously compete. Except John Dee.

"*But* the man had no political aspirations. He just wanted to get paid and stay in a position of confidence with the queen, while understanding the entire universe. He really believed he could learn the original language of God—the language spoken to Adam in the Garden of Eden—by summoning angels in séances."

"You can summon angels in séances? I thought that was about talking to the dead, who might accidentally be demons."

"Yeah, well...sometimes angels are accidentally demons, too...but he thought he was on to it. Found himself a medium and recorded every session in detail, every interaction, every elaborate set of 'holy numbers' and names that they apparently gave him. Even took down an entirely new alphabet. *Enochian* language."

"Enochian, like Enoch, like the Book of Enoch?" she said, memories flaring up from all directions.

"Yeah, how 'bout them odds," Booker said, shaking his head though there was a creeping smile on his lips.

It wasn't their first encounter with the lore of the Book of Enoch. Ridley had locked into battle before with an extremely old order dedicated to the angel Raphael. Every one of their apocalyptic beliefs seemed to stem from that apocryphal tome, which told of God-appointed divine beings called Watchers, who governed tribes of humans but led them into dark practices, sinning against their own holy mandates.

The Watchers were banished from the earth, imprisoned by the archangels in darkness. Their sentence would last until the Day of Judgment, when they would finally be destroyed by God.

Unfortunately, a very fiery creature had been determined to set them loose ahead of schedule. Ridley had picked up that mission, long before she knew how colossal it would become in the stakes of world survival.

"I maybe need to read that thing," she said.

"You're a preparation fiend. Maybe you should. Anyhow, Dee's relics and scrying—that's crystal-reading and summoning—materials and notebooks are well documented, most of them in museums. But a new notebook just surfaced."

Ridley took a sip of her hot chocolate, waiting for the *what the hell is this really about*. Booker loved dramatic reveals.

"I can't get a clear picture on its provenance, which is disturbing me, to be honest...but it's just been sold at auction by Sotheby's, in London."

"How much?"

"Forty-one thousand."

"*Why?* Who paid that for a notebook?"

"Both reasons I stole you away from a date."

"Correction: I retired from the date."

"You're too young for that."

Some teenagers jostled down the walkway toward them, their laughter echoing across the park. One of them wore a Santa hat over her blond locks, another wore a wreath around his neck as he bellowed out "Deck the Halls."

Ridley smiled to herself as they passed, taking another swig of her hot chocolate. The warmth bloomed in her chest.

"The 'why,'" said Booker, "is because there's somethin' in it that makes it worth that to one man. Marc Pearson."

"I know *that* name. He's rich and rubs elbows with all the important people and is terrible."

"Fair summary. He's a financier for the rich and famous. Shadowy origins, to be honest...I haven't been able to string together just how he got to his position, or how much he's actually worth."

"*I?*" she said. "Not *we* as in the agency? Just you?"

"Come on, now. He's an American citizen. That's the FBI's jurisdiction," said Booker, though he broke a little smile. "The load of rumors around him would break an eighteen-wheeler, though. Everything from arms trafficking to sex trafficking to being a protected asset or double agent."

"So why do you care that he bought a four hundred-year-old notebook? You have *no* idea what's in it?"

They rounded the memorial stones along the bank of the

water, each with the signature of a Founding Father etched into it. Booker looked down at them with sober respect.

"Every one of these guys..." he murmured, "like a death warrant when they put their name on that declaration. Ben Franklin was seventy. That guy there, Thomas Lynch," he pointed. "Twenty-six years old. What a move."

He shook his head in amazement and turned back to Ridley.

"Pearson's gotten into the occult, but he hasn't gone after the rest of Dee's items. Why this one? He's shown no interest in donating it to a museum. A lost notebook is one thing, but Pearson... he's just...doesn't seem the type to stock a private library. There's no history of him ever buying a book of any value." He shook his head. "John Dee's the most towering figure in the history of the occult, and frankly, he was into some..." he hesitated, "real stuff."

Booker had an exceptional Spidey-sense for the dangerous, the mystical, the macabre. He found threads in this world that led to dark and damaging places.

Running a clandestine unit within the CIA called Osprey, he assigned missions that altered history. Every one of them left a mark on the operatives who carried them out. No one came out of Osprey seeing the world the same way as when they'd entered.

"So you want that book," said Ridley.

"I want that book, but I'll settle for a copy."

She leaned back to look at him. "You have an inside guy."

He shrugged in false modesty. "You know I'm a real people person."

"Who am I running this with?"

Having settled partners was not the custom for Osprey work. Operatives were paired together for mission-specific skill sets. Things were so compartmentalized that the entire unit had never even been gathered together in the same room.

Ridley personally knew half a dozen of them, and knew *of* another four. Some of them—herself included—tended more to the military skills of the Special Ops. Some were more inclined to the nerdy and knowledgeable, but whatever the needs of a mission, Booker was a master of matchmaking.

He dug his hands deeper into the pockets of his shearling coat.

"Me."

## CHAPTER
# THREE

**ALEXANDRIA, VIRGINIA**

"You," said Ridley in disbelief. "Book, sir..."

Booker hadn't been out in the field in over a decade. Like any former operative might say, his active duty had been the best of times and the worst of times. It had grated his psyche, scarred his body, and eroded his ties to his wife and kids.

It had also been the most thrilling, most vivid and purposeful time in his life.

His years in an office at Langley, researching and plotting and strategizing missions for the operatives now under his command, had a sense of weighty responsibility to them. He was adept at what he did, with a keen eye for trouble in some of the strangest corners of the world.

A glass of Bulleit bourbon and his leather recliner were the only luxury comforts Booker usually wanted at the end of these creaky days. Yet not a week passed when he didn't ache to be out there himself alongside the doers.

"Don't think you can crack a joke about this that I haven't

already thought of," he replied, "and besides, I'm funnier than you about 'em."

She gave him the once-over. "That's no way to bond with a new partner."

"It's the start of your education on this one. I'm a dilettante when it comes to a lotta things, just finding my way through the first few layers, but I'll tell you this, I could get a PhD in all things John Dee. Been something of a fascination of mine for years, and since this guy made up his own language—or transcribed it from the angels, as he'd say—there's no amount of research you can do on a plane ride to get up to speed for it."

Osprey required a great deal of learning for every operative. Beyond just the basic mission-briefing, which was often open-ended and speculative, immersing oneself in background and opposition research was imperative. Ridley was obsessive about using every spare moment of transportation time to dig for and cram in the information. It had saved her in moments of crisis more times than she could count.

"You're stuck with me," he said. "This is the mission."

She shook her head and drained the last of her hot chocolate.

"So when do we load out?"

Her mind spun the whole ride home.

Thickly padded against the cold, Ridley skimmed through Old Town on her Indian Scout Bobber. The sleek black motorcycle had enchanted her the moment she laid eyes on it, and even in the winter, it was her transportation of choice.

She parked in an alleyway between two townhouses and walked out onto the sleepy street. It suited her between jobs, a quiet neighborhood with leafy sidewalks and an abundant population of pets. Even in this cold, there were a few pedestrians out with their dogs for a late-night walk.

As Ridley entered her front door, her own little mutt came scampering across the hardwood.

"Maddie, you miss me? *Did* you? Did you really?"

She dropped into a crouch to maul and be mauled by the wriggling happy scruff of a dog. The little rescue was the silent type, but those watchful doe eyes never left Ridley when they were together. Leaving Maddie behind was always the hardest part of taking a mission, danger ahead be damned.

Ridley snapped a leash on her and went outside. Maddie sniffed every snowbank around the block as her human sifted through what little she knew of her fresh assignment.

Booker was one of the sharpest people she'd ever known, but he was inescapably rusty. The man's girth had grown as thick as his shoulders over the last few years, and she doubted he trained with firearms or any type of weapon more often than every few months.

*An AARP liability.*

There was no room in their work for drag. She demanded as much from her teammates as she gave. It was a standard that had alienated some former partners, her relentless work ethic. Some may have thought it military residue, but there was a streak in Ridley that had always been insatiable.

She had grown up a nomad. Her mother had died in a swimming accident when Ridley was three years old. Though she had managed to save her little daughter from an undertow, she went under herself, and never surfaced. It took days to recover her body. Ridley's memories of her were snatches, impressions, quicksilver images and the sound of her voice.

The loss had destroyed her father. He traveled abroad as a project manager for a construction company. Much of his work at that time was in Europe. When his wife died, he became a shell of himself, a man who worked to the bone because he didn't know what else to do. He towed Ridley and her older brother, Alexios, along with him on his travels.

The siblings made their own path, picking up a new language every year, finding new ways to get into scraps in every city they landed in.

Summers they'd spend with their grandmother, Charis, in the Greek islands. She had a business running horseback-riding tours, so by the time Ridley was twelve, she was leading groups around the island on her favorite chestnut mare.

When the tourists had gone, she and Alexios raced bareback along the beach. They swam in the salty bright waters of the Aegean until she thought her lungs would burst. She sneaked extra *loukomades* from the counter whenever her grandmother's back was turned. The smell of the baking honey-glazed doughnut holes made her nearly dizzy with craving.

That island was the only place that ever felt like home.

Eventually, Alexios decided he wanted something more conventional. She could hardly believe it when he told her that he was going back to the States to get a law degree. How could her brother—who had set off fireworks on the banks of the Seine, who had sneaked her into a club in Berlin so raunchy that she almost heaved in a bathroom caked with powders and fluids of all colors—the brother she was always trying to out-race and out-wrestle—how could he choose such a mundane career?

Nevertheless, he left.

A year later, their grandmother died.

Ridley had been in Milan with her father. He had put his fist through a table in an outburst of grief. She'd walked the stone streets alone until the early hours of the morning, nearly catatonic.

At seventeen, she was adrift, too old to cling to the wisps of childhood and too alone to settle anywhere.

As she arrived back at her townhouse, Ridley stomped the snow from her boots and gave Maddie a nip of bison jerky. She changed into loungers and a *Stranger Things* t-shirt, then saw that there were four unread texts on her phone, all from her abandoned date.

She sucked air in through her teeth and winced at the screen.

*Oh yikes...Aiden.*

She typed back the minimum.

**Sorry, I got called away with work**

Whatever he texted back, she didn't even check. Her social night was officially over.

Ridley walked to the small desk in the corner of her bedroom, knocking the side of her head and stretching out her jaw as if she had water in her ear.

It was half-subconscious, half-ritualized, but "the water" would never come out. The slight muffle in that eardrum would never disappear.

She pulled out a small black laptop from one of the drawers and opened it. It was a "black box" that the head Osprey technician, Ted, had given to her...an anonymous ghost of a machine. It required a combination of passcode responses in addition to a retinal scan. Once on it, she could search any corner of the open internet or dark web without leaving behind a trace of her activities.

She was convinced that there was a backdoor hack to access even this device, because every fortress had a chink somewhere. She could only hope it wouldn't be worth anyone's time and effort to break hers. Ridley needed something that could be kept away from agency eyes.

Because on this device, she was putting together a file on Andreas Colby.

He was a billionaire, a real estate developer who owned properties all over the country. He owned the American football team the Miami Dolphins and the English football team Leeds United. He was on his third wife now, had four children of various interest to the tabloids, and was an avid skier, spending at least a month at St. Moritz every year.

He was also a high-ranking member of the Order of Raphael.

When the Templars had been dismantled after the Crusades, their wings fairly crushed by both the king of France and the pope, the few remaining knights had fled to Portugal for refuge. There, some of them moderated into nothing more than a social order.

Yet some of them grew ferocious, militant, and ambitious. They broke off from the moderates and named themselves after the angel that was said to have banished God's "Watchers" after they bespoiled mankind.

Today, the Order displayed a frightening reach. They seemed to be the kudzu of international organizations, a vine that could not be sourced and could not be stopped.

Ridley had discovered their existence while on her last mission. They were violent, single-minded, and maddeningly powerful. The lieutenant leading the Raphaels she encountered had unleashed an unholy terror in Jerusalem. Ridley had put a bullet through his brain.

But there was a Grand Master somewhere behind it all, living in near total secrecy. After Ridley had killed that Raphael commander in Jerusalem, she had found out that the next in the chain of command was Andreas Colby.

By the way the Order of Raphael had demonstrated its power, they were a threat to everything she worked to protect, to missions both current and future. She had to find her way to the Grand Master, no matter how long it took.

It wasn't her assignment, but Ridley couldn't let go of the Colby lead. She had told Booker about him, but had not included that she was working up a file of her own. When the time was right, she would show her work.

The progress—if she'd really made any progress at all to speak of—was laboriously slow. This would be the last night for a while that she could devote to the Colby file. It was time to hustle.

Tomorrow she'd make her last rounds at home, going to jiu-jitsu class early in the morning, swimming laps at the Olympic pool at her local gym, taking Maddie for a long, cold walk along the river, eating her traditional "last meal" of a crab cake sandwich at The Wharf, and pretending once again to the regulars that she was traveling abroad with her diplomat boss to translate his meetings.

She would pack under the forlorn gaze of Maddie. Then she'd drop off her beloved mutt at her neighbor Ana's apartment, scrub that adoring and wistful little face goodbye, and leave on the red-eye out of Dulles.

With the strangest partner-pairing of her entire career with Osprey.

The boss himself.

## CHAPTER FOUR

**EAST LOTHIAN, SCOTLAND**

Ophelia "Effie" Crowhurst swanned through the crowded Marble Hall of Gosford House, a champagne flute dangling from one hand, looking like an actress who'd just won her third Oscar. A regal brunette, she paused frequently amidst the guests to flash her huge, brilliant smile, stroke an arm, or drop a saucy jibe.

Even here within the elite of the upper crust, she was the most dazzling and vivid thing in the room.

"Jeff!" she exclaimed, stopping near a lanky man in a tuxedo. "Oh, Lily, this is wonderful you're here, too," she said to the Botox blonde on his arm.

They greeted her enthusiastically, with kisses on the cheek. They were one of the couples Effie had marked out as needing to personally greet that night. Jeff Mascom, CEO of Morgan Stanley, and Lily Mascom, married twenty-two years with five affairs between them. None of those had been with Effie, though she'd casually considered it.

"Are you and Marc joining us tomorrow at Number One?" asked Jeff.

"Oh, I don't think so, darlings, but Mathew there makes a veal sweetbread tortellini that—" she moaned and bit her lip, "will *do* things to you. Book a room upstairs for the hour."

Jeff and Lily both laughed, embarrassed but also accustomed to Effie's salacious humor.

"I'll send Marc 'round once I find him," she promised, excusing herself.

The Doctors Abroad Institute was deeply grateful for the support of Marc Pearson and Effie Crowhurst, but they may have been even more grateful for their guest list.

The gala could have been put on to save the Madagascar tomato frogs and the A-list would still have turned out. As too many charities understood, it was often less about the cause than about the scene one could create. Marc and Effie *were* that scene.

Gosford House was a palatial estate that faced down the iron waters of the Atlantic. Despite the lashing winter winds, the rich and famous had arrived at their little party en masse, a parade of stars in the darkness.

Silk and satin gowns shimmered throughout the manor. Masterpiece paintings adorned the open halls, which were decked with wreaths and baubles and bows of every Christmas sort. The lights of a giant tree twinkled in the corner of the great hall.

Effie worked her way through the guests...a Pulitzer Prize-winning author who had been making the rounds for her new book...a reclusive tech mogul whose taste for bizarre endeavors was legendary...the most high-profile defense lawyer in America, self-styled heir to Johnny Cochran...the silver-haired founder of an international modeling agency...

At least half of these people clung to dirty little secrets, and she knew them like a favorite book. It gave her a thirsty thrill to recall each one.

As she wandered into the parlor, she caught sight of a tall man with sloped shoulders, a receding hairline, and a broad-mouthed overbite. Surrounded by a small crowd, he wore a gray and red kilt with an impeccably tailored black jacket studded with silver. Despite the quality of his clothing, he still managed to look rumpled, with a goofy grin.

For the first time, Effie broke into a genuine smile of delight.

As she approached him, he caught her eye and began to beam.

"Ophelia, you vision."

"Bertie."

She greeted the prince with a kiss on the cheek. Albert was the youngest son of the late queen, the king's brother, and the boyishly charismatic black sheep of the family. Effie had known him since university, as they shared the same social circles. It was she who had introduced him to Marc. It was she who had spun his predilections into the tightest of webs, an insurance policy that would open any door in the UK that wasn't already available to her.

"Where's your shy suitor?" he asked, glancing about.

"I've a few guesses, but I know he's waiting for a special guest tonight. Very odd."

Albert's brows rose. "Oh?"

"Not that, you filthy man-stick. She's some kind of professor."

He laughed, "Of what?"

Effie took a sip of her champagne and forced a smile. "The Elizabethan-era occult!"

"Ah, Marc and his hobbies."

"I'll find you later, darling."

She squeezed his arm and glided off. Following the sound of

string music to the cavernous Octagon Room, she found a chamber ensemble set up in one corner. The room had twinkling crystals on high-top tables and walls filled up to the ceiling with classical paintings. There was a bar in front of the towering windows. That was where she finally spotted him.

Marc Pearson was somewhat unremarkable at first glance, nearly five-ten with silvery hair buzzed close to his scalp. In his late fifties, his great doe eyes now crinkled at the edges, and deep lines framed a boyish grin. He was trim and fit from his obsessive routine of morning laps in the pool and hot yoga in the evenings. He looked delicious in the scarlet smoking jacket he wore now, standing alone, waiting for a drink from the bartender.

As she headed toward him, she realized where his gaze was fixed.

The musicians in the corner sat in a semi-circle: a leading violinist, a viola player, French horn, clarinet, bassoon, cello, and double bass. They played with delicacy and vigor.

Most of them looked to be in their twenties and thirties, but the violinist was conspicuously young, an angelic-looking blonde playing with deep focus.

"Surely that's not your professor," said Effie, sidling up to his arm.

"A prodigy, to play with adults like that," said Pearson. "She's amazing."

"It's Beethoven. Opus twenty."

He gave her an impressed glance.

"You think I wasted *all* my time at bloody Oxford?"

He had risen to the top of the world in shadow, but she was still his cultural guide and social grease. Marc Pearson was a blue-collar boy from Philly who suffered from social anxiety in large groups, though he had his private charms.

In fact, the longer someone spent in conversation with Marc

Pearson, the handsomer he became. Effie knew this intimately, though she herself could hardly stand those extended one-on-ones. She would rather be the life of the party than sit down with a single person and talk for hours on end. Public charm drew adoring crowds. Private flattery took far too much effort, unless there was something tangible in it for her.

Pearson watched the ensemble in admiration as the diving, dancing strings of Beethoven's opus reached their climax. When the piece ended, he joined in the light applause.

"Who are they?" he asked. "Where are they from?"

"Haven't a clue. I'm sure Isidora booked them."

"That violinist."

The girl was indeed lovely, almost ethereal. She couldn't have been more than fifteen to Effie's keen eye, but probably even younger, for the way that young teenage girls try to dress themselves up to appear older. She was smiling in modest appreciation of the applause, bracing her violin against her thigh.

"At that age, to be playing like that..." Pearson shook his head, amazed.

Effie knew what he wanted.

She pushed herself off the bar, heading toward the dispersing musicians. It was quick work to intercept the girl.

"Darling, that was absolutely brilliant. What a performance," she said, beaming at the young musician.

"Oh, thank you, ma'am."

The girl fidgeted through her smile, used to getting such adulation but still a bit uncomfortable with it.

"No, please, no 'ma'am' for me! Call me Effie. I insist on that."

"I'm Lexi," she said in an American accent, then added, "Rapp."

"How old are you, love?"

"Fourteen."

"Mm, extraordinary. You know of Nicola Benedetti, the Scottish prodigy? You remind me of her at a young age, though you're even more beautiful."

Lexi fidgeted through a grin, her eyes going wide. "No way, she's incredible. And she's gorgeous."

"I've met her several times."

It wasn't true, but it was plausible. Effie could meet anyone in the world she desired.

"Where are you studying?" she asked.

"Edinburgh Music School."

"Oh, love, you really belong in a better school than Edinburgh. Do you know St. Mary's there?"

Lexi seemed to sense that she had just tumbled into the deep end of a marvelous world. "That's one of the best."

"You know what?" said Effie. "Marc is co-host this evening. He's such a tremendous supporter of the arts, but especially loves helping young musicians. He says that all he can give them is money, but they can give him the sublime! Actually... would you like to meet him?"

The girl's eyes went wide. "I—I still have to play..."

Effie glanced over at Marc. He was by the bar, but now a willowy young woman with soft blue eyes and the look of a model was leaning over his shoulder, speaking discreetly.

Isidora. He'd bought her in Serbia when she was fourteen and groomed her into the perfect personal assistant.

As she murmured into his ear, Marc's eyes went to the door of the Octagon Room.

The professor was here.

## CHAPTER FIVE

**EAST LOTHIAN, SCOTLAND**

MARC PEARSON SHUT the heavy oak door behind him. A glass of whiskey in hand, he turned to face his guest.

The ornate library with towering shelves and velvet couches seemed to both thrill and intimidate Professor Lianna Powell. The rich, famous, and powerful came in all shapes and sizes, but she appeared quite uncomfortable, an outsider in this opulent house.

She was nearly five-nine, a solid woman who'd grown a bit softer than she'd like over a lifetime in the classroom. Her blonde bangs and celestial blue eyes had given her a cherubic appearance when she was younger, but now her face had thickened, and the slight cleft in her chin gave her the appearance of some weary mum from a tenement project.

Now she clutched a champagne flute and gazed about the library in wonder.

"Professor," said Pearson, with a smile of genuine delight. "I'm so glad you're here. I've had enough dripping small talk for the night."

He gestured to the couches, taking a seat himself.

"Please, join me!"

"Very happy to be invited, thank you," replied Lianna, her accent pure Manchester, her voice almost shockingly soft.

She sat down across from him, careful not to muss the black and gray dress she'd borrowed for the evening. Sequins ribboned through it like tendrils of smoke, and she thought it was the finest she'd looked in years.

"*You're* the guest of the night for me," he said. "Thank you for coming."

"I spoke with Isidora, was it?"

"My assistant."

"Afraid she didn't tell me much about this. Have to say I was a bit surprised, Mr. Pearson. Professors of history at St. Andrews don't get invited to places like..." she waved a hand upward.

"You're the woman I need," said Pearson, leaning forward onto his knees, "and you look sensational, by the way."

He had a way of paying such compliments that landed. His ability to discern people's deepest needs was unrivaled. In a one-on-one conversation, he could bond with almost anyone. They'd walk away feeling like the most important person in his life.

Lianna could hardly conceal her swell of pleasure at being called sensational-looking. It wasn't the kind of word men used for her.

And Pearson knew this, of course.

"You know," he said, "I wasn't even looking for the *nearest* expert when I found you. I was looking for the premier historian for all things John Dee, and I couldn't believe it when they said you were at St. Andrews! Was the car ride comfortable enough for you?"

"Yes, yes, it was really nice. Beautiful car. Thank you for sending it."

"Well, my driver will be ready to take you home whenever you'd like. Though I hope you do get to stay and enjoy yourself for a while after we chat. You know Sam Kweku is here tonight?"

"No! Really?"

Pearson always did background on his meetings. Professor Lianna Powell rarely used social media for much else beside posting photos of the rugged cliffs of St. Andrews or mornings spent over a mug of tea in the nearby bakery. But she did post about her favorite TV show, a brutal gangster saga set in London, and those posts seemed to always include a photo of its handsome Ghanaian star.

So Pearson had of course invited the actor to the gala, though it was more as a gesture of goodwill than anything else. He had no doubts that Professor Powell would be saying yes to his proposal.

"I'll introduce you, of course! He's a lovely guy."

"Oh, I'd love that. But, Mr. Pearson, I'd like to understand why you've invited me here."

"Please, I'd like it if you called me Marc. And let me show you something."

He set his whiskey glass on the coffee table and went over to the desk. Crouching down, he punched open a safe and pulled out a pouch the size of a briefcase. He carried it back to the couches and set it down between him and Lianna.

"You probably already know about this piece, but I bought a little treasure for myself last week."

He pulled a notebook slowly from the pouch and set it on the coffee table. Lianna's mouth went slack. She reflexively grabbed his nearby whiskey glass and ran it to the desk, setting it down with her own champagne flute well out of the spill zone.

She dropped back down to the couch and stared in wonder at what Pearson had laid before her.

The notebook was thin and decrepit, probably no more than seventy-five pages. The leather binding was dry and cracked. Even before he opened it, though, she knew.

"It's the lost Dee notebook," she breathed.

Pearson delicately pulled back the front cover. "In shockingly good condition given its age. Its provenance is unclear, but it's authentic."

She bent low over the brittle pages and lifted a hand. "May I?"

"Of course."

Lianna turned the first blank page with the barest of touches. The second was filled with an elegantly scribbled cursive.

"Oh, it's authentic indeed. That's his handwriting. Oh, my God."

*The Trail to That Which is Hidden, as Instructed by The Angels to Dr. John Dee*

"I gotta say," started Pearson, "I'm just an amateur with Dee stuff, but I wasn't able to find anything in any of his other writings about this thing called 'the Devil's Eye.'"

Lianna couldn't tear her eyes from the notebook as she turned its pages. "I'll be honest, I've never heard of it, either."

There was a long pause as Pearson watched her read the handwriting of Dee, which he found nearly illegible.

After a moment, she murmured, "Bloody hell, Ken."

His brow arched. "It's Marc."

"Sorry, Mr. Marc...you've...really got something here."

He leaned forward intently. "What, what?"

A smile stole across her lips. "You've got a treasure hunt."

# CHAPTER SIX

**LONDON, ENGLAND**

Ridley couldn't remember the last time she'd been to London for pleasure, but in a city like this, it was probably best to be on the company card, anyhow.

It was an unusually snowy December in Europe, and southern England was frosted clean white. Ridley and Booker had walked Oxford Street under its curtains of dangling star lights. Christmas decorations twinkled out of the shopfronts. Even the red of the passing double-deckers seemed more festive in the veil of snow.

They'd made their way to Willows on the Roof, where they now sat in a transparent "igloo" styled as a ski chalet. Each transparent igloo sparkled with lights overhead, had two leather couches with fur throws, a small table in the center, and a little electric stove for warmth.

It was private, cozy, and a top-notch choice, as they told their contact.

Tom Sterling sat across from them, a ruddy blond chap with a pleasant but bland face. Ridley appreciated the appearance.

*He would have made a great spy. A gray man. Indistinct and immediately forgettable.*

"We've had two different scholars verify it," he said in a thick, melodic Scouse accent. "That's the hand of John Dee."

Booker worked on a stack of cheese and meat from the charcuterie board. "What's the provenance?"

"Eh, that's vague, gotta admit. We can't trace it far. Came to us through an intermediary, who found it in an old estate sale down by Fulham, near where Dee lived."

"Does it need translation?" asked Ridley.

Sterling gestured to Booker. "This bloke can handle that."

He reached into the satchel beside him and grabbed a miniature data stick, then pulled out a small printed booklet. It was thick with a plain cover.

"Printed and bound, one for you to handle. And one digital."

He handed them both to Booker, who had to wipe his hands before taking them. As he started to look through the pages, Ridley spoke through a mouthful of sweet potato fritter.

"Nothing really suspicious, then."

Sterling shrugged. "Not from our view at Sotheby's. The buyer didn't seem to have any problems with its provenance. He snapped that up right quick, just lay down a bid double the closest competition and walked out with it."

"Who was the closest competitor?"

"Auction regular. Nothin' that old eccentric won't buy. Doubt he even really knew who John Dee was."

Booker sat forward, almost stricken to attention as he stared down at the notebook in his hand.

"Dee always wanted a treasure hunt," he said in disbelief. "Looks like he made one himself."

Ridley peered over her boss' shoulder as he flipped through the pages. They were full of scribblings, tiny graphs, tables, and complex diagrams. Many of the characters were foreign to her, as if Dee had been using a wholly different alphabet.

"When you say 'treasure,' do you mean 'tin' or 'bread' or 'nuggets of wisdom?'" she said, "Because I thought he was poor and always in debt."

Booker had given her the John Dee 101 course on their trans-Atlantic flight. It had been like drinking from a firehose.

"He was...but he also did everything the spirits told him to do, or that his scryer *said* they'd told him. Looks like this was a treasure they told him he couldn't have, so he hid it somewhere."

Booker's fingers traced the words of Dee's opening paragraph.

"You horn-mad dogfish..."

Ridley cracked a fast grin. Whenever Booker hit the threshold at which anyone else would swear, he reached for a wild phrase instead.

"What is it, come on," she said.

"I've never even heard of this. He had a crystal he called the Devil's Eye, and they only used it once, and it showed 'unspeakable horror.' Spirits said it wasn't for him or his scryer, but they gave him instructions...hide it, bury it away somewhere secret. Leave a trail for the worthy, for the one meant to find it...to use it."

Sterling nodded grimly. "That part we got."

"Why would anyone want a crystal that only shows them unspeakable horror?" said Ridley.

"Someone wanted the map to it, to the tune of thirty-one thousand pounds."

Booker flipped the page and read for a moment. His partner's leg juddered with impatience, and then he actually laughed.

"Ah, sorry," he said, "but of course. Never just a shiny, expensive rock someone wants..."

"'Splain," said Ridley.

Booker placed the notebook flat on the table. On the page was an intricate drawing. It was a circular seal. The outer circle contained a heptagon; and inside that, a heptagram; and inside that, more angular encirclements; and in the very center, a pentagram. Every layer was absolutely riddled with numbers, letters, and strange characters.

"I've seen that," she said, staring intently.

"Looks like Solomon's Seal, doesn't it?" said Booker. "Close, close. Pentagrams. The modern West sees them and thinks 'Satanism,' but they go back as far as ancient Sumer. Used to be a symbol for ancient Jerusalem, even. Christians in the Middle Ages thought it was about all kinds of good things, from the five wounds of Christ to the five virtues of knighthood...then it started to get mangled. The 'wickedest man in the world' got hold of it and probably drove it into the occult for good. Aleister Crowley. He was a waste of space."

But it was Solomon's Seal that gave Ridley flashbacks. That little ring had nearly ignited the three major religions of the world.

*Memories.*

Booker went on. "But *this* is the Sigillum Dei Aemeth. Dee didn't even create the first sigillum dei—means seal of God—but this is his first, which he thought was the *true* seal. Obviously. And it's gotta be made out of wax, to the proper dimensions, to be the real thing. Aaand...this all contains the power of the Holy Spirit and, if you activate it, can control all creation and commune with the angels."

"It's a wonder that's just sitting around on the internet," said Ridley, "and everyone's just shooting each other for power instead."

"Yeah, ya think? Nobody's figured out how to activate it, or the *right* person hasn't figured out how to activate it, or—"

"It's a load of horsehit."

Sterling chuckled and leaned back on his couch. "Sorry I won't get to see this partnership at work."

Booker's voice became iron. "Ridley's seen enough of the strange and unearthly, but she always seems to restart in the same place."

She picked up her glass of mulled wine, stinging a little at the reproof.

It wasn't true, but it was close enough to the truth that she hated it. She felt like she had changed. With the things she'd seen, the unearthly forces that she'd faced...she would have to be braindead to not have been affected by it. Sometimes, though, it felt like she had just been seeing mirages in the desert. The oasis must be out there, but she was hesitant to settle on one.

"It's not about whether I believe it," she clarified to Sterling. "It's about whether the other guy believes it."

"Why would it matter if the other guy believes it, if it's not true?"

"You wouldn't believe the amount of damage a true believer can cause," said Ridley. "So, the Devil's Eye must be the missing piece, the way to activate all these holy powers."

Booker looked up from the pages with a wry grin at Sterling. "See, this is why she's here."

The Scouser toasted the air with his own cocktail.

"Appears you'd be right," said Booker. "With all the powers of the universe at his fingertips and he *hid* the thing..."

"Must have scared the fu—daylights outta him," said Ridley. "If this notebook is all about a treasure hunt, and Marc Pearson was willing to pay for it, then we're gonna have some stiff competition for it. Real quick."

"Oh, they'll be the best you can get with a bottomless bank account."

"Even he can't afford *the* best," she said, taking a long swig of the mulled wine.

"You probably wouldn't have to pay a Dee expert much...not a high-earning profession."

Booker turned the page. His brow furrowed in concentration.

"This is odd..."

Ridley peered over his shoulder. Half the page was covered with a honeycomb-like pattern. On the other half was a cluster of hexagonal columns, drawn as if to be 3D.

"He did write the preface to the English translation of Euclid's *Elements*," said Booker, "but this doesn't really look like geometry. It's more like doodling."

At the bottom of the page was written the word *HEBUDES*.

Booker's eyes lit up.

"Well it looks like John Dee went to just about the ends of the earth to hide the Devil's Eye. Ridley, when's the last time you dived?"

# CHAPTER
# SEVEN

### THE HEBRIDES, SCOTLAND

ON AN AVERAGE DAY in spring or summer, the western isles of Scotland would be sprinkled with tourists puttering around in sightseeing boats, snapping pictures of every crumbling stone, and hiking over the ragged green slopes.

On a day like this in December, though, the Hebrides islands were practically barren.

A leaden sky loomed close over the fierce iron sea. Booker sat by the motor at the back of the large dinghy, bundled in a thick parka, hood pulled up tight. Water slapped against the rubber sides as they raced along.

Ridley sat near the middle, huddled against the ripping wind in her own parka and gloves. Beneath them, she wore a diving drysuit.

She'd felt a flush of adrenaline in the first second that she'd pulled it on, but had shrugged it away to finish suiting up.

In the years since her accident, Ridley had swum bare-skinned thousands of times. It was part of her every week. She needed the water around her almost as much as she needed to consume it to live. In those same years, she'd donned a wetsuit dozens of times for snorkeling and scuba-diving.

But a drysuit...she hadn't worn one since it happened.

She hadn't *always* wanted to be a Navy SEAL, but when the thought settled on her in her late teens, it utterly obsessed her. It was an apex challenge.

No woman had ever gone through that harrowing crucible, that grit-in-your-teeth, blood-in-your-mouth, every-muscle-screaming regimen of training that produced some of the finest warriors in the world.

She knew she had rare physical capabilities. At five feet and eleven inches with a gas tank that could run for days and the upper body strength that had always rivaled her brother's, she had a solid foundation. Yet it was her mental ferocity and extraordinary swimming prowess that would distinguish her from the majority of her peers.

So she had joined the Navy. She excelled. She applied to join the SEALs and was accepted, stunning her fellow soldiers. She passed the indoctrination training pipeline.

When she was accepted into BUD/S: Basic Underwater Demolition/Sea Air Land, it made headlines on every military website in the nation. She was the great exception, a groundbreaking soldier, a frontier-setting woman whose identity was strictly kept anonymous to the public at large. None of her two hundred classmates let her forget it, nor did any of the instructors. She ate shit for it every day. Anyone who stood out as a "star" without having earned it was bound to get hammered down.

Ridley endured it all, and discovered that the physical challenges were the least of her difficulties. At its core, the twenty-four week BUD/S course was about selecting those who were the best at high level problem-solving under extreme physical stress.

She thought she'd finally found her place in the world, her purpose.

*Some people's stories don't go the way the way they're supposed to.*

The morning of the accident, the sky over the coast of California had looked nearly as gloomy as this December day above Scotland. She'd felt a pressurized ache in her right ear, just the faintest touch of what might be an infection, but every day of training had been riddled with countless aches and pains. There was no reason why this should be anything but another mark of misery along the journey.

So she'd gone on the dive that day.

*That day. That damn day.*

A rogue underwater wave—freakish and invisible—had slammed into her right side.

Something exploded in her head. The volt of pain sent her reeling, but she quickly realized it wasn't just the pain that was disorienting. Her entire equilibrium was being sloshed about, blinding her to which way was up.

By the time she found one of the underwater ropes and her teammates hauled her into the boat, it was already over for her.

Ridley would never again be able to dive to depth. She would never regain full hearing in her right ear. She would never become a Navy SEAL.

She had failed.

She hadn't realized a purpose again until Booker found her in the Navy ranks, finishing out her service, rudderless and angry.

Earlier that morning when Booker had seen her emerge in the drysuit, there was a palpable watchfulness in his gaze.

*He was probably a good operative but his poker face has gone to shit.*

She didn't let him ask, though he didn't seem inclined to.

The boss took care with each of the Ospreys. He was even fond of some of them, and had a casual, affectionate relationship with a few. Some ribbed him like a favorite uncle. But he wasn't their father. He let them be unless he saw something that would interfere with their professional capacity. He certainly wouldn't play "shrink-the-old-wounds" out in the field. Mission was paramount.

Ridley was grateful for it. That was what she needed.

The dark lump on the horizon grew as the dinghy sliced toward the Isle of Staffa. Booker finally slowed the motor as they approached.

"This looks fake," said Ridley, peering up.

Once-molten lava had emerged from the sea and cooled quickly, forming into geometric shafts of basalt that appeared as if they'd been chiseled.

It looked like a black chia pet on top of a mass of steel rods.

Straight ahead of them, a gash in its side loomed black and deep.

"You can see how legends begin," said Booker, steering for the cavern.

Ridley pulled off her coat and readied for the dive. She'd insisted on getting her equipment from Northern Diver, which supplied the UK's Royal Navy. The drysuit was triple-glued and rubber-taped on the seams, with Kevlar kneepads and hard-soled boots.

She slid a flexi-light into the pocket on her upper right arm, and a 5" SOG SEAL Strike knife into the one on the thigh. She pulled on Bio Ranger Fins, half the length of regular flippers, wide and split-finned. They were easier to navigate small spaces with and much easier to walk in.

"Look at this place!" exclaimed Booker as they reached the mouth of the cavern.

"Did Harry Potter destroy a horcrux here?" said Ridley, re-checking both the main and bailout cylinders on her small breathing tank.

"Better. John Dee hid his first clue. How the hell he even knew this place existed...wasn't 'officially discovered' until the eighteenth century."

Fingal's Cave. So strange, so harsh and beautiful and grand that it had drawn the likes of Keats and Tennyson. Mendelsohn composed an overture for it. Jules Verne wrote of it. Queen Victoria had made the journey to see it. Pink Floyd had even written a song named after it.

Booker stared up at the ceiling of the cave, a rugged rock cathedral.

"*Eternally swept by a deep and swelling sea...*" he said, "*it baffles all description.*"

"Was that Dee?"

"Sir Walter Scott. Poets live for a sight like this, but then it torments them for life. Some things just have to be seen."

Ridley slid the tank onto her back. "You're an erudite man, Book."

"You're a savvy woman to recognize it," he replied with a grin.

She pulled on the full facemask, securing the seal. That familiar *whoosh* filled her ears...though now it was muffled on the right. She grabbed a roll-top bag and attached it to her waist. Whatever it was that she was going to retrieve, they were betting on it being no bigger than an industrial pail.

"Ready?" asked Booker.

Ridley nodded and gave him the thumbs up, then tumbled backward off the dinghy.

## CHAPTER EIGHT

### THE HEBRIDES, SCOTLAND

BILL DANE POPPED a cinnamon Altoid into his mouth. He squinted out at the ocean being whipped by the wind, at the heavy gray sky. December in Scotland was not for sightseers. All the better for him and his squad of three.

Four. They had a guest along.

From where he stood high on the ferry dock, he could see the professor on the lower section, rummaging through her travel pack for something. She was the expert on this trip, and their job was to escort her to the destinations she laid out.

Dane disliked protection work. It was like having to keep his eye on two different balls at once, but he couldn't say no to this one.

When Pearson had called him two days ago, Dane picked up on the first ring. It had been four years since his last job for the shadowy financier: a basic blackmail delivery that needed a ferocious display of force. It was easy, and Pearson had paid almost triple the fee in appreciation. He'd told Dane to consider it a down payment for the next one.

This job was more complicated. It was also bizarre and unknown, not Dane's preference. He had to choose his squad carefully on this one. Small, mobile, adaptable.

In the Oceanus 28 VST boat that bobbed on the water, Fredrik Solbakken was triple-checking diving gear. Dane had packed it meticulously himself, but he always wanted a second-eyes recheck.

"Freddie" Solbakken was Norwegian, in his early forties, a former Naval Special Operations Commando, or MJK. He likely came from Viking stock, with his wavy red hair, lantern jaw, and deep-set eyes that had a wild intensity to them. He was a gear man. He spoke a few European languages and knew how to get almost any weapon he needed on the continent short of a nuke. Or maybe he just hadn't tried that one yet. Dane had worked with him a handful of times. This was the right job for him.

Behind him, talking to the professor who was still on the dock, was a lean man in his late twenties. He had close-cropped dark hair, delicately chiseled looks, and eyes that were just a bit too far apart. Alan Qualley had once been part of the best heist crew on the West Coast. When they'd gotten busted years ago, he had managed to slip the beam of the feds so well that he became suspect number one on the gang's "rat" list.

By the time the real informant was outed, the damage had already been done. Qualley left the business of robbery and went to work with Dane, taking his chilly demeanor and all of his lock-busting skills with him. They'd been on nearly a dozen jobs together, and the kid had more than proven his worth.

"Professor!" Dane called.

Lianna Powell looked up from her rummaging to where he was standing, twenty feet away.

"What do you need?" he asked.

"Nothin', thank you! Just putting my things in plastic bags for protection."

Dane checked the time on his watch, a Casio G-Shock. They didn't know how long their task would take at the destination, but he wanted to be back at the dock by nightfall.

"Check, Freddie?" he called to the boat.

Freddie raised his arm with a thumbs up. "Check complete! Let's go."

Dane strode down the dock, gesturing for Lianna to go ahead of him. "Professor."

"Please, *stop* calling me that. I've got a name, and I'll certainly be using yours, Bill."

"Lianna. Please get in before me."

She hiked her backpack over her shoulder and gave him a nod. Qualley offered her a hand to climb into the boat.

Dane pulled the line and stepped on board. Freddie at the wheel, they launched out into the open water.

Lianna had explained the mission to them in depth. She wouldn't be doing the diving herself, but the briefing had been thorough, photos included. Over breakfast, she had put up a diagram on the large TV in the conference room.

There was a strange figure on the screen, like a stick figure man with bowed legs out to the side, arms opening wide, a giant head with one eye in the center, and a crescent moon shape swooping across his forehead.

"This is the hieroglyphic monad," said Lianna. "John Dee was trying to condense the whole of nature into a single recognizable symbol. Sort of a thesis project, you might say. Wrote an entire treatise on how it contains elements and planets and the signs of the zodiac. Little fellow looks like a bit of a stodge, doesn't he? But when *you* see it—" She clicked to the next photo. "It'll look more like this."

Dane's eyes raked the picture. The stick figure had been dismembered, and the four separate elements now labeled.

The splayed legs were the *IGNIS*.

The body and straight-out arms were the *ELEMENTA*.

The circle-head with the dot in the center was the *SOL*.

And the crescent moon crown was the *LUNA*.

"Dee created puzzles," said Lianna. "He was a genius, if a pretty bizarre one. According to his writings, there are four stones at the bottom of Fingal's Cave, each with one of these four symbols on it."

Freddie seemed somewhere between skeptical tactician and bored schoolboy. Qualley watched, but his cool expression hardly ever betrayed his thoughts.

"'Course it's been a few hundred years, so it may require some digging. Once we've got the stones, they have to be placed into a column at the back of the cave. Each one should have a corresponding notch, carved out-like. Place the right stone in the right place..." She lifted her hands as though conducting a magic trick. "The first key is revealed."

"How?" said Dane.

She propped a hand on her hip and tossed the bangs from her eyes. "Well, I don't know yet. There isn't a proper explanation in the pages. Just instructions."

Freddie rolled his eyes back at Dane.

"What's the key?" asked Qualley.

"Ah!" Lianna's expression brightened. "They're *letters*—I believe like letter blocks, like children play with. Maybe smaller. But they're not English letters. They're characters from the Enochian alphabet. A whole different language."

"From where?" said Freddie.

"The angels."

The noise he made was half laugh, half grunt.

"I know, it's a bit of a faff," said Lianna, waving it off, "but we're not out here chasing angels, are we? Just stones, gentlemen."

"What do the keys do?" asked Qualley.

"That's the next question. There are seven of them that John Dee hid in seven different places. I'm workin' on where each of those are, but the instructions here say they must be done sequentially, in order, for whatever reason. And I don't want to be the one to fuck up a five-hundred-year-old treasure hunt."

The cursing from such a soft and elegant voice was startling. Dane liked her more for it.

"The keys will spell out 'M-A-D-I-M-I.' *Madimi*. The name of Dee's daughter," said Lianna. "Named after his favorite so-called angel who sometimes came across like a succubus. That's a sex demon."

"That's bad parenting," said Dane.

Lianna looked at him and let out a laugh. "Yes, I s'pose it is."

Even when seated, his posture was alert. Some of the Rangers in his former squadron used to joke that they didn't even need the K9 unit's Belgian Malinois when they had Bill Dane. All five feet and ten inches of him were compactly built. He was otherwise unremarkable looking. He kept his rust-brown hair short, likewise his thick beard. His eyes were shrewd, and the only thing that ever cracked that stoic aura was a rare boyish grin.

"And what are all the keys for?" asked Qualley.

"John Dee hid a special crystal somewhere, which has great value to the man who hired all of us in this room. And no, I don't know where that is yet. There are clues he's buried along the way that, uh...build to our finale. So it will take all the keys together to open the—whatever it is that this crystal is hidden in. *Ma-di-mi*."

Qualley looked at her, then back at Dane.

"This is weird," he said in a flat voice.

"This is the job," Dane replied. "We're getting every single key and retrieving the crystal at its undisclosed location that the professor will be providing for us."

"It's Lianna, please, not 'professor,'" she said.

He gave her a curt nod, but not of agreement, just acknowledgment.

"Why am I even here?" asked Freddie. "I'm glad you invited me, but unless it's for my jolly personality, why bring a toy-man to dig up stones that have been hidden away for five centuries?"

"We start on a boat," said Dane, "and I don't take anything lightly. And for your jolly personality."

Freddie flashed a mad grin. "I don't know why I argue with money like this."

"What is the crystal for?" Qualley asked Lianna.

Before she could answer, Dane cut in. "That's not part of our mission. We retrieve it and we get paid and we leave. Nothing changes that."

His disinterest wasn't to keep his conscience clean. It was to keep his mind clear. He wanted relevant information only, with no other concerns interfering.

Pearson had alluded to some things when he'd first introduced Dane to Lianna. The professor seemed to know why he was after this obscure old item, but Dane couldn't be sure.

He *was* sure of who Pearson was, and the billionaire wouldn't be putting this thing in a museum. It was meant for something else.

# CHAPTER NINE

### THE HEBRIDES, SCOTLAND

FINGAL'S CAVE was nearly two hundred feet deep, a narrow alley of sloshing waves with angular basalt columns jutting up along the sides.

Though the water was only twenty-five feet deep in this area, it was the length of the cave that presented the challenge.

As Ridley glided through the murky green, the only sound she could hear was the steady in and out of her own mechanized breathing.

She reached the floor and turned on the flexi-light, scouring with its beam. Algae and gunk coated most of the rock, as it surely had for millennia. This would take a level of meticulousness that Ridley had to stretch for.

Booker's voice came over her comms. "How does it look down there?"

"Good thing what I'm looking for is so new, not covered in seaweed or anything."

*Just five hundred years old instead of five million like everything else down here.*

She set about her search, yard by yard, combing with her hands, sometimes using her knife to pry away larger stones.

The timer on Ridley's tactix Delta watch glowed up at her. Before she knew it, twenty minutes had gone by. No sign of an etched stone.

*Makes sense if he left them farther in. Less chance of them getting swept out to sea.*

Four minutes later, Dee proved her right.

There, dead center in the narrow floor, was a stone the size of an apple. It was so covered in grime that Ridley's eye almost passed right over it, but then she glimpsed straight lines on it. Unnaturally straight.

She picked it up. Sure enough, both sides were carved deeply with the *ELEMENTA* symbol, the cross-like center of the hieroglyphic monad.

"I got one," she said into the radio.

"Yes! How big?"

"Palm-size. Dee was thoughtful enough to mark both sides."

"He made them to be found. Good work."

Ridley opened the roll-top bag and stuffed the stone inside. She moved on.

It took only six minutes to find the next one, the *IGNIS*. It was about the same size. She bagged it, updated Booker, and swam on.

The peaceful buoyancy of being underwater was like a salve to her. Consumed by focus on a tedious task, she nonetheless bathed happily in the contentment, the isolation, the monotonous Darth Vader rhythm of her regulator.

The third rock was half-buried under a pile. It was a miracle she saw it at all. She used the SOG blade to lever it loose.

The *LUNA*.

She could just make out the veil of darkness thirty feet ahead. The back of the cave.

"Got the third," she said over comms. "I'm running outta space here."

*If I missed one behind me...*

"You've got the eyes of a mantis shrimp," said Booker. "You'll find it."

"A mantis shrimp," she repeated.

"Best eyesight in the animal kingdom, since eagles don't really open their eyes underwater."

"That's very interesting. I'm concentrating. Over."

Twenty feet to go.

Ten feet. She was just preparing herself for the retrace of the entire cave when she saw it.

Tucked at the foot of the end wall was the *SOL,* the circular head.

"I got it!" she exclaimed. "All four! Come and get it, partner."

She swam to the surface. Booker was motoring into the cave as she removed the facemask and pulled herself up onto the nearby ledge. The SOG knife in her thigh pocket scraped against the rock.

He cut the motor, climbed out, and wedged the line into a crevasse.

Ridley held up the bag. "So where the hell do these things go?"

Booker hadn't gone into the cave ahead of her because he didn't want to stir up the silt and kill underwater visibility. Inefficient as it was, now they searched together.

Ridley stripped her tank, mask, and fins, offloading them into the boat as Booker stepped cautiously around the levels of geometric rock. In years past, he would have been nimble and sure of his steps. He wasn't quite as confident moving around in this bigger, less wieldy vessel.

But his eyes and instincts were still sharp.

"How on God's blue and green earth did John Dee get all the way out here to set all this up?" he said, hand roving the rock surfaces. "He was old as Uncle Remus by the time he even got hold of the Devil's Eye."

"Do you think you can start an old man's club with a guy who's been dead five hundred years?" said Ridley, searching the other side of the wall.

"You should put that facemask back on. Right back on."

It had been almost too easy to find those stones. Ridley had been so focused on the task that she hadn't thought how plain it all seemed. They were just lying there.

*But in Dee's time, no diving masks. No scuba gear. A practically impossible task.*

"This!" exclaimed Booker.

He made a fist and slammed the butt of it on the wall in triumph. Ridley moved over to join him.

There, cut into one of the rock columns, were four vertical spaces, like small cubbies carved into the wall.

"Uniform size. Unnaturally regimented spacing."

Ridley pulled the carved stones from the bag at her waist.

"The *luna*," said Booker, taking the crown piece and slotting it into the top cubby hole.

A perfect fit. For a second, he stared at it.

"I actually have chills. This is real. I've been studying Dee for a decade, and...this is real."

Ridley gave a grin and handed him the next stone.

*Sol.*

*Elementa.*

He hesitated just barely before slotting in the last: *ignis*.

There was a small scraping sound. Below the indented

shelves, a compartment in the rock had slid open. A moment before, perfectly concealed, it was now yawning open, the size of a P.O. box.

Ridley crouched down and reached in. Her fingers closed around a stone and she pulled it out. Booker stared at the treasure in her palm.

It was quartz, a milky, glassy stone carved into the shape of a "3."

"It's the 'M,'" said Booker. "Like a three, but backwards. *Madimi*."

He looked at her, eyes glinting as if he'd been electrified.

"One down," he said. "Here we go."

Ridley smiled in satisfaction.

Then the air seemed to shift around her. The light dimmed as if a veil had been draped over her eyes. Smears appeared, bluish-gray, like the Milky Way stretching out around her.

She looked back down the waterway.

The water was rising up. The sea was climbing up both sides of the channel as if being summoned. Ridley gaped.

Something appeared at the mouth of the cave.

Framed against the grim sky was the silhouette of a girl.

She stood on the narrow shelf of rock. It appeared that she was facing them. A thin dress whipped about her legs.

*No one lives on this island.*

The water roiled up the cave walls like the parting of the Red Sea, but there was nothing comforting about the sight as it must have been to the Israelites escaping their captors.

It was stupefying.

"Book!"

She couldn't look away from the girl, but there was a pause of silence behind her.

"What?" he said finally.

"Look!"

"At what?"

She swung around, incredulous, raising her hands in gesture. "Everything! The water! There's a girl—"

He looked at her in confusion.

"It's—are you serious?" said Ridley.

She turned around, and it was gone. All of it...the girl, the bluish haze, the water sliding up the cave walls.

The frigid sea water sloshed about in the narrow channel. The light returned to overcast. There was no sign of anyone at the mouth of the cave.

"Ridley?" said Booker.

She shook her head clear.

*The only hallucinations I ever suffered were in Hell Week. I'm not sleep-deprived. I'm not dehydrated. I'm not under the influence of any substance.*

"I don't know..." she muttered, and shoved the quartz key into Booker's hand.

He looked at her with concern, peered down at the key in his hand, then zippered it securely into a pocket.

"Let's go," said Ridley.

There was some horror in this cave. Or in that key.

# CHAPTER
# TEN

**THE HEBRIDES, SCOTLAND**

FREDDIE's black-domed head breached the water. He swam to a rock ledge, pulled himself up, and yanked off his facemask.

Dane was crouched yards away at the back of the cave, his jaw clenching and unclenching. Behind him was the empty slot in the stone where Dee's crystal had been. Lianna, in a state of wonder, was inspecting the hieroglyphic monad stones in the small cubby holes.

Freddie held something up in his hand. "Wasn't long ago."

Dane stood up as Freddie tossed the item to him. He stared down at it—a SOG Seal Strike knife. He pulled it out of its sheath. There was no damage to the material or the blade.

"There's a bit of water on these," said Lianna, looking at Dane. "Someone's *just* been here."

Dane shoved the knife back into its sheath. "Where's the next key?"

"Um, it's in Prague. Right in the center of the city. How did anyone get ahead of us?"

He offered a hand brusquely to her. "Back to the boat. Right now."

## EDINBURGH, SCOTLAND

Marc Pearson ambled along the hardwood floor of the narrow school hallway, checking emails on his phone. A small paned window overlooked a yard shrouded with a thin layer of snow. The faintest strains of Vivaldi's "Summer" pranced from behind one of the classroom doors.

Sitting on a bench down the hall was Effie, chatting quietly with a blonde woman in her thirties whose beauty had been scratched away by grief. There was a lightness in her face now, though, a hope she hadn't imagined.

And Celia Rapp looked at Effie and Pearson as her saviors... as her daughter's saviors.

The violin went quiet, and a moment later the classroom door opened. The Director of Music emerged, a thin woman in her sixties. She was chatting with Lexi, who came out carrying her violin case. The girl was a bundle of nerves and delight and insecurity. Following behind her was the Headmaster, a fellow in his fifties who actually wore tweed.

Celia leapt to her feet, beaming at Lexi. "How did it go?" she asked softly, barely able to contain herself.

Lexi bobbed her head uncertainly, but there was a shy grin with it.

"Mrs. Rapp," said the Director, shaking her hand. "We'd be very happy to have Lexi fill out a formal application. We know this process was a bit backward, but for special circumstances..."

She glanced at Effie and Pearson.

"Thank you!" exclaimed Celia. "We'll apply. We'll definitely apply!"

Lexi's eyes filled with awe.

The Headmaster shook Pearson's hand like an old chum. "Your musical taste, Mr. Pearson...you've got an ear. We couldn't be more grateful that you've taken an interest in our little school."

"We heard her play at a gala," said Pearson, grinning at Lexi. "Couldn't believe how talented she is at such an age."

"Well, we'd love to consider her for this upcoming term but I'm afraid we have no space."

Lexi's expression quavered.

"Oh no," said the Music Director, "that's not a knock against you. You've already gotten through the hardest part."

"Think of it as a chance to get even better," said the Headmaster. "Mr. Pearson here is such a patron of the arts. With a bit more tutoring, you could arrive back here next fall like a budding virtuoso."

"Okay," said Lexi softly.

"You know," said Effie, touching Celia's arm, "one of my good friends worked with a music tutor for her kids—they went on to Berklee over in Boston—and she specializes in stringed instruments. We'd be so happy to sponsor some lessons with her if you're both interested...?"

The girl felt like she was being whipped about in a dream and couldn't quite keep up. She nodded, looking between her mother, Effie, and Pearson.

"Are you serious?" breathed Celia. "Oh my God, I just—I can't believe this."

"She's in Spain for the winter, but Marc and I are going to Mallorca soon on holiday. If you have no problem flying on a private jet," said Effie with a wink at Lexi.

Pearson shrugged like he was embarrassed. "No airport lines."

"I can't go," said Celia, crestfallen. "I can't get off work."

"Oh, I'm sorry," said Effie with a look of sympathy. "Though we'd—" she glanced at Lexi, "we'd be happy to look after her. You're just about the age of my niece and nephew, you know. I don't get to play auntie very often."

Celia looked at Lexi, who locked eyes with her mother...and nodded.

"Well, that's splendid!" said Effie.

Pearson's phone began to vibrate. "Excuse me."

He stepped away and picked up the call.

"That was fast," he said into the phone.

Dane's voice came through the other end. "Who else knows about this?"

"About what—your assignment?"

"The whole thing with the keys and the treasure and the notebook."

"I have the only notebook. You have the copy. What the hell is going on?"

"Somebody beat us here by hours," replied Dane, practically growling. "They've got the first key. Somebody else knows."

Pearson raked a hand over his short silver hair, exasperation lighting the fuse of his temper.

"And they know what they're doing," added Dane. "They took the key, and they left a Navy SEAL knife behind."

"What the fuck," he muttered.

There was no way that the trail to these keys could be in any other known document. There's no way that the timing was a coincidence. It had to be from *his* notebook.

"Did you question Lianna?" he asked.

"Of course. No, she doesn't know any special ops, and no,

she didn't share the notebook or its contents with anyone," said Dane. "She's not lying. I know."

Pearson tore through the possibilities in his head.

"Every auction house keeps a photographic copy of their items," he said. "Sotheby's must have scanned the entire notebook. Someone got a hold of that copy."

"I won't ask who your enemies are."

"I prefer to think of my friends. What do you need?"

"To gather more information. They must know we're after it. They might know who we are. We don't know shit about them, but we'll find out soon."

"Fine. Report back as soon as you do."

"Yes, sir," said Dane. "This isn't a treasure hunt anymore, Mr. Pearson. It's a race."

# CHAPTER
# ELEVEN

**PRAGUE, CZECH REPUBLIC**

RIDLEY AND BOOKER arrived midday at Václav Havel Airport, where the boss took the opportunity to rhapsodize about the former writer turned political prisoner turned president.

"Never *intended* to become a dissident," said Booker as they climbed into a cab. "He just lived by truth and, under communism, that made him worthy of jail."

"You would have made a great political prisoner, Book. And for company, you could just read all the books you've stored up in your head."

"I'll get you reading some Solzhenitsyn. Is Russian on your Rosetta Stone?"

"No, and it's slid down the list of languages I want to learn," said Ridley. "I think Ukrainian has taken its place. They have all the phrases I'd want to say to Russians right now anyhow."

He chuckled and gave the cab driver an address two blocks away from their actual destination.

Ridley had spent the two-and-a-half-hour plane ride

studying map layouts of the Old Town area of Prague. When there was no time to pull out a GPS but there was a life-or-death need to navigate streets for pursuit or escape, map study was the most boring but essential tool in one's arsenal. She pored over them on the little seat tray, trying to take her mind off the discovery she'd made once they returned from the dive at Fingal's Cave.

That she had lost her SOG knife.

She'd used it on the dive, prying away at stones underwater. She'd slid it back into the pocket on her thigh, she *knew*. But it wasn't on her when they got back to land, and it wasn't in the boat.

*Just a simple knife, nothing special. No one's missing it. Can't be traced to us.*

Ridley couldn't figure out why but it was bothering her. It was some level of failure, to lose a weapon or a tool, to leave anything behind by accident.

It was only half as bothersome as the vision that kept replaying in her head...the hazy surreal air that had just *changed* around her...the strange girl at the mouth of the cave that must —*must*—have been a hallucination...*the water going up the damn walls.*

And Booker hadn't seen a thing.

*Folie d'une.*

*Folly of one.*

Though she knew she should, she just didn't want to tell him yet. Not until she had settled it a bit more in her own head.

She tried to distract herself from this pulsing worry over her own sanity by admiring the view of one of the most beautiful cities in Europe.

No matter how many centuries passed, Prague would always be suspended in the twilight of the Middle Ages. The

"City of a Hundred Spires" lay now under a veil of white. The Vltava River snaked through the heart of it, dark as gunmetal today. Christmas lights twinkled along the storefronts.

It was nearly thirty minutes later that they got out on a street corner, tipped the driver, and made their way down the block through the gray slush. They stopped when they reached a small jeweler's shop. Ornate wooden doors were flanked by window displays that dazzled behind reinforced glass.

A bell jangled overhead as they stepped inside.

It was antiquated and dark, a small space with only enough light to accentuate the shelves and cases.

Ridley glanced down at the glowing counter. The sparkle of an emerald ring drew her in like a horse to feed—until the blur of movement in the back snapped her head up.

"Can I help you?" came a man's voice in a thick Czech accent.

"Do you sell anything for Garand thumb?" said Booker. "Maybe a poultice?"

The jeweler emerged from the back. He was taller than both of them, wearing a pinstriped suit, holding a pair of tweezers in one large hand. He had a heavy, creased face with dark brows and glowering eyes.

*Not not-handsome, but that face is a whole mood unto itself.*

"I only use poultices on Thoroughbred hooves," he said.

Booker gave a nod, the contact now confirmed. "I'm Odin."

"Snapdragon," said Ridley, meeting the man's eyes.

"I'm Józef," said the jeweler. "I don't use a code name because everyone around here knows me. It's what happens when you own a shop and make wedding rings for people."

He moved past them to lock the door, then retreated to the back, beckoning them. The two operatives followed.

Józef went to the standup safe and punched in a sequence

on the keypad. The safe didn't open, but one of the counters slid across the floor, revealing a set of steps leading down into a basement.

"Come with me," he said, trotting down the stairs.

Ridley and Booker followed him into a chamber nearly twice the size of his shop. It was cool and dim, the floors and walls made of old stone, lined with shelves and drawers. Strips of light wrapped around every edge.

And every cupboard and shelf was stacked with weapons.

"*Malaka*," murmured Ridley.

There were rifles and shotguns and pistols, suppressors and stocks, flashlights for the barrels and optics for the slides.

"You said 'light and mobile and concealable.' So probably you don't want the Benelli," said Józef, waving away the prized shotgun.

Ridley went to a rifle counter and gazed down at the goods. "I really believe in us, Booker, that we can find a reason to need this MP7."

The jeweler grinned. She wondered if he knew how dour even his smile looked.

Booker picked up a Glock 19 like it was a long-lost glove. "This'll do nice and easy for me."

There was no doubt that Pearson had bought the lost notebook of John Dee to pursue the treasure it promised. The financier himself was somewhat of a recluse, not known for adventurous outings. There was little chance in their estimation that he'd be coming out "into the field" to search for it himself.

So Ridley and Booker had brainstormed what kind of team Pearson would have put together to retrieve the Devil's Eye. Former special ops, surely. At least two operators, with some sort of expert on board. Minimum of three for discretion and easy mobility. They'd be intensely motivated to not hold back... and to not lose out on the prize.

*They're behind already. Fingal's Cave was ours.*

The location of that first key had been fairly clear, as was their destination there in Prague. The two Ospreys knew they'd be running into trouble sooner or later. They wouldn't be unarmed when it happened.

Ridley's eyes roved the pistols. She picked up an HK VP9 with the slide locked back. "This is cut for optics. You have a red dot for it?"

The look of exasperation was so drawn out that it was clear he was weighing up whether to lie.

"A Trijicon. It will take a few minutes," said Józef flatly.

"Thanks," she said, adding a bit of flash to her smile. "I'll take a suppressor for it separately."

There was no way to discreetly carry a pistol with a suppressor mounted on the barrel, but she never knew when she might need to screw one on for business.

"And you have knives?" she asked.

Picking up the HK and a tiny screwdriver, he pointed to a wide drawer. Ridley pulled it open to see a parade of glinting steel. She plucked out a Spyderco Sage knife and held it up.

"Odin. Your battle axe?"

Booker took it, flicked open the blade, and gave her an approving look. She went back to the drawer, and saw the only thing she'd really been looking for: a karambit.

She picked up the curving fixed blade. It was a Boker Magnum Spike, eight inches long with a finger ring on the bottom of the handle. It looked like the talon of a velociraptor. It even had the double edge she liked.

*These don't normally come with a double edge. Thank you to whoever modified it.*

As she gripped the finger grooves, Ridley felt an immediate bond with it.

Booker eyed the size of it. "You couldn't find a machete?"

"She and I are one now."

"That's a homicidal marriage right there." He tucked the Spyderco into his back pocket. "You ready?"

# CHAPTER
# TWELVE

**PRAGUE, CZECH REPUBLIC**

OLD TOWN SQUARE brimmed with Christmas garlands, strings of lights, and angels made of golden wire hovering above the crowds. A towering evergreen in the middle gleamed with ornaments. Vendor stalls made to look like alpine huts sold kielbasa dogs, roasted chestnuts, and fried dough. Customers gathered around high-top tables with cups of beer or mugs of steaming mulled wine. Christmas carols streamed over loudspeakers, the soaring voices of a boys' choir filling the square.

Ridley and Booker wove through the crowds. Though their weapons were tucked snugly under their coats, it was time to appear as tourists.

Ridley was rarely hungry when out in the field, but the scent of chimney cakes baking at one of the huts had won her over. She tore apart the cinnamon pastry as her gaze roamed the area. Everything was calm and festive, everyone relaxed.

Booker had picked up a little bowl of hot, filled dumplings and was now struggling to keep the melted brie and berries from dribbling down his front.

"Just—really—the ideal time of year to mess with a public attraction in the middle of town," muttered Ridley.

"I brought you along for your optimism, didn't you know?" said Booker.

She laughed, and began singing along to "Good King Wenceslas" as its stately melody poured over the square.

"Hey!" she exclaimed, interrupting herself. "Wenceslas. He was Bohemian—Czech. Look at that."

"History, let's go! That's the Jan Hus Memorial." Booker pointed at a huge copper monument next to them, where a cloaked figure towered over a swarm of dramatically posed followers. "They burned him at the stake right here for being a Protestant, a hundred years before Protestantism...preceding Martin Luther."

"The guillotine was really a humane development, compared to dying of smoke inhalation or having your skin melt off."

"That Church has tried an awful lotta things to hold on to power," he said through a mouthful of dumpling. "Probably don't know the half of it." He paused, as though a thought had plucked at him. "How 'bout that Vatican Library, huh? Wonder what's in there. Maybe we'll get to find out someday."

By the spark in his eye it was clear that the "we" was Osprey.

"You doing Christmas with your kids this year?" she asked.

"Bah," he scoffed, trying to be casual about it. "They've got their own grown lives. The twins are going to spend it with Holly and her husband...think Amelia's going to her fiancé's family place in Aspen."

"You're not gonna be alone on Christmas," she said emphatically.

"Oh, no, I'm gonna be sittin' at a piano in an English manor house, in a smoking jacket, bourbon in one hand, some ham and collard greens quiche, singin' 'Merry Christmas, Baby' with Diane Bellingsworth."

"Just you and her?"

"Ohhh, yeah."

"She's fit." Ridley pulled off another shred of the chimney cake. "Where's this clock, then?"

He motioned to a corner of the cobblestone square.

As they made their way over, they noticed the gathering of onlookers getting thicker. Booker checked his watch.

"Ah. Two minutes to showtime."

They took up position at the back of the crowd and gazed up at one of Prague's most distinct attractions: the *Orloj*. The astronomical clock.

There were two circular dials on the medieval tower, one above the other, not more than two or three stories up. The lower was a golden array of zodiac signs. On the sides were noble-colored figurines: a chronicler, an angel wielding a sword and shield, a philosopher, and an astronomer.

Above this, the upper dial was a stunning, intricate astrolabe of blue, red, and black. There was a series of different circles and clock hands within the larger one. All of it was flanked by some ugly figures, including a skeleton holding a bell and an hourglass.

The tower stood at the southern wall of Old Town Hall and had loomed over the Square since 1410. The clock, which had been repaired again and again over the centuries, was a wonder of mathematics and engineering. It had somehow even survived a Nazi bombing in World War II.

"Here, watch," said Booker, pointing up.

A few feet above the top dial, two small windows slid open. As a chorus of bells filled the square, a procession of weary-looking statues glided by, turning their pious, mournful faces outward as they passed. They clutched items—a sword, a chalice, a wooden cross—and each wore a golden halo. Below them, the skeleton clanged his bell up and down.

"The twelve apostles," said Ridley.

Booker finished his last dumpling. "Eleven."

"Oh, right. One lost his place in the squad over thirty pieces of silver. No statue for that guy."

She scanned the tower. Two hundred feet up at the top, there were some tourists taking photos of the view.

Down beside the astrolabe clock, there was a door leading out to a thin railed balcony that ran along the face.

*That won't hold the boss. That's for me.*

"Last tour of the tower is in an hour," said Ridley, "then it closes at five." She peered up at the giant clock and grinned. "That thing looks like it needs a cleaning."


They waited.

While Booker had the digital version of John Dee's notebook on his mobile phone, he also carried the small printed version that Sterling had given to them. He preferred it, poring over the pages as they were meant to be seen, deciphering the Olde English spelling and parsing out his numerical tables and alphabet graphs.

On the plane ride over from the UK, he had worked on the riddle of this second location. The clues to the general area were fairly simple to break. It hadn't taken Booker long to figure out that they were heading to Prague. The second bit was the more difficult, for Dee had created a series of puzzles "only for the worthy."

*The celestial sentinel of Bohemia...*Dee had spent a great amount of time in Bohemia, trying to impress Emperor Rudolf II with his promises of alchemical wonders. When the Catholic Church accused his scryer Edward Kelly of working magically against Rome on behalf of Elizabeth I, using necromancy, sorcery, and spycraft, the pope called for their expulsion from Bohemia. That was a rocky moment between Dee and Kelly and Rudolf II.

Eventually Dee returned to England while Kelly was given the title of baron in Bohemia.

Though John Dee had felt at home in Prague for years, there could only be one place that wholly enchanted him: this giant astronomical clock tower.

From Dee's next section of the riddle, Ridley had snatched the prominent phrases: *The orb of command...the halo of greatness...in the steps of King Arthur...empress of the world...looks upon the time of holy ascension and then the time of death...*

Booker had hunched his huge shoulders over the tiny airplane tray, as if closing down the space between him and the pages would help. Even Ridley had figured quickly that the royalty talk was about Queen Elizabeth, Dee's great supporter, the monarch who visited him for supernatural guidance and spiritual instruction.

"Looks upon the time of holy ascension and then the time of death," Booker had muttered.

"Ascension to the throne or ascension to heaven," wondered Ridley. "And *then* the time of death—not *and* the time of death. They're different."

"Elizabeth I was crowned in 1559, died in 1603." Booker tapped his fingers against his half-drunk can of ginger ale. "Elizabeth and her boy-toy Robert Dudley commissioned Dee to figure out when the best time would be for her coronation... down to the hour. Astrology held real sway for the queen. She believed in her divine role in the cosmos. Maybe that's the time of holy ascension—not her death but her ascension to the throne."

His eyes lit up, like a scent hound who'd found the trail.

"And *then* the time of death," said Ridley.

*Death...look upon death...*

She pulled out her phone and drew up a photo of the clock tower. She zoomed in.

"There."

Booker peered at it.

The skeleton that hovered beside the clock face.

"The hourglass," said Ridley with a wry smile. "The hour of death."

He looked up at her as though she'd just gifted him a Rolls-Royce.

"You have brains in your head. You have feet in your shoes," he said, starting to sketch something with his pen. "Oh, the places you'll go."

Now, as twilight fell into night, the two of them watched for the last tour to clear out of the tower. When the crowds in front finally thinned, Ridley and Booker strolled across the square.

Below the golden zodiac clock was a small oaken door studded with iron. The lock was as simplistic as any Booker had ever picked. They were inside within seconds, both having to duck their heads.

The steps that greeted them were steep and carved of stone. The walls were aging plaster. The stairwell was as medievally narrow as the door.

"Lilliputians," grumbled Booker as he started upward.

They climbed until they were behind the face of the astronomical clock, where an enormous contraption of gears ticked and whirled and spun. Booker furrowed his brow as he looked it over. Ridley gaped.

"Well...complex," he said.

"No way," she said, and turned to the little door behind her. "I'm not dealing with that."

"Rid—"

But she had already pushed her way outside, and now stood on the balcony two floors up, beside the clock face.

The metal rail felt brittle beneath her. Cold air sliced across the square that was glowing with Christmas cheer.

Ridley pulled a small drawing from her pocket.

On the plane, Booker had carefully drawn out the faces of the zodiac clock and the astrolabe clock, exactly as they would have looked at the hour, day, month, and year of the coronation of Queen Elizabeth I.

Ridley scanned it carefully, then looked up at the giant dial yawning above her. There were markings on it for Gothic time, Babylonian time, sidereal time, celestial movements...she had studied the face and the mechanisms as they worked out the proper positioning, but looking at it now, she felt like it had all become ooze in her brain.

*When did all this become a wristwatch?*

They didn't have time to figure out the gears. Manual cranking it would have to be.

She drew a deep breath and reached for the first set of hands, the Roman numerals for the hour. That one was easy: twelve.

Gripping the cold metal of the sun and moon hands, she flipped it so that the sun was dominant: noon.

The inner dial was the zodiac. Ridley had to haul it hard into place.

Inside the tower, Booker had descended one flight and found the single gear he could understand: that of the golden zodiac board. In Czech, every day of the year had its own name, many of them in honor of a saint.

"There you are...Alice."

He turned the gear wheel.

Outside on the balcony, his partner was pulling the last

hand into place. She stepped to the side and surveyed the new settings.

There it was: twelve o'clock in the afternoon, January 15<sup>th</sup> in the year 1559.

The exact time that John Dee had divined for the coronation of Queen Elizabeth I.

"Come on, come on," she muttered, and looked up at the half-sized skeleton figure beside the clock.


She did not see the man emerge in the square below with his companion. His gaze locked on the clock face, and on the dark figure standing on the rail in front of it.

Bill Dane's eyes were like live coals in the darkness.

# CHAPTER
# THIRTEEN

**PRAGUE, CZECH REPUBLIC**

RIDLEY STARED at the skeleton holding its silent bell aloft.

*Come on. It has to be...*

As she watched, the hourglass split apart, disconnecting in the middle to reveal a hidden tube between its chambers.

"And then, the time of death," she murmured to herself, grabbing an outcropping of the stone column.

She hauled herself up, grateful for the carved ridges as footholds. Ridley hadn't been on a rock face in ages, but this ten-foot climb wasn't much of an ascent.

Testing each of her grips, she pulled herself up face to face with the skeleton.

"Time to let go, you dreamboat."

She yanked the hourglass out of its hand, cracking off a few metacarpals. They fell thirty feet into the snowbank below.

Ridley clenched one of the hourglass rods between her teeth as she climbed back down to the metal rail.

As she was about to break open the hidden tube in the center of the hourglass, she felt a prickle of attention...that strange compelling beam of intensity that meant someone was watching her. She looked down.

Across the courtyard, a lantern-jawed man was staring up at her.

*Special ops. It's all over him.*

She heard the door into the tower below her open.

*They're here.*

"Tango! On the stairs!" she shouted to Booker inside.

She had no idea how many there were coming into the tower. They must have thought they'd formed a trap, catching one of their targets out on a railing two stories up with the object in hand, and the other in a narrow stairwell with only one way down.

But this was not a trap for Ridley.

She only had seconds to make the first move.

Biting down on the hourglass rod again, she dropped to a crouch on the rail, grabbed the edge with one hand, and swung herself over. The sharp, cold metal tore at her palm.

The man launched himself across the courtyard.

Ridley let go of the railing and dropped twenty feet to the snowbank beneath.

The jolt was so strong that she felt the wooden rod crunch between her jaws, but she was already up, scrabbling with hands and feet to get moving.

She could hear the railing door above her open.

"Go!" came Booker's voice, booming overhead.

The stranger was closing on Ridley in a dark flash—

*Any split-second advantage—*

Launching herself forward, she whipped a chunk of muddy snow up at his face. It was indeed only a split second, but she was already running as he pawed it out of his eyes.

Ridley snatched the hourglass from her mouth as she tore

into a full sprint, away from the Christmas market. The stranger broke into a run after her.

Back at the clock tower, Booker landed in the same snowbank with a mighty thud and a groan. He dragged himself to his feet.

When Bill Dane burst out onto the railing only seconds later, he spotted Booker stumbling toward the Christmas market.

He didn't even consider the stairs. Dane dropped the two stories down and was already running full tilt by the time he registered the impact.

---

Ridley clutched the hourglass in her hand as she sprinted through the narrow cobblestone streets. They were packed with pedestrians and Christmas shoppers. It was a mad high-speed weave to maneuver through them.

She dashed by brightly lit cafés and shops with holiday carols pouring out, clipping the occasional shoulder as she went. Indignant shouts trailed behind her.

But so did the lantern-jawed man.

Turning one corner, she slipped in the snow, nearly crashing into a festive display. Heart thudding, she clambered upright and sped off again.

She couldn't afford a collision and couldn't afford to make a scene by stopping to fight her pursuer in public. She couldn't even glance back to check how far ahead of the man she was. And she wasn't sure where she was running, but knew that her direction was west, toward the river.

Cold seared her lungs as she scanned for any vehicle to hijack. There were none in sight. To her intense frustration, all these ancient streets were for pedestrians only.

She heard a loud exclamation far behind her and realized that she must have gained on lantern jaw.

*Sprint speed: still intact.*

Ridley tore down a side street.

---

Bill Dane stormed through the Christmas market, his eyes scanning madly.

His quarry was big and dark-skinned. This should have been easy. The chatter of the swarming crowds, the calls of the vendors, the whirl of Christmas carols all around him...nothing else mattered.

He was hunting, dodging between the alpine huts hawking their hot foods.

There, ahead, he caught sight of a big man in a woolen cap, the skin of his neck a dusky shade. His target hadn't been wearing a hat, but he could have pulled one out for disguise.

Dane barreled through the crowd, knocking a steaming cup of cider onto one tourist who yelped.

He didn't care. He lunged toward the black man, who turned just then to talk to his female companion.

It wasn't him.

A growl escaped Dane's throat. He whirled about, searching.

---

Ridley hurtled around a corner. Looming in the darkness ahead of her was the majestic Gothic tower of the Charles Bridge.

At the end of the cobblestone, she skidded to a halt at a crosswalk. Taxis and scooters whizzed by. It was too congested to make a dash through.

She glanced behind.

The lantern-jawed man was just coming around the corner, his eyes scanning for his target.

Ridley turned back to the street, stole a look down into the traffic, and made a break for it.

The sound of horns and skidding tires hailed down, but she was through in seconds. She ran full out toward the tower, under its yawning arch, and onto the Charles Bridge.

It was the most photographed sight in Prague, sprawling medieval stone. It allowed foot traffic only. Tonight, the lampposts were glowing under a frosting of snow. Giant statues of the saints loomed down from each railing.

Halfway across the bridge, Ridley slowed and looked back toward the tower. Her boots scuffed the thick snow. A few curious pedestrians glanced her way as she heaved for air. She had no idea where Booker was or whether he was safe, but she wouldn't run any farther.

Here, away from the dense crowds of the city streets, Ridley leaned behind the stone outcropping of one of the statues. She reached up under her jacket and slid the VP9 from its holster. Sticking the hourglass between her teeth again, she pulled the suppressor from a long pocket inside her jacket and screwed it on.

She held the gun discreetly against her leg, fighting the urge to even look at the hourglass as she held it with her other hand.

She stared down the bridge.

*Don't take your eyes away for one second.*

And then the air shifted.

The blue-gray haze didn't descend or emerge—it simply *was*. Floating amidst it were milky, sparkling swaths that looked like mini galaxies. Flakes of snow began floating upward.

It was eerily peaceful, until she saw the pedestrians passing her by.

Each of their faces were gaping masks of horror. Their jaws

hung open as if caught mid-scream. Their eyes were black holes, swirling abysses.

And all of them were craning their necks to leer at her.

A volt of fear coursed through Ridley. She gripped her gun until her knuckles went white.

*This can't be. This isn't real.*

A young couple. An old man. Three young children. Their faces ghastly, each one swiveling toward her. She had never felt so exposed. She had never felt terror seizing her like this.

Ridley couldn't bear to look at them, but couldn't bear to take her eyes away, as if they'd pounce on her and devour her soul. But she was screaming inside.

*How do I get out of this?!*

"Oh, my God," she whispered, her brow knitting in panic. "Oh my God, oh my God..."

She looked up and down the bridge for help, for any sign of a reality outside of this horror—the way the world had been only a moment before.

And then everything in sight changed back.

She couldn't see it happen. Maybe it happened exactly as she blinked. It just *was*. The night was dark, the snow was settled, lights twinkled in the distance, and happy pedestrians ambled by her on the famous bridge.

And there, emerging from under the tower, was her pursuer.

He hadn't spotted her yet, but then she saw him reach a hand into his jacket.

*Shoulder holster.*

Ridley tapped the long suppressor against her thigh, trying to regain her composure.

He wandered closer, scanning the broad swath of pedestrians, hand still tucked inside his coat.

*I've got my weapon already presented. Advantage: me.*

She was a damn fine shot with a pistol, but he was still forty yards away. She did not want to get into a shooting match with civilians in play.

Thirty-five yards now...thirty...searching for her in the dim flood of the lamps. She could see he was still breathing hard.

*Come on, come closer...*

Then Ridley spotted a dark blur on the end of the bridge, coming toward her. It was moving too fast to be a pedestrian.

With the sound of a motor.

A black Honda Rebel motorcycle was roaring through the snow toward them, a pair of broad shoulders leaning over the handlebars. Pedestrians darted out of the way in alarm.

The lantern-jawed man startled and whipped around, ready to draw.

Booker had been ready for that. He skidded to a halt a dozen yards from the man, his Glock already in hand, barrel raised.

Ridley rushed out from behind the statue, keeping the VP9 at a low ready. If she pointed it at the stranger now, Booker would also be in the firing line. Crossfire was a killer.

"Don't pull that," called Booker to the man. "Hands up and they better be empty."

Freddie Solbakken lifted his hands in the air. His glare could have burned through a redwood.

He finally spotted Ridley as she flanked him, the long barrel of the suppressor pointed at his chest.

Bystanders fled with shouts of fear. The middle of the snowy bridge was soon clear for this triangulated standoff.

"Unzip your jacket, very slowly," Ridley ordered.

Freddie opened up his jacket. Sure enough, the butt of a gun was just visible under his armpit.

"Pull that out with two fingers *only!*"

He glared at her, but did as she said without a word.

*Well, he's not deadly stupid enough to try something with two guns trained on him.*

"Drop it on the ground."

The Beretta thudded in the snow.

"Back up."

As he did so, Ridley crouched, looped one finger through the trigger guard of his discarded gun, and tossed it over the side of the bridge. It made a faint splash in the frigid water below.

"On your knees," she said.

This seemed to be the ultimate insult.

As Freddie obeyed the order, he said almost soothingly, "You have no idea who's coming for you."

Ridley held up the hourglass. "You have no idea who's ahead of you."

She stepped around the kneeling man and cracked him in the skull with the butt of her gun. Just behind the ear, sending his equilibrium sloshing off-kilter.

He grunted and reeled, dropping his hands to the ground on all fours.

Booker revved the bike toward Ridley. She swung up onto the back and he gunned it, speeding off through the snow.

As the Honda Rebel sliced off into the darkness, a solitary man stood at the other end by the Gothic bridge tower. Unlike the rest of the pedestrians around him who were still scurrying away in distress, he was calm and alert.

Deep-set blue eyes watched as the motorcycle disappeared into the distance. He watched the dizzied Freddie stumble to his feet with a bellow of frustration.

Then he slipped away into the crowds of Christmas shoppers.

## CHAPTER
# FOURTEEN

**PRAGUE, CZECH REPUBLIC**

LIANNA POWELL HAD BEEN WAITING with Qualley at a café near the Christmas market in Old Town Square. She was sipping on a mug of mulled wine when her lanky escort got a message on his phone and shot to his feet.

He dropped a few euros on the table and hustled her away so fast that the hot wine splashed her sleeve. Her irate protests meant little as he rushed her through the market.

They met Dane in front of the astronomical clock. He was pacing in the snow.

Lianna glanced up at the giant dials, then down at his fuming expression. "What's wrong, then?"

"They got here first, by minutes," he snapped. "I don't know who the hell they are. A middle-aged man with a paunch and some Amazon woman."

"Speaking as a middle-aged woman, I think we might have to start respectin' the competition, eh? Second time in a row now."

Dane's eyes flared. This soft-spoken professor was talking

to him like an errant student, without fear. Scolding him for a failing grade.

"There won't be a third," he said, his voice low.

Lianna walked toward the clock tower, staring up at it. When she noticed the piece missing from the skeleton's hand, a smile drifted across her lips.

"It was the hourglass, wasn't it," she said.

"Yes."

"Where's Freddie?" asked Qualley.

"Chasing the hourglass," said Dane. "And losing it. He's on his way back."

"Well, we closed the distance on them, didn't we? Between the first and the second," said Lianna, returning to the both of them. "Keep your heads up."

Dane let out a scoffing laugh. He couldn't help it.

"Professor, this ends for them in Kraków."

She observed him for a moment, the blazing determination, the nearly manic anger, the wounded pride.

"*Lianna*," she reminded him, but this time her smile was meant to soothe him. "And yes, let's say it does."


There were no bag checks on trains.

Ridley and Booker had stopped to buy a change of clothes each along with some toiletries. They packed everything into a small duffel and—still carrying their guns and blades—settled into a deluxe sleeper cabin for their overnight trip.

It was cramped and spare and reminded Ridley of the barracks. At least it had its own toilet and shower.

She sat on the bottom fold-out bed, eating a sun-dried tomato chicken sandwich with her left hand. The palm of her right was raw from the jolting scrape of the railing. Booker stood, leaning on the bunk ladder as he ate a buffalo chicken wrap.

"Special ops, for sure. Not American," said Ridley. "Not the one who tailed me. He looked like a Viking. I could practically see the horns on his imaginary helmet."

"Well, we know he speaks English. I didn't get to chat with mine."

"You have a locator on my phone, don't you?"

"You never thought so before?"

"I should have."

He looked at her, deadpan as he chewed.

"You know the last time I was in the field I could have made that run you did. But I'm a self-aware cat," he said, slapping a hand on his broad stomach. "I'm not keepin' up with you on foot, but I sure will by vehicle."

She thought about it. "That's a fair call. Probably shouldn't be eating that breaded buffalo chicken then, huh?"

"I'll put you back on desk duty."

"Sir."

After they'd finished eating and washed up, Ridley sat cross-legged on the floor and stared at what she'd raced across Prague to protect: Death's hourglass.

Booker had carried it since they'd dismounted the motorcycle. There was something about it that now made her shudder.

"Booker," she began.

The smallness of her voice alarmed him. He lowered himself to sit on the edge of the bed.

"I've been seeing things...in Fingal's Cave, on the bridge tonight...something is happening to me and it's—both times —I dunno—it's happened both times I've been holding a key."

"Okay. Tell me what's happening."

Ridley told him. She tried to describe every bit of her hallucinations but blundered over her own words to explain what it *felt* like.

He let her talk. As she finished, she looked up at him with a pleading gaze.

"You didn't see anything?"

Booker shook his head. "Sorry I missed it. Sorry you didn't."

"You think it's the keys? Why would it just be affecting me?"

He lifted his hands without answer.

"Why don't you get that one out, then," she said, nodding him to the hourglass.

Booker broke open the center piece as gingerly as he could. Sure enough, there, hidden in the thick neck of the hourglass, was a carved, milky-white stone.

"That's it. 'A' in *Madimi*," he said, holding it up to the light.

Ridley's whole body was rigid. "You feel okay? You don't see anything weird?"

"Nope." He gave her a sympathetic look. "Ya know what, though? Give you another example of the John Dee unexplainable. That's quartz. Ya know what it takes to cut quartz? A diamond-tipped saw. But this was the sixteenth century. Diamond-tipped saws had not been invented."

She frowned at him, then looked closely at the piece as he held it. It was cleanly cut, almost delicate.

"So what is it," she said, "magic?"

"It's..." he lifted those broad shoulders in a frozen shrug, "the kind of thing we're always lookin' for."

She tried to shake off the tension. "Almost time to open a Ridley's Believe It or Not. Think of the ticket prices! Can we bring the 'top men' out to introduce the items?"

"That's funny every time, Indy," said Booker dismissively, peering at the quartz.

Then he laid it down on the small table beside him.

If—at the end of any mission—an operative still had in

their possession any physical item with strange, inexplicable, or mystical power, it passed into the custody of the Director of the Osprey Division: Booker Douglas.

And not one of the operatives had ever gotten a hint as to where those items ended up.

*At least none have ever ended up on the news...again.*

The director could have been the most powerful man in the world had he chosen to wield a fraction of the things that had ended up in his custody. He was a rare man.

Booker glanced at his LIV Titanium watch. "Seven hours 'til we reach Kraków. I'll shower now, and that bottom bunk is mine. You don't want me movin' around above you. Wouldn't get a wink all night for the nerves. But you, uh...you tell me quick if you have any nightmares like that alternate dimension thing."

Ridley gave a salute. He went into the bathroom to wash up.

She got to her feet and went over to the table, looking at that small piece of stone. She had seen some things, but those hellscape hallucinations...

As a kid, she'd watched reruns of *The X-Files* and wondered how—after all that she'd seen—Scully was still the skeptic.

Then Ridley had joined Osprey.

It wasn't so much a matter of being unwilling to believe, but needing to be convinced to move off her own baseline. She also rarely had time to sort out the bizarre and supernatural, to reorder it within her own worldview. The mission required the work of figuring it out, but that was task-based, puzzle-oriented.

When the mission was done, shards of it would sometimes drift through her mind at night as though on a swirling river. But they were in pieces, and she could never quite put them all together.

She was open enough to the possibilities of the metaphysical, but it was always the mission she preferred, the *doing*. Let others, like Booker, wade into the wondering.

At least, this was the thought she reinforced for herself after every assignment.

As Ridley stared at the innocuous-looking quartz key lying on the table, she felt a dread unease.

She realized that this time—on this mission—the supernatural may just hound her out of her own mind.

## CHAPTER
# FIFTEEN

**KRAKÓW, POLAND**

The train reached Kraków the next morning.

Ridley had woken early, showered, and picked up two coffees in the dining car. By the time she'd gotten back to the sleeper, Booker had folded the bunks away and was sorting through their inventory out of fastidious habit.

The train slowed and stopped an hour short of their own destination. When Booker saw the sign for "Oświeçim," a solemn expression gripped him.

"What is it?" asked Ridley, noticing his shift.

"Auschwitz."

She went to the window.

From this station, there was nothing to see. No sign of the death camp from here. Yet still, she felt a ghastly chill.

In another life, on another train, the two of them might have been pulling up to that long brick building that welcomed passengers to the hell within its gates.

*Him, black. Me, a deviant.*

From which one million Jews would never emerge.

There wasn't much that could shut down Ridley, but the gruesome stench of genocide and the images that spilled through her head were enough to do it. Booker must have felt it as well.

They didn't speak again until they reached the station at Kraków.

The city was quilted with snow, already alive with morning traffic. The Vistula River wound through its center, its surface like polished tin in the light of morning.

Neither Ridley nor Booker had ever been to Poland. While they'd studied maps the night before for a general layout, she'd finally tossed the book off her top bunk, declaring it practically useless. All of the street signs would be in Polish. Though she knew seven other foreign languages, Polish was not one of them. That suddenly aggravated her.

"You know what *is* interesting," Booker had said, leaning back on his lower bunk. "This city was named for a cobbler-turned-king named Krakus."

"I award you nine points for interesting," she said dryly.

"And there was a man-eating dragon named Smok who terrorized the city and could only be placated with ritual offerings of cattle...until *one* day, Krakus the man pulled an Odysseus—"

"—Thank you for using his proper Greek name—"

"—and fed him a cow stuffed with sulfur. Smok: exit stage left. Krakus becomes king."

There was a pause.

"Okay, fifty points for interesting," said Ridley.

Booker had chuckled and gone back to reading.

He'd called in an order for a dead drop car in the Polish capital, so their first stop was to pick it up in the train station parking lot.

In its trunk was a backpack. Inside that were some flashlights, a pickaxe, a sledgehammer, a hammer, and a crowbar. Each of them was wrapped in cloth to muffle any clanking, and stuffed in alongside a length of rope and tactical gloves. Ridley sifted through all of it, ready to put the gear to work.

The last thing in the bag was a small Pelican case that held three cameras no bigger than a case of earbuds.

"I never got to the 'psychic remote viewing' part of CIA training," said Booker with a wry smile. "We go to work with good old-fashioned, cutting-edge technology."

"Hi-ho, hi-ho," said Ridley, slamming the trunk shut.

"They don't like a director being out in the field," he told her as he climbed into the passenger seat. "And they surely don't want to be responsible for somethin' bad happening 'cause they shortchanged him."

"Oh, so is that why they gave you the Bond car?" she said with an arched glance at the Hyundai.

"They only give Bond cars for Bond-level driving."

He tossed the keys to her.

"The man literally wrecks *every* car," she said.

Nonetheless, Ridley drove them southeast through the glittering white streets. The architecture of the capital looked an awful lot like a B-grade Prague to her, though it was still magnificent in the freshly fallen snow.

They passed smatterings of Ukrainian flags that fluttered out of apartment windows. Since the Russian invasion, this country had taken in over a million refugees fleeing the butchery and devastation of their homeland.

Poland itself had been set on edge by the encroaching war of conquest.

The country had been ripped apart in World War II, half of it crushed by Nazi Germany, the other half by Soviet Russia.

The Germans had built six camps here for extermination, to which they shipped three million Polish Jews for slaughter. In their broader plans for world domination, they outlined "the complete destruction of all Poles." Every Polish resistance uprising was smashed to pieces.

The Russians cut their own bloody path through the country. In one month alone, they massacred over twenty thousand officers and prisoners of war in the Katyn Forest. The heaps of twisted corpses were left in ditches, not to be discovered for years.

As World War II was won and the Axis powers defeated, Poland was caught in an accursed limbo. Stalin had promised the United States and England that he would allow the Polish government to remain sovereign. Much to the shock of everyone who had never met a mass-murdering dictator, he did not keep his word.

Poland was drowned, abandoned by the Allies to the long anguish of communism under Soviet rule. When the USSR fell, the country fought its way to freedom, to a democratic republic. They joined NATO, never again to be conquered and slaughtered by the Russians to the east.

Yet as they had watched Putin's tanks roll into Ukraine and heard the authoritarian from Moscow pronounce his life's desire to reconquer the lands that had once been subsumed by Russian rule, Poles felt this threat in their bones. They had seen this play before. If Ukraine fell, they rightly feared they would be next.

As Ridley navigated along the squiggly blue lines of their GPS mapping, she realized they were less than four hours' drive from Lviv, the western-most major city in Ukraine.

*It's a different kind of tension, being one jump away from a European war zone.*

Today at least, Kraków was dressed for Christmas in relative peace.

It took them only half an hour to reach their destination.

Ridley parked the Hyundai in front of a long yellow building. A rickety-looking tower was coming out of the back like a chimney. A few other visitors were making their way inside.

Booker pulled on his leather gloves. "Are you ready to dig?"

# CHAPTER
# SIXTEEN

**KRAKÓW, POLAND**

Ridley and Booker had arrived early for the first tour of the day. Only six other people were in line at that hour.

*Small enough group to keep track of but just big enough to peel away unnoticed.*

They were welcomed through the door by an English-speaking guide, a young woman who introduced herself as "Dag." She was lithe as a whippet, but one whose dose of coffee hadn't quite hit yet. She wore a dark coat that looked like military garb from the 19th century, lined with brass buttons and sporting a nametag.

Dag welcomed her first group of the day with some helpful tips.

"The tour is almost three hours total. The deepest part is three hundred twenty-seven meters, which is about one thousand feet. We have an elevator for some areas, if you feel you cannot walk."

Ridley nudged Booker, who ignored her.

"It's *not* cold down there. You will be happy with little jackets or sweatshirts."

They had done their homework. Booker was in dark jeans, a crewneck sweater under a waxed canvas jacket, and hiking boots.

Ridley wore some lightweight hiking shoes, a black cowl-neck sweatshirt, and black tactical pants which—while form-fitting—had enough pockets to store her life savings. Tucked well into the holster on her waistband was the HK VP9. The karambit was sheathed along her belt. She stood clutching the straps of the gear backpack that was slung over her shoulders.

"And please, keep up. We lose people down here all the time. Don't get lost. We will find you, but you will miss my beautiful speeches."

The rest of the group chuckled.

"Any questions?" she asked.

When there were none, she clasped her hands together and smiled. "Then, we'll get started. Welcome to the Wieliczka Salt Mine."

The start of the tour was the long descent down a series of narrow wooden stairs, walkways, and shafts. Peering down between the rails as they circled and circled, the darkness below seemed an abyss. It was a dizzying, seemingly endless scuffing of shoes.

Ridley hung back on one of the landings. She pulled one of the mini cameras from the bag, peeled off the adhesive back, and stuck it in the corner of the ceiling. It would face the stairs, and—if Pearson's team caught up with them as quickly as they did last time—give Ridley and Booker an advanced warning.

She re-zipped the bag and caught up to the group.

Two hundred-some feet below the earth, the tour arrived at the first level of the mine. The passages were all reinforced timber, and dimly lit. The mine had truly been transformed. Though it had been in use since the 13th century, it was now a vast underground complex.

They passed deep, illuminated alcoves that housed exhibits of ancient miners at work. There were a few Hobbit-sized doors along a narrow corridor that caught Ridley's eye, but the tour guide said nothing about them. She did encourage them to swipe a finger along a wall to "taste" it. Some tried it, to their own disgust.

It was pure salt, everywhere.

They soon passed more large sculptures that were also carved entirely from salt, noble depictions of peasant workers, ladies, and knights. There were even life-sized models of horses at work, hitched to some of the preserved mining contraptions.

*What miner in the 1200s ever thought this place would become a place for tourists?*

The group wound through huge hallways that looked like they were built with Lincoln Logs. Ridley lagged back again and set another one of the small cameras facing down the corridor.

Only a few meters past that, they finally entered the first major cavern.

On one side, under a spotlight, was a huge salt bust of a king. A giant plaque identified him as King Casimir the Great.

*This is the place.*

Ridley hung back with Booker until Dag led the rest of the tourists into the next passageway. Once they were out of sight, she dropped her backpack to the ground. He pulled up the camera feeds on his phone.

Empty stairwell. Empty hallway.

"The Great," said Ridley, pulling out the sledgehammer. "Feels like an easy one."

Booker inspected the bust.

"All made of salt. There's no part of the hieroglyphic monad here, though," he said, searching the base.

"Yeah, it said 'under,' right? Under the Great." She stepped up to the bust and murmured, "Sorry 'bout this, Cas."

He stepped back to pull out the little printed notebook from his jacket. "I don't think—"

But Ridley had already heaved the sledgehammer back. She swung with all her might and smashed it into the great king's temple.

Chunks of the rock salt flew. Booker leapt back, shielding his face.

She took another swing, and another, until she'd obliterated the memorial statue. Finally, she stood back to assess her work.

Her partner moved forward to inspect the stone carnage. "Nope."

"No—what?"

"There's nothing here. This is the wrong 'Great.'"

Ridley propped the sledge on the ground and leaned one hand on it. "There are no other 'Greats' in this whole damn mine. What are you talking about?"

Booker slapped the salt stone. His eyes were getting that gleam.

"Who would Dee have thought to be *great?*"

Ridley gestured to the shattered remains of the statue. "Well, now I'm guessing *not* Casimir the Great."

"You remember what chamber's across from this one."

Ridley hoisted the sledgehammer over her shoulder. She had worked hard on the train to memorize a diagram of the colossal mine. Exhaling a puff of air, she nodded.

"Yeah. The Copernicus Chamber."

"*That's* a great."

She cursed herself inwardly.

*For shit's sake, Samaras. You just destroyed a centuries-old statue. Why didn't you think?*

"Let's go. Let's go!" Booker grabbed the backpack and strode out of the cavern.

She gave a wincing glance at the wreckage of King Casimir, and trotted out after her partner.

They made their way through another cavern, crossed over the main stairwell again, and down a long passageway. At the end of it, they found themselves in another large chamber. Even though it was smaller than Casimir's, it still dwarfed them with its lofty ceiling and interlocking timber walls.

Along one wall, illuminated with accent lights, was a grand, dramatic statue of Nicolas Copernicus. It stood on a stone dais, one arm holding up an orb meant to be the solar system.

Booker bent down in front of it.

Below the name at the feet of the statue was a carved arch. Under the arch was a familiar sign.

SOL.

*The sun segment of the hieroglyphic monad.*

Booker pressed his fingers against the symbol. Nothing moved. Then he pitched his whole weight into it, and the symbol depressed into the arch. They heard a deep scraping, and the stone beneath the arch slid down into the floor.

The space was about three feet tall and two feet wide. Beyond it was pure darkness.

Ridley crouched down and shined a flashlight into it. A few feet behind the arch, a tunnel opened up that looked almost high enough to stand in.

"Toto, we're not in Kansas anymore," she said.

Booker's knees creaked as he stood up and pulled out the notebook again.

"This part...could really be clearer."

"Tell me what I need to know."

He gave her a look. "You think you're gonna be okay in there, pickin' up another key?"

"Well, you're not gonna get through that doorway, so necessity says yeah. I'm great."

"Your snark crap is real endearing." He turned back to the pages and frowned. "*The ring within rings, the Hebrew trinity.* A ring...I only know of one ring with Dee. He was 'instructed' to make it. Those 'angel' things gave him a whole long order—*detailed*—including the Sigillum Dei. One of them...one of them was a ring. And yes," he said, looking at Ridley, "it goes back to the Seal of Solomon."

"Of course."

*Can't get away from that damn ring. All these ancient people loved it.*

"Well," she said, dropping to the ground and sliding under the arch feet first, "I'll recognize that one."

Booker knelt down to call into the tunnel after her. "It's not *the* Seal of Solomon, it just has some connection to it!"

Ridley got to her feet in the dark space, but still had to stoop slightly.

*Not enough headroom for a modern woman.*

She aimed her flashlight down the narrow tunnel. It was wide enough for two of her, but only about ten feet long. There was a clean flat wall at the end.

Booker called in after her. "Get me on video call. I'll walk through it with you."

As she pulled out her phone, the flashlight beam swept the walls. Her hand slowed and stopped.

The salt walls were carved, every inch of them an intricate mural.

It was some of the most vivid and macabre artwork that she had ever laid eyes on. There were demonic figures strewn about, some writhing in chains, some contorted in pain. Legions of fiery angels scattered them to the pits of hell. They descended from the starry heavens, planets shining behind them, to slay the writhing enemies in darkness.

She slid out her phone and dialed her partner on video.

"Book...was Dee an artist?"

"No. Why?"

As she showed him the wall, he murmured in astonishment.

"That's like a Hieronymus Bosch. Incredible. All the apocalyptic visions Dee and Kelly were transcribing, all the battle cries for the angels...incredible."

The clock in Ridley's head was ticking, though. She walked to the end of the tunnel, inspecting the dead-end wall.

There in the middle was a ring, faintly carved, about a foot in diameter. There was a series of characters along the edge—like a clock—but these looked to be letters of a foreign language.

She peered closely at them. It was multiple languages.

"Okay, tell me what I'm lookin' for," she said, aiming the phone camera at the ring.

On the other end, Booker was looking them over. "Looks like Cyrillic, Arabic, Hebrew, Greek—that you know—Latin... Sanskrit? Maybe Chinese in there...no Enochian."

"It's the *Hebrew* Trinity," said Ridley, but she couldn't tell a Hebrew character from a Cyrillic or Sanskrit one.

"It's the PELE ring!" exclaimed Booker. "It's usually in Latin, but can be inscribed also in Hebrew. The archangels told Dee how to make it. Allegedly. It says, 'he will work wonders,' and that first letter you want is a *pe*."

*Should have learned this alphabet already...I've been useless in this mine. GET GOING.*

"Tell me like it's a clock," she said.

"The *pe* is at your eight o'clock."

She pressed hard into the carved *pe*, and a deep bellowing scrape rang out in the tunnel.

The flat wall in front of her slid down into the floor, opening up a dark passageway ahead.

But then she heard a thud behind her.

Ridley turned to look.

The entrance had sealed shut.

# CHAPTER
# SEVENTEEN

**KRAKÓW, POLAND**

Ridley stared at the vault door, her exit now blocked. She looked back at the ring of alphabet characters, then at Booker's face, shining out from the screen of her phone.

"What did you press?" he exclaimed.

"Don't worry, I pressed the right one."

*Did I?*

"This can't be right..." he muttered.

"Well," said Ridley, shining the flashlight down into the newly opened section of tunnel, "I guess I keep going. Finish the puzzle and maybe there's a way out."

She headed deeper in. The tunnel here was only a few inches narrower than the first section, but that felt ominous. The salt walls were carved with similar motifs, a mural of war between the celestial and the beastly.

"Obviously he didn't do all this digging and booby-trapping alone," said Ridley, "but still—*how* did he *do* this?"

"There's somethin' spooky just in the fact that this all

exists. Dee was poor his whole life, always scraping and pleading for patronage."

"Spooky? Yeah, it is, thanks."

The hallway curved slightly. As she rounded it, another dead-end wall appeared. In the center of this one as well was a dial-like ring.

More foreign letters.

"Time for your erudite magic," she said to Booker, scanning the phone camera slowly around the ring.

"Sor...what? You froze."

"Tell me which letter!"

"It's an...would be *lamed*—"

He was breaking up. She looked down at the phone. "Sir...?"

Then his picture moved. He was holding up a page of the notebook copy, onto which he'd drawn two Hebrew letters. Her eyes scanned them hurriedly.

"This!" he said, pointing to one of them before the picture froze again.

Just as she was about to click and screenshot the image, it blurred out.

"Shit."

Ridley turned to the wall. She didn't dare waste any more time or go back into the first section of the tunnel in case there was some trap that would lock her out of this one.

*I got this. I saw the letters.*

She looked down at the carved ring, poring over each character.

*I can cross off the Latin, and the Greek...and that one looks Chinese...*

Then she saw one that matched what Booker had drawn. She knew it.

But then she spotted another that looked like the other character that he had drawn.

*Hebrew reads right to left, but did he think of that when he wrote down the two letters? Did he write them backward for me, thinking I didn't know? What happens if I press the wrong one?*

She clenched her fist over and over, mind racing.

Then she reached out and pressed one.

A deep scraping rang out, and the wall slid down into the floor.

She exhaled in relief.

*He had faith in me. Book would have written it the Hebrew way and bet on me to know it.*

But in that same moment, the wall behind her sealed shut with a heavy thud.

The video call went completely dead. She hung up and shoved it back into her pocket. There was nothing else to do but continue on through the new door.

The tunnel there narrowed even further. Her broad shoulders brushed against the salt murals from hell as she made her way.

This one wound in S-shapes as well. She wasn't really claustrophobic, but the combination of apocalyptic art and the tight, dark space was beginning to put her on edge.

Nearly five yards in, she spotted it: the last wall. And there was the carved ring of letters.

She inspected it closely, ruling out three already.

Seven left to choose from.

She remembered Booker's writing...it looked like an "N."

And on this ring were *two* letters that looked like an "N."

"Ahh, no, damnit!"

Ridley gripped her head with both hands, the beam of the flashlight flailing about.

"There are too many languages!" she shouted at the wall.

*Focus. Choose. Please, God, wherever you live.*

She had always been brave, near reckless when facing

brushes or even staredowns with death, but she always thought it would look more like going out in a hail of bullets. She did not want to wither away and die in a hidden tunnel in a mine.

Ridley drew a deep breath, hovered her hand over the letters, and pressed one.

The wall scraped open.

She let out a laugh of disbelief and stepped into the chamber beyond.

The whole space was no bigger than a desk cubicle, and the roof so low that Ridley had to hunch.

The back of the chamber had only one thing carved into the salt wall: an archangel wielding a fiery sword, its magnificent wings spread end to end like a canopy. It looked down at the floor.

*Not enough eyeballs on that angel, biblically.*

In the middle, shining in the beam of her flashlight, was a glass case. It looked like a jewelry box.

She crouched down and peered inside.

"There you are," she murmured.

She gave a quick glance around for any hidden notches or slits in the walls. Booby traps were enough of a normal occurrence in her line of work that it was always good to check.

But John Dee hadn't devised a test for the learned and devout just to sabotage them at the prize. Ridley opened the top of the glass case.

She hesitated.

*Testing time. If these damn keys are the cause of hallucinations, I'm about to find out hard.*

She braced herself and pulled out the carved piece of quartz.

This one looked like a pair of C's linked back to back. It was the same size as the others, the cutwork almost stunning in its precision.

She shoved it down into a deep, snug pocket along her thigh, and stood up.

"Wait...exit?!" she shouted.

*Did something malfunction? What if the mechanisms are broken after centuries?*

She drew in a deep breath through her nose, expelling it slowly with determination. She methodically swept the flashlight over the walls...until one detail caught her eye.

Around its neck, the huge carved angel wore an amulet with the *SOL* symbol.

Ridley pressed into it with all her strength.

And the door behind her reopened.

She darted through it.

It was so dark beyond the beam of the flashlight that she wasn't sure how she knew the air had changed, but she knew it.

Suddenly, she was aware of the salty stale scent, the dry air in her nostrils, the uneven ground beneath her feet.

But then the walls around her seemed to ripple. Something shimmered over the apocalyptic murals.

Ridley whipped around with the light, trying to spot what it was—*where it* was. The beam caught just the tail end of something that was definitely moving—

*Is that a fucking dress?!*

She bolted to the end of the tunnel section, quickly found another angel on the wall wearing an amulet, and smashed the button. The next door opened.

Ridley felt like the wall carvings were pressing in on her. They were moving, or something was moving inside of them. She couldn't look to find out.

She smashed the next button, scampered over the doorway, and dashed down the tunnel.

When she reached the end and the small arch finally opened, she practically dived through it.

She heard Booker mutter, "Praise baby Jesus," as she scrambled to her feet.

"Here, here, here," she said, pulling it from her pocket like a burning coal.

But he was looking down at his phone, backpack slung over his shoulder, his face taut. She knew that expression.

"We gotta go," he said. "Not the way we came."

"Take this!"

She pushed the key into his hand. He shoved her toward the exit end of the huge cavern, and before she could protest, pushed the phone at her.

Ridley looked down to see the crystalline feed from the camera in the last corridor—

Where Bill Dane was leading his team toward the Copernicus Chamber.

# CHAPTER
# EIGHTEEN

**KRAKÓW, POLAND**

The only other way out of the Copernicus Chamber led them deeper into the mine. So Ridley and Booker ran.

They took the timber corridor that ramped down, back toward the central shaft with the stairs.

Yet soon as they reached it, they realized that the stairwell ended there. The steps descended no farther. The only thing available was the industrial elevator lift.

"Thank God," muttered Booker as they rushed into the cramped metal box and racked the gate shut. "These knees are rioting."

Ridley looked for the buttons. There were none.

"No, no, no..."

She caught sight of the up and down mechanism—on the tunnel wall outside the elevator. They were large metal rings attached to chains, meant to pull. It was made for a lift operator to control, not for the riders.

Booker hauled the gate open as Ridley grabbed the crowbar from the backpack.

"Grab my hand," she said.

He gripped her free hand, bracing all his weight back on his heels. She leaned out of the elevator, reaching with the end of the crowbar.

"Another inch!"

The dual chains had no symbols on them, only a word each, written in Polish.

Booker had to grab the handrail in the elevator, letting all of Ridley's weight out at a wild slant to the ground. He was thankful his strength hadn't gone the way his cardio had.

*One more inch...*

Ridley flung her wrist out, and the claw of the heavy crowbar grabbed one of the rings. She yanked.

The elevator lurched. Booker hauled her back inside as the crowbar slipped from her fingers.

But instead of moving up, they felt the floor jostle and sink. They were going down.

Booker let out a laugh that was half bitter, half gleeful. As though *this* was what it was really like to be back in the field again.

He almost couldn't hear Ridley's cursing.

As the mine shaft engulfed them, he murmured to himself. "There are older and fouler things than orcs in the deep places of the world."

She drew the HK VP9 from her belt, her eyes lit with a furious determination. "The 'fouler' part here would be me."

They could only hope that they would stop midway at Floor II, not be carried down to the very darkest bowels of the mine. The lost time itself would be painfully costly.

Booker secured the backpack, buckling even the strap that barely fit across his broad chest. He double-checked his Glock for one in the chamber, but then re-holstered it.

He knew these things were true around the world, certainly

in the Northern Hemisphere: it would be more alarming for people to see a black man holding a gun than a white woman doing the same.

The lift juddered as it continued its slow descent. With no sense of distance in the gargantuan mine, the seconds that passed felt interminable to them both.

Ridley gripped her pistol, trying to relax her stance as she stared at the walls of salt sliding by.

Though she had studied the diagrams with intense commitment, they were imprecise, lacking the details and connecting corridors that made this underground labyrinth so convoluted. There were more than a hundred and seventy-five miles of tunnels down here, though the average tour covered barely over two.

The lift slowed. She and Booker tensed.

Then the wall seemed to unsheathe in front of them, and they were looking into a huge, brightly lit gift shop.

*This wasn't on my map.*

There was a second's pause before they exchanged a glance.

"Do you want to go back up?" she whispered.

"No. We risk runnin' into them."

They stepped out.

Ridley kept her gun low, discreet against the black of her pants. There was no one in this section of the mine this early, except for one cashier behind the refreshments counter and another by the gleaming display cases.

"Think we could purchase some salt?" muttered Ridley.

Booker spotted a large LED map on one of the walls and hurried over to it. He was as disoriented as his partner.

"Here we go..." he traced a finger along the screen. "This way."

He bolted out through a brick archway, and Ridley followed him into a long, bleached timber hallway. They ran.

From the gentle slope upward it was clear they were heading the right way, and it was only a moment before they reached one of the mammoth chambers.

This one nearly stopped them in their tracks. It was practically a cathedral of bleached timber scaffolding, reaching a hundred feet high. A grand chandelier even hung overhead.

"Michałowice," said Ridley, recognizing the chamber. "Next one is Baracz."

She went across and trotted down the short stone steps into another corridor. Booker followed, doing his resolute, most prideful best to not let on how much the extra pounds and years were weighing him down.

*He's slowing. Of course he is.*

Even as her frustration flared up, Ridley managed to quench it with a stronger impulse: to get her little team to safety.

"Give me the bag," she said.

"No, I'm fine with it," he replied, trying not to wheeze.

Ridley reached out to unbuckle the chest strap but he smacked her away.

"I'm good!"

"I'm not tryin' to be nice! Just give me the bag!" she snapped.

It would have been less humiliating if she'd put him on a scale, but this was about executing a mission, not his self-esteem.

Booker wrenched the bag off his shoulders and held it out to her. Ridley slipped into it, buckled the chest strap, and moved on.

When they reached the end of the hallway, they emerged onto a wooden gangway in an immense cavern. Below the railing was a pool of water, lit from within, glowing bright emerald. The light rippled up onto the sheer walls, creating an eerie dance of shadows. A narrow, restricted walkway connected to the main one, snaking along the back of the cavern, up and up and up.

Bach's "Air on the G String" drifted from surround sound speakers, filling the chamber with an eerie, sublime calm.

Booker looked down the gangway toward the hallway exit, then nodded to the railed walkway that wound up and around the pool.

"That's a shortcut to—"

He didn't finish his sentence. His gaze caught movement high up on the dark walkway.

It was the bearded man who had come after him in Prague. He was not alone.

And his eyes had just locked onto them.

# CHAPTER
# NINETEEN

**KRAKÓW, POLAND**

"Down!"

Booker yanked Ridley behind the railing as shouts echoed through the cavern.

The wooden slats were thick, but there was space between them. It was barely concealment, let alone cover.

But then—exposed as they were on the open walkway with only a flat wall behind them—their enemies had neither cover nor concealment.

Ridley glanced out. There was the bearded man in front, the lantern jaw behind him, and two similar-looking goons who seemed like tag-alongs.

*Thing One and Thing Two.*

Well behind them was a middle-aged blonde woman, and bringing up the rear with her was a slender young man. When they saw Ridley and Booker below, the slender man pulled the woman back until they were out of sight.

The rest were drawing guns and beginning to storm down the walkway.

Ridley lifted the VP9, sighted the red dot and fired four times.

The sound was deafening, and immediately returned by a volley from the other side.

Wood splintered the railing around her. More shouts.

"I'll cover!" said Booker.

Staying low, Ridley scrambled forward. The gloom of the cavern and the dancing puddles of light everywhere helped to keep her obscured.

The walkway made two right angles as it wrapped around a square section of the wall, and then joined with the main path right at her exit point.

Booker loosed a volley at Thing Two bringing up the rear. He spasmed, grunted, and spilled over the walkway. His body splashed into the pool below.

But he wouldn't sink. The water was brine, so saturated with salt that it was impossible to sink into it. His limp body floated on the glowing surface, a trickle of scarlet streaming outward.

Ridley glimpsed the bearded man taking cover against the angled wall, barely twenty feet away. The exit corridor was nearly the same distance, but she did not want to get caught running down an open hallway.

The bearded one slid out from the edge only enough to loose some shots at her.

The bullets bit into the salt wall. One landed in the wood at her feet. Ridley slipped her barrel up and fired, forcing him back.

She had four left in this magazine, though another was loaded up in her pocket. The lantern-jawed man leaned out with an M4 rifle and fired a volley toward the gangway.

*They have superior cover. More firepower...but they're stacked one behind the other.*

Then she realized, if they were to break for it down the long hallway, Booker would need a head start.

"Hey!" she shouted at her partner over the cacophony. "Go!"

She beckoned wildly. Booker saw it in her urgency. He must have realized the same and knew that now was not a time for valiant recklessness. He nodded.

Ridley laid down a suppressive volley as he made a rush behind her. He reached the corridor just as her slide locked back.

She was already slipping in a new mag as the empty one hit the floor. For a suspended second, the only sounds in the cavern were the ethereal strings of Bach.

Booker hesitated at the sense of fleeing, but there was a reason he'd brought Ridley on this mission. Many, in fact, and she would be able to catch up to him in no time.

He turned into the long hallway and put as much speed as he could physically muster into his heavy legs.

On the gangway, Ridley was huddled below the rail in darkness, testing, waiting, timing...her gun raised, holding her fire...

Until the bearded one skimmed out to take another shot.

She squeezed the trigger rapid-fire.

He must have sensed that was coming. He had ducked lower to reposition his head. The bullets flew over him.

Lantern jaw then appeared above him, laying down a volley as Ridley flattened herself against a low rock jutting out nearby.

The bearded one used the cover fire to advance. He was coming down the walkway toward her, closing the distance to fifteen feet...twelve...ten...

She wanted to give Booker more time, but her window was closing fast and she couldn't risk burning up the rest of her ammo here.

*He better be running his ass off—*

She ripped open the backpack and pulled out the last remaining tool: the pickaxe.

And Ridley hurled it as hard as she could.

The man couldn't properly see it coming in the dark, and he was too close to duck. The iron chisel struck him in the head. Snapping with surprised pain, he reeled and stumbled. His equilibrium was lost. The railing was too low.

Bill Dane toppled over the edge and fell a dozen feet into the water below.

This was the second's worth of distraction she needed. Ridley launched herself into the hallway, hearing the shouts echoing in the cavern behind her.

She tore into a full sprint.

Dane hit the glowing pool of brine and the density of the water nearly shoved him back to the surface.

His vision was still spinning. Overhead, he could hear Freddie shouting down to him.

Scrambling in the strangely buoyant water, Dane blinked against the sting of the salt. He looked for a way out. There wasn't one. The walls were sheer for at least ten feet on every side, with nothing more than ragged divots.

So be it.

He swam to the edge and attacked the wall like an animal. Hands and feet gripping and reaching and hauling on the slightest of notches. One crumbled—he snatched for another. One foot slipped—he swung his leg even higher onto the next divot.

Within seconds, he was pulling himself up the wooden walkway. Freddie grabbed his jacket and helped drag him over the rail.

Dane was dripping wet, but didn't even bother to wipe the strangely slimy water off his face.

"Go! Go!" he barked, yanking a backup Glock from his waistband.

Freddie grabbed their extra Polish muscle. "Come on!"

Qualley had reappeared at the top of the walkway with a wide-eyed Lianna, clutching a gun in his own hand. He led her down through the cavern after the others.

Dane, Freddie, and the Pole tore down the walkway and into the corridor.

Ridley was sprinting for her life, counting the seconds until a gunshot would explode in the hallway behind her.

It was only a hundred feet to the next chamber, and there was no sign of Booker.

*Old man must have some speed left in him.*

Just as she caught sight of the bright cavern opening in front of her, a crack split the air. The timber wall beside her splintered.

She hurled herself through the doorway, and into St. Kinga's Chapel.

It was a breathtaking sight, a vast and reverent place of worship. There was an altar at the end, exquisite chandeliers made of salt crystals, and saintly murals carved into the walls. Two long stairways flanked upward, behind the corridor from which Ridley had just emerged.

Booker was stationed at the base of one, planted with his Glock at low ready, ready for what was coming through that hallway. He was still catching his breath from the sprint.

As Ridley burst into the chapel, he yelled for her.

"Up the stairs!"

More gunshots blistered in the hallway, coming closer.

She bolted for the opposite set of stairs. Taking cover behind the banister, she aimed her HK at the corridor.

*They can't be so stupid as to run right in...*

They weren't.

What came through that open doorway next was not an enemy combatant. It was a flashbang.

As the canister clattered along the smooth tile floor, time seemed to slow. Ridley and Booker both recognized the stun grenade instantly. They only needed their limbs to work faster.

They each leapt up their staircase, clamping their eyes shut, boxing their hands over their ears—

The explosion was deafening. It reverberated through the cavern with a blinding flash.

The grenade had landed closer to Ridley, and the shockwave blew her into the wall. She reeled.

She could barely hear the voice of Booker yelling through the din. Her right ear was always slightly muffled from the damage of her diving accident, but this pressure blast had just destroyed her equilibrium. She felt sick.

All she could do was force herself to crawl and stagger up the steps.

She turned and fired blindly down into the cavern.

A cacophony of shots answered her.

The audio buzz was just starting to clear. She could see Booker across the other staircase, shooting as he backed up the steps.

Ridley scrambled like she was drunk, unable to stand, letting off wild shots in the general direction of her pursuers.

She could hardly believe it when she realized she was at the top of the stairs. She'd somehow made it through the hail of bullets chipping into the salt-carved banister and walls around her. Booker was there, hauling her through the next doorway.

This one closed.

He pulled the heavy wooden door shut and grabbed the small hammer from Ridley's backpack. She could only fight the urge to vomit as he wedged the hammer into the broad door handle.

Then he grabbed Ridley and dragged her down the corridor. Within seconds they heard banging and smashing behind them. More gunshots echoed through the mine, but he had bought them the precious time they needed.

They ran and climbed, up and up. Booker tied another door shut behind them with the remaining length of rope. Ridley finally regained enough steadiness to put on some speed.

They clambered up the diabolically steep stairwell they'd gone down at first. They emerged into the entrance hall where they nearly bowled over a stunned guide and, without saying a word, sped toward the door, and finally burst out into bright, frigid morning.

"Stop! Drop your guns!"

In the parking lot in front of them was an SUV and a tactical police van. Fully kitted-out officers swarmed through the snow, their rifles raised. A few men in suits joined them, pistols at the ready.

Booker and Ridley dropped their guns to the ground and lifted their hands.

"Are you saying we made a scene?" she muttered under her breath.

He was still sweating from their sprint through the mine. "This would be the fastest police response I've seen in years."

"No...too fast. Something else happened. They knew we were here."

From the passenger side of the SUV, a woman stepped out into the snow. She was in her late forties, wearing a trim navy pantsuit under a woolen coat. Her thick dark hair was perfectly coiffed above her shoulders, and her melancholic blue gaze was strangely arresting. As it settled on the two foreigners, Ridley could feel the unmistakable confidence in it.

*This is the boss.*

"You're Americans?" Her voice was soft, with barely any hint of a Polish accent.

"Yes, ma'am," said Booker.

She nodded, looking them over as if they were oddities. "You know we don't let tourists run around our national heritage sites with guns."

"Will all respect, there are some individuals comin' up the mine right now that you may actually need your own guns for."

"Thank you. I know."

As if on cue, the tactical police unit swept into the building behind them. The men in suits remained, closing in on Ridley and Booker. Two of them pulled out cuffs.

"I'm Deputy Director Maślak," she said. "You're under arrest, obviously."

"Obviously," said Ridley as one of the suits pulled her wrists down.

A man stepped out of the back of the SUV. He wore a black peacoat, and a distressed scowl over his deep-set blue eyes.

"It's not them," he said to Maślak.

*That's a Glasgow accent. Who the hell is this?*

## CHAPTER
# TWENTY

**KRAKÓW, POLAND**

Ridley and Booker sat together in an interrogation room.

As they had been cuffed and shuttled across the city in the SUV, he'd explained in calm, civil tones that he was a CIA department director. No, they couldn't find his name listed anywhere publicly. Yes, there was an extension for them to call, if Maślak would like to use her official line to the Central Intelligence Agency.

The Scottish man stayed silent, glancing at them every few minutes.

Maślak did call the agency on the drive, relaying the identification number that Booker recited for her. They confirmed his identity. She thanked them and hung up.

"Director Douglas," she said, her striking gaze catching them in the rear-view mirror. "I think we can keep this below the level of 'international incident.'"

"Director Maślak. I think all of our higher-ups would be very happy to hear that."

They'd been thoroughly patted down, their bag and passports taken, and every weapon and item from their pockets had been removed for safekeeping...including the quartz keys.

Once they reached the station, Deputy Director Maślak had ordered their handcuffs removed, and said that she would not be separating them yet "as a professional courtesy." Then she and the accompanying officer left the room.

Ridley tapped the table impatiently, glancing at the two-way mirror beside them.

"We don't have time for this," she grumbled. "At least they must have that goon squad in custody, right?"

Booker glanced at whomever was behind the mirror. "I'd hope so. They almost triggered an international incident."

They didn't want to say much more, since they were certainly being recorded.

A moment later, Maślak walked back into the room by herself, holding a file. She took a seat across from them.

"Did you catch them?" asked Ridley.

"The task force spent an hour sweeping the Wieliczka mine. They didn't find the individuals you described. Of course, that mine has almost three hundred kilometers of tunnels, and there were already a number of tours underway before we could call them back."

Ridley snorted in frustration and pushed back from the table.

"But we have recovered the CCTV from this morning."

She opened the file and spread out its contents on the table: printed stills of black and white surveillance footage.

There was the bearded man in front, leading the team that had opened fire on them.

"Do you know them?" asked Maślak.

There was something beguiling about her. Her voice was gentle and soft, but her gaze was intensely focused.

*She must be the most successful interrogator in Poland. I'd tell her.*

"We have no idea who they are," said Booker as he inspected the photos.

"Why did they shoot at you?"

He gave a wry smile. "I'm a black man from St. Louis, ma'am. That might not mean much to you, but I've watched bullets fly since I was nine years old and no one ever could give a reason."

Booker didn't do this often, but he actually seemed to be enjoying himself. Maślak's gaze was implacable.

Ridley leaned forward, sifting through the photos. "Can *you* tell us who they are?"

The deputy director looked up to the mirror as though signaling someone.

"Why don't you tell me what you're both doing in Poland?" she asked.

"The Christmas markets here are divine," said Ridley.

She could tell Booker hated this response, but Maślak gave her a surprising, thoroughly disarming smile.

"They are delightful. It's always a task to keep them safe from terrorists now, but that's not a job for the CIA. That's on us."

The door behind her opened just then, and in walked the blue-eyed Scot.

"I'd like to introduce you to Agent Carnegie," she said.

He pulled up the seat beside Maślak.

"'Mornin'," he said.

The first thing that struck Ridley was his intensity, that shade of lapis lazuli set deep under heavy brows. His dark reddish hair was swept back in short waves. He had a stony look to him, a chiseled jaw and broad, somber mouth.

*Handsome bastard.*

"Well, you're not Polish," she said, giving him a dead-eyed look of challenge.

Before he could reply, Booker said, "You pointed them to us? How did you know anything about us being in that mine?"

"Who are you?" pressed Ridley.

He actually laughed. "Give me a minute. My name is Iain Carnegie. I'm with MI5, and I wasn't followin' you. I was followin' them."

He smacked a hand down on the photo of the bearded man.

"Not very closely, I guess," shot Ridley.

"How many rounds did you go through down there? And you only hit one of 'em?"

When neither of the Americans responded, Maślak said, "We found the body of a local small-scale criminal in the Baracz Chamber, floating in the brine pool. Since we don't know what kinds of guns these other individuals were using, we can't determine if the shots were theirs or yours, but..." She raised a hand as if to say, *obviously*.

"So who are they?" asked Booker. "Why are you following them around the continent?"

Iain straightened up. "What I'd like to know—and I'm pretty sure I get to ask because I'm on *this* side of the interrogation table—is why *they* were followin' *you?*"

"That's classified."

Ridley looked at Maślak. "Why are you working with MI5?"

"Agent Carnegie alerted us to some individuals of interest who were entering our borders," she replied.

"Look, I think we got off here a bit wrong," said Carnegie, softening. "I've got somethin' that might help you, and I think you know somethin' that would help me. I'm not tryin' to make trouble for you."

Though MI5 was as old as allies got with the CIA, the interests of their own countries were always paramount.

There was no such thing as a friendly foreign intelligence service.

"Director Maślak," said Booker, "are we under arrest?"

There was a loaded pause.

"Director Douglas, you know you have diplomatic immunity," she said. "We're only here to speak with you as...peers."

Booker stood, his chair scraping back along the floor.

"Well, then. We appreciate your consideration. We'll just get our things and be on our way." He glanced up at the camera in the corner of the ceiling. "Agent Carnegie, come grab a cup of coffee with us."

Ridley blinked at her boss as she stood up, but knew she shouldn't have been surprised.

*This is what he does. Classic spy. He's a people dealer.*

Carnegie gave a nod and got to his feet.

An hour later, Ridley and Booker sat on a bench in Jordan Park. She held her steaming cup of flat white while he winced at the burning first sip of his cappuccino. A handful of skaters glided by on the ice alleys that wound their way through the park.

"Is this the first time you've ever been caught up in a foreign country?" she asked Booker.

"By the country? Yes." He gave a dark chuckle. "By a militia? No."

Maślak had returned everything to them except their guns.

"Unless we're driving you straight to the American embassy, and then we will hand them back to you at the gate," she'd told them.

"Grinch," Ridley had muttered to herself.

So she sat now with her Magnum Spike karambit reaffixed along her belt, and the three precious quartz keys tucked snugly in her deepest pocket.

Iain Carnegie came striding up clutching a steaming cup of his own. He brushed snow off a large rock next to them and took up a perch on it.

"I know you don't want to be here another minute," he said. "Neither do I."

Ridley nodded deeply.

*We're being delayed. We're losing time. If they sneaked out of that mine, they're already ahead of us.*

But to forego gathering intel on their enemy would be indefensible and idiotic. They were barely halfway through this mission, and they needed background on the team that had attacked them twice.

"Starting off on the same page. Excellent," said Booker.

Carnegie went on. "I want to tell you this first: I've not been followin' *you*. I've been trackin' *them*. And *they* are ferocious."

He pulled out his mobile phone, swiped about, and handed it to them. On the screen was a surveillance-style photo in clear color, taken from some yards away. It was the bearded man.

"That's Bill Dane. Former US Army Ranger who got out and went mercenary. He's one of the most focused and relentless sons of bitches I've ever seen in action. Swipe there."

Ridley slid to the next photo. Lantern jaw.

"Freddie Solbakken. Former MJK—Norwegian Naval Special Operations Commando."

*He must have been the one to dive Fingal's Cave.*

"He's a gear specialist, worked with Dane a handful of times. They seem to get along, and Dane doesn't get along with many. Go again."

The next photo was of the lean, chiseled young man.

"Alan Qualley. Like the quiet boy genius. He's a heist man, great at pickin' locks and solving puzzles. Dane trusts him."

"So why is an MI5 agent tracking them?" asked Ridley. "Don't you have a backlog of terrorists to take care of?"

Carnegie looked at her for a moment. His eyes were piercing.

"They're working for a very bad man. No one in the world wants to touch him—and I mean the *world*—and I can't abide it anymore. He's hired this vile lot of killers to do somethin' for him, and *that's* a lead to catch him out."

"Marc Pearson," said Booker, as though it was the final line of an epic.

Carnegie's jaw clenched reflexively. "Yeah."

"There's one more ID you can give us," said Ridley.

She swiped again and held up the screen. There was a photo of the middle-aged blonde woman, the one they'd glimpsed only briefly in the Wieliczka Salt Mine.

"She doesn't look like a mercenary."

"Ah, yeah," said Carnegie, rocking back and taking a sip from his cup. "Her name is Lianna Powell, and this is where I'm askin' you: why is a professor of the Renaissance and Elizabethan England travelin' with these mercenaries?"

Ridley caught a whiff of his drink. "Is that hot chocolate?"

"Yeah, I don't like coffee. You people are all mental. Look, now I've shared my lot with you. Tell me what you're doin' out here, why Dane and his crew are after you, and why they got a professor with them."

Ridley and Booker exchanged a look.

And he told the MI5 agent, without pause. She was surprised by how much her boss and partner was willing to share, but realized there was nothing confidential in it, and one would have no real intel without Dee's notebook.

Carnegie listened implacably, sipping his hot chocolate, interjecting with only a handful of questions.

When Booker had finished, the Scotsman looked between them for a moment.

"So you believe in this. The Devil's Eye, the Sigillum Dei, all these pieces of quartz you're findin'."

*Always the question.*

But he had said it without either scorn or fascination.

"This is what we do," said Booker, his expression weighted with experience. "Most of our operations...will never be disclosed, God willing."

Ridley shot him a quick look and decided to put it out there. "You remember Jerusalem?"

At that, Carnegie's eyes flickered with realization and shock. "That was you?"

It was the cataclysmic incident that had shaken the world and spawned a hundred thousand conspiracy theories. The day that Ridley and her partner Henri had just barely prevented a supernatural destruction. It was the most public revelation of their work that had ever been seen—and seen it had been, on hundreds of cellphone recordings that had lit up the world within minutes.

She raised her hands in admission. Booker looked annoyed, but it was the fastest way to establish legitimacy. Besides, there was something about Carnegie that just seemed...*steadfast.*

"'Right, then," he said, "so you're trackin' these key things, the bad lads are trackin' behind you, and I'm trackin' them. I've got a proposal then." He leaned forward on his knees. "I finish this race with you. We work together, each gets better odds, and we all get what we need in the end."

There was a pause, but then he stood up and started backing away.

"I'll let you two discuss!"

As he wandered toward the rink, out of earshot, Ridley looked at Booker. He didn't meet her eyes, though. Instead, he drew a deep breath and looked out over the happy Christmas scene before them, the lights strung over the ice, the mittened skaters drifting and twirling on the ice.

"You're not serious," she said, realizing what he was deciding to do.

"It's gonna be a 'yes.'"

"Sir! We don't know anything about him!"

"I sent a message to an old contact at MI5. He couldn't send over Carnegie's file, of course, but knew of him through a friend. He vouched for him, but...lot more than that, look what happened in the mine. I left you against superior numbers because I couldn't keep up. Inexcusable," he muttered, shaking his head, "and dangerous."

"I can handle that—"

"You need another set of legs that isn't all tired and thick from neglect."

The edge of self-contempt that bled into his voice alarmed her. He could be self-deprecating at times, but she'd never seen him like this.

"We're not just doin' him a favor," Booker went on. "He's gonna be following us anyway, so we might as well use him on our side...'cause we sure could use him."

Ridley looked across the park at Iain Carnegie. He'd propped his arms along the alley fence, gazing out at the skaters. She could just make out the solemn set of his brow in profile.

She sighed. "Okay, let's go get our Scotsman. No bagpipes."

# CHAPTER
# TWENTY-ONE

### RUŽOMBEROK, SLOVAKIA

Bill Dane pulled off his salt-caked jeans and threw them into the corner of the dressing room. He stripped off his long-sleeved shirt in disgust. Grabbing one of the wet wipes he'd brought in with him, he swiped down the lean muscles of his torso. He leaned over and poured the rest of a water bottle onto his head, shaking out his short hair and scrubbing at his beard.

The brine had made him smell like the rank seashore.

But that treasure hunter duo had made him as testy as a bull shark caught in a creek. Who were they? An old man with a belly and a giant of a woman who outran Freddie. Both American, by their accents. They were both obviously trained, but she looked military. The military wouldn't send out a man so out of shape or old into the field, though.

That left private contractors or one of the alphabet agencies.

Whoever they were, they'd made off with the third key. Just a step ahead—again. They were on to the fourth.

Or were they?

No way the tactical police that had swarmed down into the mine were there on the side of the Americans. They would have brought in a bigger force on the front end, not waited for a firefight. If they'd been caught at the top, they might still be in Polish custody.

But you could never count on someone who wasn't you.

Dane tugged on a hunter green T-shirt, a charcoal sweater, and black jeans. He tied on a pair of hardy boots.

It was time for reinforcements.

He left his old clothes in a pile on the dressing room floor and walked out.

In the back of the women's section, Lianna Powell set a hand on one of the racks and drew a slow, steadying breath.

After the adrenaline had dissipated, a daze enveloped her that she hadn't been able to shake. Her words had wobbled when she tried to speak during the drive out of Kraków, but her armed escorts had been so aggravated about their failure that her voice was lost in their arguing.

Only two weeks ago, she had been sitting in her office at St. Andrews on a blustery winter afternoon, sorting through her mail. There in the stack was something unusual, a gold-embossed invitation to a gala hosted by the billionaire financier Marc Pearson and his socialite partner, Effie Crowhurst.

Lianna had to put on her glasses to double-check the name on the card, and would have thought it was a mistake had there not been a smaller note tucked inside the envelope.

Handwritten, it said:

*"Dear Professor Powell, I've become a great admirer of your work on the corpus of John Dee and would be delighted at the opportunity to meet you. It would be my honor if you would attend this event so we might be able to speak in person. I eagerly await*

*your reply. (And I'll send a personal car for you on the night) — Marc"*

It was so formally phrased and yet warm, personable. Clever, she'd thought. It certainly felt like it had been crafted for a professor of Elizabethan England.

For the next thirty hours, she kept the note and the invitation on her desk, glancing at it in disbelief throughout the day. When she finally responded, she included a short note of her own.

*"Dear Mr. Pearson, I'm honored by your invitation and will happily attend. Thank you. Please be in touch about the car."*

She included the phone number to her office and signed it rather formally, *Professor Lianna Powell*.

Then she realized she'd need to buy a dress. She hadn't been in need of a new outfit like that in a decade. Since her divorce a few years back, she hadn't found a single occasion that would warrant a brand-new look.

Not that prior to her divorce it would have meant much, either. It had taken her too long to come to terms with something she'd probably always known at the bottom of her heart: her husband's eyes had never lit up at the sight of her, even when she was the fittest girl in the county. They'd never lit up at the sight of any woman. She'd finally let it go—let him go—and after stewing in her own animus and self-pity for a year, wished the best for him, that he might one day find the partner who *did* light him up, and be the man he'd never been able to be for fear of judgment.

Still, she thought spikily from time to time, it's a cruel and selfish thing for queer lads to marry women they don't fancy. He'd wasted the best years of her life, and now in her fifties, she'd felt it was a lost cause to even make the effort.

Until that invitation arrived, and she felt a fizz she hadn't known since she was a much younger woman.

She'd have to delay getting a dress for as long as she possibly could, though. She couldn't bear going to get fitted in this state. Over the next eleven days, she ate almost nothing but hard-boiled eggs, chicken, and lettuce.

By the time she went to get an outfit, she felt miserable. Only the sight of herself in the shop, donning a dress that was one size smaller, made all of that gnawing hunger and terrible sleep worth it.

She'd been awed as Pearson's personal chauffeur pulled up to Gosford House, a beacon of bright, grand elegance in the whipping cold night. She was even more awed when she walked through the front doors to the extravagance inside, a lavish Christmas gala swirling around her, filled with fame and royalty.

Lianna Powell—the girl from a sagging textile town outside Manchester, who'd fallen in love with useless old books from hundreds of years ago, then fallen in love with a man who'd divorced her for the chance to date other men, who'd seen the newest Sherlock Holmes half a dozen times for the delight of watching Benedict Cumberbatch, who'd ordered curry takeaway more times in a month than she'd gone out in a year—had never felt so out of place.

But when the debonair Marc Pearson himself had pulled out a long-lost notebook of one of the most astonishing minds of English history, Lianna Powell had never felt so enraptured.

Marc Pearson could move effortlessly amidst all the trappings of wealth and beauty, but this...*this* was her world. No one knew it better. As she dived into the words of Dee, on the very pages he'd touched and upon which he'd scrawled his genius, Lianna felt herself come alive.

And when Pearson had invited her to follow in the very footsteps of Dee, paying her generously to solve the alchemist's mysterious puzzles and retrieve his treasure, she could scarcely believe this was real life. She was going on an adventure. Not only was she invited, but she was *needed*. For the first time in so long she couldn't even remember, she felt vital, important, respected by important people—people who really *mattered* in this world.

She'd gone home elated and packed immediately.

When she'd been introduced to the team that would escort and protect her, however, she'd wondered what kind of undertaking this would really be. Freddie Solbakken was a hard man, like she'd imagined a Viking would be. Alan Qualley was curious but aloof. And Bill Dane...he was vivid and fierce. She'd never met someone with so much concentrated intensity.

Though they treated her with respect, there was no deference. They were clearly answering to Pearson's directives, and understandably. But there was something unnerving about them all.

When they'd reached Prague, Qualley had taken her off to sit in a café in Old Town Square while Dane and Freddie scoped out the astronomical clock and figured out how they might best infiltrate the tower. She'd known nothing of the chase that ensued until well after the mysterious "other" duo had made off with the quartz key, and Dane and Freddie had returned, perplexed and furious.

Though giving chase to someone was a wholly different thing than pulling a gun and shooting at them.

She had been descending the narrow walkway in the salt mine when the first shot blasted through the cavern. Qualley had immediately pulled her back to safety. Lianna didn't know who'd shot first, but it hardly mattered. She couldn't even see *who* was shooting at them.

Dane had hired two Poles to accompany them into the mine. "Extra hands and eyes," he'd explained to her. It was clear when they drew weapons that they'd been hired for reasons other than having functioning digits and eyeballs.

When a bullet hit the one just ahead of her—when he spasmed and fell forward—she felt the air vacate her lungs. She would never forget the sight of his body plunging into the pool of brine, the sound of the splash when he hit the water.

The cacophony of shots that followed nearly deafened her. She rushed back out of the chamber with Qualley. A gun had appeared in his hand, as well, and by the tense way he watched every exit, she realized he'd been expecting this.

Lianna had watched her father pass away in a hospital bed after a terrible stroke had sapped him of everything, but she'd never seen someone die violently in front of her.

She'd never seen someone killed.

Hours later, as she stood amidst the women's pants in a little clothing store in a small town in Slovakia, she felt her mind still being tossed about. She was in a storm she couldn't comprehend, on a vessel that she didn't understand, being crewed and captained by dangerous men. Not one of them had been rattled by the shootout, or by seeing a colleague shot to death in front of them.

"Hey."

His voice cut sharply through the daze. Lianna startled to see Dane standing a few feet away, pulling on a quilted woolen jacket.

"You okay?"

She couldn't tell if there was a note of genuine compassion in his question, or if he was just checking on his assets.

"Yeah, yeah," she said, straightening up. "I'm all right."

Dane sensed she was coming unmoored. Fair. Not many professors of the Renaissance or old England had been in a firefight.

"We're going next door. Let's get you something to eat," he told her.

She met his eyes with so much earnestness that he was taken aback. "What are we doin' here? What's all this about and why are there people out there tryin' to kill us over an old John Dee puzzle?"

He looked at her for a moment, feeling a pang of actual sympathy. He had to wrestle his gaze away.

"I don't know. But Pearson warned there might be others after it. It's priceless, isn't it? People do dangerous things for priceless stuff. That's why he wanted dangerous men."

"Maybe we should try to find out who they are," she pleaded. "You don't *have* to kill them. We can beat them, bargain with them."

"They have the first three keys," he said, his voice hardening again. "We need to do more than beat them to the next one. We need all of them."

She realized: this is who he is. This is why he's here. He's a killer. She was on the quest of her dreams with killers. And Pearson had hired them for exactly this.

"Come on," he said, gesturing for her to come. "We're going next door. Get you a poppy seed cake at the bakery."

Her nod was resigned. She said quietly, "I could use a cuppa."

They left the shop and walked a short way to the café, where she spotted Freddie and Qualley already at a table, devouring some pastries.

Dane opened the door for her, but didn't follow.

"I'll join you in a minute," he said.

She went in. Damn that miserable diet of hers. This was a day for cake.

Outside, Dane pulled out his phone.

He dialed Marc Pearson.

# CHAPTER
# TWENTY-TWO

**PALMA DE MALLORCA, SPAIN**

The Arab bathhouse was one of Effie's favorite places in Mallorca. So Pearson had rented the whole of it for their small list of VIP guests.

It was a maze of quiet, intimate spaces. There were steam rooms with tawny stone walls, arched doorways hung with curtains, and candles on every carved bench.

Leaning along the wall in one of the rooms, wearing nothing but towels around their waists, were a senator in his sixties, the head of an international modeling agency in his fifties, and a financier in his thirties. All were sheened with sweat. Only the torso of the fit young financier looked better for it.

Keeping them company were four young women with towels wrapped around their chests. They hardly said a word as the men talked and laughed with each other, but they knew to position themselves nearby and never look distracted.

In a nearby room with a shallow soaking pool, Moroccan lamps all around the edge cast latticed light along the burgundy walls. Marc Pearson reclined in the water. Next to him was Sean "Redhand" Darius, a musician in his forties who had made the transition from snarling hip-hop to a more domesticated, lucrative pop music producer.

Effie—in a bikini that bordered on "why bother"—floated atop the underwater marble step across from them. Beside her was Lexi, in a yellow one-piece bathing suit, keeping herself submerged up to her neck.

She'd never been in a bathhouse before. She'd never been to Spain before. And she certainly had never met a celebrity like Redhand before. Effie and Marc had been treating her lavishly well.

Lexi's mother had driven her to the small airport where her fourteen-year-old daughter got to board a private jet with her violin case in tow. During the flight, Marc and Effie had coaxed her with a wink into having a glass of extremely expensive champagne with them. She gagged a bit on the dry bubbles, but smiled and drank the entire flute of it.

Once in Mallorca, they'd taken her shopping for a new bathing suit. Effie insisted on pulling five or six and accompanying her to the dressing room to be "the fashion judge." She was the most stylish person Lexi had ever seen, but even as she insisted on buying two of the bikinis, Lexi pushed to include a one-piece.

Effie knew when to give a little with teenage girls who were self-conscious, even one who had the looks of Lexi Rapp. So she bought all three for her. Let her wear the one-piece first. This would be a breaking-in process.

Now, as Lexi floated herself as low as she could get in the water, she still felt Redhand looking at her occasionally in a way that made her nervous. Part of her was fluttering that someone so famous would look at her like she was worth his attention, but the other part wanted to sink even lower...beneath the surface, out of sight.

"She's an amazing musician," Marc told Redhand, nodding to Lexi across from them.

He raised his brow. "Oh, yeah?"

"Oh, incredible violinist. She's here with us to meet a tutor before going off to one of the best music schools in the world."

Marc smiled at her. She gave an awkward smile back, and glanced at Redhand.

"You know I started using string instruments before Kanye did it," he said. "He took samples from all the old shit, the good shit. I went straight for the fresh strings. Young hungry talent. They put it *down* for some of those tracks."

Lexi had no idea what to say, but then Marc's phone buzzed on the table at the end of the pool.

"Hey, man, no phones!" said Redhand, indignant that he'd had to leave his in the locker room.

"What can I say, the host makes the rules!"

Marc Pearson climbed out, water pouring from his hip huggers. As he grabbed a towel, Effie gave Lexi a look of exasperation.

"The problem with having business around the world?" She leaned in conspiratorially. "He gets these calls at *all* hours."

Pearson draped the towel around his shoulders and grabbed his phone.

The screen read: *Courier*.

He picked it up. "Tell me good things."

Even the flicker of hesitation on the other end of the line made Pearson suddenly sober.

"You know, sir, I only tell you true things," said Dane.

Pearson walked away from the pool out into an empty hallway, warm with the light of candles alone.

"What's true that you would be calling me about?" he said.

"There are others. They had a head start on us and got to the items first. There were—encounters—and I know they're professionals. Tactical training. Obvious knowledge base."

Anger flashed through Pearson. "How the fuck did they get that notebook! I paid a lot of goddamn money for that!"

It wasn't a question, and Dane knew better than to try to answer it.

"I need to hire more hands," he said.

"How many are on this team that's gotten ahead of you?"

There was a hesitation.

"Two, sir."

"Aren't you three?" His tone was chilling.

"Yes."

"How many keys have you gotten?"

"We're on our way to the fourth location now."

Pearson always heard what people didn't say. "How many *keys have you gotten?*"

"None. They have all three."

He'd never known Dane to be bested like this. He tried to hold back his steaming fury.

"So how many extra hands exactly would you need to take on two guys?" he said quietly.

"I've got a connection in Budapest. He can supply us with some muscle, but it depends who's available. With your permission, I'll send you the details as soon as I make contact."

"Get them. You shut down these thieves. They're taking what's mine."

"This won't end well for them," said Dane, his voice quiet and measured.

That was the Bill Dane he had hired.

"Keep me updated," said Pearson, and hung up.

He drew in a deep breath through his nose, held it, then

slowly exhaled through his mouth. And again. Then he turned and walked back to the pool.

The senator, the financier, and the agency head had migrated in as well with their posse of girls. Pearson was mildly annoyed as they piled into the water, their boisterous laughter filling the small space, but he was as much in the hospitality business as he was in the finance business. The spa treatments here were high class. The amenities were top notch. The food they would have later at dinner would be Michelin-starred.

The girls…they were talented, but not Pearson's. They came from the modeling agency and understood that their work here had little to do with their ability to walk a runway.

He grabbed a small cup of tea off an ornate silver platter on the nearby table. He dropped back into a chair, pulling out the sprig of fresh mint to sip on it.

Reset. Focus. Engage.

From the pool, Effie could see his expression, which would have looked like mildly aloof boredom to anyone but her. To her, it was one of raging disappointment in someone else's failure.

She glanced at Lexi beside her, who had grown increasingly uncomfortable with the influx of older men stepping into the pool.

Effie leaned in to her ear.

"You want to get out of here, love?"

Lexi turned to her with a fast nod of relief. Effie grinned and gave her an affectionate rub on the back of her shoulders.

"Come on, then. Let's get massages and then find some baklava."

They stepped up out of the pool. Redhand's gaze followed them for a moment.

From his chair at the end of the pool, Pearson watched as

Effie first handed a towel to Lexi, then wrapped one around her own taut waist.

As she guided their young charge out into the hallway, her eyes met his. They didn't even need a nod of acknowledgment. It was already there.

Effie always wanted to go first. It made sense, since a young girl would always feel safer and more comfortable with a woman. Her guard would be down. Physical affection was easier to initiate. She would offer to "teach" the girl things, show her what pleasure could mean.

Eventually Effie would groom the girls for him. She did it well, but Pearson had come to believe that was more of an excuse that she gave to both him and to herself. The truth was that she wanted—deeply wanted—and her needs were almost as insatiable as his.

He sipped his tea as Effie vanished with Lexi, marveling at the kind of woman he'd found to be his partner.

# CHAPTER
# TWENTY-THREE

**BUDAPEST, HUNGARY**

Ridley had never been to Budapest before, and she knew only four phrases in Hungarian: *Szervusz...Hogy vagy? A nevem Ridley...Viszontlátásra.*

Hello...How are you? My name is Ridley...Goodbye.

She didn't think it would get her very far. For all the languages she'd soaked up while bumming around Europe as a teenager, Hungarian was isolated, impractical, and famously one of the most difficult to learn. Thankfully, as in almost all of Europe, it wouldn't matter. The English language was the way of the world.

Booker had arranged to stop at a safehouse thirty minutes outside Budapest. It was more of a mini air hangar, which seemed devastatingly conspicuous to Ridley, though sometimes it was the appearance of not trying to hide that made a place seem innocuous. To outside eyes, it was an old, out-of-use hangar that had been converted into a private welding and metalwork business.

They pulled up at dawn, just as violet smudges were

forming in the sky. As they stepped out of the car, their breath formed thick puffs of frost.

Inside the safehouse was a man who went by the name Adam. He was a heavily tattooed American in his forties, with a Boston accent that had mellowed around the edges. And he had been expecting them.

"Mercedes-Benz GLE Coupe," he said, going to the end of the hangar and whipping off a cloth cover like a magician's unveiling. "She's fuckin' gorgeous, but not *too* much."

Ridley was happy to see that that the small black SUV appeared appropriately used. Anything with shiny new paint would be a beacon for suspicion or theft.

"What's the fuel capacity?" asked Booker.

"Twenty-two gallons. Nineteen miles to the gallon," said Adam, "and oh, my God, don't blow her up or run her off a bridge like a crash dummy test. I'm sick of that movie spy shit."

Ridley laughed and looked at Booker. "Told you about James Bond."

She saw Carnegie discreetly eyeing the rest of the hangar, and she didn't like it.

"Kit?" said Booker.

"Oh, yeah!"

Adam beckoned them over to a worktable. From beneath it, he pulled out one small duffel bag and one backpack and unzipped them. Booker began unpacking the backpack piece by piece. Ridley sorted through the duffel.

"Happy fuckin' Halloween," said Adam with a devilish grin.

It was a collection of tactical gear. Grappling hooks, nylon cord, gloves, flashlights, headlamps, two small pickaxes, a Leatherman, a medical kit, road flares, duct tape, a water thermos, and a compass.

"Trick or treat," Ridley murmured, sliding on one of the pairs of gloves for size.

Carnegie sized her up. "You look like O.J. Simpson, except—the glove *does* fit?"

She grinned and flexed her fist in it. "If these are murder gloves, they'll be used on killers, rapists, and abusers only."

He lingered for a moment, then gave a hard, appreciative nod.

"Ballistics?" Booker asked Adam.

He pulled out two Pelican cases and set them on the table. "I had to go some places to get these."

---

Every major city in Europe seemed to be built around a river, but few were as famous as the one that split the city of Budapest.

The mighty Danube was majestic and serene, and as dawn crept over the city, the ice floes on its surface began to break and drift downstream. The streets began to fill, and this city—one of the most densely populated in Europe—started to teem with its daily business.

It would be another few hours until they could meet with Booker's arranged contact. In the meantime, he insisted on breakfast. The trio parked the Mercedes in a garage with on-site security, stashing the duffel and backpack in specially built compartments hidden under the seats.

They walked down the banks of the Danube past Parliament. The building was nearly a thousand feet long, a neo-Gothic colossus of cream spires and rust-colored cupolas. Booker was enthralled by the architecture. He kept stopping to gaze upward and marvel.

Ridley fought shivers. No matter how many cold European cities she'd lived in through her younger years, it was Greek island blood in her veins. Her mother's Icelandic genes...sometimes seemed as distant as the memories of her.

Carnegie glanced at Ridley. "You think God made snow beautiful so we could bear with winter?"

"No. Obviously so we could have snowball fights."

"You don't have to stop with a ball. I threw a whole snowman's head at boy in primary school once. That's how you get the nickname 'Frosty' for the rest of your schoolin'."

"You or him?"

"Oh, him, thank God."

At that moment his eyes settled on something ahead on the ground, and his expression suddenly fell.

There on the concrete embankment were rows of shoes. Each was detailed cast-iron, rusted, facing outward as if the wearers had suddenly leapt out of them. They looked old-fashioned, mid-century.

Carnegie crouched, staring silently down the row.

*What on earth—*

She heard Booker's voice softly beside her. "The Shoes on the Danube Promenade. In World War Two, pro-Nazi militiamen lined up Jews along this spot right here...and they shot them. They were beating and killing Jews all over the city, but they just thought—here, cleanup would be easier. The Danube would wash 'em away. But they made them take off their shoes just before. Shoes were valuable."

Ridley looked down at the pair nearest to her. They were so small, lined up haphazardly as if a parent had hurriedly yanked them off a child's feet at the barking orders of an executioner.

*Those would fit a three-year-old.*

She swallowed back a thick, sudden, stinging grief.

Crouched beside them, trying to angle his face away, Carnegie wiped at his eyes.

The three of them were there for a moment. The Danube drifted silently by.

These shoes would never move.

They walked on, eventually stopping in a café where Ridley got an omelet, Carnegie asked for bacon and eggs, and Booker ordered *hortobágyi húsos palacsinta*.

"Meat pancakes," said Ridley, reading the English translation off the menu.

"Don't knock 'em," said Booker.

Carnegie looked at the menu again. "Ach, I shoulda gotten that."

"I cannot eat meat before coffee," said Ridley, scoping for the pot she hoped was already headed her way. "But tell me—us—more about this woman we're supposed to meet in an hour."

It was a late briefing, but Ridley had been too preoccupied on the trip studying maps of the area in Budapest they were heading for. This one would not be easy.

Booker glanced around. The only other diners in the place were an old Japanese couple sitting in the opposite corner, but still he kept his voice low.

"I did her a mighty favor one time—a long time ago, but these Hungarians have long memories."

"I thought you'd never been to Hungary before."

"Haven't. Her nephew got caught up with some Albanian gangs that tracked him to Germany. Long story, but I went into a bad place, found this dumb kid, and—well, some gang in Albania is still missing their hitmen."

Ridley whispered loudly to Carnegie. "He looks nice, but..."

"Oh, I don't know," said the Scotsman. "He's got some shark in his soul."

"Great White, you think?"

"Nah. Mako."

Booker snorted. "Get outta here. Y'all need to watch more Shark Week...can't recognize a bull shark."

"The real Jaws was a bull shark," said Carnegie. "It swam up a creek in New Jersey and ate some boys."

"Ate a few, bit a few," said Booker. "Ten miles inland."

"You're moving this conversation into telling us our woman is a shark, then," said Ridley.

The waiter appeared, delivering their steaming hot plates of breakfast. Ridley eyed her boss' meat pancakes with suspicion. Booker unrolled his utensils from the napkin.

"If *I've* got shark in my soul?" he said. "No, no, she's an orca. The apex predator."

# CHAPTER
# TWENTY-FOUR

**BUDAPEST, HUNGARY**

"They call her 'The Godmother of the Unsavory,'" Booker told them.

Katerina Horváth looked like something between a career parliamentarian and a high school teacher. But she couldn't be missed.

As the trio arrived in the Fisherman's Bastion courtyard at Buda Castle, Ridley spotted her instantly. Through the crowds of tourists in their parkas, amidst the snow-covered spires and stone turrets, stood a woman nearly as tall as her.

Straw-blonde hair waved down just past her shoulders. Dark brows framed a pair of blue eyes in a face that was both beautiful and weathered. A blue scarf was bundled around her neck, and she held a digital camera that she was using to scan the courtyard. It took only seconds before her canny gaze landed on them.

"Booker," she called, smiling as they approached, slinging her camera behind her shoulder.

"My favorite blonde," said Booker, leaning in to exchange a

kiss on both cheeks. "Of course you picked the best view in the city. Meet my colleagues: Ridley and Carnegie."

They shook hands. Katerina seemed to size up Ridley in particular.

"You remind me of my niece," she said.

"So she's a badass polymath knockout," said Ridley.

"Well, she's funnier than you."

*That was funny.* But Ridley refused to laugh.

"Let's talk," offered Katerina, gesturing to the stairs leading up to the parapets.

The four of them climbed to one of the semi-circular turrets. It all looked like a fairy tale castle, especially now, cloaked in white. The oldest parts had stood on the Danube since the 13th century, once home to the Holy Roman Emperor. When the Ottomans sacked the city hundreds of years later, they let it go to ruin.

It wasn't until the 17th century that a collected army of European Christians took it back. They rebuilt it, but the cycle of destruction continued in World War II when it was seized by the Nazis. Eventually, the Soviets rolled into Hungary. Buda Castle was the last stand of the German and Hungarian holdouts.

The Red Army destroyed almost the entire place. The only thing left intact was the underground crypt.

*Thank God John Dee didn't hide his key inside that castle.*

Once they'd made it into the enclosed turret, Katerina settled with her back against the wall. She glanced out one of the firing ports as if doing surveillance, then turned to Booker.

"I don't ask you a lot about it," she said, "but there's something very strange about what *you* ask."

"We're not here to get involved in anything you're runnin'," he replied, leaning against the wall beside her. "We just need a very good tour guide and a couple of extra hands that know how to handle, uh—walking trouble."

"Yeah, you're going to have trouble. This is why I want to know what you're really doing here."

Ridley and Carnegie stood to form a semi-barrier of privacy against the few tourists that wandered through the turret.

"What do you mean, we're 'going to have trouble?'" said Ridley.

"You can't put your question in front of my question," Katerina grinned as if amused by a child. "And for that, now I have two questions. Who are you?"

She turned to Carnegie. He returned an almost shy smile.

*Was that a charm play? Is he flirting?*

"I don't even know who you are," he assured her. "I'm only here because the Americans and I have a nemesis of *mutual interest*."

Katerina looked at Booker. "So you tell him and not me?"

"Some billionaire has a fetish for the occult," said Booker, folding his arms over his broad chest. "He's on a scavenger hunt —which I love—but he's using some bad cats to play for him. So we're gonna just stay a step ahead and make sure he doesn't get what he wants."

She chuckled.

"There isn't even any money in it!" he said.

"So, okay, big American spy...maybe you don't know this: your 'bad cats' know some bad cats here in Budapest."

Ridley straightened up in alarm.

Katerina went on. "I have very little mice with very big ears, and they can go everywhere. You're not the only ones who came to Hungary to hire some help."

"Who?" said Ridley. "Who do they have? How many?"

Katerina's blue gaze locked on Ridley, who suddenly felt the potency of this woman's status.

*Godmother of the Unsavory.*

"We're not the most powerful ring in the city. I know that. I say that. Because I don't sell girls. Whatever else you want? I get it, but no girls, and no boys. You know *that* before we talk about mafia."

"Okay, sure. Okay," said Ridley, genuinely taken aback by the ferocity.

"Tibor Sátor runs the worst. They're called the Bloody Tens—and it's for a really stupid reason—but he's the one giving your billionaire five of his most medium men for a job tonight. They've been out today buying digging tools, and their shopping list looks a lot like yours."

"Medium men, huh?" said Booker. "So you must be lending us five of your best."

"Four. One of them used to work there as a—what do you say—cleaning man..."

"Janitor."

"Yup, janitor. He knows all the halls and rooms. Another man is a piece of steel. He'll walk through fire for us. And then one of them is my second cousin. Maybe he's not the best, but he's my cousin, so," she shrugged, "you get him. Milos. And he's very loyal."

"How 'bout that shopping list?"

"They'll have it for you tonight. You'll meet at the street entrance at eleven o'clock, with tools. Everyone will be gone, people asleep, vampires out. It will be perfect."

"Eleven is too late," said Ridley.

"It's not too late."

"Yeah, it is."

She and Katerina locked eyes as though they were ram's horns. The Hungarian woman folded her arms.

"The policeman who lives on that street leaves for overnight work at ten o'clock, but sometimes he's late. Tibor sends out his men at midnight. I fit you in when you won't get arrested and you won't get dead. That's not too late. That is just on time."

Booker glanced at Ridley. He knew that behind her slightly irritated expression was a fresh tide of respect.

"And the fourth man?" he asked.

"Woman. You're going with me."

"You're coming? You go out on the streets still?"

"This is my city, and you came into it talking about treasure, asking for my help. You think I won't be there to see it for myself? You do not understand Budapest. You do not know Hungarians."

Carnegie and Ridley exchanged a glance of admiration.

*Godmother.*

"I can't claim to," said Booker.

He was unbothered by her inclusion but bristled at the accusation of such cultural offense.

"We're 'long in the tooth,' I hear," said Katerina. Her sly smile softened him, "but we are boss. We're the ones who have seen more of all this."

He leaned back to get a good look at her. "Are you nicer than you used to be? Are you gettin' soft in the heart these days?"

She chuckled, but there was still a hardness in her eyes. "I'm more persuasive now. And better looking—but so are you!"

"You're definitely a better liar."

Ridley shifted on her feet, tiring of the flattery fest. "Have you been in the caves before?"

"Of course I have," said Katerina, "but the other ones around the rest of the castle. Not this place. I'm not a tourist, and only tourists go into Dracula's Labyrinth."

# CHAPTER
# TWENTY-FIVE

**BUDAPEST, HUNGARY**

The waiting was always a trial of its own.

Ridley had learned to adopt "practiced relaxation" as a way to cope, bringing her physicality under control first. Her mind would follow. She would breathe in through her nose—deep and slow—hold it for several seconds, and then exhale slowly through her mouth. Tactical breathing.

Katerina had suggested they go see the Hungarian State Opera House in the hours until operation.

"It's very beautiful for Christmas," she told them. "Nutcrackers everywhere."

Out of principle, Booker wouldn't go to the places suggested by criminals. Instead, he and Ridley and Carnegie ran a standard Surveillance Detection Route to root out anyone that the Godmother had put on their tail. Friendly or not, Katerina wouldn't simply let some foreign intelligence agents roam her city without knowing exactly what they were up to.

Sure enough, they were being followed by a man with salt-and-pepper hair. They decided not to alarm the Hungarian mafia queen by shaking him. No reason to risk spooking her out of their arrangement. Besides, they'd be doing completely innocuous things from now until then. As long as their tail stayed out of earshot, it was an acceptable arrangement.

The trio walked through the city that teemed with Christmas and tourists. Carnegie insisted on stopping in an apparel store for a fresh change of clothes. Then he realized he wanted to clean up before donning them.

So they ended up at the Szechenyi Baths. Even in such brutal temperatures, the vast outdoor pool was filled with people. There were marble railings and towering fountains all around it. Behind that sprawled a classical building of canary-yellow, which looked like an old tsarist palace and housed a dozen more thermal spring baths.

"I'm not in the bath mood," Booker had told them when Ridley and Carnegie agreed that it was a perfectly good way to wash off.

He sat with their bags near the gargantuan outdoor pool, able to see the entire courtyard from his bench. His two teammates donned swimsuits, rented towels, and slid into the hot water amidst the crowds of bathers.

Ridley dipped her head back until the warmth seeped up her scalp. When she pulled forward, squeezing her hair out, she felt Carnegie glance away discreetly.

"Okay, William Wallace," she said, "There's something bothering me."

It had been bothering her since they met with Katerina, much of the reason being that she was mad at herself for not thinking of it sooner.

"Hopefully not me."

"Not liking coffee does give me trust issues, but you said about Marc Pearson that 'no one in the world wants to touch him'…and here you are shacking up with foreign officers—

strangers—chasing his goon squad across Europe when for all you knew it was a wild goose chase."

His gaze radiated the anticipation of her question.

"Does this mean that MI5 decided to touch him? Or did you decide to take your own working vacation?" she said.

"Can't believe it took you this long to ask me."

"I'm kicking myself."

"They'd recall me in a blink if they knew who I was after, but wouldn't the CIA do the same?"

She frowned. "We're here on official business."

"He's your boss?" said Carnegie, dipping his head toward Booker in the distance.

"Yeah. We're insulated—operations are self-directed, for the most part."

"And you think if the director of *your* agency found out whose tail you were on that you'd still be out here?"

Ridley glanced over at Booker. He was bundled up on the bench, looking casual but forever situationally aware.

She dipped lower into the water. "That's not how we work."

"Well...I saw Jerusalem, like every other person on this planet. You're tellin' me that was all okay with your boss's boss?"

"That operation was successful," she said coolly.

*The CIA Director handed us half our hides on a plate for those scenes of devastation in the city.*

"So what is it about Pearson that puts him on the untouchable throne? You're sayin' the mightiest intelligence agencies in the world are afraid of him?"

Carnegie's expression tightened.

"It's fuckin' blackmail."

"Blackmail of who?"

He looked at her. "Everyone. That's his real business—collecting evidence that would destroy or imprison powerful people 'round the world. So he's an asset to everyone, and a threat to all."

She and Booker had done their homework, but there was little actual substantiation in the dossier they got through official channels.

*Did the CIA seriously scrub those to cover for him?*

"Did you ever come across something in his background called the 'Order of Raphael?'" she asked.

"No...haven't. That sounds like a cult."

"Eh...it sort of is. Long story, but they like getting powerful people to be part of it."

"Pearson doesn't share his power," said Carnegie darkly.

"You're willing to lose your job over this," she realized out loud.

"By Christ and Highlands whisky, yes I am."

Ridley looked him over as though she'd never seen someone like this before. His eyes were kindling like live embers as he bobbed just above the surface. Water dripped down the divots of muscle near his collarbone.

"Why him? There are a million and one pieces of vile shit in the world," she said.

"Because he abuses young girls! He sells them to his rich and famous friends. He breaks them in himself, sucks them dry, and kicks them to the gutter when they *age out*, so they can move on to becoming drug addicts to deal with the pain or street prostitutes because they think they're not worth anythin' more."

His voice was thick, quavering with anger. "You may be on some mad quest about angels and demons and sorcerers, but I'm just here to destroy that man's flesh and blood and bone."

She felt like she'd never believed someone's conviction as much as she now believed his. Wrath rippled from him.

One thought slashed through her mind.

*Marc Pearson will die in horror.*

"I can leave him for you," she said, buoying the mood.

"Oh, would you?"

"Sure, yeah, I'm pretty generous."

Carnegie slicked his hair back with both hands and flashed a crooked grin at Ridley. It seemed like an effort to reassure her that he wasn't just a walking vengeance demon.

He didn't tell her about how many nights he'd lain awake in the dark thinking of how he could get his hands on Marc Pearson...how long he'd kept an ever-expanding file on the billionaire...how he'd wept after meeting a pair of sisters who'd been abused...or how he'd put his fist through the wall upon later hearing that the younger one had committed suicide.

He knew that even at this moment—as he was floating in a Hungarian bath—there was a girl out there caught in Pearson's spidery clutches. He preyed on the ones who needed help: money, attention, opportunity...or a father. Those were his favorite.

It didn't matter to Carnegie now what other roads he may have taken in life: what family he may have had, what promotions he might have earned, what parties he could have attended. He had leapt onto the deadly bullet train that was Marc Pearson's criminal enterprise, and he wouldn't let go until he'd ripped up the very tracks on which they were speeding.

He glanced over to see Ridley watching him, as if she was trying to read the subtitles on his vehemence.

"You can call me Iain," he said. "I know it's hard because you look at me and think, 'Oh, my God, it's James Bond!' but that's just a natural reaction and most—*most* people get over it."

She feigned a gasp. "But what if I don't?"

"Oh, then we gotta spend more time together. That shine'll come off right quick."

"I'll work on that, Iain, and don't worry about those slips of trying to say 'Ridley' and it just comes out 'Gal Gadot.'"

His laughter was interrupted by Booker's voice calling, "Towels out!"

They looked up to see him standing by the nearest edge of the bath.

"She's pushed up the meeting time. Our friends are on the move."

# CHAPTER
# TWENTY-SIX

**BUDAPEST, HUNGARY**

The sun faded, the temperature plummeted, and the twinkle of lights across the snow shone in the darkness.

They waited on a street corner for the Godmother to arrive. Ridley and Iain had donned their new clothes: sturdy, warm, practical. Booker was bundled in his bomber jacket, doing a shiver-stomp routine to stave off the intense cold.

The Godmother was on time.

A gray SUV pulled up alongside them and the driver's window slid down. A blue-eyed man behind the wheel sized them up.

"Come on. She wants to talk to you. In."

His accent was so thick that it sounded like he had tar stuck in every corner of his mouth.

Booker pulled open the back door. Katerina glanced at him from the passenger seat.

"All of you in," she said.

They piled inside, despite the brief hissing squabble between Ridley and Iain over who would jam into the middle against Booker. She gave him grace and agreed to. It was her partner, after all.

"This is Milos," said Katerina when they'd pulled the door shut.

"I'm her cousin," announced Milos from the driver's seat.

"My other men are already there. Zsolt used to work in the caves. He knows the way. Ferenc is a...he's what I need. What *you* need, if Tibor Sátor was paid enough to send his best."

"He'd be paid well to," said Booker.

"Good," grinned Katerina. "I hate that gargoyle and I love killing his best men."

*Looks like a music teacher, acts like Griselda Blanco.*

"The tools you need are already there," she went on. "You have your own weapons?"

Booker and Ridley clapped their hands over the bags in their laps.

"Okay. Let's start your treasure hunt."


Ten minutes later, they climbed out onto the sidewalk.

The street was narrow and sleepy. Had there not been a couple of flags over the unassuming entrance, it would have looked like just another apartment door with some iron grating above it that read:

PANOPTIKUM — *Labirintus*

They cast eyes up and down the street as the black gates swung open. Inside was a very short man, prematurely balding. He beckoned them in.

Katerina stepped through first, speaking to him in Hungarian.

*Hungarian is like codebreaking. I didn't get a single word of that.*

The only light inside was coming from an electric lantern on the stairs.

"This is Zsclt," Katerina said to the others as he pulled the doors shut behind them. "His English is very bad. Don't even speak to him, it's so bad."

Booker and Ridley exchanged a glance in the semi-darkness. This much collaboration meant very little control, which meant she was already uneasy.

They lowered their bags and began to draw out their gear.

Ridley strapped a drop-leg holster around her thigh. She did a barrel check on her SIG Sauer M17 and tested the light mounted to its rail.

Booker fitted a headlamp around his skull, holstered his Glock 19, then slung a Benelli M4 across his broad back.

"Double, double toil and trouble," he murmured.

The sight of this big man coming down a hallway with a pistol-grip shotgun cradled against his huge shoulder would be piss-your-pants-but-put-it-in-the-movie-trailer scary. Ridley thrilled a bit at seeing him donning field gear again.

She clipped a flashlight to her belt, secured the karambit blade in its sheath, and stuffed some road flares into a back pocket.

Iain tucked away his own Walther PDP 9mm. They'd given him the "extra" pistol since he was a foreign tagalong.

"None of you brought silencers?" said Katerina, threading a suppressor onto the barrel of her HK MP7.

"They don't fit well in holsters," replied Booker.

"Oh, my God. None of you have fired a gun in a fucking tunnel before?"

It was more a statement of disgust than a question. There were times when Ridley was actually grateful for the slight muffle of hearing damage in her right ear.

Katerina pointed to a little camera affixed to the ceiling. It was aimed at the door.

"We have one on both ends of the street, too. Milos is

watching in the car outside. He will talk to me here," she told them, securing a wireless earpiece.

"Would be a shame to bring all these toys and not get to use them," said Ridley.

Booker frowned at her. "Cut that crap and go play *Call of Duty* if you're so trigger happy."

"You *wanted* to be here," she muttered, annoyed at the reprimand.

*The play-acting had him feeling the old way. Imminent threats have him insecure about whether he's still up for the action.*

The Godmother looked her up and down. "I can get some extra work for you after if you want to hurt people."

"Really generous, thanks."

Booker glanced at his watch. "We have fifty-two minutes until Dane and his friends are supposed to show."

"Zsolt!" called Katerina.

The former janitor grabbed a large duffel that clanked as he carried it. He led them down the whitewashed stairwell and through a low-ceilinged doorway. The walls turned to dark stone as they descended farther into the caves.

Though he had turned on some of the lowest accent lights throughout the labyrinth circuit, the only decent way to see was with their own sources. He carried the electric lantern. Booker had his headlamp on, and Iain brought up the rear with an Olight Warrior flashlight of his own.

"They made a whole market out of that Transylvanian guy," said Ridley as they passed a sign painted with a cheesy vampire.

"Vlad Țepeș was really kept down here, huh?" said Iain. "No wonder he turned into a bloodthirsty impaler."

"No, I think that's *why* he was kept down here."

The caves beneath Buda Castle had been there for hundreds of thousands of years. Only in the medieval age did inhabitants of the area begin to dig and link them together. Under Ottoman rule, harems of Turkish women were kept down there. Later they were used as wine vaults and then much later during World War II as bomb shelters.

But they had also been used as torture chambers, and as a prison of near-unimaginable gloom.

In 1462, Vlad III, that fearsomely cruel Prince of Wallachia, had traveled to see Matthias Corvinus, King of Hungary. He needed funding to continue his war against the Ottoman Turks. Since the king was reluctant to continue such military campaigns, he was easily swayed by the presentation of forged letters by Vlad's enemies, "proving" that Vlad had colluded with the Sultan in secret.

Matthias accused him of treachery, had him arrested on the spot, and—according to the royal biographer—sentenced Vlad III to ten years imprisonment in the caves beneath the palace.

There were fair reasons to believe that he was in fact kept in this stale darkness, but it was nearly impossible to confirm. Whatever the truth of it, this labyrinth felt...terrible.

Ridley tried to shake off the eerie sensation. They'd studied the layout from a basic map and knew they were headed into the corridors to their right. The entry to the chamber they were looking for would be in the farthest corner.

As they veered to the right, Ridley startled at the faint outline of a man standing in the hallway, a flashlight dangling at his side, an MP7 slung across his chest.

Katerina greeted him. "Ferenc."

With a quick exchange in Hungarian, she introduced him to her foreign trio. Ferenc looked like he was built of steel, right down to his jaw. He greeted them in decent English.

"Ferenc will take the rear," said Katerina.

"I've got it," said Iain.

"You did. Now he takes it."

Ridley could practically feel Iain bristling, but they had no time to argue and really no choice. The steely Hungarian brought up the rear.

"Book, show Zsolt on the map where you need to go."

Booker leaned in to his map with the smaller man, with Katerina translating for them.

The beam of Iain's light strayed across a sign on the wall. Ridley caught the words: *Maze of Darkness.*

Just below it was a quote.

*"Let us descend into the blind world."*

*Dante: Canto IV: First Circle.*

"Let's," she said under her breath.

Zsolt nodded at Booker, said something in Hungarian, and headed down the tunnel to their right.

As they followed him, the accent lights along the walls disappeared, and the only thing they could see ahead was the bobbing of his lantern leading them into Dracula's Labyrinth.

# CHAPTER
# TWENTY-SEVEN

**BUDAPEST, HUNGARY**

Ridley, Booker, and Iain had studied this section of the Buda Castle Caves enough to orient themselves to Dee's directions. They knew it was going to be a bizarre walkthrough given the displays, which were all designed for tourists who wanted to be spooked.

It was nevertheless alarming when they came upon the first of them.

Carved into the rock on one side of the hall was a prison-like cell. Behind the iron bars was an array of shockingly lifelike mannequins. They were dressed as soldiers and looked like they'd been frozen in the middle of an argument.

Ridley could hear Iain swear behind her in a bare whisper. She compulsively swept her own flashlight over every corner of the cell.

*As if there's someone hiding in there? Come on, Samaras.*

Zsolt led them on into the Maze of Darkness. This section of the labyrinth was purposefully kept so black that night vision wouldn't have worked there. Their lamps and lights bobbed along as the dingy stone corridor narrowed around them.

Their guide at the front said something to Katerina in Hungarian.

"Don't shoot Attila," she told them.

"Who?" said Booker, but then he jolted— "Shit!"

At the end of the tunnel stood a figure. Ridley's hand flinched toward her weapon.

He was wearing a black cloak, the hood draped down over his eyes. His skin was black. He stood in front of a black-gated crevice in the wall. The sight was scary enough for Booker to burst out with the rare curse.

"Attila," said Zsolt, casually gesturing at the black figure.

Ridley sized up the mannequin as she passed. It was unnervingly tall, its face too lifelike, its cloak too textured. She didn't want to take her eyes off it even as she turned down the adjoining tunnel.

*I've seen worse among the living.*

Zsolt stopped a few yards past the black Attila. He exchanged some words with his boss in Hungarian again.

Katerina turned to Booker. "This is the place you wanted?"

Booker aimed his headlamp down the corridor, to where it formed another L-shape at the turn. He looked at the compass on his watch.

"That's the northern-most point?" he asked.

"He says it's the farthest you can go here."

They made space for Booker to move forward, inspecting the corner closely. He scanned the entire wall, the ceiling, the floor...nothing. In the meager light, a frown seeped across his face.

"Nothin'—*nothing?!* Can't be right..."

"What are you looking for?" said Katerina.

"The sign for *elementa*. It'll look like a cross—a square one."

She snorted. "You can't be serious. You know how many times they have digged out these tunnels? Destroyed? You think you can find a carving from hundreds of years ago?"

Booker gave her a dark glance. "They're all intact. I'm tellin' you. Somehow."

"Your treasure is bullshit. Someone playing with you."

*How could Zsolt have measured exactly how far this is?*

"Ask him," said Ridley, "where is the next place that's farthest north?"

Katerina had an exchange with Zsolt, who raised a hand as if he'd realized something. He started down the tunnel ahead.

"This is a rat trap," muttered Iain as they followed his bobbing light.

"Come on," said Ridley. "Focus."

"Oh, I've got the back of your head, Wonder Woman. I'm focused."

But she felt the same, an intense discomfort with being stacked single file in a tunnel.

Their shoes scuffed against the stone floor. Another cell appeared on their right, and as Ridley caught sight of what lurked behind the bars, her hand shot to her holster.

Standing side by side, deep within the black cave, were two children.

*Fucking mannequins!*

They wore threadbare togas that made them look like ancient slaves, but their skin was *blue*. Their heads were bald and nearly bulbous, but it was their eyes that were most unsettling. In the flashlight beams, they glowed white.

Iain let out a laugh. "Braw. Top stuff."

Ridley relaxed off the grip of her SIG. "God—and I mean this from the bottom of my heart—*damned* haunted house."

After a moment, they turned again. This tunnel was wider.

Accent lights dotted the floor, casting a weak yellow tint on the rocks around them.

On one of the walls was a bizarre relief, a half-human, half-stag creature rising up on his hind legs. From its head sprouted huge antlers, and a man's face looked directly out at passersby.

They sought no explanation for this one.

The team was quiet as they came to a T. Zsolt led them down to the right, but he didn't warn them about what they would see.

Ridley spotted something on the wall ahead. Booker turned to look at it, his headlamp casting a full beam on a bristling display of rusted spears.

Behind it were rows of spikes. Impaled on each one was a ragged, bloody head. Their faces were twisted, almost melting in expressions of agony.

Bringing up the rear, Ferenc mumbled something dark.

It should have felt like being in a bad horror movie. Instead it felt like descending into the circles of hell. Whether the dread was in the walls or in her mind, she bit down mercilessly on her nerves.

*Stop, Samaras. You're being a child. Settle down right now.*

"Well, if they were real, they'd smell," said Booker dryly.

"Heads on spikes are good for the enemy," said Katerina. "Maybe we bring them back."

It wasn't quite a joke.

Past the decapitated heads, they found a larger cavern. Branching off of it in the northern direction was a long tunnel.

Zsolt gestured to it with a shrug and made some remark in Hungarian.

"He says it's a dead end," Katerina relayed in English. "Don't worry. There's nothing to surprise the tourists."

She took the lantern from Zsolt and told him to stay back.

Booker grabbed the duffel from him. They followed the Godmother into the darkness.

The tunnel narrowed, but then nearly thirty meters in, opened abruptly into a rectangular chamber. It wasn't much bigger than a restaurant walk-in, but they spotted it quickly: ELEMENTA.

*The earth symbol in Dee's hieroglyphic monad.*

It was the size of a cell phone, jutting out of the lower half of the farthest wall. Booker set down the duffel full of tools and took a knee to run his fingers across the wall. He tried pressing into the carving, heaving his whole weight against it.

"*Looks* exactly like the one in the mine," he said. "Should just—*give*..."

It didn't budge. He got back to his feet.

"How 'bout a toy?" said Iain, opening the duffel.

Ridley reached for the sledgehammer. "May I?"

He handed it to her, a little smile glinting in the darkness.

"Give me the space."

As the others stepped back, she swung the hammer like she was taking a monster shot in croquet and slammed it into the stone symbol.

It depressed like a heavy button. A scraping sound grumbled from deep within the rock.

"*I'm pickin' up good vibrations,*" Ridley sang softly.

The wall split, as though there had been an invisible seam there all along. The two halves rotated slowly inward.

What lay beyond was pure blackness.

# CHAPTER
# TWENTY-EIGHT

**BUDAPEST, HUNGARY**

THE OPENING WAS small enough to remind them that many hundreds of years ago, people were several inches shorter.

Katerina murmured, "So there was a treasure room here all this time."

"John Dee liked a mystery," said Booker, his headlamp finding nothing here but curving rock walls.

She gave an order to Ferenc, who went to plant himself in the tunnel as a sentry. She checked over the comms with Milos's status aboveground.

"We're all good," she said. "Go on."

Ridley dropped the sledgehammer back in the duffel, which Iain hoisted onto his shoulder. Katerina pulled out her own flashlight.

They followed Booker into the open chamber.

Milos sat in the front seat of the SUV, smoking his third Lucky

Strike of the night. The front window was cracked for air, and every few seconds a cold wind would slice in.

He was irritated by having to do the most boring job of the night: lookout. But he was plenty relieved that he didn't have to go into the tunnels.

Even when they played as kids, his older cousin could see the panic in his eyes whenever he was caught in a small space. Katerina would try to distract him, talking him through his anxiety until he could free himself and breathe steadily again. As she looked out for him then, so she did to this day.

The street was quiet, snow drifts piled up along the curbs. Christmas lights glowed out from the front windows of sleepy houses. One of the things he was keeping an eye on was the policeman's home.

The occasional car rolled past where he was parked on the side of the road. Milos would feel the distinct urge to duck down and hide his face. It was familiar to more than a few cops in this city.

He squinted as a set of headlights came toward him. Another car rolled past—a KIA— heading toward them. This one was going too fast.

There was a skidding of tires as the oncoming sedan swerved to avoid the KIA, but it couldn't get clear. Only twenty meters from where Milos sat, he heard a faint *crunch* as their bumpers collided.

The driver of the sedan leapt out, livid with astonishment. He was wild-eyed, with red hair and a wide jaw adding to the look of someone you didn't want to anger.

The KIA driver climbed out, his hands raised in apology. He rattled off something in Hungarian that the other man clearly couldn't understand.

As they approached each other, Milos tensed. These things could explode in an instant. He wasn't able to make out the words they were exchanging, but kept his eyes riveted on their body language.

He was so intent on the furious drivers that he barely glimpsed the suppressor on the barrel of the gun that slid through his open window.

---

The chamber was much bigger than they had expected, as though Dee had discovered an entire cave and then somehow sealed it off.

It was domed, circular, nearly thirty feet wide. Running around the edge of it was a gutter carved into the wall. Dusty mirrors were positioned at strange angles and various heights around the entire space.

In the center was a huge round stone. It was perfectly shaped, taller than any of them, and there appeared to be texture carved into it.

Booker stepped up to it, peering closely with his headlamp.

"It's a globe," he said, "but the proportions are all off...this is what their maps looked like in the sixteenth century."

Iain stared around at the mirrors. "They're all sorta aimed at the globe."

"*Catoptrics.* The use of mirrors. Dee was obsessed with light—intensifying it, manipulating it. Thought you could imprint energy on things with it. Not so far off."

"Imagine if he could see lasers," said Katerina.

"Exactly!"

Ridley inspected the gutter along the wall. It looked like a water trough but it was filled with black ooze. Scattered above it were little holes that looked like vertical vents.

*This is an old trick.*

She pulled a flare from her back pocket, uncapped it, and

struck. Red light erupted from the end. Ridley dropped it into the trough.

Flame ripped down the line of oil. The chamber was instantly encircled by the blaze. The arrangement of mirrors itself seemed to ignite.

Iain reached up to touch one. "They move."

"I think *this* game is afoot," grinned Booker. "Okay, clean 'em off, brush off the dust. We need this light stronger."

They set about scrubbing them clean as he pulled out the Dee notebook and flipped through the pages.

"A globe like this can only be one thing—I think. Sir Francis Drake. The circumnavigation."

"Like we're playin' a bloody video game," said Iain. "What does that have to do with your man?"

Booker chuckled, like the Scotsman had no idea what he'd just asked for.

"When Elizabeth I took the throne, there was no British Royal Navy. The Spanish ruled the seas and therefore the New World. Dee believed that King Arthur had reached the Americas long before Columbus, making him the rightful ruler, making Elizabeth his inheritor, making *her* the empress of the world. He thought there were still colonies to be found through the Northwest Passage for her to claim, but they just needed a force capable of getting them back.

"He was the first person we know of to use the phrase 'British Empire,' declaring that all England needed in order to challenge the might of Spain was a great navy...this little island...amazing. So he proposed it all to the queen, this plan for colonizing the New World—didn't happen to mention that all these ideas came from his 'angels'—and wrote up four volumes on it, down to the *specifications* for the ships!"

Iain was listening intently.

*Most people don't handle the Booker TED talks this well.*

"He thought the Northwest Passage was needlessly dangerous, but wanted to know if America was a separate landmass from Asia. He thought to go south, below the Americas, come around the other side. And Elizabeth's inner circle found and financed a former slave trader and privateer—Francis Drake. She didn't actually commission him formally, but...no question she sent him out."

Ridley looked at the giant stone globe. "So we're recreating his route?"

"Seems so. Get these mirrors in the right spots to illuminate his landings..."

Katerina seemed a bit awed that any of this was real, but she dutifully took up position at one of the mirrors. Booker skimmed hurriedly through the notebook until he reached what he had been looking for: the hand-drawn map.

"Here we go," he said. "Landfall in England—obviously—then Sierra Leone..."

"Where's Sierra Leone?" asked Iain.

"Western coast of Africa."

Ridley looked at the globe's version of South America, a squashed chunk of land nearly unrecognizable. "If you say anything in South America—"

"Argentina, Chile, the Strait of Magellan—"

"Really, we're just wingin' it."

"You'll get it!"

They tilted mirrors, argued, and readjusted, until they had almost a dozen circles of light beaming down onto the globe.

Iain reached up to swivel the last mirror. As the light hit San Francisco, they heard something crack deep within the stone.

The globe split open. Four sections fell apart like sheaves, revealing a small pedestal within.

Perched on the top was a small piece of carved quartz.

*Don't touch it!*

Ridley felt an almost physical pang within her, a revulsion at the sight of the key. But Booker breathed a sigh of relief and went to pick it up.

"That's it?" said Katerina in disbelief.

"Worthless if you tried to sell it," said Booker.

Iain looked from Booker to Ridley in disbelief over the actual prize. "We're done here, then?"

Ridley grabbed the duffel. "Yeah, done here."

She strode out of the chamber, leaving the rippling firelight. As she went back into the darkness, one thought clanged in her mind.

*We have to get out of here.*

# CHAPTER
# TWENTY-NINE

**BUDAPEST, HUNGARY**

Outside the chamber, Zsolt was leaning against the wall like he was waiting for a pizza.

"Okay?" he said to Ridley as she emerged from the chamber.

She was surprised to hear him speak English, but then again, "okay" was pretty universal.

"Yeah," she said. "Time to go."

*Sure he didn't understand that.*

Booker and Katerina appeared. Iain followed, carrying the equipment bag. Zsolt rejoined them as they headed back down the tunnel for the main labyrinth.

"You are saying it's not even a gem?!" exclaimed the Godmother.

"It's true," said Booker. "It's not a treasure, but it's valuable to *our*—"

As they crossed into the T intersection of the tunnels again, Katerina stopped short.

"I don't believe you."

Her voice had gone cold.

Ridley looked at the Godmother, who—even in the glowing beams of the flashlights—looked imperial, like a fading Russian tsarina who still wielded her aristocracy like a headsman's axe.

"You want to take it to a jeweler?" said Booker. "We'll go right now."

"No. Give it to me."

Booker stared at her. She locked her gaze onto him, and without breaking it, gave an order to her men in their native language.

A volt of alarm shot through Ridley. Her eyes flitted between Zsolt and Ferenc. Each of them had shifted, as though staging their posture into something more threatening.

Ridley's hand dangled down by her thigh holster.

Booker calmly clocked the situation. He'd been in more conflicts in more different languages and cultures than Ridley would see for decades.

"Okay," he said, reaching slowly inside his jacket.

He had zipped and velcroed each of the quartz pieces inside of a cross-body sling, kept snug to his torso. Now he pulled one out and offered it to Katerina.

She took it. And then her expression began to melt.

Her gaze drifted down the tunnel. Horror seeped across her face. Her mouth dropped open. Her eyes grew wild.

*She's seeing something we can't.*

"No, no!"

A stream of garbled, hysterical Hungarian escaped from her —and she bolted past them down the tunnel.

Zsolt and Ferenc cried out in alarm, but they weren't any faster than Ridley, Iain, or Booker, who took off after her.

Katerina didn't have a flashlight on her. She careened through the darkness as they tried to track her with their own. She was wailing—shouting at something, as if trying to flee and fend off at the same time.

*She's stuck in it. She's seeing what I saw.*

The younger operatives quickly overtook Booker, sprinting and veering around corners. It didn't take long to reach Katerina.

She'd be dangerous. She was hallucinating, terrified, and would surely lash out at anyone in her delusions.

So Ridley lunged at her back, wrapping her in a bear hug, pinning her arms to her sides, and the MP7 on its sling to her back. Katerina howled and thrashed, still clutching the quartz piece in one hand.

"Get the key!" Ridley yelled at Iain.

He clamped a hand around her wrist and pried open Katerina's finger. She kicked out at him like a woman possessed, but he quickly ripped the quartz piece from her.

She went suddenly limp in Ridley's arms. All struggle had been sapped from her. She sagged and quieted. Ridley lowered her to the ground.

The Hungarian woman looked dazed.

Ridley's eyes snapped up to Iain, expecting to see him reacting with the same terror...but he was standing alert and clear-eyed, chest moving with quick breaths.

She looked back to their guide, who now looked more like a frightened child than the Godmother of a Hungarian criminal cartel.

Booker skidded around the corner. Zsolt and Ferenc jostled past him to reach their boss, but Ridley pushed them off to give her space.

"Katerina," she said in a soft voice.

The woman finally focused on her.

"It was hell. I saw it," she murmured.

"I know. I've seen it, too."

Ridley helped Katerina to her feet.

"This happened to you?" said Iain sharply.

"Whenever I've held one of the keys? Yeah."

He looked down at the quartz in his hand, then at Booker. "But not you."

"I didn't know if it was just Ridley, but...looks like Madimi has got a problem with women," said Booker.

*That's it?!*

"That bitch!" said Ridley.

"Well, she is—really you'd say—probably a *demon*. I wouldn't expect much from her behavior now."

---

In the darkness, a group of eight was treading down the tunnel. All clad in black, using the barest of light to guide them, they passed by the half-human, half-stag creature on the wall.

At the front, Dane's submachine gun gleamed. The barrel of the Scorpion EVO 3 nosed ahead of every curve in the corridors.

Over his shoulder, Freddie took the lieutenant position, his eyes hungry for violence.

Dane heard the faint murmur of voices ahead. He stopped and held up a fist. The others halted behind him. Turning around, he pointed to one of the other men and beckoned for him.

From the back, a Hungarian man with thick stubble and the neck of a rhino moved forward. On his back was strapped a metal pack. He pulled an oxygen mask down over his face, stepped in front of Dane, and lifted a heavy metal nozzle.

---

Ridley and Zsolt were helping Katerina to her feet. Booker was opening the pouch on his body sling.

"No more sharing," he said, extending a hand to ask for the key back.

But Iain wasn't looking at him. He was looking past him, his face going slack.

"Move!" he shouted.

Their heads turned in the direction of his stare, just in time to see the orange bloom coming around the bend.

It felt like time had slowed, like they were moving but stuck in quicksand. Ridley shoved Booker down the hall at the same time as she felt Iain hauling her by the collar. Zsolt shielded Katerina against the wall, but Ferenc was the farthest from them—the closest to the section of the tunnel they'd come from.

He had barely turned around when the flames surged around the bend, engulfing him.

He exploded in shrieks of pain, his limbs blazing—flailing—

Katerina screamed, "*No!*"

But Ferenc was only a pillar of fire and screams.

Her expression hardened. She swung her MP7 up from its sling and fired three shots. Ferenc's howling stopped as his flaming body dropped to the ground.

# CHAPTER
# THIRTY

**BUDAPEST, HUNGARY**

Ridley, Booker, and Iain barreled down the black tunnels with Katerina and Zsolt. The beams of their flashlights bobbed as they ran.

The rock walls around them splintered as gunshots seemed to explode from everywhere. Ridley and Iain twisted around to return fire. They heard a cry of pain: *someone hit.*

They hurtled through a wide hallway where the giant head of a king's statue was submerged halfway into the floor.

Ridley spun around, letting off a volley in the direction of their pursuers.

In the jerking beams of their lights, they saw the next section of the tunnel had another long row of iron bars. Behind it were nearly a dozen people—mannequins—in satins and lace, embroidered gowns and coats. Their faces were painted, their wigs were styled, and they stood in eerily lifelike poses.

The gunshots were deafening now. Ridley still couldn't see the shooters beyond the bends and curves, but then it all went quiet.

*Bullets don't go around corners...but fire does. It's coming.*
"Go, go, go!" she yelled.

Booker turned and blasted off a double with his shotgun.

The fire came roaring down the tunnel in a terrifying bloom of light. This time, their section was wide enough that it didn't fill the space completely.

They threw themselves against the far wall as flame sprayed into the display of mannequins.

The heat was unbearable. It scorched the rocks around them.

Ridley fired blindly toward the flamethrower but knew her enemies were still behind cover. She glanced at the display behind the iron bars.

The mannequins looked like human torches. Then her eyes fixed on something within the concert of fire...

*No. It's not real. That's not real.*

There in the back of the inferno stood a woman.

She was young, wearing a robe that looked like a dress. She was untouched by the flames. Her dark hair streamed down past sculpted cheekbones. Her skin pulsed a sickening bluish-grey. And her eyes glowed white.

When they fixed on Ridley, she heard a voice echo through the tunnel.

*"Swim...you can swim...but you left me to drown, little Rid...you climbed out of the water and let me die below it..."*

She slammed herself back against the wall. It felt like someone had stirred her guts with a hot poker.

*Mom.*

In this moment, she could see only this abomination of a woman...but she could hear only the voice of her mother.

Iain was scrambling to his feet when he saw Ridley—frozen against the wall, staring at the fire in horror.

"Come on!" he shouted.

She didn't respond. He grabbed her and hauled her away, dragging her into the next tunnel as another stream of fire roared toward them.

Ridley snapped to as she was moving, as they burst into a low-ceilinged hall. In the middle was a huge square pillar covered in ivy.

The flamethrower exploded behind them, pouring into the wide grotto.

Ridley and Iain dove into the near corner as the flame shot past them. They heard a howl of pain from beyond the pillar—Katerina.

Zsolt rushed to her, shouting something in Hungarian. He took his boss' gun and then shoved her into Booker, gesturing madly for them to run. He looked at Ridley and Iain and did the same.

They made a break for the next section.

Zsolt planted himself behind the pillar, Katerina's MP7 clutched in his hands. He ducked out, fired off a volley, and slipped back behind cover.

Fire surged into the hall again, even farther this time. The ivy lit up, and in an instant the entire pillar was flaming behind Zsolt.

The last glimpse Ridley had of him—the former janitor, the loyal accomplice—was a brave man pouring sweat as the room burned around him.

The rest of them heard the blasting echo of gunshots as they sprinted around the next corner—

Their guide was now gone. They could barely keep their flashlights steady enough to see as they ran. Booker's headlamp had slid off long ago. The acrid stench of burnt hair went with them.

Booker spotted a sign on the wall, an arrow pointing to "EXIT."

It was another seventy feet through the twisting darkness, staying ahead of the squalls of flame. They were punctuated by volleys of automatic gunfire.

Bringing up the rear, Ridley and Iain could hear the bullets chip into the stone around them. They shot back—blind—into the bowels of the labyrinth.

And then they were there—the bottom of the stairs. They rushed up. Ridley posted at the corner of the hallway as the last man, when she realized Iain was doing the same.

"Go!" he said.

"You go!"

"Nope!"

*Unbelievable, stubborn bagpipe—*

"Come on!" Booker bellowed at them.

They exchanged a glance, then charged up the steps together, ran out the gate, and slammed the doors behind them...but they didn't have the lock.

Booker backed away at an angle, aiming his Glock at the entryway. Any second now, they'd appear...

Ridley looked straight up. "Give me a lift!"

Iain didn't even have to look up. He laced his hands together and dropped them low. Ridley stepped up, launching herself above the doorway. She snatched one of the iron-rod Hungarian flags from its pocket and leapt back down.

She jammed it through the loop of the door handles and backpedaled down the sidewalk. Then she turned and ran with the others.

They could hear the clanging of the iron gates behind them, and the rising shouts of Dane's fury.

They ran toward Milos's vehicle. Only when Katerina slowed did Ridley realize why that smell had lingered with them through the tunnels...

The Godmother circled to the driver's side, and they saw her face.

Her hair had been burnt down to the scalp along her left temple. The flesh of her ear, cheek, and jaw were a gruesomely mottled red. The skin shone raw in the streetlight.

"Katerina..." said Booker.

The pain must have been screaming, but she only looked at her cousin slumped in the front seat, his blood and brains spattered across the windows.

"All of them," she said.

"I'm sorry—but we have to get out of here," said Booker, "or it will be all of us."

"Tibor Sátor." She swiveled her head toward him. "He dies in a thousand pieces. You kill the rest of them."

She opened the driver's side door and gestured to Milos.

"Put him in the boot."

# CHAPTER
# THIRTY-ONE

**ZAGREB, CROATIA**

RIDLEY, Booker, and Iain left Budapest in the middle of the night.

It took less than four hours for the Mercedes Coupe to reach Zagreb, but they couldn't run endlessly on adrenaline. It was too early for a hotel. CIA safehouses, though, were never out of operation.

They found it downtown, a nondescript two-story home crammed into a long block. The housekeeper was a scruffy man in his fifties named Elden. He looked a month away from retirement, but still greeted them with hot chocolate and tea in the kitchen. After running them through the layout of the house, he shuffled back to his room.

Booker was fast to bed. Ridley noted how gingerly he moved, and also how much he tried to not show it.

*The field is punishing on the young, but it's cruel to the old.*

She showered, scrubbing off the stink of smoke and gasoline. She'd brought a spare change of clothes from the car, and the clean fabric on her skin felt like pure cashmere.

No amount of creature comfort could clear her head, though.

Ridley knew she should take every spare moment to sleep and recharge. As Iain went to take a shower, she sat at the table in the dim light of the kitchen, nursing her now-lukewarm hot chocolate.

*Code black. You froze. You were useless—worse than useless...a liability.*

The code black of situational awareness and combat readiness meant a catastrophic incapacitation due to fear or overwhelming stress.

She had never frozen in combat before. She lived her life between threat levels yellow, orange, and red: aware, alert, and active. She had never seen black before. No one ever wanted to see code black.

Yet she had frozen in that tunnel at the sight of that ghoulish apparition.

*No. You froze at the voice of your mother.* Mom. *That ghost—fucking—woman—demon cursed all women who touch the keys, and then messed with your head because inside you're still such a child.*

*You almost became ash, like Ferenc. You almost made Iain ash. Like Zsolt.*

Was the retrieval operation a success? Yes.

Was it one of the costliest she'd ever been on? Catastrophically, yes.

Three Hungarian team members: dead. The Godmother of the Unsavory: scarred for life.

*Is this how the rest of this is gonna play out, Samaras? In your head. Hallucinating—putting the rest of the team in jeopardy.*

The cacophony of thoughts was only broken when Iain appeared in the kitchen, freshly dressed.

His dark hair was curly wet and his eyes were bleary from

lack of sleep. He picked up his mug of hot chocolate, went to rummage around in the cupboards, and pulled out a bottle of vodka.

Without a word, he held it up for Ridley.

She shook her head.

"Right then," he said.

He poured a liberal splash into his mug and then replaced the liquor. Iain took a swig, and Ridley could feel his openness toward her.

She felt something tugging at her to speak, but she quickly grappled it down. Instead, she lifted her mug to sip.

He took his cue to leave, but then stopped in the doorway.

"You know polar bears actually have black skin? They need it to absorb every bit o' heat they can from the sun. Their fur isn't even white—it's transparent, so it's actually just reflectin' the snow."

She just stared at him.

"And when they can't find seals to eat, they can eat berries," he said, gazing across the kitchen as if lost in the idea. "Can you imagine what kind of berry mustache that would leave on a polar bear?"

Without even a glance, he walked out.

Ridley gave a soft snort of laughter. And then she realized he'd thrown the railroad switch on her rampaging brain. Now she was sitting here imagining a berry 'stache on a polar bear.

She shook her head and looked toward the door.

**BUDAPEST, HUNGARY**

It had taken Dane and his team only moments to break through the jammed gate of Dracula's Labyrinth, but by the time they burst out onto the street, the operatives were well gone.

Dane's rage didn't explode; it only coiled his springs more tightly.

For all the firepower he'd supplied, the extra men he'd paid for, and the thorough calculations of exactly what it would take to get that key, they had missed. Despite catching two of the Hungarian meat sacks, the flamethrower had fallen short. The fire was devastating, but it had held them back for the precious seconds it took to torch everything in its path.

It was the perfect idea. The execution had failed.

Now they were a step behind.

Again.

They returned to the auto shop that Tibor Sátor had allotted them for the job. The Hungarians went grumbling into a lounge room in the back looking for food and drink.

Qualley uncapped a water and sank silently into a chair. Freddie collected their gear and began organizing the weaponry.

Lianna had excused herself to the toilet. She'd been quiet all night, apprehensive about the operation and perhaps even horrified by the firepower.

Dane watched her close the door. He didn't like her demeanor and didn't trust her silence. He'd registered her unease. If they'd gotten to any of these keys first, she could do her work. Then she'd be happy. Now she was just judging them all for their violence.

He went into the back office and pulled out his phone. It didn't matter what time of the night it was or what time zone Marc Pearson was in.

He dialed.

The billionaire's voice came over the line, clearly muddled from sleep.

"They were ahead of us," said Dane.

"Bill," said Pearson, "I understand this is probably stranger than any job you've had before, but I wanna be clear on something. What the *hell* is going on out there?!"

"We need better resources. We need to get to the next location before them and fuck the torpedoes, sir."

Lianna appeared in the office doorway with a strange expression on her face.

"Is that Mr. Pearson?" she asked softly.

Dane gave a nod. It was dismissive, so he was more than a little surprised when the professor walked over to him and reached out a hand for the phone.

"I'd like to speak to him."

He gave a baffled scowl, but for some reason he didn't understand, allowed her to take the phone.

"Mr. Pearson," she said, walking away to speak. "I'd like to discuss the terms of my employment."

"Lianna, it's nice to hear your voice. You sound upset."

"That's very astute of you, yes. I spent the evening in a cave, Mr. Pearson, where I had to twice step over a burning body. I'll assume you've never been around a charred human being before, but I won't describe the smell for you."

"That's awful. I'm—"

"No please, let me finish."

Dane's temper spiked as he heard her recount the specifics of their failed mission to his employer.

"I took this odd proposal of yours because you were onto something exceptional—once-in-a-lifetime, I'll give you that—but the reality has been nothin' like that. You've had no use for a scholar or an expert this far. It's all just a—an exercise in hooliganism. And *killing*, and I've had all that I can possibly take of dead bodies and bullets and burning flesh on this bloody mission, Marc Pearson!"

There was a thoughtful pause on the other end, then Pearson spoke.

"I can't imagine what you went through tonight, Lianna. I'm very sorry. There have been some obstacles—unforeseen, I'll certainly give you that—but you are the most important member of this team."

"No. No, that's not good enough. I'm right here experiencin' all this and that's simply not the truth. I don't appreciate the flattery when you're telling me to disbelieve my own eyes."

By now Dane was looking on in amazement, listening to how this unassuming middle-aged woman was speaking to one of the most elite of the world's elite.

"I can see how your experience doesn't make it feel that way," said Pearson. "I can only tell you how highly I value you... and I have a lot of value to offer *to* you. For what you're going through, I don't think my initial offer was fair. How about two million?"

Lianna straightened up, her expression frozen.

"I don't understand," she said. "We haven't gotten a *single* key and throwin' more money at me won't help with that."

"I totally agree, but that's a separate issue I'm going to be discussing with Bill Dane there. What I want to do right now is make sure you're comfortable and that you're being valued for your expertise and your willingness to step into these tough places. What do you say, Lianna...two million pounds?"

She hesitated. "And two million pounds for what—for doin' the job or for you accomplishing what you'd like out of all this?"

"You just doing the job I asked you to do. The rest of it, I'm taking care of."

There were a hundred thoughts in her six second pause.

People were dying around her. She was working with violent men, probably psychopaths. They'd just killed two men and were mercilessly determined to kill more. They were looking for something secretly powerful on behalf of a billionaire, which she did know—in her very quietest Jiminy Cricket voice—was rarely a good thing.

But he wasn't paying her for any of the killing. He wasn't asking her to commit any crime, or even to cover for them.

Two million pounds.

She had never been to a tropical island, but she'd fantasized about stepping out of a bungalow in the morning in Bora Bora, taking in the lush green islands and hearing the bright water lap against the dock. She could help her cousin settle the debts she'd been saddled with since her husband died last year. She could pay her nephew's tuition at uni. She could retire and spend her days buying books and fine teas and scones and sitting in a garden just poring over them.

This was not how she'd expected her life to go. But here it had gone.

"All right. All right, then," said Lianna. "Two million pounds. Thank you, Mr. Pearson. Goodnight."

She handed the phone back to Dane, who was nearly dumbstruck. Then she walked out of the office.

"Dane?" came Pearson's voice over the line.

"I'm here."

"What the fuck is going on?"

"They're ahead of us. We need better transportation to the next location. Right now."

"You have the money to—"

"A private jet."

"I don't have a private jet sitting around in Eastern Europe. Real sorry," said Pearson sarcastically.

"You must have a friend or two who does."

There was a pause on the other end.

"And I'm hiring another hand," Dane continued, "and he's gonna cost, but I need him."

"Is he better than the goddamn clowns you just hired there?"

"I know this guy. He's a specialist."

"In what?"

"In every way you'd want to kill someone."

Another pause.

"Don't try to gouge me on this, Dane."

"Give me Shao and the jet and this all turns around."

He could almost hear Pearson thinking.

Finally the billionaire said, "Get him. I'll get you the plane, and you get me *those keys*."

Dane felt a rush. "This will be over in Venice."

# CHAPTER
# THIRTY-TWO

**VENICE, ITALY**

Ridley could not remember Europe ever having so much snow. Even The Floating City lay under a glaze of white.

The sky was iron-gray as they arrived. Water sloshed angrily beneath their water taxi. The streets and canals were eerily quiet, but that was to be expected at this early hour. Given the weather forecast, it would probably stay quiet. Venetians did not like snow-clad days.

There were positives to streets that were packed with people. Losing a tail and creating a distraction would certainly be easier, but for their mission today, they wanted to draw as few eyes as possible...in the most public place in the city.

*Better if it was deserted, but there's no rewinding to the pandemic, or fast-forwarding to the apocalypse, in which case...who cares anyhow?*

They disembarked with their backpacks on the San Marco stop, tipped the taxi driver who looked miserable in this cold, and walked into the most famous place in Venice.

St. Mark's Square was a sprawling, grandiose piazza.

Napoleon had called it "the finest drawing room in Europe." It was one of the most magnificent sites in all of Italy.

Ridley had been there only once before as a teenager, when she and her older brother Alexios had eaten their bodyweight in pasta, stolen a gondola, and tried to get the vast flocks of pigeons to take flight in choreographed batches.

Now that same square that was usually teeming with both tourists and birds was nearly empty. A veil of snow and clouds loomed over the brick bell tower, over the long arcade buildings that flanked the piazza, over the Gothic splendor of the Doge's Palace that faced the water, on the towering Christmas tree topped with a star, and over the grandest sight of them all: St. Mark's Basilica.

"It opens in two hours," said Booker, gazing up in awe.

Ridley glanced down at her phone. "Let's go meet our man of the hour."

On one of the days that they had been in Venice, she and Alexios had passed by a young curly-haired vendor who'd whistled at her. After a few exchanges of playful shit-talking in Italian, they realized that the teenager was actually a pretty charming rascal.

He told them his name was Ezio and he swiftly tried to sell them a lineup of trinkets. When they refused, he started asking them about their favorite American TV shows. He was a few decades behind the current runnings, but he could sing every word of the *Friends* theme song.

Eventually he cajoled them into a game of *scopa*, introducing them to the forty cards in an Italian deck. As if he was a savant, Alexios whipped them both, game after game, until Ezio and Ridley finally ganged up to take him down. That day had begun a friendship that spanned over a decade.

And one of Ezio's cousins was a caretaker at St. Mark's Basilica.

They met him at *Porta San Pietro*—Saint Peter's Door. He was a husky man in his forties with a thick mop of black hair and traps like a prize steer.

**ITALIAN:** *"You are friends with Ezio?"* he said, looking Ridley up and down.

In her boots, jeans, and winter coat, there wasn't much to see, but she indulged his Italian ogle just for the sake of moving on.

**ITALIAN:** "Yes, we were friends as kids! You're Stefano?"

**ITALIAN:** *"Oh, my God,"* he said, then quickly crossed himself in repentance. *"He should have married you. His wife can't even figure out how to use a hairbrush. Come in!"*

He nearly pulled her through the doorway. Iain shot him a look as he entered, and Booker brought up the rear. Stefano pushed the great doors shut and locked them.

**ITALIAN:** *"Do you speak English?"* asked Ridley.

**ITALIAN:** *"Of course!"* said Stefano, grinning. *"I only wanted to hear you—a beautiful woman—speaking my beautiful language."*

Ridley smiled. "I think I've run out of Italian."

She looked up, and the Basilica took her breath away.

Gilded domes soared overhead. Frescos of biblical scenes adorned every angle…shimmering tile mosaics that depicted everything from the Garden of Eden to the crucifixion of Jesus. It was a splendid monument in blazing Byzantine glory, now decked in lush garlands and bloodred poinsettias.

*This must be what they mean when they say "the heavens."*

"Christ," muttered Iain, his eyes drifting from one wall to the next.

"Come," said Stefano, leading them into the church. "He said you need a ladder? I have a ladder for you."

"Does it go six meters?" asked Ridley, "and can we take it to the outside balcony?"

"Yes, it's seven meters big. You want to go outside in this weather?!"

"It's not really a 'want,' but a 'need.'"

"You want to sit on the roof? You want hot dogs, beer with that?"

She clapped him on the shoulder with a smile. "You've never been to America, have you?"

"No, but I know New York. Yankee Stadium." Then he began to sing, "*I did it myyyy*—"

"Mr. Stefano!" said Iain at such full blast that his voice echoed through the basilica. "We want to be outta here by the time visitors arrive—don't want you to be in any sorta trouble."

"Yeah, yeah," grumbled the Italian. "We have to go up to the museum. It's seven euros, you know."

He led them to an iron-gated door, unlocked it, and began to climb the narrow stone staircase. By the time they reached top he was gasping for air with a distinct smoker's wheeze.

"Ladder is here," he said, opening the door to a small utility closet.

Iain stepped in to grab the ladder first. He hauled it out, brushing off Ridley and Booker who tried to help.

"It gets bigger," explained Stefano, drawing his hands into a wide gesture, then chuckled. "It's a man ladder."

"*Expandable* might be the word," said Booker.

"Yeah, of course. Expandable."

He carried on through the church's museum, galleries that contained tapestries, giant codices under glass, wooden thrones, and four life-sized bronze statues of horses midstride.

"The Horses of St. Mark," said Booker, slowing as he passed. "They were in the Hippodrome in Constantinople when it got sacked...someone brought 'em here in 1200-something and stood them up on the terrace outside."

"These are the real ones," said Stefano, turning around to speak loudly. "The ones outside are not real."

Booker tried to keep his steps urgent, but he had to get it all out.

"Napoleon stole them to use on the Arc de Triomphe—"

Ridley shook her head. "That little ass-bag."

"—but eventually brought them here. So yeah...these fellas right here," said Booker, gesturing to the regal animals, "these are the original four. The mighty quadriga."

Iain paused for just a moment by Booker, adjusting the ladder in his grip. "You might even call them *steeds*. Think they've earned it?"

"I don't do that or Ridley might think she needs to hop up there and ride one right outta the church."

Iain glanced up at Ridley, who was following Stefano out onto the gallery.

"She rides?"

"Eyes on target, lad."

They rejoined their guide on the walkway looking down over the vast golden expanse. Near the high altar, statues of the apostles stood atop a series of columns, all in an orderly row.

Within a few hours, there would be lines of tourists waiting to get beyond them, to get close to the Palo d'Oro. This altarpiece was a mural of gold enamel, painted with scenes of the saints, studded with emeralds, sapphires, rubies, and pearls.

Today, there was an elaborate nativity scene set up near the altar.

Stefano was trying to prove something with his hands. "I say, I hear his ghost!"

"The ghost of Saint Mark is not here hanging out with you, Stefano," Ridley said. "Balcony. Come on."

He continued to rave about how he heard noises and saw

strange things there after hours, but a moment later, stepped up to a wooden double door at the front of the church.

"You can go outside. I will stay in here, warm."

Ridley pushed open one of the doors and a cold blast of snow swirled in. She stepped out onto the *Loggia dei Cavalli*, where she stood beside the four bronze replica horses. Before them sprawled the piazza, veiled in white.

Booker stepped out onto the balcony, turning back to help Iain fit the ladder through the doorway.

Craning her head back, Ridley gazed up at the front facade of the basilica above them.

"For all the lion and the lamb talk in the Bible, seems nobody really wants to be the lamb," said Ridley.

"But how'd he get *wings?*" wondered Iain, expanding the ladder flat on the balcony.

"Some of the visions in the Bible describe a multi-faced being with wings," said Booker. "One of those faces was a lion. Or—multiple choice here—wings were often seen as a symbol of divine presence, so the lion could have just gained wings through the power of Christ. Mark took up the symbol sometime, somehow."

"But Mark—you're saying Mark, the guy that wrote a gospel and walked around with Jesus—somehow ended up in Venice, Italy?" said Ridley, helping Iain lock out the last rungs of the ladder.

"His body, allegedly. The real man ended up in Alexandria, founded the church there that became the Coptic Christian Church. Probably founded Christianity in Africa, actually... killed as a martyr though, by some angry mob who dragged him through the streets and tortured him to death.

"Only 'bout eight hundred years later, some Italian merchants smuggled his body—or his relics—out of Alexandria to here. They built a tomb, claimed the lion, and made a holiday for him. Later, this whole place."

The three of them lifted the ladder, positioning its full length against the front face of St. Mark's Basilica.

"And this is where John Dee found a spot to hide something, seven hundred years later," said Ridley.

"Time is like a great blob that eats everythin'," said Iain, rattling the metal rungs to check their stability.

Booker pulled out the Dee notebook and went to the tabbed page.

"*Before a canopy of gold he stands...Below the saint's feet, in sacred lands...With wings that shield, in silent grace...His eyes gaze upon the Venetian face...One hand at peace...One hand to mark.*"

Ridley shucked her backpack into the snow. She pulled out a small pickaxe and a chisel, then looked up.

At the highest point of the facade above them stood an ornate marble statue of St. Mark. Angels with golden wings flanking him.

Below him, emerging from the blue facade, was a golden winged lion, and beneath one great paw, a book whose pages read:

*PAX TIBE MARCE, EVANGELISTA MEUS*
*Peace unto you, Mark, my evangelist.*

Ridley held the tools out to Iain.

"This is your play," she said, noting his expression of surprise. "Go get it."

He nodded, took the pickaxe and chisel from her, and slid them into his belt. He began to climb.

# CHAPTER
# THIRTY-THREE

**VENICE, ITALY**

Ridley glanced at Booker, who was studiously watching Iain pull himself up the rungs.

"Proud den papa," said the boss. "All the cubs playin' together so *nice*."

"Proper grizzlies, we are," said Ridley, "but also, Madimi is a torturous bitch who hates women."

"Also that."

To be sidelined in any circumstance was nearly unbearable for Ridley. She always wanted to be in the game, to make the play. To be taken out for reason of her gender alone was detestable.

*To be taken out by a ghost-demon-spirit is flat embarrassing.*

Above them, Iain climbed to the top of the ladder. He came straight up in front of the out-facing book under the lion's paw.

Carved into its golden pages were the letters: *PAX TIBE MARCE, EVANGELISTA MEUS*

"Anythin' in particular I might be lookin' for?" he asked.

"A button would be *ideal*," Booker called back.

"Hit it with the axe," said Ridley.

Iain muttered to himself as he pulled out the chisel and pickaxe, "Bloody haver..."

He tested the edges of the stone pages, then began to tap the chisel into every angle of every letter.

On the balcony below, the other two could see nothing of what he was doing. Only the clinking of the chisel carried on the thin cold wind.

Ridley looked out across the piazza, to the bell tower, the Doge's Palace beside them, and to the Grand Canal beyond.

A spear of alarm jabbed at her.

*Where's Dane? Why isn't he here already?*

She reached for the SIG Sauer M17 under her jacket, easing it from its belt holster.

"What is it?" said Booker sharply, snapping to attention as he scanned their surroundings.

"I don't know..."

She went to the door and tugged it open. Below a clear plastic flooring, she could see the narthex entrance beneath her. Past that, the basilica was still quiet. No sign of Stefano.

But that prickling alarm wouldn't let up.

She heard Iain's voice. "Got somethin'!"

Ridley stepped back out onto the snowy balcony.

"This is it!" he exclaimed.

He tucked the carved stone into a small velvet jewelry bag, then stuffed it into the pocket of his jeans.

Booker called up to him. "What was the trick?"

"The *'E'* at the end of *MARCE* and the *'E'* at the beginning of *EVANGELISTA*. Tapped 'em all."

He had just started down when a gust of wind rattled the ladder.

At the same moment, a chunk of blue stone exploded from

the facade next to his head. The sound of a loud *snap* echoed across the piazza.

Iain didn't even look. He clamped his feet outside the vertical poles and shot down them like a slide as a second bullet clipped the rung just above his head.

"Sniper!"

The three of them dropped below the front arch of the balcony, behind the towering horses. They pulled their guns.

"The belltower?" said Ridley.

"Too high for a decent angle," said Booker. "Probably the roof of the arcade."

"Which side is gonna matter a lot."

The arcade housed museums and cafés, exhibition venues, and even at the far end, a police station. It formed a U-shape around the piazza, both ends coming up nearly to the basilica.

Whether the shot had come from the right or the left side was a crucial distinction. Pick the wrong side and they'd pick your skull with a bullet.

"Bait," said Ridley.

She grabbed the backpack from the snow, took the pickaxe from Iain, and stuck it on the wooden handle like a tent pole. She stuck the dark bag out just beyond the cover of their balcony section, to the right.

A thin line of fabric exploded into threads. Another loud *snap* across the piazza.

"Well, not the *best* sniper," said Iain.

She gave him a look and held the bag out to him.

"Nicked it on the temple," he conceded. "So he's on the right side, then. Northwest. Probably."

"That's a high-end suppressor he's using," said Booker.

They scanned the balcony. The rail in either direction beyond their position was waist-height, made of stone posts with plentiful gaps between them. At the ends, though, the balcony turned the corner and wrapped around each side of the basilica.

*Real cover. Cover you can actually use to escape.*

"Into the church," said Iain.

Crouching, he moved back and pulled open the wooden door to the basilica.

*No. Too easy.*

"It's a trap!" said Ridley, but he was already stepping inside.

On the upper balcony of the basilica, Iain could see down through the protective glass sheeting to the main entrance of the church. He could see across the massive gold domes. He could see the museum exit that Stefano had led them through.

And a flash of movement inside the last exhibit hall—

He had only an instant to determine if it was the Italian caretaker, to shoot or not shoot. That split second was clarified when he saw a muzzle whip upward.

He dropped below the stone balcony as a volley of bullets exploded the wall behind him.

Outside, Ridley and Booker hit the deck.

"It's a *trap!*" she yelled again in frustration.

Iain came diving out through the doorway, nearly landing on Ridley, and kicked the door shut behind him.

"Oh, it's a trap?" he said.

"Only place to go is south along the balcony," said Booker. "If the sniper is to the northwest, it's the best chance—only chance."

Ridley nodded. "Rolling cover. You first."

"No. Key holder first," he said, looking at Iain.

"You need the most cover and the first element of surprise. You go. We'll lay down fire here."

Booker clenched his jaw, but it was the right call. "Low and fast."

"Iain, put a couple through the door," she said. "Keep them back."

Ridley and Iain got into position. Staying under cover of the arch as far as he could, Booker moved down the left side. He glanced back.

She gave him a nod, then aimed her SIG over the top and squeezed Iain's shoulder.

The rounds exploded into the cold air. His shots tore through the wooden door. Hers ripped across the piazza, toward the roof of the arcade building, toward the hidden menace.

*Just enough. We just need a few seconds.*

Booker was running, staying as low as he could without landing on his face.

Forty feet.. thirty...twenty...ten...he skidded around the corner and went flat against the wall, his heart hammering in his chest.

"I'm clear!" he shouted back to the other two.

Behind the horse statues, Ridley looked at Iain. "You next."

"Afore God and my mother's grave, I won't. You go."

"I'm touched by the chivalry, but you have the key. If you die here—last and noble—we're all fucked and this whole thing tilts in Pearson's favor. Just go."

He gritted his teeth and shot off a few more through the door. They could hear shouting on the other side, echoing through the colossal church.

"Sorry, Mum," he muttered, then glanced upward. "And God in heaven."

*Could God in heaven come down here for a minute—*

"Go!"

She whacked him on the back and loosed another volley in the sniper's direction. Iain launched himself as she fired.

This time, despite the bullets coming at him, their unseen shooter got off a quick double.

One of them chipped off the balcony rail as Iain flew past it.

*That's not a real sniper. It's someone sniping* with *a rifle.*

Iain slid around the corner beside Booker.

"Rid!" shouted Booker, slotting in a fresh magazine. "Go!"

He angled out and unleashed a volley.

She sprinted, half-bent, snow exploding beneath her feet. In the cacophony of gunshots, she couldn't hear the quiet crack of the sniper rifle, but she felt the sear of its bullet as one ripped a chunk of stone from the wall only an inch in front of her.

*Fifteen feet...*

She knew that she would make it.

Iain swiveled out from behind the corner and unloaded a volley toward the sniper.

She dove behind him.

As soon as Ridley hit the stone floor, she was scrambling back up again.

At the end of the short balcony was a low slanting roof. Beyond it was a series of tiered levels leading back up to the great snow-covered domes, all connecting to the adjacent Doge's Palace.

*Like they were built for climbing. That never happens in real life.*

"Let's go!" said Booker, already heading for them.

With Ridley bringing up the rear, the three of them began their ascent. At any second, she expected the ambush group inside the basilica to emerge around the corner. They rotated through taking up a firing position. As two climbed, one would train their weapon on the balcony behind them.

It was a good thing Booker was still as strong as a silverback. His speed and mobility were an issue, but his capacity to give the other two a boost—or even to pull himself up—was impressive.

Ridley had just clambered up under the rail of the third level when Iain shouted behind them—but his own voice was drowned out by gunshots.

They were here, shooting from the balcony corner.

She dropped low, fired her last two rounds, and reloaded. The slide snapped back into place as she scoped the balcony.

Booker was shooting from nearby. Iain was the lowest down.

"Get up here!" shouted Ridley, unloading another volley of suppressive fire, forcing the enemy back behind cover.

With a burst of effort, Iain scampered up as if he'd been infected with the Spiderman bite. He stopped beside Ridley, but she nudged him on.

"Keep going—you have the key! Go!"

This time he didn't hesitate to do what he hated.

He left her side to climb up to the next level. As soon as he'd reached the large dome, he fell behind cover and aimed back at the balcony. From there, the clear line of sight was getting smaller. Still he fired.

Booker waved Ridley on. She made a dash upward, flattened herself against the backslope of a roof, and loosed a volley of bullets while Booker pulled himself over the next tier.

Each one of them was now behind cover. Knowing his duty, Iain peeled off, starting down the slanted roof toward the Doge's Palace.

Then he slipped.

# CHAPTER
# THIRTY-FOUR

**VENICE, ITALY**

THE SNOW SLID out from under Iain's feet and he tumbled down the slanted roof. He only stopped when his ribs slammed into a metal rail at the edge.

"Are you okay?" Ridley yelled.

"Good to go," he groaned.

He put his hand to his pocket to check for the key—and there was nothing there. His head whipped about. The snow had avalanched down with him. The little pouch with the key could be buried anywhere.

"It's gone. Shit!" he shouted. "Fell outta my pocket!"

Ridley crouched on the crest above him.

"Just now?"

He was scrambling about, sifting his hands through the piles of snow. "Yeah, had to be!"

Gunfire behind them. It was getting closer.

"Move now!" bellowed Booker.

Off to their right, they saw him drop down a level.

*Can't leave it for Dane and his minions...if they happen to stumble onto it right here...*

Ridley scanned frantically. She could hear Iain's scoff of disgust at his own mistake. Then she saw it.

Another level down, on a small ledge, the dark corner of a jewelry pouch peeked out from a snow drift.

"It's there! I got it!"

She scampered down, hot-footing each step as if the touches would burn her feet. She landed hard on the ledge and snatched up the pouch.

She pried open the drawstring.

There was the key, safe and sound.

In her hands.

*Oh, no.*

She turned to Iain, nearly twenty feet above her now. "I can't carry this!"

"I'll come down!"

As soon as he started to move, a volley of gunfire exploded overhead. A bullet bit at the metal railing beside him, and he dove for cover—away from Ridley.

*MOVE. NOW. It doesn't matter if you have the key if they put a bullet through your spine!*

Ridley couldn't follow Iain toward Booker without putting herself out in the open. They'd been divided.

It was time to go.

She had to get down off this roof, with or without them. She shoved the key pouch into her deepest pocket and snapped into high gear.

Jumping across a gap in the roofing, she skidded on the snowy surface...slid down another section...and ran.

Ahead to her right were the terracotta roofs of the Church of San Teodoro. She sprinted for them and leapt.

She landed hard, scrabbling against the snow slide she had just caused. A gunshot cracked behind her.

There was no more cover ahead. Ridley sprinted to the edge of the roof.

Below her was a canal…five stories down.

She hesitated. Climbing was not one of her best skills. She didn't know how many enemies were pursuing her, or their weapons capabilities. She *did* know that she had only nine rounds left in the magazine of her M17, and that she carried the key.

So Ridley went.

She holstered the SIG and began scaling down the balconies and window railings as fast as she could go. Hands already half-numb from the cold, it felt like every grip she took was perilous.

*At least no one's pointed a gun over the side of the roof yet.*

She would be the fish in that barrel.

Ridley looked down to gauge her next hold, but the bottom two stories of the building had nothing at all. The windows had flat hex grates on them, no shutters, no sills, no ledges.

"*Malaka,*" she hissed to herself.

There was a narrow walkway along the canal. As she clung to the metal rail outside the third-story window, her mind was spinning.

She could leap for the canal to give herself a safe landing, but in these temperatures, it would be near-instant hypothermia. She could absorb the twenty-foot drop to the stone beneath her, but that would likely crack an ankle.

And that was it. Those were the options.

A few pedestrians were finally braving the weather at this hour of the morning. A single gondolier was drifting down the canal. No one seemed to have noticed the dark-haired woman hanging off the side of the building.

Though an ankle break was a possibility, hypothermia would be certain.

So she lowered herself as far as she could, feet dangling, and dropped.

Mid-air, Ridley spun to one side. There would be no face-to-wall incidents today. She landed on the balls of her feet, dropping into a full crouch as the impact jolted up her bones. She winced but sprang forward, stumble-running onto the short bridge beside her.

They always set a rally point wherever they worked. In case of separation in Venice, it was the Church of the Pietà, to the east of the basilica. Shorefront, quick access to the open water, not far from the piazza of St. Mark's.

As she reached the crown of the bridge, a flash off to her left caught her eye.

Sprinting down the stone sidewalk was a man in dark clothes. She didn't recognize him from Dane's crew, but there was a pistol in his hand, and his eyes were fixed on her.

She bolted just as he raised his weapon, and pulled her own SIG from its holster.

Ridley ran backward, firing off a shot to force him to slow down, then she tore down the alley ahead.

Her heart thudded in her ears. What short streets there were in Venice had little curve or warp to them. Being caught in a straight line in a narrow space was a death trap when your pursuer had a gun.

She burst out into a small, nearly deserted courtyard with three diverging outlets.

*Where, where—pick a lane!*

She went forward left, dodging by some startled pedestrians, but dropped down into cover behind a snow-covered kiosk. From there, she could see the mouth of the alley she'd come through.

*Eight rounds left, and no idea how much ammo he's carrying. Can't afford an all-out firefight here.*

To her disappointment, the man didn't come running out. Only a young couple emerged from the alley. They seemed spooked by the sound of her gunshot, gesticulating as their voices bubbled over each other.

Her pursuer walked calmly behind them.

*Clever boy.*

He was about five-foot-nine, probably Chinese. His dramatic black eyebrows framed a handsome, stony face. He was lean and narrow, and something about the way he walked held a latent menace. This was a capable man—his every glance and step was sharp.

And he was making his way across the courtyard behind a set of human shields, searching for her.

Ridley had no choice but to hold position quietly.

There were three escape routes from here: one straight shot on her right, one behind her, and one below her heading to the right. It would have to be the one behind her, that still allowed a half-measure of cover while moving. But she wouldn't make it unless she drove her pursuer behind cover.

Finally the couple ahead of him veered off into an apartment building, exposing him totally. He drew up his Beretta to a ready position by his chest.

*Thirty-five feet...*

Ridley whipped the barrel of her SIG over the kiosk and squeezed off two shots—

She had always been a "backward" shooter: average with a rifle, ace with a handgun. Hitting a target at this distance should have been a sure thing.

*This* target had the reaction time of a fly...or he felt that a shot was coming through God-only-knows what kind of sixth sense, and dodged behind another kiosk.

She missed, but at least he had cut off his sightline for that precious second.

*GO.*

Ridley launched into the alleyway behind her. A gunshot exploded through the courtyard and she could hear a bullet punch the wall.

She sprinted, shoes pounding through slush. She could see the water ahead of her—

But knew that he'd be on her tail, in the alleyway, with a clean shot at her back through the narrow straight. She heard his thudding feet and stole a glance back. It was him, and only him, in the alley.

Ridley lifted the SIG over her shoulder, tilted just down, and shot blind—three times.

The noise nearly blew out her good ear.

He shot back just as she burst out of the alleyway onto a strip of dock and dove to the right.

There was a motorboat bobbing just ahead, covered in a tarp. She leapt onto it and dropped low, taking aim at the mouth of the alley.

He was not that stupid to run out into the open after her. He held cover behind the wall and fired out at her. Ridley couldn't afford to shoot back.

*Only three rounds left.*

The narrow canal was quiet as a cemetery. There was another small boat across it that she could jump to, but not without opening herself up. And she couldn't untie the boat cover without exposing herself to a bullet. She was trapped.

She glanced down into the black frigid water...and time seemed to stop. The gentle sloshing appeared to freeze.

Fear hit Ridley like a shard in the chest. Emerging from the depths of the canal was a face. It was the image of a nightmarish giant—a woman with black swirling hair, gray skin pulled tight over razor cheekbones, and eyes that glowed a frost-blue.

They stared right at Ridley.

*Madimi.*

Her mouth gaped open.

Ridley clamped her eyes shut, drew a quick breath, and shook her head. When she opened them again, she refused to look back into the canal.

Time seemed to restart.

*This is all for the key. He needs it. That's leverage.*

Ridley dug her hand into her pocket. She squeezed the key out of the pouch into the bottom of the pocket, then pulled out the empty velvet piece and held it over the water.

"You want this?" she called to him. "I think you need it."

A beat of silence.

"You know you die if you drop that," came the voice from the alley. A faint eastern accent, but it wasn't Chinese.

"I've weighed my options, and this is the one we're both stuck with!"

"What do you want?"

"For you to not shoot me, chuckleshit. Drop your gun. Kick it off the dock into the water, and then show me your hands around the corner."

"And you shoot me? No."

"I'd rather not deal with a death in Venice. Brings too much heat."

*Maybe in the leg or something...*

When he didn't respond, she got sharp. "I have the prize, I make the rules. You want it? I'll toss it on the dock when I see your gun hit the canal."

She heard the *thunk* of his gun on the ground, then saw the Beretta skid off the dock. It splashed and sank in an instant. No doubt he had another weapon on him.

"Hands, *right now!*"

She saw one hand emerge, then the other. She would need this delay.

She tossed the empty velvet pouch onto the dock a dozen feet away. It fluttered down into the thin layer of snow.

"Fetch."

As she saw him emerge, it was this instant or nothing. Ridley stood, eyes gauging her leap to the boat across the canal.

In the half-second it took to glance back at the man who was kneeling down for the pouch, she saw his hand draw something from his ankle.

And then it was flying at her—a blade.

She reeled—dodging it by a millimeter—but Ridley's launching foot slipped on the edge of the boat.

Her arms spun—clutching for balance—but there was nothing there.

She fell backward toward the canal.

Her head cracked against a docking post and she tumbled into darkness.

Ridley hit the freezing waters with a splash.

# CHAPTER
# THIRTY-FIVE

**VENICE, ITALY**

IAIN SPRINTED across the courtyard of the Doge's Palace, gripping his Walther 9mm, head swiveling to spot incoming threats. Booker's shoes thudded rapidly a few yards behind him.

They had descended the three-story chapel of the doge as fast as their limbs would allow. Thankfully, the ornate stonework offered hand- and footholds everywhere.

As soon as they hit the ground they took off, running to the colonnades that bordered the courtyard.

They each slid behind a thick stone column—then looked back at the Doge's Chapel.

Descending the walls like dark ants were two of their pursuers. A third stayed high as a sniper.

"Let's go," said Booker, launching off the pillar.

They sprinted toward the courtyard exit, Iain quickly outstripping the older man.

They could hear some faint shouts behind them, but no gunshots. They were surely saving their bullets for a better sightline.

Iain burst out onto the waterfront. The Grand Canal was still quiet, a heavy gray and white veil covering the city.

The Church of the Pietà was just over three hundred meters east from their position, but the entire length of that run would be out in the open.

Booker barreled up alongside him.

"Get to the rally point," he told Iain as they sped up. "I'll divert them."

They broke apart.

Iain hit the burners. He'd always been a decent runner in football, a winger who could tear down the flanks, but he'd never hit a high gear like this before. It wasn't just the concern of a bullet punching through his spine, but Ridley was on her own. They'd lost a teammate, and somewhere out there she was in a chase for her life, with the very item that they had been dispatched to retrieve.

He hurtled past the few pedestrians who had bundled up and braved the snowy cold. Sounds of alarm faded behind him as they spotted the gun in his hand.

He didn't want to see Ridley in his mind, but there she flickered for a moment...squeezing out her dark hair as she surfaced in the Hungarian baths...slotting her SIG Sauer into the holster on her thigh...

Iain's heartrate was like a jackhammer in his ears.

His legs became pistons.

Booker had run to the docks and down a small wharf, using the posts and display maps as concealment.

He couldn't start a boat chase here. Being on open water with God-knows-how-much fuel in the tank would just be more of the same chase, with less resolution.

Just as he pulled the tarp off one of the water taxis, he heard their pursuers bolt out from the courtyard of the Doge's Palace. They must have immediately spotted Iain down the waterfront.

Booker dropped low behind cover.

"Separated!" shouted one of the men. "I'll find the big man. Go!"

Two of them took off after the Scotsman. The third went into hunting mode, scanning the other way on the waterfront, glancing into the alleys.

It gave Booker a moment to slip into the water taxi. This type usually had a key left stashed on the boat. It took only seconds for him to find it in the cockpit.

With a glance over his shoulder, he realized with a jolt that the man stalking the docks for him was Bill Dane. He wore a thick woolen pea coat and carried a Glock G19.

Booker would have to time it perfectly, moving like the panther he hadn't been in years.

Keeping as low as he could, he watched Dane's head turning...as soon as his shoulders shifted to look away, Booker started the engine.

For a split second, Dane couldn't tell where the noise was coming from. In that instant, Booker threw the throttle forward and leaped back onto the dock.

He crouched behind the empty ticketing booth as Dane caught sight of the boat zooming out into the Grand Canal. He sprinted to a motorboat and ripped off the tarp.

As he jumped into the cockpit, Booker emerged from behind the booth.

He breathed in relief as Dane revved the engine and took off after the rogue—and empty—water taxi.

Iain barreled into the Church of the Pietà and heaved the

massive wooden door shut behind him. He scanned the sanctuary as his lungs raged for air.

It was empty.

From behind one of the red tapestries on the side emerged Booker. His gun was still clutched at a low ready.

"Eliminated?" he asked.

"No," gasped Iain. "I lost 'em in the alleys...totally gone. Yours?"

"Took off chasing a boat that had no captain."

"No Ridley?"

"No."

His voice was steady, but Iain could see his jaw flex with worry.

"She's got the key...someone was on her tail, right?" said Iain.

"I got a glimpse, but—just a glimpse. Cover the door."

Iain gripped his pistol as he cast an eye to the entrance.

Booker pulled out his phone and opened up his tracking app. He stared at it, mouth tight. He didn't say anything for several seconds, until Iain couldn't take the silence anymore.

"Mate, what?"

"I've got her on here. Her tracker's not moving."

"Where is it?"

Booker started for the door but couldn't look up to meet Iain's eyes.

"Rio del Vin. It's a canal."

# CHAPTER
# THIRTY-SIX

**VENICE, ITALY**

THE WORLD RIPPED open in front of Ridley's eyes.

Water spewed from her mouth. Violent coughs racked her body. Her gaze spun as she pushed herself up to sit.

She could still see the canal in front of her, but she was now on the stone beside it.

Kneeling beside her was a woman in her thirties, her long dark hair partially wet. She was wiping water from her mouth, and a look of exhausted relief beamed from her eyes.

She put her hands on Ridley's back to help stabilize her as she sputtered out the last of the water.

"*Meno male*," the woman murmured. "*Hai bisogno di un ospedale!*"

"Where's—"

Ridley whipped around, looking for the man who'd chased her down. No sign of anyone else along the canal. Then her hands went to her pocket.

The key was gone.

She frantically checked again, then lurched to the side of the canal, looking down in desperation.

The woman beside her yelled and hauled her back from the edge, as if she was afraid that this waterlogged rescue case was about to throw herself back in.

"Are you American?" she asked, almost accusingly.

**ITALIAN:** *"Yes, but I speak Italian,"* said Ridley. *"Where's the man who was here?"*

**ITALIAN:** *"The bastard that pulled you out of the water first? He took something from your pocket, and then dropped you back in!"* said the woman.

"Damnit!"

Ridley staggered to her feet, and just then realized that she was shivering. Wholly soaked in the frigid waters of Venice.

**ITALIAN:** *"Did you see where he went?"* she asked.

**ITALIAN:** *"No, Your Majesty. I was saving you."*

Patting through every pocket, Ridley realized that her phone was missing, too.

*At the bottom of the fucking canal. And whoever that was has the key. And I'm about to go hypothermic.*

"Look, I can speak English," said the woman, trying to calm her down. "You need to go to the hospital. I think you have blood on your head."

As she pulled out her own mobile—

"No!" said Ridley. "I'm not going to the hospital. I need to get back to my friends. We got separated..."

"You are not." There was some unexpected fire in this stranger. "I cannot have it. I saved you from the canal and you freeze to death on the street?"

She began to dial, but Ridley lunged to put her hand over the phone.

"Please," she said, quieter, looking into the woman's eyes.

Her teeth were beginning to chatter, her words stuttering

out through the shivers. The Italian woman searched her face for a moment, hesitating.

"But you can't stay in those clothes."

"I know. Is there a shop near here for clothes?"

"Not near here," she said, but then pointed upward behind her. "But I live near."

She grabbed Ridley's wrist and began tugging her toward the apartment building.

*I am going to go into shock if I don't get warm. Just go with her, Samaras.*

With desperate reluctance, she followed this woman to a narrow door. As she was unlocking it, Ridley had a piercing thought that the woman could be one of them. A whole ruse, designed to get her into a secluded place.

*Why wouldn't she just let me drown in the canal then?*
*Because we have the rest of the keys they need.*
*That's a hostage deal.*
*You are being stupid.*
*Stupid, but stupid which way?*

She had little choice but to get warm as quickly as possible. Calculated risk.

So Ridley followed her rescuer up to her second floor apartment, now nearly seizing with cold. It was a cozy little place with a fair view of the canal. As soon as the woman had shut the door, she turned to her half-frozen guest and pulled off her jacket.

"Come on. Take it all off. I will get you blankets."

Ridley began peeling off her soaking clothes, which had already begun to stiffen. As she struggled with the last leg of her pants, a gray-and-white cat sauntered by, then jumped up on the windowsill to stare at her.

The woman came back with a heap of blankets. As Ridley wrapped herself in the thickest of them, her host pulled a pair of wool socks on her feet, then smushed a woolen cap on her head.

"Something hot t-to drink," said Ridley. "No alcohol."

Alcohol was fake warmth and would only impair heat regulation.

The woman heated water in the microwave and had a mug of tea in front of her guest in no time. She sat down on a hassock as Ridley began to sip.

After a moment of watching her, the woman finally said, "I'm Aurora."

"Ridley."

"Is that your first name or your last name?"

"First name."

"Aurora Cantore."

Ridley eyed her. "Ridley." Then she glanced at the cat, who had settled into a contented loaf. "Who's that?"

"Phoebe. She was—" Aurora glanced back, "a very smelly cat when I got her. Now. My partner left some clothes here, if you are okay with clothing for men. He's like your height—and we need to find your friends, but you have no phone."

Ridley could feel her body going from a stabbing cold urgency into merely an extreme shivering chill.

"I need to get to the Church of the Pietà."

Aurora raised a brow. "You want to thank the Virgin Mother for saving your life? How about you buy me a coffee first for doing that."

Ridley tried to laugh. "I'm not religious. I just need to meet my friends."

"Maybe you *should* light a candle. You almost drowned. Why? Why were you in the canal?"

"I just slipped. Icy on the dock...am I a stupid tourist?"

It wasn't her best work, but her brain was still thawing.

Aurora's gaze on her was unblinking. In another circumstance, it would have been a sultry look.

"Sure."

*She doesn't believe it.*

"When you're warm, I'll check your head. You were bleeding. I think you got shot."

Ridley's eyes snapped up.

"Shot?! Shot in the head?"

Aurora nodded with new certainty. "I heard them, and I'm *not* a stupid tourist. There are reasons that someone refuses so much to go to the hospital when they're injured."

"I was not shot in the head."

"You should call your friends."

She held out her own phone to Ridley.

*Of all people...why couldn't my rescuer have been a cantankerous stoic who minded their own business?*

"I don't know their number. It was just in my phone."

*Of course she knew their numbers, but she wasn't about to plug them into a stranger's phone.*

Aurora gave her a pitiable look and stood up. "I'll get you clothes. Then we'll go to the Chiesa della Pietà."

When she'd disappeared into the bedroom, Ridley's eyes began to roam the apartment. Though there was little space in the compact Venetian style, much of it was taken up by books...rows of them, stacks of them, piled on top of every conceivable surface.

And as she looked closer, she saw the names on the spines and covers: Robert Ludlum, John le Carré, Ian Fleming, Daniel Silva, Mick Herron, Isabella Maldonado, T.R. Hendricks, Gregg Hurwitz, Brad Thor...all of them thrillers. Espionage. Action.

Aurora was a spy junkie.

"*Gamó tin týchi mou,*" Ridley murmured.

*Fuck my luck.*

Forty minutes later, Ridley stepped into the Church of the Pietà. She wore a pair of slightly baggy pants strapped up with a belt, and a gray quarter-zip sweater that looked almost fashionably loose.

Behind her was Aurora. Whether she had any suspicions about Ridley or just felt the thrill of this stranger's urgency, she insisted on traversing the snowy alleys of Venice with her. Ridley had adamantly protested the company, but also had to concede it wasn't her city. The Italian woman declared she was taking a walk in the now-sleeting conditions, and just happened to be going to church.

But Booker and Iain weren't there. Only a few devout morning worshippers who were bent over the velvet pews.

Ridley's mind was a flurry of possibilities.

*They didn't make it. Only one of them made it but he went out looking for me. Both of them made it but went out looking for me—even though one of them should have stayed back. Why would they do that—if they thought I was dead. Booker tracks my phone...which is at the bottom of the canal...*

She had to focus. In any of these scenarios, without any form of contacting them, she had only one resort that would make sense to both her and to them.

Ridley obsessively committed to memory the location of the CIA safehouses in every location they traveled to. It was part of her preparation on every mission, to study maps until she could draw them in her sleep, and to remember entry codes until she could recite them backward.

Venice had one such safehouse. It had to be the next place that her partners—if they were still alive—would regroup. They would expect her there.

And she absolutely could not tolerate an Italian civilian going with her.

"What will you do?" asked Aurora as they headed back out onto the waterfront.

"Drink coffee, I think."

"There's a beautiful trattoria across the bridge."

Ridley turned to face her full on. She felt ridiculous, a deep chill still icing her bones, wearing the oversized clothes of this woman's boyfriend, standing there in Venice looking as unglamorous as anyone could be in the romantic Floating City.

"Aurora, I do owe you my life—"

**ITALIAN:** *"You owe me a coffee. But you have no money. So I'll buy you one."*

*Borderline stalker behavior. This can't be right.*

"I—I know where my friends will be. Thank you for everything. If you give me your address, I'll have these clothes sent back to you by the end of the day."

"Ridley..."

Something prickled in her. It was the first time this woman had called her by name, and there was a weight to it that she didn't like.

"Someone was shooting at you and your friends, I think. And now you're looking for a safehouse, but maybe you want to be careful on these streets."

Aurora unlocked her mobile and held out the screen for her to see.

Ridley's face went to stone.

"Someone is going to recognize you."

# CHAPTER
# THIRTY-SEVEN

**VENICE, ITALY**

OF COURSE there were surveillance cameras around St. Mark's Basilica.

The question was how this attractive spy junkie with a cat and clear attachment issues came by a still shot of Ridley crossing into the church—within two hours of it happening.

"I'm a—you call it 'accountant,'" Aurora told her. "For the police, and I work at *Polizia Locale Sezione San Marco*."

The police department located at the end of the piazza...in front of St. Mark's.

"We hear a lot of noises in Venezia, but not a lot of guns."

In keeping with her professional skillset, Ridley was an excellent liar, even when under stress. But this one...this one was a fun new challenge. She took a slow breath before responding, as though bracing herself to divulge the truth.

*The best lie is one mixed with truth.*

"You're right that someone was shooting at me and my friends."

"And one of them—the man—took something from your pocket in the canal?"

"I'd assume so, unless you have really desperate and evil pickpockets running around."

Aurora seemed terribly pleased with herself for piecing together this real-life thriller.

Ridley went on. "I think *they think* that we're after the relics here. Old Saint Mark's bones. We're not, but there was no discussing that with them. They must be part of some religious order. Fanatics."

Aurora's eyes went wide.

"The Order of Raphael?"

Ridley had to wrestle down the shock of hearing that name. "The who?"

The odds of an accountant sitting in a police station in Venice knowing about the Order were mind-boggling. Either she was a spy, or the Raphaels had really slipped when they helped to nearly destroy all of Jerusalem's holiest sites.

*After seven centuries, they got a coming-out party they never wanted.*

But Aurora didn't want to divulge any more of her clandestine reserves. She shivered, tugging her scarf tighter.

"Some people I heard about...maybe they're not real."

"Well, I'm not heading to a safehouse, no," said Ridley. "I'm heading to a house that belongs to a friend of a friend. I figure it's the only other place in Venice my friends would go right now. If these crazy men are still hunting us...you're right. I need to get off the streets."

"The police are looking for you, too."

"Even better! Look, I don't want to put you in any danger—"

*—this woman would probably impale herself for some real-life danger—*

"—but would you be willing...would you help me figure out who that man was who knocked me into the canal? Maybe he *is* part of that Order you said. I never saw him before today, but he must be on the same surveillance tapes near the basilica, right?"

Aurora hesitated, but Ridley could see it in her eyes: she was hooked.

"I can't access those things. I'm just an accountant."

"That's not—no way. You were smart enough to figure out all of this. If they can't see how much spy-shit talent you have..." Ridley shook her head. "I'm sure you're good with numbers, too, but some Italian agency is missing out."

"What do you want me to do?"

"Just get me the best image you can of the man who did this to me. He looked Asian, maybe Chinese."

"And how do I get it to you?"

Now she sounded skeptical.

"Meet somewhere nearby?"

"Yes...yes. Meet me at La Palanca."

"How much time do you need?"

"Two hours." She fished into her purse for some euros and pressed them into Ridley's hand. "To get across the canal. See you then."

The sleet had relented by the time Ridley found a gondola to take her across the Grand Canal.

When she finally arrived at the address of the safehouse, she punched the passcode into a digital pad at the front door. A voice came over the intercom.

"*Buongiorno. Stai vendendo qualcosa?*"

"I have Neapolitan Mastiff puppies for sale."

It wasn't even one of the more bizarre passwords she'd

given for entry at a safehouse. One guy in Portugal had made her sing "Bohemian Rhapsody."

The door buzzed open. Ridley trudged in.

The man who met her in the front hall looked so much like Fredo in *The Godfather* that she stared for a moment.

"Come on," he said, beckoning her into the house. "Your friends are here."

As Ridley walked into the sitting room, Booker rose to his feet. He hauled her into a bear hug before she could even finish her greeting.

"Invincible," he exclaimed under his breath. "Of course you are."

"I'm lucky, and very, very cold."

As Booker released her, Ridley saw Iain rising out of his chair.

It had been a while since she'd seen that look on someone's face. Like everything he'd hoped for in the world was there in front of his eyes.

He couldn't say anything, but pulled her into a hug. When he clutched the back of her head, she felt a ripple, as if she'd passed from the shallows into a deep current of...something.

But he pulled back quickly. When he saw her expression, he knew.

"They have the key," he said.


Ninety minutes later, they sat inside the small café on the waterfront, with espressos, a tea for Iain, and some hot slices of quiche. A handful of other diners were happily tucking into lunch plates. Most looked like tourists and spoke a smattering of languages.

When Aurora Cantore entered, she quickly spotted Ridley and headed over to the table for some brief introductions.

"The woman who saved my life," Ridley told them as Aurora sat across from her, beside Booker.

He straightened up and squared his shoulders as she settled in beside him.

She was doing an excellent job of playing it cool, but clearly enjoying the most exciting excursion of her year. She pulled a tablet from her bag and opened it up. When she laid the device flat on the table, they saw an enlarged photo from a surveillance camera.

"That's him," muttered Ridley.

It was as blurry as hers had been, but it was unmistakably the man who'd chased her into the canal and left her for dead.

"And I got an identification for him," said Aurora. "His name is Shao Luming."

Ridley, Booker, and Iain exchanged glances of surprise.

"Thirty-one years old. Chinese-born but raised in Indonesia. Trained a lot in silat and knife-fighting, went into KOPASSUS—the Indonesian Special Forces—but he didn't stay long. A few times he was caught and they questioned him for crimes but never went to jail. That was a long time ago. He didn't leave the crime life. They think he's a mercenary now, and he just got better at not getting caught."

*Spy novels really come through.*

"Wow," said Booker. "You're—uh—this is amazing work."

She grinned.

"There were a few flags on him," she said. "The authorities wouldn't let him in this country without watching him, but they don't know he's here. I don't think you will tell me who's chasing you, but I hope you know what you're doing. I think this one is a very dangerous man."

# CHAPTER
# THIRTY-EIGHT

**VENICE, ITALY**

Until eighteen hours ago, Lianna Powell had never been on a private jet.

When she had first set foot in the Gulfstream, she was properly awed by the luxury, the smooth creamy leather and gleaming hardwood.

This time, she only had eyes for the piece of quartz on the table in front of her.

The stone glinted atop the dark cloth. It had been shaped into a delicate, curling figure that appeared to be a "3," but Lianna knew it wasn't a digit. It was the "M" of the Enochian alphabet. John Dee's Holy Grail. The language of angels and the Garden of Eden.

Across the table from her, sitting erect in an ivory-colored leather chair, was Bill Dane.

"What can that do?" he said.

She could tell he was unimpressed. His jaw was tight, his eyes unblinking.

"Well," said Lianna in her calmest professor voice. "It's

impossibly small for a piece carved so precisely. In fact, quite impossible that it was carved at all! Quartz is rather hard and very brittle. It must be cut with diamond blades. And do you know when diamond blades were invented?"

"That question is a trap for stupid."

"I'm sorry, Bill. That was rhetorical. They weren't used until the early 20th century."

She pulled out a magnifying lens from her knapsack. In the seat behind her, Freddie guzzled a whiskey double and Qualley played a game on his phone.

"John Dee did something extraordinary here," said Lianna, "and I haven't a clue as to how. But everything that's written in his journal has been true and accurate. I've no reason to believe that the power of this key would be anything different."

"Like I asked before, what can that do?"

"When collected with the other five, they'll be aligned in the correct order to spell out the name of his favorite spirit—*Madimi*."

"You don't know where they'll have to be aligned."

She looked up at him pointedly. "Not yet. We need to find what's in Vienna. *That's* where we'll find the last piece we need in order to find out where Dee hid the Devil's Eye."

From the back of the plane emerged Shao Luming. He was really quite handsome, with his full lips and vaulting black eyebrows, but he scared her. Dane was one thing, intense as a war dog. Shao seemed more like a cobra—a relaxed creature whose threat still seemed obvious.

He settled into his seat, removing a sheathed blade from his waistband and tugging down the hem of his gray turtleneck. He laid the piece on the table in front of him, paying no more attention to it than having removed it for comfort.

Lianna felt that ripple of present danger. The weapon was nearly nine inches long, and from the angular end of the black sheath, she wondered if it was a tanto knife. She'd been to an exhibit the year before on feudal Japan and found herself fascinated by the collection of swords and knives they'd used.

Turning her focus back to Dane, Lianna went on. "However, we're all caught in a stalemate of sorts...because we need *all* the keys."

"That was all she had on her," said Shao, gesturing to the quartz key.

"Maybe the others are carrying the rest."

Dane's jaw tightened even further. His failure in taking out their other two targets was viscerally shameful, especially in light of how successful Shao had been.

"If they're smart, they wouldn't be," he said. "Why carry them around? You could just stash them in a safebox. No risk."

"Suppose that would make our task a wee bit harder then."

From behind them, Freddie's gruff Norwegian voice cut through. "Or they destroyed them. What would they need the keys for if the only point is stopping anyone else from getting that fucking Eye?"

The thought hit Lianna like a bolt to the chest. She had never considered it before, that anyone so clever and dogged in pursuit of these precious items would actually *destroy* them.

"No," she said, shaking her head. "No, they wouldn't. They just couldn't. Anyone who knows and cares this much about John Dee could never."

Dane sniffed. "It's power. You don't destroy your own leverage. They have the keys. And we'll meet them again soon. But first we meet Pearson. He's coming to Vienna."

### SLOVENIA

In the front seat of their rented Audi, Ridley nestled down

into the heated leather and opened a small packet of Biscoff biscuits.

"Merry Christmas," she said, offering one to Booker in the driver's seat.

He dipped his head in thanks and took a bite. Christmas carols bobbed and jingled softly through the stereo.

Iain was sleeping in the backseat in an awkward pile of limbs. The ruthless pace of this treasure hunt had left them all beaten and exhausted. It would have been easier to take a plane to Vienna, but with Ridley's photo already circulating through the Italian police force, that was no longer an option. Instead, it would be a long drive northeast through the snow.

"You warm yet?" asked Booker.

"My bones are on thaw," she said through a mouthful of Biscoff. "Did you really think I was dead?"

"Water ain't got you yet. You're like a horseshoe crab. You could survive an extinction level event in $H_2O$."

"I couldn't find a place for that on my resumé."

*I couldn't keep a damn stone in my pocket. No one can count on you, Samaras, if you fuck up something like this. You had one assignment.*

Booker took a sip from his energy drink. "Did you see her?"

*Here's the psych check-in.*

"The demon bitch? Yeah. For a second, in the water...I guess until I knocked myself unconscious and fell into her gigantic face."

*Doesn't get much more pathetic...*

"Is it getting worse?" he asked.

She thought for a moment, recalling each time she'd fallen under that eerie spell.

"Yes. The first time she was just a little girl, standing at the mouth of Fingal's Cave, remember. In Budapest she was—"

*The young woman standing in the flames...*

*Dark hair and jagged cheeks...*
*That pulsing blue-grey of her skin...*
*Her eyes glowing white.*

But the most grotesque of all of it: mimicking the voice of Ridley's dead mother.

But she said none of that.

"—in Budapest she was definitely older."

Booker nodded soberly. He knew that she had seen horrors, but even in this private moment, would not speak them.

"The way Dee wrote about her through the years was of her growing up. A girl first, then a 'nymph' as old men liked to call teenage girls back then, and then 'nubile,' and we all know what that means."

"Barely grown woman he'd like to—"

"I don't know why it happened that way...maybe seeing a kid at first throws you off guard. You feel like they need help or protection, so you have no defenses up against anything they do or say."

"Have you never seen *The Shining? The Omen? Children of the Corn?*"

"Be helpful, Rid."

"You're probably right. Her growing up gives him a sense of closeness, like he's raising his own kids in real life. Then the pervert part, where all that warps into lust and she can seduce him into some really bad acts." She chomped on the last of her biscuit. "There's a term for that, you know."

"Just because I don't cuss like you doesn't mean I haven't heard every foul thing in the English language. I don't need your dirty dictionary reading."

She glanced back at Iain. He was still asleep, his curling hair rumpled against his jacket-pillow. The intensity of his every expression—the *aliveness* of his whole face—had melted away into a pure, childlike stillness.

Until a week ago, she'd never even seen his face. Now...

Combat bonding had been her primary form of relationship for so long now that she could hardly relate honestly to anyone outside of that. She knew it wasn't healthy, but if she couldn't bond with people like that, what could she really do?

*Dates with duds. Empty flirtations with beach babes. Men who didn't know, women who couldn't understand...and vice-versa.*

Ridley had never gotten to serve in full military combat, but she'd come to see how badly a former soldier could struggle with reconnecting to civilian life. No one else could possibly understand the bonds formed under such stress, in the valley of the shadow of death.

But this one...Iain Carnegie was different. And whatever was coming, she really needed that difference to stay dormant.

"You must be glad I'm stubborn as rust on a ten-speed," said Booker, noticing her attention.

She darted him a look of faux surprise. "I'm not measuring tartans for a kilt or anything."

"You know, I always wanted to spend Christmas in the Highlands. Some castle, couple servants to get that hearth fire goin' in the morning...smell that slab bacon and fresh corn muffins...dog by my feet when I get up, lady by my side like a fine Christmas morning present."

"Angela Bassett or Michelle Pfeiffer?"

"A man does not complain about the color of the wrapping."

"Did you sing carols around the baby grand the night before?"

"Mmm-hm. I got some Bing Crosby in me."

"You're Bing Crosby frosted with James Earl Jones, boss."

"You seein' family?"

Ridley's father, Nikos, was a distant man. Since the death of his wife, he'd drifted from his children as he'd drifted around the world working on large-scale construction projects. He'd been living in Dubai for the last few years, but neither his son nor daughter had been to visit him yet. The invitations to do so had been feeble, and the responses half-hearted.

Ridley couldn't imagine a much worse choice for the holidays than spending Christmas in a seething desert with a distracted father who never knew what to do with her.

"To be determined," she said. "My brother invited me to Disneyworld with his family, but I think I'd rather drink gutter water."

"My kids loved that place. If you're under ten, it's magical."

"No kids for you this year?"

"Ah..."

As far as Ridley knew, he'd always had a fairly good relationship with his adult children, a daughter and twin boys.

"They'll be at Holly's new place with her new fiancé. Did they invite me? Sure did. Would I be caught dead there? Don't let them take my body."

Skimming quickly off the topic, Booker glanced into the backseat, seeing only Iain's boots.

"I know you never tangled with anyone on a mission before," he said, "no matter which team they play for. I have no doubt you're in game-time mode now."

She couldn't tell if that was admiration or a warning.

*Both wrapped up. He knows how to work his operatives.*

"I'm sayin' this because that man's about to see you in a gown, Ridley, and Lord knows what that's gonna do to his constitution."

# CHAPTER
# THIRTY-NINE

**VIENNA, AUSTRIA**

Vienna was one of the finest cities in Europe, and Christmas was the finest time to be in Vienna.

The city played host to some of the most lavish holiday balls in the world. Tomorrow night, Marc Pearson and Ophelia Crowhurst would be attending the most opulent of them all. Also on the guest list was the Royal Prince Albert, Duke of Edinburgh.

Their analyst back at the Osprey office had been screening a countless number of channels for the billionaire's name. He lay low in general, using his own plane and staying only at his own homes around the world or at those of friends, but almost never in hotels. He generally surfaced in public only for events that Effie coaxed him into, so it was significant when his name popped up somewhere.

Thankfully, it wasn't hard for a CIA division director—no matter how discreet his profile—to get a few invitations to the Vienna Opera Ball.

They would have a night off from their relentless chase

anyhow, because their very destination point—the Hofburg Palace—had been shut down for the night. The government had lent out its jewels from the Imperial Treasury there to an exhibit in Salzburg. There was enhanced security in the area as they were returned tonight. Not even Dane and his cronies would dare attempt to infiltrate the place.

So they had tonight to attend a ball, and tomorrow, to find the final key.

The streets of Vienna were draped in lights: curtains, chandeliers, netting, braided ropes of all sorts. Department stores were decked with glowing oversized ornaments. Thick, bristly wreaths hung from shop windows. Towering evergreens were wrapped in string lights and studded with shiny baubles. Pedestrians bundled against the cold, milling through the Christmas markets, clutching hot drinks and shopping bags.

Ridley had been here as a teenager. Most of her memories of Europe starred her and Alexios romping around like two Artful Dodgers and storming up trouble, but in Vienna…

She remembered her father taking both of them to an elegant old coffeehouse where they drank milky *franziskaner* like grown-ups, then to see the magnificent Lipizzaner horses perform…the riders' epaulettes flashing atop their stallions… she thought she could do that, too. Her father explained that women weren't allowed in the Spanish Riding School.

Years later, she would discover that women weren't allowed in the Navy SEALs either. She stepped straight up to that wall and began swinging for its demolition.

It was only a malfunction of the sledgehammer that stopped her from becoming the first. Or would she have eventually failed on her own?

Acutely reminded of having become neither a Lipizzaner

rider nor a SEAL, Ridley made her way through the streets of Vienna to the Golden Quarter shopping district. Still wearing the oversized men's clothes of Aurora Cantore's partner, she walked into a boutique—and a tide of unmistakable looks surged her way.

*So this was Julia Roberts in* Pretty Woman...*without that amount of pretty.*

But Booker had handed off the almighty business credit card to her. She garnered a bit more respect once she began speaking German to the employees, and even more when she gathered a rack of gowns to try on.

She was picky but impatient, a terrible combination. The saleswoman kept flattering her each time she appeared in a new outfit, but interestingly, the level of the compliment always corresponded with the price tag.

Then she tried on a sleek, one-shouldered piece of deep emerald.

Ridley didn't think her looks were much, but her figure could carry a few things. She walked out of the fitting room and caught sight of herself in the mirrors.

Iain's face flashed across her mind...*the way he looked at me when he realized I was alive...*

This was the dress.


They climbed out of their luxury Uber that night, wrapped in long thick coats against the December night. Guests were streaming out from the long line of limousines. Valets in green jackets were hustling around in the snow. Behind them loomed the Vienna State Opera.

As they stepped onto the sprawling red carpet, Iain offered Ridley his arm. She laced hers through the crook of his elbow. He had lightly gelled his thick auburn waves, which somehow made his deep-set eyes seem even more intensely blue.

She glanced at his white tie and tails.

"My penguin escort."

He looked offended. "You're lucky to have found an *emperor* penguin tonight, ma'am."

From behind them, Booker smirked and straightened his own white vest. As they entered the opera house though, his look of amusement became one of awe.

A green carpet wound up the marble staircase, and as they climbed it, a splendid palace opened overhead. There were Grecian statues looking poised and nonchalant, vaulted ceilings painted like the heavens, carved balconies stacked floor after floor, and glowing lamps cradled in gold sconces.

"What ho!" murmured Booker. "You know this place was destroyed in World War Two? American bombs took out the whole theater."

"Story of the continent," said Iain. "'Destroyed in World War Two.' Fuckin' Germany."

"Don't let Austria off that easy. They were *enthusiastic* supporters."

A coat-check girl greeted them in the foyer. As Ridley shrugged out of her long wool coat, she saw Iain lean back as though stepping out of a blast radius but unable to look away from the flash.

Booker chuckled, "Cleopatra has arrived. You know you don't have to work the honey trap, Rid."

*Honey trap:* the use of seduction and the lure of a romantic or sexual relationship to obtain information, sometimes referred to as "sexpionage," and a favorite tool of the Russians.

"Honey, I am Venus flytrap material."

She straightened the one-sash shoulder of her silk gown. Iain had to shake his head clear.

They funneled in with the crowds heading for the auditorium, already scanning for any sight of Pearson.

As they climbed the stairs, Iain tugged at the hem of his vest. "Actually get a bit nervous at this sort of things. I'm just a minger from Glasgow."

"You look handsome," she told him. "You're all right."

He grinned at her.

Then they walked into the theater—and emerged into something enchanted.

The seats and stage had been replaced by a hardwood ballroom floor. Ornate wreaths hung from every balcony. The boxes, draped in red velvet and reaching five tiers, were stuffed with the richest and most famous guests, with buckets of champagne propped on their balconies. Gathered along the sides were thick crowds. They were leaving open the center of the floor for something grand.

"We made it before the program started," said Booker as they descended the red-carpet stairs.

As usual, Ridley had done her preparation for this one. This wasn't simply a gathering of people to dance. There were well over a thousand guests in the opera house tonight, but they'd be nothing more than an audience for the first hour.

*Endurance...if Shackleton could do it, I can stand here in a dress for an hour watching a fancy parade.*

There was a finely dressed woman going about with a microphone, spotting famous faces in the crowd and beckoning along her cameraman for interviews. Booker, Ridley, and Iain sidled down to the floor just as the orchestra at the far end struck up the Austrian national anthem. Everyone rose to their feet.

When it finished, the music melted into a quick, bright piece, and the procession began. Over a hundred debutantes paraded out onto the floor with their escorts. Each wore a white gown, opera gloves, a Swarovski tiara, and clutched a small bouquet. Their male partners wore tails and white gloves.

Ridley murmured into Iain's ear. "You don't do this debutante stuff in Scotland, do you?"

He shook his head. "Just men in kilts blowin' into bags."

She laughed.

A children's ballet company took the floor next. As they performed, Ridley's eyes roamed upward, scanning the boxes. In the middle loge was the president of Austria and his entourage. She spotted a woman she was sure had to be Brooke Shields. George and Amal Clooney had a box with their friends. In another was the novelist Daniel Silva and his wife, the CNN reporter Jamie Gangel. Ridley saw retired prime ministers, a player from the Austrian national football team, and even recognized some foreign business magnates.

Then she saw him.

In a third-tier box halfway down the floor, sat Marc Pearson. Beside him, Effie Crowhurst leaned elegantly against the rail.

*Ferenc being torched into a pillar of flame...Zsolt holding the line to die in the inferno...*

The memories flashing in her mind began to glaze into a cold hatred. A man who thought he could do anything and get away with it.

*He* has *done anything he wanted and gotten away with it—*
*But not this thing.*
*NOT THIS THING.*

She nudged Booker, who followed her eyes up to Pearson's box.

"He'll come down," Booker whispered. "Effie never misses a chance on the dance floor."

Iain noticed their attentions and looked up. Just as he

caught sight, an angelic blonde girl slid in and took her seat between them. At this distance, he couldn't quite tell her age.

The wait was excruciating. Adult ballet, children's choir, a violin solo, a tenor and soprano duet...each culminated in a wave of applause, until finally came the *Fächerpolonaise,* the introduction of the debutantes.

The *Hofdame,* a woman in a billowing red gown conducting their choreography, stood at the front of the ballroom on a podium. The black and white lines of the debutantes with their escorts stepped and twirled and turned, all in coordinated grace.

"Ah, that's beautiful," said Iain.

He gestured to a couple on the end with Down's Syndrome. Ridley thought he looked more delighted by that than anything else they'd seen together.

Then the Waltz of the Danube began, and the young couples went swirling across the floor. The ushers collected up the velvet ropes, and the rest of the guests melted onto the floor to join.

Iain straightened up and smoothed out his vest. "Not sure if you can handle this, but I did waltz a couple of times in primary school." He turned to Ridley and offered up his hand.

"One can almost smell the elegance." She took it. "See if you can keep up with 'the Ginger Rogers of the Crip walk.'"

They floated into the waltz, his hand against her back. As they glided across the floor, her eyes kept flitting to Pearson's box. Each time Iain swung around, he glanced up as well, but the scent of her perfume was distracting—the sudden closeness, holding her hand outstretched in his, the dip of her collarbone above the emerald neckline—

Then he felt her hand clutch his tighter. As she leaned in close to his ear, he struggled to stay focused.

Until she said, "He's coming down."

# CHAPTER
# FORTY

**VIENNA, AUSTRIA**

BOOKER HAD BEEN WATCHING Pearson's box. When he saw the shady financier stand with Effie and lead their young blonde companion out of sight, he switched into another gear.

He slid through the crowd to get a better view of the stairs that led into the ballroom. There was no part of this operation that required meeting Marc Pearson.

But there was the man who put this entire deadly chase into motion, and Booker wouldn't waste the opportunity to keep eyes on him and everyone he spoke to.

Turns out, that would be a lot.

Effie appeared like a bird of paradise, all radiant smiles and coquettish charm in her peacock-blue gown. It seemed like there wasn't anyone in the room she *didn't* know, or anyone who didn't want to meet her. Pearson accompanied her, gladhanding and complimenting guests at every turn.

And then there was the girl with them. Booker could only catch glimpses of her amidst the general height of the crowds, but she appeared to be no more than a teenager. She was dressed in a red-and-white gown that made her look like a very young Grace Kelly. She drifted about with Pearson and Effie, with them introducing her to everyone like a prized debutante.

He'd watched people for a living, surveilling, reading body language and figuring out what motivated them. There was something not right about this scene, like the girl was being forced to play a happy part onstage after the worst day of her life.

Booker wasn't the only man taking up space with shoulders like a former linebacker, but he was one of only a dozen black faces in the opera house. It wasn't the kind of crowd he could disappear into, but he still moved easily through it, greeting strangers as though he knew them and leaving many a confused guest in his wake. He kept himself in Pearson's periphery.

Out on the floor, Ridley and Iain finished their waltz and slid back to the sidelines.

"I don't see any security on him," Ridley murmured into Iain's ear.

He glanced at Pearson, who was meandering through the sparkling array of guests.

"Don't see his attack dog, either," said Iain.

"There's no way they're *not* meeting. They're not in Vienna at the same time without Dane crossing paths with the boss."

"Wager he cannae dance worth shit."

"But now he has a key."

"Doesn't matter."

She looked at him. "Doesn't matter?"

"No, it doesn't. They were always gonna come for us anyway, since we had all the keys at first. Now we're in the same position, really. We need somethin' they have, so we've got to go after *them*."

"It *matters* because now we've got to watch our backs and *also* formulate a plan of action to take theirs."

"Take their backs?" he said.

"Yeah. Take their backs, steal what they took, leave them crying."

"Spoken like a Viking. You could be my people."

"My mother's Icelandic."

"Where they ferment sharks. And *eat* them."

She laughed. "I'm not that Icelandic."

Then her eyes caught sight of Pearson. He was walking straight at Booker.

"Mr. Douglas!"

Marc Pearson grinned that polished, bone-white smile at the CIA division director, striding up to him as if this was a long-awaited introduction. Booker recovered his shock within a blink.

"I'm so glad to run into you like this," said Pearson, extending his hand.

Booker shook it like any good diplomat would. "Marc Pearson."

"So you're traveling for work, but what are you doing at the Opera Ball?"

Straight to it. No sense in pretending.

"Group dances and white ties with tails really get me in the Christmas mood."

Pearson laughed as if an old friend had cracked a joke, and Booker could see immediately how he ingratiated himself into so many people's lives.

"Well, of all the balls in all the houses in all Vienna, you walked into mine," said the billionaire. "You're not following me, though, I know. You're just following instructions. Yep...

four-hundred-year-old instructions from a guy who dined with angels."

"You're makin' it sound weird, but you're a guy who hired killers to chase those instructions around the world."

"Let's be a little more fair, here, Mr. Douglas. I hired them before I even knew they'd have to contend with *other* killers. I think the balance is about right."

"I guess you're building your own Sigillum Dei, then," said Booker. "Down to the last instruction."

"I've loved being successful in my work, you know, but it's been a little boring moving money around and telling other people where to put it. I was ready for something else."

"Regular blackmail got boring so you needed a more intense high."

"You love this stuff," said Pearson with a conspiratorial smile, "and look at you, back out in the field after all these years!"

That made Booker's senses prickle. He'd lived most of his life behind a wall of anonymity. When he became the Director of Osprey, the clandestine nature of his division meant he was all but invisible to most people even within the agency. Pearson was flexing connections that only a handful of people in the world outside of government would have.

"I'm just enjoying my travel," said Booker.

"How 'bout your friends?"

Pearson gestured—right at Ridley and Iain.

---

Ridley saw Pearson's eyes switch straight to her from across the room.

"Goddamn Italians," she muttered. "They leaked our pictures."

Iain had noticed, too. "Those scrotes..."

"They want to know who we are? Let's go make an impression."

She grabbed his hand and started toward her boss and the billionaire.

"Marc—hope you don't mind me calling you that—I don't think we need the politesse. Your boys have shot enough rounds at us in the last week. We don't need all this playacting."

Booker's sonorous voice alone commanded a certain amount of respect. He watched for any flicker in Pearson's eyes, any shift in his demeanor to such a serious address. There was nothing.

"I don't really like pretending, Director. I like making things into reality."

"You think you can recreate the Sigillum Dei and stare through an ancient stone and suddenly have all the secret knowledge of the world?"

Pearson smirked. "You traveled half the world to stop me from doing that. Obviously *you* think I can. And information is the most valuable thing in the world, didn't you know? You're in the Central *Intelligence* Agency. Intel. Secrets. Control people's shame and you control them. It's sort of...my business."

Ridley and Iain approached just in time to hear him finishing his little speech.

"Your business," said Iain. "Which one?

Pearson looked at him. "All of them, Mister Carnegie. Anywhere humans can act, they can act badly. Bad acts make for good secrets, and I've got nets everywhere for collecting. Ms. Samaras?"

*So he knows all of us. He wants* our *secrets.*

"Is that a question?" she replied.

"No. You've all just got such...interesting stories to tell!"

Pearson's eyes switched to Iain, who visibly hardened. And Ridley hated him.

"Men with money have such ideas," she said.

"And women without it come begging."

*Don't spit in public—you can't spit at a ball—*

Booker could see that look on Ridley, as if she was about to break down a brick wall with her head.

"You must have thought you'd hired the best, but the best weren't for hire," he said.

Pearson chuckled, "That's quite a line, yeah, what a mistake I made—ah! I could only get the Muppets!"

Effie sidled up to him, all slink and verve.

"Oh, I've heard about you!" she beamed. "Spooks and a Scotsman running all 'round the Christmas markets! God, you're all a bit better looking than I'd imagined."

Her eyes raked up and down each one of them.

"Ms. Crowhurst," Booker said coolly.

And then the young blonde companion appeared beside Effie. There was something unmistakably *off* about her. As if the pieces underneath that ethereal exterior had been shattered and shaken.

*She looks like the child of Brad Pitt and Grace Kelly. If this isn't Effie's niece...this is very bad.*

"Lexi," said Pearson delightedly, "come meet a very accomplished man. This is Mister Booker Douglas, a director in the CIA, and these are his associates, Ridley Samaras and Iain Carnegie."

Her suspicions twisted quickly into dark certainty. The proof of Pearson's bent for young girls was standing right there before her eyes.

*He flaunts it in front of everyone.*

"Hello," said Lexi, managing a polite smile at each of them.

"Hi," said Ridley.

"Lovely people," said Effie, "this is Lexi. She's a fantastic little violinist. With us on a music scholarship! You know how generous Marc is as a patron of the arts, *especially* young promising artists. Well, we heard her play and I just insisted she come along for the experience here."

Ridley glanced at Iain. He was looking at Lexi, his jaw clenched like a pitbull's. In that moment, his eyes could have razed a building.

"Pleasure to meet you, Lexi," he managed to say to the girl.

"You'll see her playing the Philharmonic in a few years," said Pearson. He beamed with pride, and Ridley wanted to knock that grin off his face with her elbow.

Lexi squirmed a bit in the way teenage girls do when uncomfortable with a compliment.

"Mr. Carnegie," said Effie. "Would you allow me this dance?"

She lifted one hand, as though draping it over the space between them. Iain had hardly reacted when she was moving toward him, and suddenly they were sweeping out onto the dancefloor together. Iain went waltzing away with her.

Pearson smiled at Booker and Ridley. "She's a force. *La Niña*. I'm sorry to have to leave you, but I've got a room full of people here that I must visit with. Doctor's orders."

He placed a hand on Lexi's back. Ridley could have sworn she saw a flicker of something desperate in the girl's eyes.

*I can't save you. How do I save you?!*

"Please forgive me," he said.

*I will never.*

And with a Cheshire cat smile, he led Lexi away into the crowd.

"Oh my God," hissed Ridley. "He's a shitty Hannibal Lecter... just eats girls' souls instead of men's livers, doesn't he."

Booker nodded out to the dancefloor, where the radiant Effie was swirling around with a stone-faced Iain.

"What does that make her?"

"The White Witch."

*What does she want with Iain?*

## CHAPTER
# FORTY-ONE

**VIENNA, AUSTRIA**

"You move like a real man."

Effie practically purred in Iain's arms. He seethed.

"Where are Lexi's parents?" he said.

"Her father died recently, poor love. Her mother was so thrilled by Marc's offer to pay for schooling...she couldn't thank him enough!"

She looked him in the eye, and there it was. All of it. She was flaunting their power over the girl. She was taunting him with it.

"What's wrong then, love?"

"You. And him. Everything about you."

"Oh, surely not *everything*. You've only seen some parts of me. You've a bit more assessment to do."

She slid in closer, giving a squeeze with the hand that was draped along his upper arm.

"You're ruining the frame," he growled, and immediately reset the distance between them.

"Did you have dance lessons as a boy?"

"Some."

"Or did you play a musical instrument?"

"A little."

She cocked her head at him. "Where did you put those fingers then, strings or keys or brass?"

"You think you're interrogating me?"

"I like to find what people get really...let's say what they get worked up about."

"You're not askin' because you want to know them. You're askin' because knowin' turns you on. You're an exhibitionist. You'd never ask these questions in private."

"Of you? Oh yes, I would."

But she seemed struck by his analysis. People didn't speak to Ophelia Crowhurst this way.

"I prefer musicians," she said. "The young ones are so enthusiastic. Their fingering might not be as precise but they're so open to instruction. So fresh...just delicious."

The words slithered and curled out of her. Iain squeezed her hand until she winced. He could have crushed every bone in it. His voice came out in a snarl.

"You think you can hide behind his money and his perversions. I see you. I know what you do to children."

"Let go—"

She tried to wrestle out of his vise grip.

"You're wicked. And you won't survive this."

"Stupid threats. You shouldn't say such things."

She was staring at him, all social graces evaporated, no hint of her effervescent charm to be seen.

"Mr. Carnegie, we will destroy you."

"I know. But I'll take you with me." He pulled her in close. "And the hounds of hell will gnaw on your heart."

He stepped back and relaxed his grip. The music wound to a close.

"Pardon me," came a posh male voice behind him. "May I cut in?"

Effie flipped the switch, her face brightening instantly.

Iain turned and found himself face-to-face with Prince Albert, the Duke of Edinburgh. He was a tall man with sloped shoulders, a receding hairline, and a broad-mouthed overbite. Despite the quality of his bespoke white tie and tails, he still managed to look rumpled. He had been known in his youth as "the rascal prince," which was a palace-managed, public relations-scrubbed way of referencing his debauchery.

He had been friends with Effie Crowhurst for decades, part of a social elite in England that was almost impenetrable to outsiders.

But not Marc Pearson.

"Darling!" exclaimed Effie, who quickly gave him a kiss on each cheek. "Yes, the gentleman was just leaving."

She shot a bladed look at Iain.

"Thank you, sir," said Prince Albert, pleasantly unaware of this stranger's contempt.

Being this close to both of them was overwhelming—repulsive. Iain stepped back.

"I'm sure your lady friend will be happy to get you back," said Effie, glancing over her shoulder as Iain turned away. "Enjoy your night!"

He nearly tore through the crowd to get away from her, furious that he couldn't find words enough to rip her apart, raging that she was dangling their latest victim in front of the nation's elite and no one could—or would—see it.

Iain's teeth were grinding as he found Ridley and Booker along the edge of the dancefloor, sipping from champagne flutes.

"Where's Pearson?"

"Seems to be making the rounds," said Ridley.

"He hates groups," said Iain, searching. "He'd rather get somebody one on one and seduce their ego."

"What did she want with you?" asked Booker.

"To make sure I knew what she's doing to that girl. Lexi."

His words nearly spewed with venom. Ridley held out her champagne to him. He grabbed the flute and swigged it in one gulp.

"What *she's* doing? I thought she just recruited for Pearson," said Ridley.

"No. She hurts them. *She* fucking abuses them, too."

She shouldn't have been shocked. With all that she'd seen in the world, with all the faces of evil she'd looked upon, she knew in her head that there was no exclusive claim to it by gender, race, class, or background. But this one wrenched in her gut. A grown woman should be the one protecting a girl from the lair of a male predator. She should be her guardian.

*There must be another circle of hell. Dante did not understand this one.*

She grabbed Booker's champagne from his hand and downed the remainder.

"They break them and trade them to anyone rich and sick enough to get in line." Iain's voice was shaking.

"Deep, slow breath," said Booker quietly. "That may be valiant fury but it won't do a damn thing here."

Ridley glanced at him. Even the mildest curse from his mouth meant a level of molten anger within.

"He's not getting the Eye," said Ridley. "He's not."

"That man with all the power of all the knowledge in the world?" muttered Booker. "Blackmail on every human being... he'd get away with even worse."

"If anyone fuckin' cared to begin with," said Iain.

Ridley's eyes swept the room looking for the girl again.
*Lexi.*
But then she stopped in shock. At the sight of a face she hadn't seen in years.

# CHAPTER
# FORTY-TWO

**VIENNA, AUSTRIA**

Ridley had to look twice, past the swirl of waltzing couples and glittering tiaras that passed before her.

She muttered, "That *is* him."

Iain searched for whomever she was looking at, but she was already crossing the room.

As she approached a young couple, the man caught sight of her. His blue eyes widened, and he stepped forward to pull her into a hug.

"Oh, my God!" he exclaimed in a cheerful Austrian accent, then whispered in her ear. "Are you undercover or can I use your real name?"

"Real name."

"Okay, *we're* undercover! I'm Dieter."

He stepped back beside his partner. Otto Seiwald was a sight for any eyes needing a pick-me-up. With his curly blond hair, square jaw, and open expression, he exuded "Golden Retriever." No one would have made him for an agent with the

*Bundeskriminalamt,* Austria's Criminal Intelligence Service known as the BK.

"Ridley, this is *Lina.*"

The woman with him was a dusky stunner. She reached out a hand to shake Ridley's, flashing a brilliant, dimpled smile.

"Nice to meet you," she said.

**GERMAN:** *"It's a pleasure to meet a partner of Dieter."*

Lina was surprised to hear such convincing German from this American.

**GERMAN:** *"You're unexpected,"* she replied, getting a smile from Ridley.

"What are you doing here?" asked Otto.

"I'm here with some friends of mine." Ridley gestured back to Iain and Booker. "We were in Vienna and realized we could go to a ball. When we heard who would be here—George Clooney, Brooke Shields, Daniel Silva, Marc Pearson...we just had to come see for ourselves."

He gave her a look of understanding. "We heard the same thing."

When Ridley had last encountered Otto Seiwald, he was a sharp, eager young intelligence agent cutting his teeth in the Stolen Property Department of the BK. She was searching for the same expensive ivory chest that he was when they crossed paths in a standoff that was aggressive but strangely jocular in nature. Ridley had liked him immediately.

Though she eventually beat him to the stolen item, all she wanted was what was inside. She shipped the chest to his office with a handwritten note in German and a triumphant little stick figure drawing.

The last she'd heard, he had been promoted into the Joint Operational Office, which bore the awkward acronym of JOO. While responsible for combatting human trafficking, most of their work was dealing with the smuggling of migrants from third-world countries.

*If they're here keeping tabs on Pearson, too, this is much, much bigger than that girl, Lexi.*

"He stopped for a bit of a chat with us," said Ridley. "You, uh—you ever met him?"

"Not yet, but I intend to ask Ms. Crowhurst for a dance tonight."

"Enjoy that. She stole away my partner for a really, really unpleasant waltz. Though she might prefer a dance with you." She nodded at Lina.

"I'm ready for that," said the Austrian woman with a smile.

Ridley glanced back to see Iain watching her intently, while trying to mask the fact that he was.

*Pretty shitty spy when he's watching me...but I can't introduce them yet. I can't compromise their cover.*

She'd come to trust Iain with her life on this operation, but he was still with a foreign intelligence agency. To mix him with the BK was not her place. Not without just cause.

"How long are you here in Vienna?" asked Otto.

"Another night."

"Will we run into you again...?"

*He wants to know if I'm gonna make trouble in his city.*

"Oh, Dieter," she smiled. "You know you're my favorite Austrian. Also, Arnold, but mostly you."

With a straight face, he flexed a hulking pose. "I don't see the difference."

Though amused, Lina rolled her eyes.

Ridley glanced back at her own teammates, just in time to see Booker pulling a cell phone from his pocket. He glanced at it and went stone-faced.

She tensed.

And then he looked straight across the ballroom at her.

"Excuse me," she said to the Austrians, and slipped off.

Her mind tumbled through possibilities, most of them vague but dreadful, until she reached Booker. He was still holding his phone, as though not sure what to do with it.

Ridley had to lean in close before he spoke.

"From the agency. I have to call in."

Booker excused himself, stepping off the floor. Ridley looked at Iain, who was just as baffled as she was.

"I've never been in the field with him before," she said, "but I don't think this is good."

*His kids? His job performance? The Italian government lodging a bitchy complaint?*

Iain's gaze locked onto something across the floor, and his face darkened. "It's *him*. Whatever it is, he did it."

Ridley glanced behind her.

There was Marc Pearson, standing with a champagne flute in hand, chatting with one of the EU prime ministers. Beside him, Effie was luminous as ever, enchanting the small crowd gathered around them.

Ridley was about to protest, to say that despite all the ways that evil organized itself, it was still an equal opportunist...but then Pearson looked straight at her and smiled.

*It is him.*

Ridley wondered if Otto and Lina were watching this, but couldn't give them away by even looking in their direction.

Booker returned, expressionless.

"I'm recalled," he said to them.

"You're *what?*" said Ridley.

"That was Conway. They're pulling me from the field."

"Why? Did he say?"

Ben Conway was Deputy Director of the National Clandestine Services within the CIA. Traditionally, he used a light hand in overseeing the Osprey division. They were always different, their assignments difficult to understand. It wasn't like him at all to yank Booker like this.

"It wasn't his call—came straight from the Director."

The Man in Black, CIA Director Jude Fraser himself. He was a political savant, but not one given to meddling the way some insecure men were.

"Who turned the blowdryer on him?" said Ridley.

"Had to be a senator. Or someone higher."

"And this was urgent?" Iain asked.

"They've got a plane for me tomorrow morning." His jaw clenched.

*No. NO.*

"Sir, we can't do this without you," said Ridley. "You know the works—the puzzles—everything Dee. We need you tomorrow night."

"Stop."

That stern basso rebuke was enough. This wasn't the place to talk about it.

Ridley searched the crowd for Marc Pearson.

She found him. He was talking to Prince Albert. Then Lexi appeared at his side, looking awed—and terrified—by being so close to a member of the royal family.

Ridley glanced at Otto and Lina across the room.

*They're seeing this—*

And then Pearson introduced Lexi to the prince. And he took the hand of this girl and kissed it. And Ridley knew what would eventually happen to her.

Pearson's eyes found them across the floor thick with waltzing couples. A smirk tugged at his lips. He lifted his champagne flute as if to toast them from afar.

Something ignited inside of Ridley, some fuse. She didn't know how long the line was, or how fast it would burn, but she knew what would happen when it ran out.

# CHAPTER
# FORTY-THREE

**VIENNA, AUSTRIA**

BOOKER SET his copy of John Dee's notebook on the hotel coffee table.

"I'm leaving this with you."

"I have the digital backup," said Ridley.

She had draped herself on the corner armchair, her feet dangling over the arm. She was still in her dress, though now feeling closer to becoming a pumpkin than a princess.

Booker was packing what little he had into a small bag.

Iain sat on the floor, his back against the wall, arms propped atop his knees. He had pulled off his tailcoat and now sat looking rumpled and moody.

They'd spent the past hour poring over the pages of Dee's notebook, every clue and possible solution torn apart for inspection. By the end, Ridley felt like she was finally picking up on patterns and coded associations, but Iain's efforts ended in muddled frustration.

"It's like a raccoon on acid tryin' to scribble out a horoscope," he had grumbled.

"You need to start drinking coffee," she said.

"I'm catchin' up. Didn't realize how mad this is."

Nor had Ridley, but she was determined to grasp it—to walk into the Hofburg Palace tomorrow night and walk out with the last of the crystal keys. There would be little time to operate within the grounds.

"The keys all had to be collected in order, per Dee's warnings," Booker said. "This is the sixth—the final—but where the actual Devil's Eye is located? Still unsolved for."

"What the hell do you think it really is, though?" said Ridley. "Even if you want to say it's some demon-powered stone, *where did it come from?* How did this weird English polymath ever get his hands on it?"

He looked at her over the pages of the notebook. "Origins unknown. What I wouldn't give to find out. I'm an origins man."

"*Dear diary,*" started Iain.

As they'd left the opera, they picked up some frankfurters smothered in sauerkraut and mustard. Though none of them were drunk, it was the hangover food they needed. Each of them felt stained with something vile.

It had seeped most deeply into Iain. He'd gone dark as soon as they left, hardly speaking until they wound their way back to the hotel. Ridley slid a few jokes his way and even sang along to a Christmas carol in her best German, but he was stoic nonetheless.

He had worked through it by the time they got into the notebook. Now it was almost three in the morning, and there was little else to do but sleep.

"I don't understand why they pulled *just* you," said Ridley from the armchair. "If Pearson had such a problem with us and could flex his influence that fast, why not call us all off the trail?"

"He needs the keys," said Booker, finally taking a seat on the edge of the bed. "If we all leave the field, so do the keys. I just want to know who he went through...somebody put pressure on Conway. It was his call in the end."

*Conway covers for Osprey when he can but not when he thinks it will actually blow back on him.*

"Or Pearson is messing with us."

"After getting rid of *our* John Dee expert, he thinks we'll fail," she said.

Iain held up a finger as though voting. "That one. People are toys to him."

No one spoke for a moment.

Then Ridley got to her feet and stretched her legs. "He has no idea the mistake he just made."

A faint smile tugged at Booker's lips.

"He surely doesn't."

Before the sun came up the next morning, Booker was gone. He would be back in his office at Langley by midday.

Ridley and Iain started their countdown. They had until four-thirty to ready everything they needed...assembling their toolkit, plotting their entry and exit points, and refreshing themselves on everything they'd gone over with Booker the night before.

Mid-morning, they ran reconnaissance.

The Hofburg Palace was a historical landmark. It had stood since the Middle Ages, once home to the kings and emperors of the Habsburg dynasty. Since the end of World War II, it had been the residence of the president of Austria, though it was broadly open to the public every day.

Even on this bright, cold day, the main entry was brimming

with tourists. Ridley and Iain made their way through the palace wing by wing, taking photos and typing notes into their phones, mostly admiring the grand courtyards—and the Winter Riding School.

The memories of seeing the Lipizzaners as a child came pouring back on Ridley. She caught the thick, mingling odors of hay, manure, and horsehair. The clop of hooves and whickering of the great animals drew her in like a spell.

*Not here for them...not here for them...just here for their stables.*

Adjacent to the stables was the Swiss Wing, the oldest section of the great palace. It housed the treasury where the royal jewels were kept, and a gothic chapel where the Vienna Boys Choir sang Mass on Sunday mornings.

But it was the red and black gate leading into the old wing that most interested the pair. Built by an emperor in the 16th century, the *Schweizertor* looked more like a Roman arch than a Gothic gate.

"Of course it had to be right next to the wing where they keep the jewels," said Ridley under her breath as she surveilled the high walls. "*Verdammt.* Can't just have a quiet night in Vienna."

The courtyard behind them was sprawling, and a road passed through it. There were six exit points, well spread out, but shockingly few security cameras.

They knew Dane and his team would be there tonight.

*Dane pulled in an extra man with that speedy little knife-chucker, and then his boss took out one of ours.*

"It's not enough," she said.

"Enough what?"

"You and me." She turned to face him. "We need more."

"More...?"

. . .

"You are looking for what?"

Otto Seiwald crinkled his brows and sat back in the cab of their horse carriage.

"It's not really important *what*," said Ridley, "but that I *am* looking, and Otto—you're the only person in Austria who can help me."

"I think you're really not giving credit to the black market here. You can find *anything*, you know. Like hitmen and professional puzzle solvers and human punching bags. Maybe you need all three?"

Outside the covered carriage, the muffled clop of hooves blended with the sounds of traffic and Christmas music. When Ridley had asked to meet somewhere discreet and soundproof, Otto had been thrilled with his own idea of a covered carriage ride. She had to admit it was a good choice for a clandestine rendezvous.

**GERMAN:** *"You are everything I need!"* said Ridley. *"But also maybe your partner."*

**GERMAN:** *"You liked her? Everybody likes her. First because she's beautiful and then because she is so good at being a spy."*

**GERMAN:** *"Will she do it?"*

**GERMAN:** *"Nadine? Yah!"*

"Her real name is Nadine?" said Ridley. "Okay. Good. Splendid. We need you in four hours."

Otto draped a hand over his eyes. "Oh, my God."

"I know, yes, I'm very sorry. This was unexpected. Very unforeseen circumstances. Very unfortunate."

He looked at her from beneath his fingers. "Okay, but this is actually kind of exciting. And I *do* owe you because you did give me that chest in the end. But your partners are okay with this?"

"Partner. My boss is gone. It's just me and a Scottish agent on this one."

"You're working with a Scot and an Austrian? What is happening here in Vienna?"

*Just tell him, Samaras. Desperate times.*

"The BK really put you on Pearson?" she asked.

Otto seemed taken aback. "The Joint Operational Office investigates credible charges of human trafficking, and Marc Pearson...he has connections to some evil modeling people in Europe. Really bad. We don't want that in Austria."

"Consider yourself special in the world, *mein freund*. So far, it seems like no other intelligence agency wants to touch him."

She wasn't going to tell him about what had happened with Booker. That would spook any foreign operative, hearing that America's premier agency did Pearson's bidding, even going so far as to pull one of their own directors off his tail.

"Are you..." he leaned closer, conspiratorial. "Are you rogue?"

"No. This is my assignment. I swear, and I know—"

"—spies swearing honesty—"

"I know, but here we are. You ask, I answer, we work it out on the streets."

"But you're CIA and you're going after Marc Pearson."

"Not exactly, no. We're going after something that he's also going after."

"A girl?"

It felt like someone had set off a tripwire in her stomach.

*Not a girl. Not* the *girl.*

"No," Ridley said. "That's your job."

*Her name is Lexi.*

The carriage hit a dip in the road, jolting them both.

"If we're successful," she said, "he'll be furious. An angry man is more likely to make a mistake. So we could all make the argument that this would help clinch your case against him."

"It's not a case, really. More 'an investigation.'"

"You can nail him to the wall."

*Liar. You know you won't leave him for Otto, or anyone else.*

But she could see it was tempting him.

"Yah, okay," he said finally. "What else do we need to know?"

Relief swept her.

"That you'll need firepower, and suppressors to go with them. Can't be disturbing the horses."

"Or the president's palace security?" He nudged a brow upward.

"It's on our wishlist."

"You cannot take any guns into the palace."

She gave him a disbelieving frown.

"You cannot," he said. "This is one of my terms. I'm an officer, Ridley. I can't just go around collaborating with foreign agents who illegally carry firearms into the president's residence. God, my English has gotten good."

"Okay. Fine. Whatever."

"You know that *Krampusnacht* is tomorrow night? Kohlmarkt Street. It's near the palace."

"Ah. Krampus. Yes."

She cursed inwardly at herself for overlooking such a factor. Crowds should always be accounted for.

Krampus was the demonic, horned goat-like monster of lore who was the antithesis of St. Nicholas. He punished bad children each Christmas season with lumps of coal and general terrorizing.

Every December in Austria, there was a parade for him. Participants made their own costumes and prowled down the street to the delighted horror of onlookers. Most wielded whips and carried woven baskets on their backs...all the better to haul away the bad children.

"Maybe Krampus will do all the work for us," said Otto. "Maybe they take your enemies to hell in a handbasket."

"Not before we get something from them that we need."

"Oh, my God. *Now* you tell me that."

# CHAPTER
# FORTY-FOUR

**VIENNA, AUSTRIA**

It began to snow that afternoon.

Ridley and Iain were not going to risk infiltrating the grounds after hours, when the public gates were closed and security was locked in for the night.

Instead, they bought tickets for the day's second-to-last guided tour of the Spanish Riding School. The stables were fastidiously kept by a legion of grooms and riders, but no one would be paying much attention to the walking machine out behind the building.

The contraption looked like a giant fenced carousel. They would put a horse in each section and set it to speed like a treadmill. The stallions would stride along to its pace, getting in their daily exercise. The whole thing had high solid sidings and door releases that could be opened from the inside.

It didn't take much to slip away from the guided tour, into the small courtyard behind the Riding School, and into the mechanical walking machine. Ridley and Iain settled down low with their backpacks, well out of sight, bundled against the cold.

Iain leaned in to her good ear. "You wouldn't rob me of the chance to make a dashin' exit from here riding on a white stallion now."

"If you can't make it do the leaps, do you think you really deserve to?"

"Do you think that kind of negative affirmation is helpful?"

She grinned. "We have a lot of time to pass."

Darkness fell early. They wouldn't have to wait long.

When Dane got a message from Pearson that their rivals were now down a man, he felt a surge of energy—and that snapping jab of failure.

Dane couldn't eliminate any of them. His boss had done it in a phone call.

Suddenly his reinforcements felt pathetic. He had called in Shao for his deadly skills. But now even Shao had gotten his hands on a key, while Dane still hadn't.

He ate his own resentment like it was motor fuel. Time to go again. Time to do something different.

Dane had taken lunch with Lianna that afternoon. As they sat across from each other over plates of Wiener Schnitzel and fried potatoes, he grilled the professor.

"The last key tells us where it is?" said Dane.

"Yes, it should," replied Lianna through a mouthful of fried onions and sour cream. "Dee was trying to lead anyone who could follow this trail to—to understanding. It was his obsession: understanding. The world, the cosmos, God, power..."

"You think he got anything right?"

"Oh, well, yes, I suppose. Yeah. I don't think he made sense of it. His sorcery led him away from the true understanding of mathematics and science."

"But that's what we're all out here chasing: his sorcery, not his fucking periodic table of the elements."

"It's money, Mr. Dane."

She paused at hearing her own words. She didn't like them, but went on.

"He's constructing for us, teaching us along the way, checking our understanding of his own journey for knowledge. His hieroglyphic monad created to encompass all elements of the universe, his divination for Queen Elizabeth to ascend to divine power, the *PELE* that proclaims God working wonders...I might not understand the Lion of St. Mark, to be quite honest... but *this* one—for this key—we need to recognize the angels that *he* recognized. He wrote their names into the Sigillum Dei. We'll use those names tonight."

"We won't."

She tilted her head. "What's that now?"

"We're not going to the gate," said Dane.

***

The gates of the Hofburg Palace closed at five-thirty. The courtyards went quiet. Half the windows grew dark, and the rest glowed softly through the veil of drifting snow.

Ridley and Iain emerged quietly from the horses' walking machine. They'd been huddled close for warmth as the temperature dropped. It had felt strangely comfortable to Ridley. She'd only known this foreign agent for a week, and knew that in-the-trenches-bonding was stronger than just about any other type.

Still, that sense pervaded, keeping her calm as she ran through everything in her head that Booker had gone through with them...over and over again.

*The most public place yet. The highest security. The least time to work.*

*Booker brought you into Osprey because you can do things like this. Let's go.*

Ridley tucked a mic piece into her left ear—the good one.

"Hansel?"

Through the earbud, Otto's voice came back. "In position. All clear."

"Copy. Gretel?"

It was his partner Nadine who answered, "Gretel in position. All clear."

"Copy. We're a go. Over."

She and Iain slipped inside the stables. It was dark but for the accent lights along the corridor. Horses rustled and snorted in their stalls. There would be a groom on site, staying in the small apartment at the far end, but there was no sign of him now.

They crept outside into the courtyard of the Swiss Wing. This weather had changed things. Instead of the dark clothes they'd first collected for the nighttime mission, they'd gone out last-minute for a pair of white quilted jackets. Now they moved like ghosts in the snow, packs of equipment strapped to their backs.

The two stepped under the archway of the *Schweizertor*, quickly scanning the vast courtyard ahead.

No sign of movement. No sign of any guards.

Ridley and Iain dropped their bags along the wall and unpacked them.

The trickiest thing to find and pack had been the collapsible mini ladder. They needed to get at least sixteen feet out of it.

*Treat foreign agents as well as you can. One day you give them an ivory chest—and then one day they give you a perfectly sized compact ladder.*

She and Iain pulled it to length and propped it against the side pillar. It was high enough for the climber to reach the lower ledge.

"You read off the angels," said Ridley. "I'll be in the heavens above you."

"God, you're a weapon," he muttered, pulling out his phone.

She shed her outer gloves for a "stickier" inner pair. The webbed rubber would offer better grip, especially in this weather.

Ridley began to climb.

Just above the archway was a row of golden heraldic sigils, then a ledge above them. Atop that was a double panel with a gold-on-red inscription praising Emperor Ferdinand I of Austria, split by a huge royal crest. She passed the ledge, but then realized there was a thin mesh netting around the top level.

She dug out the Magnum Spike karambit from its sheath on her belt.

"A knife for all seasons," she murmured, and began to cut.

On the ground, Iain glanced left and right down the closed street that cut across the courtyard. Both gates were closed. Otto and Nadine were each posted outside of one.

There was no sign of Dane or his team.

He pulled out his mobile and began zooming in on the digital photos he'd taken of Dee's notebook.

Up top, Ridley flung aside the netting and pulled herself gingerly up onto the narrow ledge. What she hadn't been able to see from the ground was that both of the burgundy panels were made up of narrow, cut segments, almost seamlessly joined together. On each one was a single Latin letter of gold, as though someone was writing with a child's blocks.

"The first one is *Zadkiel*," called Iain.

She reached for the first "Z" in the inscription and rammed

the butt of the karambit into it. It gave way, slotting inward like she had pressed a button.

"All that prep for this?" she called back to Iain.

"Gettin' a wee bit ahead of yourself...*Samael*."

The names of the angels of the pentagram on the Sigillum Dei. Different versions had different names attached, and better or worse handwriting had been used to transcribe them. Booker had pored over every available option and whittled down the alternatives. This would be a simple trial and error.

Ridley pushed the first "S" in the line.

Its segment sank back into the panel.

She grinned down at Iain. "I make it rain!"

He called back up more letters...*R, M, A*...until they reached *Gabriel*. Ridley mashed in the "G" and listened for the sound of stone against stone.

But there was no sound at all. Nothing moved.

"What happened?" hissed Iain.

She hurriedly scanned the letters, reading them back to him. They were all correct.

"Maybe one of them jammed?" she said.

"Nah, after all these hundreds of years, how could anything have ever gone *a little bit* wrong?"

"Helpful."

She was already tapping and hitting every segment she'd pressed, even using her blade to jimmy the edges. "There must be other letters!"

"Is there anythin' else you have to press or hit—"

Ridley was gripping the ledge tightly with one hand. She couldn't back up for a wider view, but she tried to mentally zoom out.

*It's here somewhere. The key is here. You can get it. Where would it be...never far from the puzzle...FIND IT.*

She found herself staring straight at the center of the gate's arch. A crown above. An eagle below. A shield on the eagle's chest.

Reaching forward, she felt around the edges of the shield.

She pulled, yanked—and it gave way, cracking in her hand.

Ridley had to fight to regain her balance. Tossing away the broken shield, she peered into the revealed space, squinting in the darkness.

"Was that—" started Iain.

But he was interrupted by the sound of Nadine's voice in her earpiece.

"I have a suspicious person, male, in Michaelerplatz."

*The courtyard outside the northern gate. They're here.*

"Copy," said Ridley. "Treat him as a high threat!"

She struggled to sheathe the karambit, but had to free her hand to grab the mini flashlight.

"Let's be quick about this," said Iain.

The beam of Ridley's flashlight flooded the broken crest—and a small piece of quartz glinted in its light.

"You absolute minx," she murmured. "There you are."

She grabbed the key from its carved socket, pulled her glove around it like a doggy bag, and dropped it down to Iain.

He snatched the glove out of the air, jammed it into a pocket, and zipped it tight.

Ridley peered back into the broken space.

*It's supposed to be here—we need the next location—*

"*Verdächtige* is moving in," came Nadine's voice. "Fifteen meters...now there are two males."

There was a tiny etching on the interior...Ridley pulled out her flashlight and looked closer.

*Where St. Peter watches over the rulers of the Empire*

That was it. She recited it back to herself twice.

"Gretel," came Otto's voice, strained with fear, "weapons?"

Nadine responded, "Unknown. Ten meters."

Ridley scampered down the ladder and grabbed her pack from the ground. "Hansel, abandon position! Get to Michaelerplatz. Gretel, we're coming to you. Over."

She and Iain ran for the south end of the street that bisected the courtyard.

"Hansel," said Ridley, "you copy?"

For a few deathly seconds, there was no response.

Then came Otto's voice.

"Suspicious persons in the Heidenplatz. Ten meters out."

# CHAPTER
# FORTY-FIVE

**VIENNA, AUSTRIA**

ON THE NORTHERN side of the palace, Michaelerplatz was bustling with people.

A dozen Christmas market stalls glowed in the courtyard. Horse-drawn carriages circled the cobblestone. Pedestrians milled about, though the crowds were smaller than average due to the snow pouring down.

It was through this thick veil that Nadine had spotted the suspicious persons.

She'd been slowly eating a giant pretzel by the outer ring of vendors' stalls when she saw the first, a striking Asian man with thick, vivid brows. Even under the coat and scarf, she could tell he was athletic, with a tightly coiled stride. He lingered by the carriages, discreetly keeping an eye on the gate.

And he wore no gloves.

Gloves might get in the way of holding a weapon.

She called it in over the comms, but it wasn't more than a moment before he was joined by a younger man. This one was lanky, with delicately handsome features. They exchanged a few words, but neither took their eyes off the gate.

Then they began to move closer to it.

"*Verdächtige* is moving in," she said quietly over comms. "Fifteen meters...now there are two males."

Then Ridley told her they were headed her way, then Hansel announced that there were more suspects on the other side of the palace. Nadine needed to move.

She stepped forward, pulling out her phone like an oblivious tourist. Wandering toward the gate, she slowed and paused three meters from the suspicious pair. She held up her pretzel and attempted to take a grinning selfie against the palace backdrop.

Feigning disappointment with the first attempt, she tried again. Checking her phone, she was still unhappy. She glanced up at the two men.

"Excuse me! Would you take a photo of me?"

She rushed up to them, phone held out, a gorgeous grin lighting her face. She knew what she had. People just behaved differently around beauty. Especially men.

The sharp-featured young man moved to take the camera from her.

"Sure, yeah."

"Thank you! You're American?"

She backed up only a few feet.

"Yeah," he said.

The Asian man's eyes were now flitting between her and the gate. So he *was* distractible.

"I love it there!" said Nadine. "Could you get one of me like this?"

She held up her pretzel to take a huge, theatrical bite.

Qualley snapped a photo.

• • •

Ridley sprinted with Iain across the courtyard, reaching the gate in seconds. He formed a stirrup to launch her over the top of the iron grating, then hauled himself up.

They landed in the thick carpet of snow outside. A few people glanced their way in perplexed suspicion but did nothing. The weather offered little visibility. Perfect for this rather obvious escape into a busy area.

Their eyes raked the courtyard.

"Gretel, where are you? We're here." muttered Ridley into the comms as she and Iain slipped into cover amidst the vendor stalls.

Just then, Otto's voice came through. "Heading to Michaelerplatz—suspects in pursuit!"

Whichever of Dane's team were here in Michaelerplatz and whichever were chasing Otto from Heidenplatz, all of them were about to converge.

*In public. Gamechanger.*

Iain spotted Nadine first.

"There, by the carriages. She's right next to them."

Ridley saw Nadine bidding two men a cheerful thanks. She appeared to be offering to buy them something from the market, but she could only hold their attention away for so long.

Shao's eyes were scanning...until they caught Ridley.

The sight of her was like a trigger. He was immediately in motion, striding toward them, his hand sliding into his pocket.

"He's made us—heading this way," she said. "We're on the move."

*Get off the X. Don't be a stationary target. MOVE.*

Iain and Ridley bolted through the market.

. . .

Nadine knew the second that Shao spotted her teammates. He was off.

The skinny one was only a couple steps behind, but she had to do something. She stepped in front of him, her cheerful demeanor melting away. From her pocket she yanked an ID badge.

"Offizier Prinz, Criminal Intelligence Service."

The bewilderment on his face quickly shaded into panic.

Qualley tore off across the market.

She sprinted after him.

***

Otto burst into Michaelerplatz, looking about wildly for the others.

Behind him appeared Bill Dane and Freddie Solbakken, trying to draw as little attention to themselves as they could while they rushed through the crowds.

Ridley's voice came through his earpiece. "Down Kohlmarkt! Over!"

She and Iain were running straight into the Krampus festival.

***

Within a few seconds, Ridley realized that Shao was the only one chasing them. Qualley had dropped off somewhere.

*Ambush?*

*Nah, he won't be fast enough. That twiggy son of a bitch isn't built for sprints.*

Shao was fast. He had run her down in Venice. But here, there were obstacles, people...publicity.

There was also no way for him to know which of them had the key.

They ran for the avenue straight ahead. It was packed with people, and glowing red.

Otto dodged through market stalls, trying to shake the two men on his tail.

"Gretel? What's your position?"

Nadine called back through the comms. "In pursuit of a suspect!"

"What the hell are you doing? We're not trying to catch them!"

"Habsburgergasse, going north!"

Otto broke to the right, heading in her direction. Then he saw Dane and Freddie split apart, probably to set up a pincer trap.

He picked Dane to chase after.

The entire street of Kohlmarkt had been taken over by Krampusnacht. Crowds lined the sides behind metal barricades. There were torches and flares and the banging of cow bells slung on belts. Marchers thumping away on animal hide drums, performers swinging sparkler batons, and small floats that looked like cages from hell.

Through the thick snow came the lunging, staggering procession of Krampuses. There were hundreds of them in shaggy costumes, carrying pitchforks and whips, horns curling above their heads. Each mask was different, but every one was a gruesome, leering face—demons, all of them.

Some would rattle the barricades, some would climb over to terrorize onlookers, some snapped their whips and pushed into the crowds. It was almost like they were possessed by their own devilish intensity.

It was into this nightmare parade that Ridley and Iain ran head on.

"We're splitting them up!" she yelled to him over the clamor.

"Or they're separatin' *us!*"

He glimpsed Shao behind them, getting jostled in the crowds. A second later, Freddie appeared.

"We've got another one," shouted Iain. "Solbakken's here."

*You should have killed him on that bridge in Prague, Samaras. You should have thrown him into the river.*

Oncoming Krampuses barged into them, pushing and sneering into their faces. Ridley and Iain tried to weave and dodge around them while keeping an eye over their shoulders, while trying to not get separated.

A giant cart came rolling toward them with an enraged-looking monster atop it. He was shaking a bloody pitchfork at the crowds.

They split to either side of it to get out of the way.

Shao was somehow closing in on them, his eyes fixed unblinking under those black brows.

The tinny clanging of the bells—the thundering drums—the blinding fountains of sulfur—the growls from every lurching Krampus—their whips snapping—the flares blooming red—it was all a grotesque and hellish cacophony.

A muted buzz hummed in Ridley's right ear. Adrenaline pulsed through her limbs. She glanced behind.

Freddie was charging straight on, bullying aside each of the aggressive Krampuses.

She turned back to the oncoming parade—and the air seemed to thicken. Everything slowed.

A cold chain of dread tightened around her chest as the bluish-gray veil descended.

And there she was.

*Madimi.*

A dozen feet from Ridley.

She looked older this time, a grown woman. The long dark hair and sculpted cheekbones. Glowing white stare. But now she was naked. Her entire body was smeared with blood.

The snow and scarlet light of the flares blurred over her like a death shroud.

*Don't freeze, you coward—don't freeze!*

Ridley couldn't tell if time had really slowed—or if she alone was frozen in this eerie nightmare.

Then each of the Krampuses turned slowly...until every hideous face was staring at her.

*I'm not even carrying the key!*

Fear rose up her throat. She had no way to get herself out of this.

The leers and snarling fangs seemed to engulf her.

And Madimi watched.

Then something clicked in Ridley. Anger surged, and she lunged forward. She had no idea what she would do if she reached Madimi, or what the demon woman could do to her, but it wasn't a formed thought. She was just an attack dog unleashed.

It was never going to work to lay a finger on Madimi, but the instant she charged forward, the spell snapped.

The clatter and banging resumed. The Krampus parade careened onward, jostling Ridley.

She whipped her head about, searching for Iain in the rumble of costumes and flame and snow and noise.

*You lost him. You lost your teammate.*

Her eyes never found her partner, but they did land on Shao. He was rushing at her, closing on twenty feet...fifteen...

*MOVE.*

She had no choice.
She ran.

## CHAPTER
# FORTY-SIX

**VIENNA, AUSTRIA**

IAIN BULLED through the Krampus parade, scanning desperately for Ridley. They'd been separated by a huge wagon float for only a few seconds, but somehow she'd vanished.

One of the angry costumed marchers shoved him off, then cracked at him with a cat'o'nine tails.

Iain bellowed in angry disbelief and pounded a fist into the man's solar plexus.

He staggered in the snow as Iain took off. He had no time to get into a fight here. Freddie was storming through the parade after him, crazed eyes fixed on his target.

He had to find Ridley.

Nadine could have run down a deer.

But this night, she backed off her quarry. If her target didn't think that a government agent was chasing him, he would regroup with his team or take refuge in a location that he thought was safe.

It was time to stop chasing him, and instead follow him. This was easier in the heavily falling snow. It took a few well-timed pauses as he looked back for his pursuer, turning her face away and casually interacting with a stranger. Finally, he slowed.

But he did not stop. She slipped after him as he made his way briskly across Graben Street.

Toward Peterskirche.

St. Peter's Church.

Halfway down Bräunerstraße, Otto wished he'd spent more time on the track. Dane was disappearing rapidly into the thick snowfall, sprinting as if the hounds of hell were snapping at his heels.

At least between the weather and the Krampusnacht parade a few blocks away, the crowds were thinner. He couldn't call in for official reinforcements, for he had no explanation for why—as a BK officer—he was chasing this man. But if he didn't do something to catch him soon, he'd soon lose his target completely.

"Stop!" he yelled, struggling for breath. "Police!"

Dane disappeared around the block.

Otto's lungs burned as he willed his heavy legs to go faster.

Ridley raced through the wide streets, under giant suspended chandeliers, past glowing shopfronts and twinkling Christmas trees, toward the towering Cathedral of St. Stephan, its lacy spires illuminated against the night.

The cold air seared her chest. Her muscles were screaming but she barely paid them mind. Pedestrians gave small cries of alarm or threw bewildered stares as she tore past them.

*He's drafting behind me through the crowds.*

She dodged around a horse-drawn carriage, spooking the big harnessed animals. Sprinted along a row of market stalls. Slipped around a group of laughing teenagers.

But she could not shake him. He was closing in on her.

She had studied the streets around the Hofburg Palace as she always did, in case of something just like this. Past the cathedral, though, she hadn't committed anything to memory. From here on it was the gamble of a turn.

*If he catches you—*

—the thought hit her like the clang of a bell, loud and sudden and sure—

*—he will kill you.*

The cobblestone avenue split into two smaller streets. She went left.

---

Iain was running for his life, and he despised himself for it.

His impulses were screaming at him to turn and fight. His head was telling him that he had the entire collection of keys on him save one. He couldn't risk a showdown.

He had to survive. Had to find Ridley. Had to not be stupid and prideful and turn into a needless fight.

So Freddie chased him, from the parade, down another pedestrian street, past St. Peter's Church—

Iain was faster, but not by much. There were too many variables for it to be about straight speed. Pedestrians and snow and benches and dogs on leashes—

His brain blistered at the thought that he didn't have a gun on him. If Freddie did, he only hadn't pulled it yet because of the risk of being caught in public like this.

Shoot a man on the street in Vienna on a snowy evening and there will be witnesses.

But he had to separate—somehow—from this Danish madman.

Iain skidded to a stop as the street opened onto an avenue. A procession of headlights rolled by.

He turned around.

Freddie slowed. His wild eyes were shining, red hair caked with snow. He pulled out a collapsible baton from his jacket and snapped it open.

Ridley veered around the corner and down another side street—and stopped.

A giant iron gate towered before her. There was no other way out.

*This is what you get for not memorizing more of the map—*

She whipped around to see Shao coming around the corner.

*And YOU DON'T HAVE A GUN.*

She couldn't tell if her enemy had one or not, but she couldn't waste any precious seconds finding out. The one who moved first in a fight had an advantage.

Ridley yanked the karambit from its sheath. She slid her index finger through the ring at the end of the hilt and clutched it reverse grip—tip down. Her very own raptor claw.

From his belt, Shao drew out a massive tanto knife. The blade was angular, its tip like a sharp prow, and he held it like a hammer. He oozed fluid confidence.

*Advantage: him.*

With a tanto that long, the distance was his. She needed to pull him in closer...and yet getting closer to a knife fighter was mortally dangerous—even when you won.

*No huge lunges—he'll be looking for a big opening.*

She slid forward in the snow. He didn't step back.

*He doesn't respect you.*

Ridley spun the karambit around her hand—finger in the retention ring—flailing it toward Shao at full extension.

He flinched back, and she went.

His tanto knife flashed forward.

Everything flew—

It was all faster than what she remembered of blade fighting. Parries, slashes, blocks, thrusts. She was carving, arcing the blade, slipping to the side. Shao was driving into her, working to get to an angle.

*Hands up, forearms up, protect the face and neck and trunk—*

He flicked the tip of his knife at her. The sharp angle bit into the back of her hand, banging against the small bones. She yanked her hand away.

Shao unleashed a flurry, forcing Ridley backward.

She blocked his slashing arm—he stabbed down toward her thigh—her leg shot back—but he had just nicked it through her pantleg.

*Not the artery—he didn't get it.*

She went for a low backhand cut. He grabbed her wrist. She flailed the karambit over the top of his hand and yanked away—*slice*.

Blood spattered onto the snow.

Shao burst into her, staggering her backward, but he'd gone off balance. She hauled his arm across his body, wrenched him forward, and put all her weight on the back of his shoulder, forcing him down to one knee.

Ridley went to slice up across his throat—when Shao switched the blade from his pinned hand to his free one—and thrust upward.

She reeled back just in time to save her face. The blade stabbed in beneath her clavicle.

He shoved her back and leapt to his feet. He looked balletic now, feet pivoting in the snow, battling her hand and forearms to try to get to the outside, to take her back, to slash her throat.

Ridley felt him go up a gear. At least Shao hadn't hit vital muscle with that stab to her chest.

She passed his arm away with her hand, hooked her karambit around his forearm, then grabbed the back of his collar. She was about to hook his leg with hers and sweep it out from under him, but as she started to yank him backward, he stepped out, turned—and rammed the tanto up at her ribcage.

She felt like she was in slow motion as she twisted away from the lunging weapon, but it wasn't enough.

The hot pain of the piercing blade took Ridley's breath away.

---

Iain's backpack lay in the snow beside him as he and Freddie grappled on the ground.

Iain was fighting to control the hand with the baton in it, Freddie fighting to free it.

Finally, Freddie wrestled it away and in the same second—cracked it against Iain's head.

It struck just behind his ear, like a wrecking ball to his equilibrium. He stumbled in the snow.

Freddie kicked him away and stood up.

He stood over Iain, both of them trying to catch their breath, and growled, "Give me the keys. All of them."

"You scabby bawbag—I'm not carryin' all the keys! You think I'm that fuckin' stupid? Where's yours?"

For a split second, Freddie had to recalibrate a thought...and that was just enough.

Iain hurled a handful of snow in his face.

Freddie pawed it furiously out of his eyes as Iain grabbed the strap of his backpack and swung it as hard as he could.

It hit Freddie in the head. He stumbled—tripped—

And fell backward into the street.

Into the oncoming hood of an SUV.

Freddie's hips jerked sideways with a nasty *crunch*. He flew back, hitting a stone pylon and crumpling into the snow.

The driver jumped out in horror.

Iain didn't stay. He picked up his backpack. As he stumbled away, he could hear the anguished moans of Freddie Solbakken lying broken in the street.

---

Ridley leapt back from Shao.

He advanced. She could see her own blood on the dark tanto blade.

*You've got this.*

But she knew she couldn't afford to take another stab like that. She was bleeding from the top of her thigh, the back of her hand, her collar, and now from her torso.

*You can beat him.*

But then a terrible thought came, and she couldn't bat it away even with the chip on her shoulder—

*Can I?*

Shao lunged forward, his straight blade flying in like a saber. She parried it aside with her own curved edge and went for a mid-torso slash—he had to block with his own forearm.

The karambit ripped open his jacket sleeve. The slit bloomed dark red.

Ridley rammed her knee up into his groin.

Shao grunted—half-crumpling—but the tanto came stabbing across her vision. She blocked his swing with the forearm of her knife hand, then captured the inside of his arm with her karambit and sliced it away.

She swung for his throat—

He dodged his head back—

She stepped off to the side and slashed hard across his ribs—hard enough to tear through his coat, through his skin, and draw a line of blood.

He grunted, as much out of anger as pain, and reeled back.

Ridley saw it: an opening.

She stepped into him—they swung and stabbed and slashed...backing him up—

As he went for a jab, she passed his arm across her, slipped off to the side, and tore the claw of the karambit up the inside of his thigh.

Blood flowed like a broken pipe, pouring down his leg into the snow.

*Artery.*

Now he had nothing to lose. Now he would be most dangerous.

And it showed. He went into a berserk offense.

Ridley nearly stumbled against his speed—until she nicked the back of his knife hand again.

He snatched it away as she stepped in, forcing him back against the wall.

She brought the karambit down toward his heart as if she was about to smash an ice block—

Shao caught her wrist.

He brought the tanto up to stab her in the neck.

She grabbed his forearm, blocking it.

Standoff.

She needed more force. She needed one more hand.

So Ridley sank her teeth into Shao's knife hand to hold it in place.

She pulled her own hand away from his forearm, rammed it onto the back of her hilt, and used the strength of both hands against his one—forcing through his block.

The tip of the karambit sank into Shao's chest.

A gasp of disbelief escaped his lips.

Ridley drove forward, felt him breaking...and sank the whole of the blade into his heart.

It gave a grisly wet crunch as she twisted it.

Shao's eyes went glassy.

He slid down the wall and crumpled into the snow.

His blood—and hers—stained the ground a shocking red. The falling snow was already beginning to cover him.

Ridley stepped back and felt the surge of sudden pain.

*Not pain—injuries. They need medical.*

But she had to find the others first.

"Hansel? Gretel?" she said over the comms. "What's your position?"

---

Otto rounded the corner where he'd last seen Dane.

He gasped for breath as he scanned the broad streets. The snow was making it hard to see, it was so damn thick.

He wondered if he should have shouted that he was police. Who stops for the police when they are already running?

Trotting down the broad pedestrian street, he wondered what Ridley Samaras had gotten him into...what he'd gotten himself into—and Nadine!

Then Ridley's voice came through his earpiece. "Hansel? Gretel? What's your position?"

"This is Hansel," he said quietly into the comms. "I'm on Graben going east toward Stephansplatz...in pursuit...of a very, very fast suspect."

"I think—I think I know where that is. I'm coming to you."

He neared a section with sparse crowds. Everyone was so bundled against the cold and snow that it would be hard to ID anyone beyond their clothing.

"I can call this in, an *alarmfahndung*," said Otto.

"No!" said Ridley. "Let me come to you."

And just as he heard her last word, from the edge of an alleyway right beside him stepped the man he'd been searching for.

Dane grabbed Otto by his collar, yanked him in, and with all his strength, stabbed a chisel through his ear.

# CHAPTER
# FORTY-SEVEN

**VIENNA, AUSTRIA**

As fast as she could run on her bleeding leg, Ridley hobbled and ran back to the busy plaza by St. Stephan's Cathedral. With every step she felt like Shao's blade was slashing open her rib cage again, but she had to find her teammates.

*If Otto was chasing Dane, it would be better to not catch him.*

She reached Stephansplatz and slowed. She scanned the vendors and crowds and twinkling lights through the thick curtains of snow.

No one running. No disturbances.

"Hansel?" she said into the comms, "what's your position?"

With every second of silence that followed, her dread compounded. She trudged through the white carpet, searching, leaving a trail of red drops behind her.

Then she spotted something by the corner of one of the buildings—a large heap in the snow, being gradually buried under the falling snow—almost human-sized.

She rushed toward it.

As she got closer, she could see blond curls matted with blood.

"No," she breathed.

Dropping to one knee, she pawed away the snow.

Otto Seiwald's eyes were frozen open in death.

"Elle!"

She heard Iain's voice through her earpiece, calling her undercover name.

"Stephansplatz, the south side," she mumbled, then, "Gretel? Wherever you are...you need to come."

She couldn't stay by his body. She couldn't afford to be implicated or detained by authorities.

She told Nadine where he could be found. The Austrian officer's voice was stricken and empty as she clarified what Ridley was telling her. She would call it in to the BK.

Iain found Ridley across the square, leaning against one of the great cathedral pillars, bent over, holding her side. Blood was soaking her clothes.

She announced it before he could: she needed medical immediately.

He helped her to the street and hailed a cab to the hospital.

They told the attending nurses and doctor that she'd been attacked by a disturbed-looking homeless man with a knife. Yes, they'd already filed a police report. No, they didn't want any further followup. Just stitches and glue.

They stopped for fresh clothes, then checked into the Park Hyatt. Iain told Nadine where to find them. Ridley showered, relishing the steaming pain of the cuts on her side, her hand, her thigh, her collar, as though each second was penance for the death she'd brought about that night.

*He was your friend. He did this for you because he was your friend. You used your friend to death. You knew how dangerous Dane was.*

*I'm going to fucking kill him. If I have to burn myself alive to set him on fire, I will kill him.*

She sank her head under the scalding stream.

Ridley had been out of the shower for only a few minutes when there was a knock at the door.

When Iain opened it, his jaw went slack in shock.

It was Nadine.

And standing next to her was Lianna Powell.

---

"You knew. You knew they were coming after us tonight."

Ridley could hardly stand still, prowling the short length of the hotel room. Though she limped a bit through it, her brutal stare was fixed on Lianna.

The professor sat at the end of the bed, looking almost timid. Iain stood with his arms knotted across his chest. Nadine leaned against the desk, her expression vacant.

She had tailed Qualley to St. Peter's Church, where he immediately went to this middle-aged blonde woman amidst the golden soaring opulence. Nadine recognized her from ID photos that she and Otto had been briefed with. As soon as Qualley retreated to make a phone call, she swooped in, flashed her badge at the professor, and whisked her quietly away.

Nadine had thought she'd inflicted a great blow to the enemy—to steal away their expert, their guide. That feeling of triumph evaporated the moment she found Ridley in Stephansplatz...the moment she saw the American's face.

Nothing would make Otto's death *worth it*, but they would squeeze every breathing word from this woman to get to the men who killed him.

"I knew they were comin' after you," said Lianna in a quiet

voice, "but I didn't know who *you* were. You're just the other team trying to kill us at every turn."

*That's damnably fair...don't show it. Don't give her that.*

"He stabbed an officer of the Austrian intelligence in the head with a chisel! You know what kind of man he is by now."

"And you know who you're *workin'* for!" said Iain.

"I was hired to decode the notebooks of John Dee. I saw nothing offensive in that, nothing dangerous. I had no idea what this—what all this was goin' to be about."

"You're helping Marc Pearson become even more powerful," said Ridley.

Lianna looked genuinely surprised. "It's just a stone. It's a precious old stone with a remarkable—*remarkable*—story attached to it. It's not worth much to add to the collection of an odd, interested millionaire."

Given the deadly serious looks around her, she realized she had misread the room.

"You help *us* now," said Ridley.

Lianna nodded quickly. "Sure, yes. I'm absolutely willing to."

Ridley grabbed the bedside notepad and wrote something on it. She ripped it off and handed it to the professor.

"What does this mean to you?"

On the paper she'd scribbled: *Where St. Peter watches over the rulers of the Empire*

"Ehm..."

They all watched her. Iain was oozing contempt. Nadine still appeared like a black hole of grief. But Lianna mostly felt the ferocity of the Amazonian woman burning into her.

"Now it's not...it initially reads like it's referring to Saint Peter's Basilica, which is what you'd probably first think. '*The rulers of the Empire*' could plausibly have been referring to the popes, who are in fact buried at St. Peter's. Most of them, anyhow.

"*But*...John Dee wasn't Catholic. The Church itself persecuted him. They accused him of all sorts of heretical practices: witchcraft and sorcery and the like. Very contentious relationship. I cannot imagine he would ever take something of such exalted importance—as he clearly saw the Devil's Eye—into the Vatican."

"Great," said Iain. "Scratch one world heritage site off the list. Now we can really whittle it down."

Despite the circumstances, she had slipped into full professor mode, shooting him a look as if quieting a student who was snarking in class.

"It *is* a process of elimination sometimes. But here," she said, sitting up straighter, her whole demeanor coming alive, "he capitalized '*Empire*.' It's true that in those days, many writers capitalized with seeming abandon, but not Dee. He was precise. He was also the first person to coin the term 'the British Empire.' The first to even propose it could be built to such proportions as to *be* an empire.

"He wasn't talking about Christian rule, but the rule of England. The monarchs of the British Empire."

"Then what about Saint Peter?" said Ridley.

"Well..." Lianna smiled as though about to fulfill all of their dreams with a perfect reveal. "Do you know that there was once a monastery in London called Saint Peter's Abbey—"

"I really did not," said Iain.

She ignored him. "First built perhaps in the tenth century. It came to ruin, but nearly a century later, Edward the Confessor rebuilt it to serve as his own burial site. It grew and grew from there.

"And today we know it as Westminster Abbey. Where sixteen English monarchs are buried."

Ridley and Iain exchanged a look.

*She sounds certain. And it makes total sense. Dee taking it all the way back to the heart of England.*

"So the Devil's Eye is at Westminster Abbey," said Ridley. "That place is a colossus."

"Ah yeah, that's the trick, isn't it? This is the vaguest part of the notebook, but it *does* contain the clues. Seven clues throughout the abbey. All this time we didn't know what space it was we'd be looking at, but now...now it will all make sense. One more riddle left."

"One more goddamn riddle," muttered Ridley.

"Solve that and we get the location of the Devil's Eye *within* the Abbey?" said Iain.

Lianna nodded. "It seems so. But...it won't do any good without all of the keys."

Ridley's jaw twitched. "Without Dane's key."

There was a long beat in the room, as if they were each turning this over in their heads.

"How in bloody Hades..." said Iain.

Ridley looked up at him. "We were always gonna meet again."

"So we tell him where we're goin'."

She gave him a single nod. Then she looked at Nadine.

"If you want to come with us, you'll see him die. I vow it. If you can't come...he'll hear Otto's name just before his soul plunges to hell."

Nadine took a moment to respond. "I'll decide tomorrow."

Ridley held out a palm toward Lianna. "Your phone, professor."

She hesitated.

"Your *phone*," said Ridley. "You think you deserve our trust? You won't be telling Dane the location until we're in the air tomorrow morning."

Lianna pulled out her mobile and gave it to Ridley.

"I'll watch her tonight," said Nadine. "We'll be just down the hall."

Ridley called Booker. No matter the hour, he picked up.

She gave him the full debriefing, her voice heavy. He listened, but he wasn't the consoling type. He laid no blame on her, though he also couldn't tell her that it wasn't her fault. He was amazed at Nadine's initiative in her stealth capture of Lianna. And most of all, he was relieved that they had figured out the final location.

"Don't wreck Westminster Abbey, aright? That's as much an order as I can make it."

"We'll be like churchmouses. Mice. Churchmice."

"You've also got another problem. Soon as you tell Dane, he's tellin' Pearson. He'll be getting set up for some terrible ritual. He must have had his Sigillum Dei made already—perfect replica to spec or none of it will work. On the terrible chance that he gets it..."

"He can't get it. We have five keys and he has only one. Not happening."

"Glad to hear that. Anyway, we'll still track his plane, see where he's heading to next. He wouldn't stay in Vienna for this. He'd want to be closer to his world of power."

She clutched her head in her hand, exhausted. "Tell me tomorrow if he's moved. Any more info on how he pulled you out of this?"

Booker had been officially remanded for "harassing behavior" and ordered to stay within the continental United States until a more thorough review could be concluded.

"Best I can figure, it came from someone on the Senate Intelligence Committee. You know how many favors and connections Marc Pearson has offered around the world? How do you think powerful people become powerful?" he'd said. "The more I fight it right now, the more heat and light I generate onto you two. And you gotta stay out there to finish the job. I'll run quiet cover here. You get that stone, Samaras."

"Sir."

They hung up.

Iain had ordered room service. Ridley wanted nothing more than to crawl into bed and sleep for eleven hours, but her Navy training had taught her to eat whenever you could. They downed cheeseburgers and tomato soup in near silence.

They hadn't discussed sleeping arrangements, but when Iain started propping up the sofa pillows, Ridley nodded him instead to the bed. He found an old Barbara Stanwyck movie on TV, *Christmas in Connecticut,* and set the volume on low. The two fell asleep to it, close enough to feel each other's warmth.

That night, it was Ridley's mind that was plunged to hell.

## CHAPTER
# FORTY-EIGHT

**BRATISLAVA, SLOVAKIA**

Dane barely slept at all.

After killing the intelligence officer in the center of the city, he couldn't risk staying in Vienna. Not even in Austria. He was sure he'd found a blind spot for CCTV when he'd dragged the man around the corner of that building, but he couldn't bank his life or freedom on it.

Qualley was in a pathetic state. He'd been useless since realizing how much he fucked up in losing their only irreplaceable team member. But with Freddie now lying in a hospital with a broken femur and their professor guide vanished into the night, Qualley was the only team he had left.

They fled across the border on the last train of the night, east to Bratislava.

Vienna had been a failure.

He didn't even know where they were supposed to go next. Wherever it was, Dane at least knew that no one else could get the Devil's Eye, not without the one key that was in his possession.

By seven in the morning, he'd finished off his second cup of coffee in a café, trying to plot their next move, when his phone rang.

He picked up to Professor Lianna Powell.

### MANCHESTER, ENGLAND

Marc Pearson, in a burgundy sweater and woolen peacoat, sat in the back of an S-Class Mercedes Benz gliding through the Northern Quarter. Beside him, Timothy Bunton, the Chief Executive Officer of Manchester United Football Club, swiped away an unwanted email on his mobile phone.

"We're working on that deal with Elcomm. I want it finalized before the second quarter, but unless you can budge those obstinate bastards..."

"You have to work them in person. Unless you're face to face, they'll just drag you out. They like the old-fashioned barter."

"We'll invite them. Will you be here on the weekend, then? I'd like to introduce you to someone. Another American, bought Leeds United years ago. You know Andreas Colby?"

Pearson shook his head. "Sorry. I'm getting some pre-Christmas rest and relaxation up at Balmoral."

"Ah, the prince, then. You and Effie?"

He smiled. "My girl Friday."

They passed a massive sky-blue billboard with a Viking-looking player charging at camera with broad outstretched arms: Erling Haaland. It proclaimed *"MANCHESTER IS BLUE."* Bunton glanced at it with disgust.

"Oh, for God's sake...we'll be wiping that out next week. Come down for it! The Manchester derby is our Boxing Day match. Doesn't get bigger than that."

"If you have the cure for my Christmas hangover, I'll take it."

"Bring Effie," said Bunton, then chuckled. "She's a hangover cure all on her own."

Pearson would play the game, but recently his thoughts were hovering over only one thing: getting the Devil's Eye. Despite Bill Dane's failure to this point, he knew that man would pursue his quarry to any corner of the world. He would kill himself to make this right and retrieve what his employer demanded.

Pearson only needed to be ready when the Devil's Eye was finally brought to him.

A few minutes later, Bunton's chauffeur dropped Pearson off at the Manchester Craft and Design Centre, an upscale indoor market. Waiting outside was his assistant, Isidora.

She greeted him with a kiss on the cheek, then led him into the brick warehouse that was decked with Christmas garlands, bows, and lights. They wove through the labyrinth of boutique cafés and artisanal shops until they reached the closed door of a discreet workshop.

They knocked and were quickly let in by a short Pakistani man wearing a leather apron. His pleasantries were brusque, and he wasted no time in getting to business.

"You're taking it today?" he asked.

"Not me, but if everything is correct, I'll send a car around for it this afternoon," said Pearson.

The shop around them was filled with wood carvings and metal etchings, works of art built with the worn hands of a craftsman.

"Okay then. It's ready," said the craftsman.

He led them to his small workshop in the back.

On the table lay a huge wax disc. Nine inches in diameter and nearly two inches thick, it was covered in intricate markings: rings and heptagrams and pentagrams, names and letters and strange symbols.

It was John Dee's Sigillum Dei Aemeth. The very table needed for the Devil's Eye to work.

Pearson leaned closer, examining it. Isidora pulled up a photo of the original for him to compare.

It was an exact carved replica. Pearson stood up and looked at the craftsman.

"This is perfect. Just what I asked for. Isa, let's give him an extra hundred pounds."

The man's eyes widened.

"I will wrap it up very safe for you," he said.

Pearson gave him a friendly grin. "I'm sure you will. I'll have someone come by in an hour. The money will be in your account by the time my man walks out with it."

By itself, the Sigillum Dei was useless, not much more than a trinket of the occult. With the Devil's Eye, it was the door to everything he wanted.

But like John Dee, he needed a scryer to open that door.

Effie Crowhurst sat in the small concert hall at the Royal Northern College of Music, pink woolen coat beside her, one leg draped casually over the other. She was browsing through the Christmas wishlist of one of her distant nephews, listening to the violin music that filled the space.

By a music stand in the center, Lexi was dicing out a series of the devastating runs in Paganini: 24 Caprices, Op 1: No. 2 in B Minor.

Her instructor, a pinched-looking woman in her sixties, watched her like a peregrine falcon would a farmyard chick. She'd stop Lexi frequently to correct her, pick apart her bow work, or dissect imprecise fingering.

The young girl's frustration had begun to simmer. She couldn't get it. Couldn't concentrate, couldn't distinguish the notes. She couldn't.

As tears of anger began to brim, the tutor became even more demanding, raising her voice in an attempt to rally her young pupil. It backfired.

"I can't do this!" Lexi burst out, ripping the violin from her shoulder. "I'm not ready yet."

Effie looked up in alarm. The instructor—whom she was paying very well—glanced at the wealthy socialite, who gave a swift shake of her head.

"Today is not the day to be perfect," said the older woman. "Today is the day to find your mistakes. You will be ready when you need to be. Take this home and practice what I told you—look at all of your notes, remember not to get caught in the transitions going up. Practice. I'll see you for another lesson after the holidays."

Lexi mumbled something as she tucked her violin into its case. She snatched the sheet music from the stand without even raising her eyes to the instructor.

Effie got to her feet and slipped on her coat.

The girl was quiet on the ride back to the hotel, gazing out the window at the array of Christmas cheer that seemed to cloak the city.

"We've officially invited your mother up to Balmoral, then," said Effie, "for Christmas."

"She's working Christmas Eve," Lexi said quietly.

"We're sending a car for her the moment her shift ends! She was just *thrilled* at the idea of spending Christmas in the queen's favorite holiday home. And meeting the queen's son, of course. Real princes aren't easy to come by these days."

"She'll be thrilled, yeah. She will be. Thank you."

That was the kind of risk that made Effie feel the thrum of

being alive, though there was little risk in it *truly*. Lexi would never tell her mum about the sort of relationship she had with the socialite and the billionaire. The girl would never do that to her own mother, ruining the generosity they were showing her, wrecking her chance to meet royalty, destroying her sense of her own child, blowing apart the holidays...she simply wouldn't.

Establish a close connection with Lexi's remaining family, make them indebted with gratitude, and be safe knowing that the girl would feel so much guilt about upsetting all of it that she'd keep silent.

Marc had been so consumed with this pet treasure hunt of his...he'd grown moodier with every bad report from his mercenaries. He still carried on with clients and friends and networked like a snakecharmer, but beneath the surface, interest had brewed into obsession. He *really* believed that this John Dee had hidden a key to supernatural knowledge and left breadcrumbs to it all over Europe.

She'd been left to groom the girl for introduction into their world, to properly teach her what Marc wanted and how he wanted it. Effie considered herself a natural teacher when the subject matter interested her.

Lexi Rapp was perhaps the most fascinating of all the girls they'd had. This one was a prodigy at everything, and she still had no concept of the extent of her talents. This one, they would have to keep.

Effie was determined.

When they got back to the hotel penthouse, she offered the idea of some tea and Jaffa cakes. Marc was still out, and the girl needed an uplift after that miserable music lesson. She'd coax her later into practicing massage.

Lexi said sure, but as Effie ordered down to the concierge, she disappeared into the back bedroom with her violin case.

Once inside, Lexi shut the door and pulled in deep breaths. She dumped the case on the bed. Fought back tears. If she let them go, they would drown her.

Instead she pulled open the case, looked at the notes on the Caprices that she'd stashed inside, and tossed them to the floor.

Lexi picked up the instrument. She set the violin to her shoulder, hovered the bow for a moment, and began to play.

This was not for any audition. Not to impress. Not to improve. Not to practice.

She played from memory, "Chaconne in G Minor."

She shut her eyes and bled through the strings. She ripped the piece open and played it for every terrible thing storming inside of her.

## CHAPTER
# FORTY-NINE

**LONDON, ENGLAND**

"Likely as no that it's somewhere in stone. It wouldn't be lyin' out in the open for hundreds of years."

Iain stood in the aisle of the DIY store looking up at an array of chisels. Wham's *Last Christmas* played through the tinny speakers overhead.

"How much would we have to pay a stonemason to desecrate England's holiest site," Ridley muttered as she passed behind him carrying a crowbar.

"At Christmas. With Mary, Joseph, and baby Jesus lookin' on."

"We could use that A-team. Does baby Jesus do 'smiting?'"

He reached for a medium-sized chisel. "That'd be the only thing on my Christmas list."

At the end of the aisle, Lianna was absorbed in her mobile phone. Nadine could not come to London. The BK had pulled her back to the office for their investigation into Otto's murder.

"Hey, Powell," Ridley nearly spat her name. Lianna had

been nothing less than quiet and agreeable since they'd taken custody of her. Still, the reality of her association was like bile in Ridley's mouth every time she spoke to her. "Have you figured them out yet?"

"I believe...it appears we're looking for a collection of letters within the Abbey. The location of number six is very vague—the most difficult. Number two is ambiguous but there's really only one of two places it could be referring to."

She looked up in time to see Ridley give her a terrible smile.

"Carry on," she said to Lianna, who turned away like a scolded puppy.

Iain moved close in to Ridley's left ear.

"It would be better if she *wanted* to help us, you know," he murmured. "I know what she's done, too. I know I want to hate her for takin' the money of that sick wicked bastard, but she's our expert now."

Ridley felt the back of her hand ache where Shao's tanto had taken out a chunk of flesh and bruised the bone. She felt like spitting icicles in response.

*What's your mission here, Samaras?*

"Yeah, okay," she said quietly.

She met his eyes. For a second, she thought they were as blue as the seas of the Cyclades. This man could strip a person's soul bare with the intensity of that look. She wanted to stay in it but needed to turn away. She touched his arm, only for a second.

"We have to go," she said, and walked off with the crowbar.

Tickets to Westminster Abbey were thirty pounds. They declined the guided tour.

With the thin layer of glittering snow across the grounds and the Christmas tree outside the main entrance and tourists wandering in and out, it was the picture of Yuletide London.

Ridley, Iain, and Lianna walked in midday with nothing in hand but John Dee's notebook, a pen, and a notepad.

The grandeur that soared above them was breathtaking.

Lianna's eyes lit up as she looked to her right. In an alcove beside the entryway was a boxy, fairly plain wooden throne atop a dais.

"That's the Coronation Chair! Every English monarch for over seven hundred years has sat *right there* upon that chair to be coronated. Oh, it's magnificent."

"There are gonna be a million things in here you want to gawk over," said Ridley. "You're free to do that on your own dime. Get us to where we're going." She glanced at Iain, then added, "Please."

"All right, I hear you," said Lianna. "This way to the Pyx Chamber."

As they made their way through the Nave, they passed statues and inscriptions, effigies of great royals, biblical sagas in stained glass. There was no space wasted in this colossus.

"They fit three thousand dead people in here?" said Ridley. "Really?"

"Over three thousand three hundred. Some are ashes, of course. George II was the last English monarch buried here. Before you were even a country, actually."

*I'll shove the Star-Spangled Banner so far—*

"Here?" asked Iain, pointing to a sign that said *PYX CHAMBER*, gently steering Ridley to the right.

They walked through a small vestibule, reaching a door that looked like that of a dungeon keep. It was thick oak with iron slats across it, six locks, and then another reinforcing oak door inside of the first.

"So this must be where they kept the cookie jar," said Iain.

Lianna laughed. "Not far off. At first it was just the undercroft beneath the monks' dormitory, but then the king made it into a strongroom for his valuables."

Ridley touched the row of locks, then muttered close to Iain as he passed. "Good thing we didn't try to break in for this clue."

Inside, it was a small stone chamber with low vaulted ceilings. It was clearly one of the oldest parts of the Abbey.

Lianna cast suspicious glances at the tourists milling around. She waited until they had left the room before pulling out Dee's notebook.

"This one...I can't believe he wrote these all so plainly. Everything else has been a riddle, but he's very specific when it comes to the location of these..."

She flipped a page.

"There—the pillar. Should be at the base of this pillar here."

There was only one in the room, a massively thick stone column. Ridley jumped over the barrier fence and crouched down, scanning.

Until she saw a faint carving on the far side, near the floor.

"It's just a circle," she said, taking out her cell to snap a photo. "An 'O,' maybe?"

"Yes, should be a letter," said Lianna.

Ridley hopped back over and showed the professor.

"Yes, all right. One out of seven. Let's go find some more letters!"

Lianna beamed like she was on a scavenger hunt with friends. It irritated Ridley, but she did love the feeling of success.

They moved on to the Chapter House next door, an empty octagonal room with soaring stained glass windows. Above the door inside was a splendid carving of Jesus sitting on his throne, surrounded by adoring angels.

Just below his feet was carved a single letter: *L*.

They went back into the main abbey, to the South Transept, where Poet's Corner was flush with the great literary talents of the kingdom.

"We're searching for *the* poet," said Lianna, keeping her voice hushed around the throngs of other visitors. "There are so many buried here, though."

"Well, who before the mid-1600s?" asked Iain.

"Chaucer! Of course. It had to be Chaucer. He was the first one buried here, 1400 or so. Yes."

His tomb was so central that it had obviously been an early installation. Behind the ornate ancient woodwork, below the stone plaque commemorating him in Latin, was chiseled a very faint *V*.

Lianna actually pumped her fist.

"These next four should all be very close, right in a row," she told them.

They were.

In the lavishly decorated Cosmati Pavement in front of the High Altar: *E*.

On the tomb of Edward the Confessor, it was smaller and more obscure, but there it was: another *E*.

In the Lady Chapel, the Chapel of Henry VII, between two specific stained glass windows: *H*.

"Doesn't this feel a bit too *easy?*" said Ridley under her breath to Iain.

They gazed up at the fan-vaulted ceiling with giant gold pendants hanging from it.

"Yeah, it does. Maybe it's the reward for gettin' this far. John Dee, the Merciful."

*That's not it...*

Henry VII's grandiose tomb had been barricaded many years ago, so that a gorgeously carved cage of dark wood now ensconced it. Still they were able to peer and zoom in enough with a phone camera to find it: *A*.

"That's it," said Lianna as she jotted it down on the notepad. "Seven letters. What on earth is it...E, L, O, A, V, H, E."

"So that's not English," said Iain. "My Latin's a wee bit peely-wally."

Ridley stared at him.

"You can use that one," he said. "No charge."

She turned back to Lianna. "So what language are we gambling with here?"

"I don't think—I mean it *could* be Latin, but I think it's perhaps something...older. One moment."

She wandered toward the nearest seat she could find, absent-mindedly sitting on the sumptuously cushioned kneeler in front of the chapel altar. She huddled over the notepad, trying different combinations of the letters, muttering to herself. Until finally she looked up at them.

"I think it's Hebrew."

"Dee knew Hebrew?" said Ridley.

"No, not according to any of our sources or his own writings, but if it is, I believe this one says '*Eloha ve,*' which means 'God and.'"

Ridley threw her hands up in exasperation. "It was too easy until it got offensively obtuse. What does that mean?"

"God and..." murmured Lianna, raking through all her years of study, of poring over words and charts and maps. "'*For* God and country' was quite common, mostly in Latin, but Dee...no."

Then she sat up as if she'd been plucked. She shuffled quickly through Dee's notebook, checking page after page.

"Oh, my God, yes. Yes, there it is!"

She looked up at Ridley and Iain, her eyes wide. She'd just solved the greatest mystery of her life.

"He used this refrain a dozen times at least, 'God and the

queen,' 'God and the queen.' There was only ever one queen to John Dee. His beloved queen, his student of the mystical. It's with her. Of course the Devil's Eye is with her! It all started and ended with her."

Ridley's jaw went slack, but her eyes were glowing.

"It's buried with Queen Elizabeth I."

# CHAPTER
# FIFTY

**LONDON, ENGLAND**

THROUGHOUT WESTMINSTER ABBEY, the tombs of many of the great English monarchs were displayed as grand marble sarcophagi on which the public could see their resplendent effigies.

But at least half of them did not contain the actual remains of the king or queen as advertised. Those coffins lay below the floor of the Abbey, in burial vaults that had not been accessed in a hundred and fifty years.

Elizabeth I was buried beneath the Lady Chapel, below the dedication of her tomb, but there was no real entrance to the vaults. They could only be accessed by digging away the mortar and pulling up the floor stones piece by piece.

"If this was the 40s, we'd only have to drug the guard and his dog and pick the lock," Ridley said as they sat in a café jingling with Christmas cheer.

She and Iain and Lianna were huddled over mugs of hot chocolate and a map of Westminster Abbey. They'd ended their tour that day with a sightseeing expedition to find security cameras inside and outside of the building. There were plenty, including one inside the Lady Chapel enclave where Elizabeth I was buried.

There was no way to do this without hacking into that system.

And that meant a call to the Osprey office. Ridley stepped outside to make that one, pacing around in the frosty sunlight away from the flow of pedestrians.

"Rid," said Booker in a grave voice after she'd told him about their conclusion. "You're going to desecrate the grave of one of England's greatest rulers, inside a church?"

"Well...yeah. I'm not gonna smash her bones, if that's what you're worrying about. You have any other suggestions? Telekinesis? The law of attraction?"

She could hear him trying to suppress a pained groan.

"I can't authorize Ted to break the security system there," he said. "No. That's the British government. After what happened in Jerusalem, my butt would be in the gutter if Conway or Fraser found out."

*Deputy Director of the CIA's National Clandestine Services Ben Conway. Director of the CIA Jude Fraser. Sneak by the big dogs.*

"We'll outsource it," said Ridley. "Just let me talk to Ted. Hackers all know each other. They form these little secret online clubs, don't they? I'll just ask him for a name, but won't tell him what it's about. He'll have plausible deniability."

The silence meant she'd hit on something.

"You don't even tell him where you are right now," said Booker finally.

"Sir. It's Ted. If *you* can track my phone, he can find out what color underwear I have on right now."

"Don't tease him. Man sits behind a desk all day."

"He's my digital hero."

"I'll put you through to him. Keep it need-to-know."

"Understood and agreed. Oh, but I have to ask him to do one more thing for us. We need Bellerophon."

The sun had set by the time the Abbey closed that evening.

Ted the Osprey technician had done quick work in finding them a hacker inside the UK. She would be thrilled to break the Westminster security system and loop the camera feed. Of course the money would have to come from their division budget, but it was at least one degree removed from total liability.

Their hacker had given them a specific window. They would have between nine and one in the morning to do all their business. The exterior guards changed over at one a.m. They didn't want the risk of having any of the replacements wander into the Abbey for a first check.

It was two minutes past nine when Ridley, Iain, and Lianna parked their van by the northern entrance.

The lock was surprisingly routine. Iain was able to pick it apart within two minutes. With a large duffel in tow, the three of them slipped into Westminster Abbey and pulled the door closed behind them.

Ridley glanced at her Delta watch. They had an hour and forty-nine minutes to work before Dane's arrival.

"This old pile of stones is a lot nicer without all the bloody tourists in it," said Iain as they made their way to the Lady Chapel.

Lianna gazed around her. "I'd love to come here for their Christmas vespers. I'm sure it's lovely."

*Christmas in jail if we get caught here.*

They reached the raised tomb of Queen Elizabeth I and dropped the duffel. Iain pulled it open and handed out dust masks and goggles. He pulled on a pair of kneepads. Then he drew out a battery-powered angle grinder with a diamond-tipped blade.

"A'right," he said looking up at Ridley. "Let's go find our girl."

The grinder buzzed to life. He knelt, lowering it to the floor. It bit into the line of mortar with a screech.

As Iain ground away at the floor stones, Ridley wandered out into the main sanctuary and the nave. She was on alert, her eyes restless.

*Thank God it's freezing outside. The guards are cozy and warm and deaf to it all in their little huts.*

Nearly half an hour later, she checked back into the Lady Chapel. Iain had been blasting away at the mortar and pulling up one small stone at a time when Ridley got a text.

**Bogey 5 mins out. LR71HLH and LX66ZMD**

*He's an hour early. Of course.*

She waved to Iain to quit. He shut off the grinder.

"They're almost here. Call your guy," she said.

He yanked out his phone and made a call. She read him out the numbers. He repeated them to his contact on the other end of the line. Though Lianna knew what they were doing, she seemed nervous. It was all coming to a head.

Then Ridley's phone rang. She picked it up but said nothing.

"I'm at the north entrance," came Dane's voice.

The very sound of it lit her blood like Greek fire. The sight of Otto's bloody hair and frozen face skittered across her vision.

"It's open," she managed to grit out. "Come to the high altar. *Only* you."

She drew a Glock 17 from beneath her jacket and went out to wait for him in the dim sanctuary.

*Keep that finger off the trigger, Samaras. Don't fuck this up now—you can handle it! Complete your mission.*

A moment later, the massive wooden door cracked open. Dane slid inside.

Ridley tensed.

He swung the door closed and strode forward, empty-handed. He stopped a dozen feet away from Ridley. His eyes dropped to the pistol in her hand.

"You know I don't have the key on me."

"You know I won't let any of your henchmen in here," she said.

"I don't need them. It's already in here."

*Didn't see that coming.*

"Get it, then," she said.

"Let me see what you have first."

This was inevitable. He needed what they had and they needed what he had. The moment of contact had to happen, but what happened next...there was no arrangement, no collaboration. It was bound to explode, but when and how—neither could be certain.

Ridley escorted him back to the Lady Chapel, walking well behind him, her gun at a low ready position.

They entered the small side enclave, which was now looking like a disastrous home repair project. Stones were stacked atop each other and dust coated everything.

A dark space yawned open in the floor.

Dane looked at Lianna. "Professor."

She paled, but managed to nod back at him. "Bill."

Iain's expression was scorching. He checked on Ridley to see how she was faring with Operation Do-Not-Kill-Him-Yet.

"Where's the key?" she said.

"If I don't come out of here alive in fourteen minutes, my men outside kill every one of you," said Dane.

"What-the-fuck-ever," snapped Ridley. "*Where* is it?"

He took a step back, reached behind the black stone griffins on the nearby Montague memorial, and pulled out a small wad of bubble-wrap.

"I'm going down there with you."

Ridley looked at Iain and Lianna and cocked her head: *okay.* She holstered the Glock.

"You first," Iain said to Ridley.

She looked at Dane. "And you second."

He nodded.

Iain tossed her a headlamp from the duffel. She tugged it on and lowered herself down into the darkness.

# CHAPTER
# FIFTY-ONE

**LONDON, ENGLAND**

THE TUNNEL WAS LOW, forcing Ridley to hunch over. It was impossibly still and black. The air was stale. Somehow it still smelled like the death of centuries.

She shuffled forward, half-crouching. They were in an aisle, with vaults on both sides. Each one was almost entirely bricked up. There were no markings to tell them who was buried inside.

Dane climbed down behind her. Lianna followed him, a bit clumsily, wearing a headlamp. Iain was last into the cramped space, also sporting a headlamp and holding a small sledgehammer.

"Powell," said Ridley, "where is she?"

"Oh, I don't—*I* don't know. These vaults are really quite mysterious."

It was frustratingly true. Little was known about the layout down here. Whatever records had been kept, they had not been made public.

Iain hefted the hammer in one hand. "Time to get to know the monarchs."

He smashed at one of the walls until the stones crumbled apart, then gestured for Lianna to climb into the space. She looked terrible doing it, but managed to get in.

"No," she said, making her way back out. "She's not here."

"She's gonna be one of two coffins in a vault," said Ridley.

She'd done what homework she could, and knew that Elizabeth I had initially been buried alongside her grandfather and grandmother, Henry VII and Elizabeth of York. A few years later, though, the reigning king James I ordered her coffin moved to another vault. For four hundred years, she had been sharing a burial chamber with her half-sister, Mary I.

They carried on down the aisle, the beams from their headlamps sweeping across the ancient stones. Iain smashed open the next vault—but it wasn't that one, either.

It was the third.

As he finished crashing the hammerhead through broken bricks, Lianna leaned forward to peer inside.

She gasped. "Here she is!"

Ridley and Iain pulled the loose stones away. All four of them squeezed in.

The roof was slightly arched, though barely five feet high. It was no more than ten feet long and six feet wide.

In the middle were two coffins, one stacked atop the other.

The top one was dressed with red velvet that had thinned and frayed. Carved into the elm wood was a Tudor rose. Below it, "*1603*." And on each side of it an initial, "*E*" and "*R*."

"That's her?" said Ridley.

Lianna nodded, her face flushed with excitement. "Elizabeth Regina. That's *Queen* in Latin. It's her."

"So we—" said Iain, looking at Ridley, "we open it?"

"Yeah, we open it."

Dane reached for the top first. Ridley and Iain jumped forward to put hands on it. They all lifted.

At the sight beneath it, Iain winced away. Ridley and Dane were unflinching, though when she looked down into the coffin, she was appalled.

Whatever had happened to this queen's corpse...she was not intact. Darkened skin tissue was everywhere, spattered and dried along the lead lining of the coffin.

"It's like she...exploded," said Ridley.

"Rumors are she did," said Lianna, "as she was being transferred to Whitehall by barge. She'd been lying in state for days. The gases from rotting tissue probably built up and burst—all that pressure."

Iain feigned retching.

Ridley couldn't believe she was looking down at the body of one of England's most famous rulers, but she gave herself only seconds to marvel. Dane's eyes were already hunting for something else in that coffin.

And there it was at the feet of Queen Elizabeth I: a hexagonal stone the size of a grapefruit.

It was Iain who snatched it up first. He turned it over in his hands, headlamp shining down on it.

It was polished as smooth as marble, but on each of the six sides was an indented carving. Every one of them was the outline of a strange character.

The Enochian letters.

The keys.

Iain looked up at Dane, his headlamp nearly blinding the mercenary. "It's time."

"Yours go in first."

"Does it matter?" snarled Ridley, whose deadly anger suddenly surged to the fore again. "Give it up. We're all here to see this thing opened."

He didn't budge.

Iain handed the hexagon to Ridley. He continued to glare at

Dane, refusing to peel his blinding light from the man's face while he dug into his pocket for the quartz pieces.

He drew out a pouch and poured the keys into his palm. He extended his other empty hand to Dane.

Dane pulled his own piece out of the bubble wrap and gave it to the Scotsman.

They hovered over the big stone, sifting through the pieces and fitting each into its matching notch. They all fit perfectly, almost snapping into place.

As Iain went to place the last key, he hesitated. He glanced up at Ridley, who met his eyes under the beam of the lamps. She clutched the polished hexagon in both hands.

*This is it. I'm already holding it.*

*Will Madimi show—*

Iain inserted the last piece of quartz.

The stone unlatched. The sides separated into four parts like flower petals.

And sitting inside was the Devil's Eye.

It was the size of a plum, translucent, and almost seemed to glow with its own light.

"All this trouble for you, little blob," muttered Ridley.

She reached in—hesitated—and then picked it up.

Nothing happened. Relief flooded her.

*Go rot in a rancid eternal tub, Madimi.*

"That's really it," said Lianna in a hushed voice. "All this trouble for that simple little beauty."

Dane stared at it.

*What's his move now?*

He had assembled some of the filthiest gangsters-for-hire in London for tonight's work. They'd pulled up in a couple of SUVs to stake out the Abbey, to outnumber and trap Ridley, Iain, and Lianna, and to steal the prize from them. It was a decent idea.

*A shame he has no idea how much money he just wasted.*

Because they had Bellerophon.

It was the next generation of Pegasus, the most insidious and effective spyware ever created for hacking an unencrypted phone. It required nothing more than the phone number itself. Once the program was embedded, it took *everything*, from keystrokes to contacts to photos. It could activate a microphone and camera to remotely record. Best of all, it left no trace at all.

From Lianna's cell, they'd been able to get Dane's number, and they set Bellerophon loose in it.

They'd been able to track every call and text that he made or received. It was a simple thing to coordinate with their hacker: tracking down the men he'd hired for extra firepower. It wasn't hard from there to take down their descriptions and track their movements to the Abbey.

When Ridley had gotten a text from their hacker-for-hire that the gangster crew was only minutes away, it had been a straightforward thing for Iain to make a call to one of his contacts in the Metro PD. They were extremely interested in the plate numbers and location of some of the most notorious criminals in the city. The arrests were standard procedure, for "trespassing."

*He has no men left outside, and he doesn't even know it yet.*

"May I touch it?" asked Lianna, her gaze fixed on this mythical stone.

Ridley held up the Devil's Eye for the professor to brush her fingers along.

"Okay, that's too much," said Ridley, pulling it back. "Vacate the premises. Everybody out."

Lianna and Dane climbed out of the burial vault first, then Ridley clutching the Eye, then Iain. They had just started their crouch-walk back down the cramped aisle—when Dane reached out to Lianna.

Alarm shot through Ridley before she even realized what he was doing.

He had handed her a small respirator mask. Lianna immediately placed it over her face—

"No!" shouted Ridley, lunging toward them.

But before she could reach the pair, the low ceiling above their heads exploded.

# CHAPTER
# FIFTY-TWO

**LONDON, ENGLAND**

The floor of Westminster Abbey blew apart.

Stone crashed into the burial vaults between Ridley and Iain. Chunks rained down, knocking them both to the ground.

Stunned, Ridley struggled to fight through the hail of rocks. She heard muffled ringing in her ears as she choked on the stone dust—and realized she was no longer holding the Devil's Eye. In the explosion, it had clattered from her hand. Meanwhile, her ankle had been pinned by the pile of stones.

She squinted through the murk to see Lianna picking up the precious crystal from a heap of rubble. The professor met her eyes over the breathing mask. She looked almost apologetic.

Which sent Ridley into a raging scramble, trying to reach the Glock inside her jacket—

She wasn't fast enough. Dane pulled and pushed Lianna down the aisle, back toward the hole they'd dug into the floor, and they vanished up into the Abbey.

Iain crawled over the pile of destruction, shaking plumes of dust from his thick hair. He reached Ridley and cradled her face quickly, checking for injury.

"You're okay?"

"I just need my ankle back—"

He helped dig away the stones until she could pull her leg free.

"What the *shit!*" she exclaimed.

They helped each other to their feet, and then hauled themselves up through the newly made hole in the ceiling.

They emerged in the Lady Chapel just in time to hear the sound of the cold air whooshing into the Abbey from the north entrance.

Still hacking up dust, they ran for it—

Outside, into the crunching snow and darkness—

A dark gray BMW SUV was revving to life in the yard. Ridley didn't recognize its license plate.

*There was a third vehicle.*

*Qualley.*

Iain sprinted for their own KIA Sportage, parked on the back end of the Abbey. Ridley's fingers twitched, wanting to pull her Glock, but that would be their destruction.

Westminster Abbey may have had security that was easily bypassed, but the sound of a gunshot across the street from the UK Parliament would bring the whole Metro PD down on them, and no connection of Iain's within the department would be able to cover for them.

She ran down the narrow road, following the sight of the BMW through the cover of trees. She watched it veer left down the A3212, heading north.

Ridley looked back for Iain, willing him to get there faster. It was an agonizing few seconds before he drew the KIA up next to her. She leapt inside, and they tore down the street.

"North is Downing Street," said Iain. "West is Buckingham

Palace. They can't be that daft to run into the highest security in London. They're goin'—"

"Over the bridge." Ridley gazed up at Big Ben on her right, looming over the Thames.

The lights of the BMW ahead cut left at Parliament Square, right into the throng of traffic that ringed the small green. It weaved and dodged through the hail of horn blasts.

Iain blazed after it, swerving to avoid the angry cars left in Dane's wake.

"Watch out—they're still going right!" said Ridley.

The BMW skidded right, heading for Westminster Bridge.

*That bridge is flooded with vehicle lights...*

"Bloody shits," said Iain, realizing the same thing.

"It's packed."

But Dane was going for it, taking the gamble that they wouldn't follow. And the path of least resistance? One of the wide pedestrian lanes.

Laying on the horn, the BMW ripped into the narrow section barricaded by iron pylons.

"He's clearing the way," said Iain. "We won't hit anyone!"

"Iain, we can track his phone! We don't have to—"

But he had already steered them onto the bridge.

The BMW's horn blared—plowing into the sparse crowds.

Pedestrians flew, throwing themselves at the railing, darting through the pylons.

Their screams—and the two SUVs hurtling the wrong way across the bridge—sent traffic screeching. The sound of metal crunching metal punched the night.

Iain white-knuckled the steering wheel. He sped up, trying to draft as closely as he could to Dane's vehicle to keep from hitting anyone in his wake.

*No innocents—no innocents—no innocents—*

Dane kept speeding up.

Ridley heard the thud of a body ahead on the bumper of the BMW. A man went spinning into the pylons—

Iain swerved to avoid him—clipped the stone rail—and fought to right the KIA—

They were nearing the end of the bridge.

"The break into traffic—" said Ridley.

"Disaster?"

"Could be."

She gritted her teeth as she saw the pedestrians shrieking, hurling themselves out into the traffic of the bridge rather than face the rampaging SUV coming at them.

They were closing on the last seventy feet of the bridge... fifty...thirty...

And then the BMW lurched.

It wrenched sideways—skidded—and came to a dead stop with its nose facing out to the river.

Iain stomped on the brake. Ridley was thrown forward, bracing with her forearms just in time to keep from smashing her face on the dashboard.

They screeched to a halt.

The BMW was blocking the entire pedestrian walk, wedged between the pylons and the rail. There was no way past.

On the other side, Dane, Qualley, and Lianna poured out onto the bridge. Dane paused only long enough to pitch two cell phones over the bridge.

*His and Lianna's. Clever boy.*

Ridley tried to throw open her door—but they were jammed too close to the pylons. She bellowed in frustration, smashing it repeatedly against the iron barriers.

Iain leapt out, but Dane and the others were already darting through traffic.

Ridley clambered over the console and stumbled out of the driver's side.

She was only in time to see Dane pull a gun on a driver, hauling him out of his vehicle. Qualley jumped behind the wheel. The others slipped into the car and started their bumper car-weave through traffic.

*Gone.*

"Damn you to your last fucking breath!" shouted Ridley.

*They're gone.*

Their taillights disappeared down the bridge.

"We have to go," said Iain, whipping his head around for any sign of the police.

They slid around the hood of the BMW and broke into a sprint. In the darkness, one could hardly tell they were covered in a layer of stone dust.

They looked like any other panicked pedestrians running for their lives.

*They won.*

*You lost.*

*They have the Devil's Eye.*

# CHAPTER
# FIFTY-THREE

**LONDON, ENGLAND**

The nearest CIA safehouse in London was in Kensington.

They'd found their way in with a passcode, and the housemaster greeted them on her way out the door. She was heading to the Christmas fair that filled Hyde Park, just across the street.

Iain sat on the floor in front of the coffee table, field-stripping his Glock 19. He was in such a fury that it looked like he was ripping the gun apart piece by piece.

Ridley set a cup of hot chocolate in front of him. She clutched a coffee in her still-bandaged hand.

"Thanks," he mumbled.

On the TV, the doe-eyed Loretta Young gazed at Cary Grant as they sat on a bench in the middle of a snowy park. Iain kept glancing up at the screen as if the black-and-white Christmas movie was the only thing that could soothe him.

Ridley's phone buzzed. It was a message from Booker.

**Remain in place. Talk at 2300 EST.**

"We're staying here tonight," she said to Iain. "We'll have

more information in the morning. Four in the morning, to be exact."

"What are you doin' for Christmas, Rid?"

He didn't even look up as he asked.

"I don't know yet," she said. "What are you doing?"

"You know what I'm *not* doin'—I'm not gettin' raped by an old man."

He smashed the barrel down onto the table.

Ridley was standing over him and it felt wrong. She backed up and lowered herself to the floor, propping her back against the armchair.

"It's the girl," she said quietly.

"Lexi. Yeah, it is."

He hadn't touched his hot chocolate.

"How long have you been after him?" she asked.

"Two years."

*Two years—of* this?

"He's a soul-eating goblin," said Iain. "Him and his fuckin' bloodwitch, they were...hell, she *told* me—bragged to me—what they were doin' to that girl!"

She clutched her mug but couldn't bring herself to take a sip.

"You've been hunting this guy for two years..." she said, "but the Security Service won't touch him? So why are you after him?"

His eyes were swimming in rage.

"Because nobody saved me!"

Iain dropped his head, as if a dam within him had collapsed. He gripped the gun slide in one hand so hard he could have broken it.

"Nobody came for me. Nobody stopped the man—"

Ridley felt paralyzed, rooted to the floor, but then somehow she was moving. She set down her mug and went to him. The back of her throat thickened and her eyes felt full as she lowered herself onto the couch.

*What could I possibly…*

There were no words for a human being rending themselves in front of you.

She slid a hand onto the back of his neck and felt him shiver. Then she pulled it away and slipped her hand into his, lacing their fingers together.

He dropped the pistol slide from his other hand…and pressed his palm against his mouth, trying to turn his face away from her.

It had always been the Devil's Eye for her. And then the death of Dane.

For him, it had always been Lexi.

*And how many others…*

She sat with him as he gagged back a sob, as he clenched his jaw and grasped her hand tightly.

*Whatever happened to the man who did this to Iain Carnegie… I'll make it worse for Marc Pearson.*

*There's no justice like hell.*

They slept beside each other that night, but neither slept well.

Her own failures—losing the Devil's Eye—Otto's death—the specter of Madimi—all ricocheted in Ridley's head. Iain's blackest memories frothed up in his mind.

Both of them squirmed and tossed. Occasionally one would rise from the murk of dreams just enough to reach for the other, to pull them in close, all drowsy limbs and tousled hair. The knife cuts on Ridley's ribs and leg and hand and collar would sting her awake if he brushed them, but she didn't pull away. The pain was part of it.

The alarm that jarred them awake at three-thirty was like a

brutal invader of this twilight zone. They dragged themselves dutifully out of the warm bed, exchanging a few glances as they dressed and made their way out to the kitchen.

By the time Booker's face appeared on her cell phone, Ridley was sitting at the table with a mug of coffee. Iain was eating some teacakes he'd found in the cupboard.

"Are you tryin' to make things more interesting for yourself?" said Booker, but his tone was not one of amusement.

"Sir," said Ridley, "you know I'm not done."

"No, you sure aren't. You just added ten thousand feet to your climb, Samaras."

"They tossed their phones last night. They must have had a suspicion."

"Suspicion is all. Maybe six people in the world could detect Bellerophon on their phones, but that doesn't matter now."

"Goin' old fashioned?" muttered Iain through a mouthful of biscuit, marshmallow, and chocolate.

"No. We're tracking Pearson's jet and flight manifest. It's scheduled to fly into Aberdeen tomorrow night."

"He doesn't have a place up there, does he?" asked Ridley.

"Nope. The only time he flies to Aberdeen is when he's visiting the prince at Balmoral Castle."

*A castle. The royal family. This really did just get more interesting.*

"Why would he take the Devil's Eye up there?" she said. "Why not just grab it and use it in whatever disgusting billionaire's lair he's in right now..."

"Without the Sigillum Dei, it's just a stone," said Booker. "He needs the ritual. He needs a scryer. He wants the whole occult experience. Makes sense he'd want to include someone from the English monarchy in it."

"A Christmas scrying?" said Ridley dryly. "Marley's got nothin' on Madimi."

"You held the stone?"

"Yeah."

"Did you see her?"

She felt Iain's eyes on her, concerned.

"No. I thought she might burst out of the queen's corpse, but there was nothing."

Booker furrowed his brow in thought. "She can't be done...I don't trust that. No."

"Book, in case we don't—if we don't get to stop him before he uses the Devil's Eye—what's our last resort?"

He leaned back in his desk chair. "There's nothing on that. John Dee never got that far."

"Do we even know where this stone came from?" said Ridley.

"I've been scouring his writings, but they're dead quiet. I don't know, either. No mention of this Devil's Eye *anywhere* but here." He wagged the notebook for camera.

Iain spoke up. "Do you think...what if it actually works?"

They both looked at him.

"Yeah," said Ridley. "This shi—stuff gets really weird."

"But..." Iain went on, "you think he can get all the secrets of the universe, like—God's eye—just by lookin' at a board through that crystal?"

Booker stared at him for a moment, before saying, "We plan for contingencies, Agent Carnegie."

"Aye, right." He raised his tea cake like a toast.

"There's nothin' in that notebook about the Devil's Eye granting any sort of physical superpower. Pearson traffics in information—that's what he's after here. If the devil decides to give him a set of horns for Christmas, well..."

"Shoot him in the head," said Ridley. "Oh, I'm sorry, haven't had enough coffee yet."

She took a swig.

"You could really find work as an exorcist," said Booker.

A great missing jabbed at her—Henri.

Henri Michel had been her partner in the hunt for the jinn that took them all the way to Jerusalem, where some of the holiest places in the world converged. He was a Christian, but that word on its own felt too light for the strength of his convictions. His faith—while not hers—was something she had come to rely on in their time together. It was there, bowed and unbroken, at the brink of ultimate and desperate destruction.

She didn't realize until this moment just *how* much she had relied on it.

*Henri would know what to do with all this spiritual stuff.*

*Why does it always come to that?*

A quick pang of guilt cut through her wondering. She could feel Iain's arm just grazing her own. She didn't want to think that he "wasn't enough partner."

*I can hoard partners in my own mind.*

"I can no more help you break into a national monument in an allied country," said Booker, "than I can help you break onto the grounds of a royal family residence—private, by the way. I don't want to know what you're doing or when or who you're doin' it with, but Marc Pearson cannot have that Devil's Eye."

"That's all you want for Christmas?" said Ridley.

"All I want for Christmas."

He actually grinned, the kind that looked like a belly laugh within a smile.

"And then both of you can get home for Christmas," he said. "Or wherever."

"Copy that."

"Tell me what you need to and nothing else. Now go on and clean this up."

"Sir."

They hung up.

Iain looked at Ridley. "He's a bit more like 'boss' when he's in his office, then?"

"That's my boss."

She met his eyes. He held up the rest of his teacake as an offering. Ridley took the last bite from his hand.

A faint smile tugged at his mouth, but then his eyes drifted down to her collar, to where Shao had stabbed her with his tanto blade.

"Is that—how are those cuts healing?"

She tugged down the collar of her T-shirt and grazed her fingers across the cut, which had been glued back together at the hospital.

"Doesn't hurt like the ribs," she said. "Look bad?"

He leaned forward. "Nah. Healing like Wolverine."

Their eyes met, and it was sudden—that electricity of being so close, that feeling of realizing it in the same moment.

Ridley could have leaned down to his lips. Iain could have reached up and skimmed his fingertips across her collarbone.

Instead, he stood up quickly.

"Sun won't rise here for another four hours," he said, going to fill a glass of water at the fridge. "Enough time to gather some bampots and a wee collection of arms."

She touched the neckline of her T-shirt back into place.

*That was too close.*

*But it wasn't enough.*

"Your Scottishness just bottles up inside you and then pours out all at once, doesn't it?" she said. "I've got a couple unsavories in London I can call, but—not for at least three hours, or they'd probably put a hit on me."

"Nah, this is Scottish work." He chugged the water. "I've got some lads in Edinburgh. We can take the first train up this mornin'."

She looked at him for a moment, and couldn't read him. His

eyes were that dazzling dark blue, but there was something moving behind them, like something had been dislodged.

*You can trust him—trust that he wants Pearson more than anything. So you know what he'll do when he gets there.*

*He owes you nothing more than that.*

Iain felt her trying to get a read on him.

He set his mouth in a crooked, playful jut and said, "Let's go get some gangsters."

# CHAPTER
# FIFTY-FOUR

**EDINBURGH, SCOTLAND**

Ridley and Iain arrived by train at midday.

Like nearly all of Europe, it was frosted with a thin layer of snow. Slush covered the cobblestones, and on this iron-gray day, starry lights beckoned them along the old sloping streets. Thick garlands and glittering trees adorned shopfronts.

They saw more than one child running around in Hogwarts robes. Edinburgh may be ten thousand years old, have one of the most recognizably epic castles in the world, and have served as a hub of the Scottish Enlightenment, but these days it was almost as well known for being the birthplace of Harry Potter.

Ridley appreciated the magical aura in one of her favorite cities in the world. It was all quaint, moody, and magnificent.

Coats wrapped tightly up to their chins, she and Iain hiked the ten minutes from the station to one of the less obvious places for meeting a pair of gangsters.

They walked into Makar's Mash Bar four minutes after noon, shaking the snow from their collars. They were led downstairs, where the only people in this spillover dining room were sitting at a corner table.

The two men got to their feet when they spotted the approaching pair.

One of them was a titan, his buzzed head nearly brushing the low ceiling. His face was craggy, with thick brows and a broad mouth that looked ever ready for a smirk.

He greeted Iain, clasping his forearm with a bear grip. "Well, mate."

"Tavvie," said Iain with a grin.

Craig McTavish, the six-foot-five gangster from Glasgow—and there was only one—looked Ridley up and down.

"Who's your hen then?"

"I'm Ridley." She stepped forward and extended her hand.

He shook it with a mixture of "amused" and "impressed."

"Craig McTavish. You're a lass of Carnegie's here, you can call me Tavvie."

"I'm not 'a lass of,'" she said, "but I'll call you that."

Iain whacked the back of his hand against Tavvie's chest. "You should know better."

"I perpetually don't!"

Iain moved to greet the second man with a meaty handshake. He was about Ridley's height, with a close-cropped beard and dark skin.

"Odie," the man introduced himself. "We're not friends—" he pointed to Tavvie, "just colleagues."

Odion Musa, Nigerian, raised in London. He'd risen through the police force to Detective Inspector but was bounced out after a scandal involving the theft of drug money.

"I'm *not* your friend," said Tavvie as they all sat. "I'm your stepdad."

"You're a wanker."

He grinned. "Call your mum, then, go on."

"You all look like steamin' idiots already," said Iain. "You interested in a bit o' business, then?"

"Is she comin'?" asked Tavvie, dodging his head at Ridley but looking at Iain.

Ridley drilled her gaze straight at him. "I'm gonna be your fly-half. Your point guard. Your playmaking midfielder."

He looked at her, giving up a bellowing laugh. "Fuckin' lass, here...all right. Let's play."

The barrier of pleasantries and shit-talking was broken.

Over heaping plates of Scotch eggs, haggis, lamb shank, and gravy stacked atop potato mash, the four of them got down to business.

Iain had vouched for Ridley, but before Tavvie and Odie spoke a self-incriminating word, they demanded to know her profession. She would only say that she was freelancing from an unnamed alphabet agency. Despite all their prodding and guessing, she refused any more. They eventually relented and agreed to hear her proposal.

Ridley gave little background, but when she finally told them that the target would be Balmoral Castle—with a member of the royal family in residence—she saw Tavvie and Odie exchange a stunned look.

"Get away with ye," said Tavvie.

"Are you not havin' a laugh?" said Odie.

"Are you not up for it?" asked Ridley.

*Prick their egos. They'll jump for it.*

"Bet your right ass we are," Tavvie replied. "We'll need another man, though."

"How do you see it?" said Iain.

Odie spoke up. "The RPS doesn't—Royal Protective Service—they don't run grounds security outside places like Buckingham Palace and Windsor. They keep it to personal details. And Albert...that prick. His family's cut his detail down. Probably 'cause they don't want any more eyes on the shit he's into."

Ridley glanced at Iain. He didn't look at her. But they both knew what Odie meant by that.

*Open secret. The royal family doesn't work to stop* him, *just the stories about him.*

"How many in a detail?" Iain asked the former cop.

"Three, probably. Four at most. Maybe they'd leave a man at the guard house, but I've been to Balmoral. It's fifty thousand acres, mate. You can walk right into that property."

"Not even perimeter cameras?" said Ridley.

"It's two-and-a-half kilometers long. Nah, there aren't cameras along that perimeter. Forest, river, farmland...and the royal family doesn't spend much time there. Not since the queen died."

"Others live on the estate, though, year-round?"

"Yeah. Not in the castle itself, but nearby."

"Servants?" asked Iain.

Tavvie gave a dark chuckle. "They call 'em 'staff' now, don't they."

"Half the castle, man. They've got an entire wing to work from," said Odie.

"Do you know how many?" said Ridley.

"Nah. I can turn up a few stones, though."

"You're tryin' to get in there before Christmas?" asked Tavvie through a mouthful of haggis, mashed turnip, and whisky cream sauce. "You're askin' a lot."

"Tomorrow night," said Ridley. "Non-negotiable."

He looked at her like she was mad, but then his eyes started to glint as if he was turned on by the madness.

Odie snorted in disbelief.

Ridley looked from one to the other. "And all through the house, not a creature was stirring..."

"Except for the prince who found some mice," said Iain.

"Who's pickin' up my tab?" said Tavvie.

Ridley smiled. "Depends on how many dishes you eat."

"And I'll have sticky toffee puddin' by the *platter*."

"We'll get your wire info as soon as we settle a fee."

Tavvie and Odie looked at each other.

"All right, then," said the giant Glaswegian, who then shook his head. "You mad bastard, Carnegie. Who coulda thought, from you gettin' your angry little ass handed to you in jail, to stormin' the gates of the castle..."

Ridley's eyes climbed to Iain's face, but she didn't let her expression betray a thing in front of the others.

*Jail...but he's MI5.*

She took a bite of her lamb and horseradish mash to dispel any sign of surprise.

"Everything criminal that I know I learned from you, daft scunner," Iain said to Tavvie.

"I'm just tryin' to finish my meal," said Tavvie through a full mouth, lifting his hands in innocence.

"Give us a few hours," said Odie, who was swigging his water as if he needed a reset. "Takes a bit o' thought to do somethin' this stupid."

"Meet at four," said Ridley.

"Seven," said Tavvie.

She cocked her head at him. "Six."

"Not every day you get the woman sayin' 'go faster.'"

"Not every day a man's tryin' to get paid for it."

He laughed with that broad, goofy grin. "Six, fine. Fine."

They ordered the sticky toffee pudding and asked for it to be brought on a platter.

. . .

Ridley went for a workout in the small hotel gym. She needed a moment away, to lose herself in the total focus of physical demand.

Iain went for a run in the cold.

She beat him back to their room, showered, then spent the rest of the afternoon poring over maps of Balmoral Castle and the surrounding area with its narrow access roads. She wanted to know every meter of it. It would be nothing like her usual memorization of city blocks and street names, as the vast estate was mostly wooded.

*It's Sherwood Forest with a castle.*

Iain worked over a diagram of the castle itself, his brow furrowed into a near scowl. He was sketching out different iterations of tactical approaches, scenarios based on personnel, positioning, and weather. Every now and then the two would trade an idea or talk through a challenging aspect, but for the most part, it was quiet in the room.

Except for the old movie that Iain put on the TV at low volume. Today it was *Remember the Night*, a Christmas rom-com with Barbara Stanwyck and Fred MacMurray.

"You love Stanwyck, huh?" said Ridley, lifting her head at one point to glance at the screen. "Second movie in days."

He sat back in his chair and sighed. "I'd spend Christmas with her."

Then he met her eyes and smiled. It was so little but so unguarded—it broke into her like a ray through cloud cover.

*This is not a good feeling. This is not how you operate during a high-stakes mission.*

*No more, Samaras. Choke it off.*

"You nail this and I'll help you put together a dating profile," she said. "Seeking fierce and warm and brassy and witty. May occasionally lapse into setting up her lover to kill her husband."

"That's the catch," he said, pivoting back to his drawings. "You know I'm glad the queen's dead. I'd feel actually kinda crap about raiding her favorite place if she was still alive. Where are you thinkin' for the approach?"

"Southeast. Hope I'm gonna like the plan your gangster boys put together, though."

"I trust their instincts."

"Do you? Infiltrating the residence of the British royal family? That's blackmail material on an MI5 agent."

"Tavvie's mum is Irish," said Iain, lifting both hands. "So *he's* no monarchist."

"Reassuring."

"If anythin', I wouldn't be worried about them backin' out. I'd worry about them goin' too hard in. They're vicious bastards when it comes down to it...especially Odie."

Ridley cocked her head at him. "Yeah, about that 'befriending vicious bastards'..."

"You're wonderin' about the jail thing, aren't you?"

"I clocked it, yeah."

Iain leaned back, raking both hands through his hair.

"Not a glamorous crime. I was an idiot when I was young and I drove drunk. Got nabbed for it...mouthed off to the cop a bit...got a dab of extra time in jail. Was good for me, really. I needed it. I read *Man's Search for Meaning* and it changed... everything. Also, got me a couple really great contacts in the criminal underworld. Really helpful."

She cocked a brow at him. "Are you gonna get away with all this? Your 'vacation' activities?"

"I'm back in the office on Boxing Day."

*The day after Christmas.*

"Guess we'll know then," he said, then tapped his pen against the sheets of paper in front of him. "As long as this doesn't go sideways."

"Send your boss a gift basket."

"May need to send him the whole Glendronach distillery."

Ridley glanced at the clock. They had two and a half hours until they regrouped with Tavvie and Odie.

"Come on," she said, getting to her feet. "We're gonna need warmer clothes."

He rose as she walked past him. "In general?"

"For the snowmobiles."

# CHAPTER
# FIFTY-FIVE

**ABERDEENSHIRE, SCOTLAND**

Snow lay thick across Cairngorms National Park, with its rugged hills and grassy lochs.

Pearson had landed at Aberdeen with Effie and Lexi. Isa had joined them as well for this "heathen holiday," as Prince Albert had jokingly named it.

A pair of Range Rovers drove them through the wild white mountains to Balmoral. They were ushered through the front gates and wound down a long, wooded drive. Lexi thought the lampposts glowing in the snowy forest made it look like Narnia. Her dad had read the books to her when she was little.

When they reached the stately gray castle, the chauffeurs pulled up under the carriage porch.

Valets carried luggage upstairs while a butler took their coats. In the entrance hall was a majestic fireplace with a mantle of Queen Victoria's royal insignia carved into wood. In nearly every corner, there were busts and statues, spears and flags. The walls boasted a parade of two dozen mounted stag heads.

The butler led them to the drawing room, where hot tea and scones and jam were set out by a white marble hearth fire. A Christmas tree twinkled in the corner, perfectly trimmed with red and gold.

Lexi gazed about the high-ceilinged room, awed by the thought that she was standing in a queen's house. There were portraits framed on the walls and photographs propped on side tables—most of them black and white—of the royal family throughout the generations. There were tartan couches and a gilded mantelpiece clock and thick drapes along the grand windows.

She picked a cinnamon scone off the silver tray tower.

Effie went to the bathroom while Pearson went to warm his hands by the fire. Isa was already speaking to the butler about her boss's food preferences.

When she'd first met the young ash-blonde beauty, Lexi thought she'd found some kind of kindred spirit in the world of Marc Pearson.

She had been wrong.

Isidora Rosić had been "hired" by Pearson when she was only fifteen, lifted out of a swirl of poverty in Serbia by the promises of a rich financier. But she never ended up on the runway. She did end up in his bed, running his calendar, and training herself in massage so that she could both adequately service his wants and train other girls to do the same.

She had not received Lexi warmly. Maybe she saw the young girl as a replacement or some kind of competitor. Whatever it was, she had remained cordial but chilly, making it clear that she was neither a shoulder to cry on nor a friend in a time of need.

When it became clear that she would be joining the Balmoral trip, Lexi had been relieved at first. Maybe with Isa around, Marc and Effie wouldn't be so interested in her. They'd call the older girl into their rooms, or into their baths, and leave her alone.

Maybe they'd do that.

But it had already left Lexi feeling even more alone, knowing there was one more person here who didn't care about her or anything that was happening to her.

Her mother would be coming to the castle soon. She couldn't tell her mother, of course. She could never tell her mother. She would destroy all her dreams, ruin the idea of being her "little girl," and wreck all the opportunities that her mom had worked so hard to put in front of her—opportunities like a sponsored education at St. Mary's.

No. She wouldn't tell her mother.

She bit into the scone—and almost spit it back out in her hand. It was like a chalky edible rock. Maybe that's why there was so much jam served with them.

Pearson waved off the butler and poured himself a cup of tea.

"What Christmas songs can you play?" he asked Lexi.

She tried to cover her mouth as she replied through a full mouth, "Carol of the Bells?"

He laughed. "Is that a question for me?"

"Sorry. I mean I can play that."

"Would you like to play later, for the prince?"

Her stomach wrenched.

*For the prince. Would you like to do something...for the prince.*

She knew suddenly what was coming—why she'd been brought along to this place. It wasn't just to keep Marc or Effie "company" in the way she'd been doing. They'd also been training her.

Lexi froze halfway through chewing.

"If you want me to," she mumbled.

He stirred a spoonful of sugar into his tea and smiled. "I can't wait to hear it."

"Marc!" came a voice from the doorway.

Pearson turned to see a man stepping into the room. He had thick, wavy dark hair, wore a cable-knit sweater, and sported a pair of Prada glasses.

"Joe!" said Pearson, going to greet him with a hearty handshake. "I didn't know you'd made it here already, with the weather back in the States."

"I wouldn't miss this." He grinned, and then his eyes fell on Lexi. "Hello."

"Ah, Joe, this is Lexi. She's the most amazing young violinist you've ever heard. She'll play for us later."

Lexi gulped down her mouthful of scone. She wished she had a glass of water.

"Lexi," said Pearson, "this is Joe Nassar. He's a tech maverick, startup genius, man for all seasons. He also loves classical music."

Joe extended his hand. She had no choice but to shake it and smile politely.

"Nice to meet you," she said.

"Yeah, likewise. Pleasure. If Marc here says you're good, you must be *really* good."

"Thank you."

To her relief, he turned an excited smile back to Marc. "Is it here yet?"

"Later. Don't worry—you'll be there for it!"

"I'm just excited, man. Ready to see this."

Marc laughed and clapped him on the back. "I told you we should have closed our deal before Christmas. This could have been the celebration party!"

Lexi slipped away to gaze intently at the pictures on the other side of the drawing room.

Maybe there were places to hide in this castle. Maybe there *was* a wardrobe where you could burrow so deeply you'd find a whole new world on the other side of it.

Her daydreaming snapped when Effie's voice came dancing through the room.

"Bertie would like to know who's up for some cross-country skiing!"

She was draped on the arm of their host, Prince Albert himself. He always looked rumpled, even when wearing white tie and tails. Now, in a red sweater and a kilt, he seemed positively woodsy in the laziest of ways.

"We've got a bit of daylight left," he said cheerfully. "Not terribly cold yet. Snow is flawless. We'll gin up a bit of an appetite and indulge ourselves in more gin later!"

His gaze caught Lexi.

"Oh, hello again, my dear. What do you say? Fancy a bit of the outdoors?"

She wanted them all to stop looking at her.

Instead, she said, "Sure, yeah."

Dusk crept over Balmoral like a lilac gray shroud.

Lexi had been fitted with the smallest skis and poles they had available, ones that were used by the eldest royal—the boy who would one day be king. She wondered if he would ever have any idea what had gone on here...the girl who had been brought to the castle and slid across the estate on his skis.

Prince Albert had wrangled Effie and Joe Nassar and one of the officers on his Royal Protective Service detail named George. Lexi tried to stay closest to him.

They circled all the way out to the River Dee, which wound around nearly half the property. The others had just moved on when something tugged at Lexi to linger for a moment.

Despite the echo of Effie's exuberant laugh and Albert's exclamations of where to look next, the world ahead of her had that wonderful muted stillness that only came with snow.

Then, across the bank of the river, appeared a stag.

She had never seen one in real life before. It was gorgeous. He snorted gently and it looked like fog.

Lexi had no phone to take a picture of it. Effie had long ago confiscated it, explaining that privacy was paramount when traveling with someone like Marc Pearson, meeting the people he introduced her to.

She shifted on her skis. The stag looked up at her and froze. She clutched her gloved hands around the poles and stared back at it.

Leave here, she thought. Get away.

"Lexi, darling! Don't lose us!"

Effie's voice shattered the spell. The great animal startled. It bolted, cantering through the snow, away from the banks of Balmoral.

"Coming!" called Lexi.

She slid forward, following in their ski tracks.

By the time the five skiers returned, darkness was nearly upon them.

They came in through the Kitchen Court in the rear wing of the castle, where the small number of staff resided. They shucked their gear and went to freshen up for dinner.

Lexi had been given her own room, more for appearances than anything else. It was next door to Marc and Effie's. Even as she changed out of her damp jeans and sweatshirt, she realized she was tense, holding her breath.

If one or both of them didn't walk through that door right now, it would only be a matter of time. She knew they would come at night. They had every night since that first time in Mallorca.

And then she remembered Prince Albert. She was sure she understood why she'd been brought here. And Joe Nassar?

She gritted her teeth and hurried to pull on navy pants and a white sweater that had a blue snowflake knitted onto the front. Her mother had given it to her for Christmas last year, saying it made her think of "Dance of the Sugar Plum Fairy." It had been their family tradition to see *The Nutcracker* on stage every year. If she hadn't loved the violin so much, Lexi would have liked to be a ballerina, though she thought she could never stay skinny enough to be one of them.

She brushed out her tangled hair and hurried downstairs before anyone could find her in her room.

One of the butlers greeted her politely, giving a dip of the head as she passed. Did they know, too?

Lexi slipped past the drawing room, where she could hear voices inside. She went toward the library.

She slipped through the doorway and stopped suddenly.

Sitting on the couch, in the midst of the rich tapestries and walls packed with old books, was a stranger.

He was probably in his forties, with wisping curly brown hair and a crooked mouth. He wore a thin leather jacket and a scarf draped casually around his shoulders. When he saw her, he smiled, and his mouth became even more crooked.

"Hi."

"Hi," she said.

Her muscles were tight and bunched. She couldn't tell if he was here for why the other men were here, but there was something really unsettling about him.

"I'm Vicente," he said.

His accent was faint Spanish.

"Lexi," she said.

"Lexi...you're the musician?"

She nodded. "I play the violin."

"Ah, I hope to hear you play tonight."

Then she noticed what was on the coffee table in front of him. It was a large circle, gray, with a geometric mess of symbols and letters and shapes carved into it in the smallest detail.

Vicente watched her eyes taking it in.

"You wonder?" he asked.

"What is that?"

"It's the sigil of God."

"Did you make it?"

He smiled. "No, but I'm the only one who can use it."

# CHAPTER
# FIFTY-SIX

**ABERDEENSHIRE, SCOTLAND**

Night fell over the Cairngorms. Two black Land Rover Defenders wound through the mountains.

Tavvie drove one, with Ridley and Iain as passengers. In the second was Odie and their tech man. Both vehicles were loaded with gear, and each towed a trailer with two snowmobiles on it.

They reviewed their logistics and then reviewed them again, talking through potential obstacles and contingency plans.

With half an hour left to the drive, Ridley grew antsy.

For the first time, the thoughts of *what if* nicked at the edge of her mind.

*What if he uses the Devil's Eye? Will we be able to tell? Will the world change? Could we ever undo it?*

*What if Madimi is there...what if she traps you in her cold upside-down hell...*

She needed to stop the thoughts. Putting in a pair of earbuds, she found Muse's "Algorithm" and hit play.

She gazed out the window, lost in the dark rock synth, watching clouds scud across the moon and their shadows swirl on the glowing snow.

At Balmoral, dinner was served at eight. As was custom, each guest changed into formalwear.

Effie had bought Lexi a scarlet dress with white trim. She'd said it was a proper Christmas outfit. She'd said so while standing in the dressing room with her, running her hands along the material...with Lexi in it. Effie had made her model it for Marc later. Marc had made her take it off in front of him.

Now she sat in that dress at the table of a prince, where kings and queens had dined for generations. She'd been seated next to Prince Albert, who wore a dinner jacket and kept leaning into her with side comments he thought were clever, or touching her arm and calling her "love."

The spread in front of them was full of things she'd never even seen in real life. The servers brought out silver platters and bowls of prawns, roasted venison and crispy potatoes, brussels sprouts and chestnuts, turnips and parsnips and cranberry sauce and gravy. She had no appetite for any of it.

Marc was deep in conversation with the man from the library, Vicente. Effie was swiveling her charm effortlessly between the prince and Joe Nassar. Isa sat quietly at the farthest end, picking at her food the way a model would.

The servers had just begun to clear away some of the dishes when the head butler bent discreetly by Albert's ear and said something to him.

"Thank you. Show them into the—uh—the drawing room," said the prince. He dismissed the butler, then turned to his guests. "Well, well, our little party is growing! Marc, your friends have arrived."

Vicente looked at Marc.

Marc Pearson's eyes lit up.

"Tell the one named Bill to wait in the library," he said.

The Land Rovers came up from the south.

They plowed through the dense forest paths and passed onto the private royal property of the British monarch. There was no way to tell the perimeter except by GPS.

Tavvie pulled the team off-road into a clearing by the Princess Alice Memorial. They were a five-minute walk from the castle—enough distance to set up their equipment without noise bleed.

Ridley and Iain followed Tavvie out of the vehicle into the crunching snow. They had dressed for the cold, but not for extremes. They needed mobility inside the castle, so they'd layered carefully. Long underwear, cold-weather boots, thin snow pants, wool and fleece pullovers, trim jackets, and tactical gloves. All of it black.

From the car behind them, Odie walked forward with a man built like a fire hydrant. Eddie Masters wasn't even five and a half feet tall, but walked with a swagger and a scowl to make him seem like the top lad in any gang.

"Put me in, gaffer," he said in the thickest Scottish accent Ridley had ever heard.

Odie checked his phone. "We're five hundred yards."

"My little birdies can go for a mile."

Iain looked at Ridley, and then Tavvie. "Let's unload, then."

They pulled down the snowmobiles first. Then Eddie took several Pelican cases from the trunk. Each had been carefully packed with drones and their attachments. He began to piece together his setup, placing each one in formation, talking to them softly.

The rest of the team brought out their own equipment.

They pulled on light tactical vests, loading them up with tear-gas grenades, small GPS devices, extra ammo, handcuffs, and combat gauze.

As Ridley picked up a rifle she thought was a B&T TP9, she realized that it wasn't the civilian semi-automatic version, but rather the fully automatic military-grade version: the MP9.

*These fellas got the goods in less than twenty-four hours.*
*These are bad men.*

She loaded a thirty-round magazine into it. Screwed on a chunky suppressor. Folded the side-collapsing stock until it became hardly more than a compact handgun.

"Pretty, huh?" Iain said, grinning at her in the faint light of their working lantern.

"It's a party-crasher. Since I'd never get a royal invitation anyway."

They loaded their thigh holsters with SIG Sauer M17s. Iain slid a Gerber Strongarm knife onto his belt. Ridley adjusted the sheath of her karambit.

*Shao's blood—*

She'd cleaned the blade thoroughly, but it never felt like she'd gotten the blood off. She didn't mind.

*Carry the blood of your enemies into every battle.*

They donned their headsets and did a communications check. All was good to go.

Iain shifted so he could lean in close to Ridley's good ear.

"I know Dane is yours."

She didn't look at him, but moved in toward his cheek, speaking so the others couldn't hear. "Most romantic thing anyone's ever said to me. You get Pearson and take him to hell in a handbasket."

They pulled apart and looked at each other. Tavvie, who

was glaring at their private conversation, handed them both the last items of their gear list.

Ridley and Iain fitted the straps of their M50 gas masks to fit, and stashed them away on their snowmobiles.

Then each of them pulled a black balaclava over their face.

# CHAPTER
# FIFTY-SEVEN

### ABERDEENSHIRE, SCOTLAND

MARC PEARSON DIDN'T RUSH to finish dinner. Instead, he seemed superlatively relaxed. He even indulged in the Christmas pudding, which the servers flambéed before serving to the guests. The flames made his grin grow ever wider.

It was Joe Nassar who could hardly wait, fidgeting in his seat and craning his neck to look out into the hall. Effie, who was ever indulging her partner's strange fascinations, was now enjoying her cognac, looking impossibly languid in the velvet dress she was wearing. Prince Albert—surprisingly for someone so gangly—loved his food. He had two helpings of the Christmas pudding and a side of mince pie.

When the servers brought out drinks, Marc asked for a glass of Macallan. Then he told them to pour some brandy for Lexi.

She stared at him. He just smiled back, encouraging her like he was the fun uncle letting her get away with it.

She couldn't say no, so she took a sip. It was foul. Her face must have given her away, since the grownups laughed at her reaction.

But she thought that if she kept drinking, things later might not feel so bad. So she was determined to finish her glass...and then maybe some more.

Albert called for a glass of brandy to be brought to him in the drawing room, and then he stood up. Everyone else rose immediately to their feet.

Lexi pushed back from the table, nearly spilling her glass.

"Shall we let Marc greet his guests, then?" said Albert.

"Let's go!" said Joe, practically leaping into the hall.

Marc paused at the doorway and beckoned to Vicente, who smiled his crooked smile and went to join the billionaire.

The party moved back to the drawing room. Lexi entered behind Isa, carrying the glass of brandy that was now burning her throat.

Sitting on the couch was a blonde woman in her late fifties with a thickset but angelic face. Lounging on the other end was a skinny guy with pinched features.

When Prince Albert walked in, the woman shot up to her feet. A look of astonishment took her over.

"Your Royal Highness!" she said.

"Hello, there," said Albert with a smile.

The skinny man awkwardly followed her lead, standing up as well.

"Your Highness," said Marc, "may I introduce Professor Lianna Powell—"

She gave a weak curtsy.

"—and this is Mr. Qualley. Sorry, I can't remember your first name...?"

"Alan," said the man in an American accent.

"And this is obviously His Royal Highness Prince Albert, Duke of Edinburgh. Now, if you'll excuse me, I'll be right back."

He beckoned Vicente to go with him. They went into the adjacent library and shut the door.

Effie took her usual social lead. "Well, we've just finished dinner but would you like some tea and cakes?"

"Oh, thank you, I'd love some," said the professor.

"No. Thanks," replied Qualley.

Albert motioned for one of the butlers to see to it.

Lianna looked at Lexi.

Lexi knew that she stood out in this group of adults. She knew the woman would wonder why she was there and who she was related to. The professor glanced down at the snifter glass in her hand full of dark liquid, and then back up to meet her eyes.

Lexi didn't want to deal with another stranger, another grownup judging her. She looked away.

Joe Nassar piped up enthusiastically. "So, are you guys the ones who found the gem?"

Lianna hesitated. "Ehm..."

"Go on then," said Albert.

He lowered himself into a grand armchair and looked expectantly at his guests.


Ridley, Iain, Odie, and Tavvie pulled on their snowmobile helmets. They mounted up and started the vehicles. They were electric, which made them heavy but quiet. Quiet and concealment were what they needed. There would be no headlights tonight.

*Thank God for the moon and its great amplifier: that winter wonderland.*

Tavvie took the lead as the four furrowed through the snow, weaving around tree trunks and ducking low branches.

The lights of Balmoral appeared like tiny beacons twinkling in the distance. They were approaching on the north side—as close as they could get to the castle while still under cover of the woods.

"Eye in the sky," Ridley called into her comms, "are you airborne?"

"Fly, my pretties," said Eddie over the radio.

The small fleet of drones rose into the night sky and vanished over the treetops.

From his setup in the back of one of the Land Rovers, he captained their flight. He sat in front of a series of video monitors, clutching at a handheld that looked like a video game controller.

"They're informants. They're spies. They're couriers. They're even little kamikaze pilots," he said over the comms.

The video feed on each one was virtually the same. They saw the long lawn of the Balmoral grounds...and then the castle came into view.

"I keep 'em in formation—flyin' on a single pilotin' system—'til they're ready to go their own ways. See, here we are. Time to break off, little birdies."

Everything he did next seemed perfectly orchestrated. Eddie sent one drone high over the royals' wing of the castle.

He directed another to hover over the servants' wing of the castle.

He sent one to scope out the farthest wing—the ballroom.

He kept another in reserve, stalling it over the nearest treeline.

He sent the last drone to track a slow, repeating path along the garden. This one stayed at a distance from the castle, but it went low enough to read the thermal outlines of anyone inside the entrance hall, the library, the drawing room, and the billiards room.

"Bloody shitstains," he muttered. "There are a lot of people in this place."

Tavvie pulled to a stop amidst the trees, fifty yards from the nearest wing of the castle. They had all heard Eddie's declaration over comms.

"How many is 'a lot?'" asked Ridley.

"I got three in the billiards room. Three in the library, and… seven in the drawin' room."

*That's almost exactly what we gamed out, dumbass.*

"And there's some activity in the dinin' room. Probably staff, lots o' movement in and out. Clearin' dinner, I'd wager."

"Copy that," said Ridley.

She killed the snowmobile engine and pulled off her helmet. The others did the same.

"Can't go through the ballroom," Iain said, muffled through his balaclava. "Takes us down the same corridor as the staff comin' from the dining room."

"Who do we think the three in the billiards room and the three in the library are?" said Ridley.

"RPS boys in the billiards room," said Odie. "Bet my life. They've got used to entertainin' themselves in rich houses. Love a game of billiards."

"Okay," said Iain. "Library? Not touchin' that guess."

Even in this near-darkness, he could see Ridley's eyes glitter.

"Something wicked this way comes," she said.

Eddie's voice came through their earpieces. "Wait now… library's clearin' out. Those three are headin' back into the drawin' room."

. . .

All eyes turned to Marc Pearson as he emerged from the library. Behind him, Vicente was carrying out a large circular disk, the strangely marked one that Lexi had seen on the coffee table.

The third guy with them was the most tense and intense man that Lexi had ever seen. He was fairly plain—maybe a little handsome—but looked like he could tear through a door with his teeth.

"Gang," said Marc, "meet Bill. The man whose work has brought us all to this room, for this moment."

Bill gave a brisk nod, paying no more attention to the prince than to anyone else. Then he planted himself in a corner, his back against the wall.

Vicente placed the giant wax disk on the coffee table. He knelt in front of it.

"Professor Powell," said Marc, "why don't you tell the rest of the guests here what this is."

She stood up from the couch. She needed to feel more comfortable, like she was addressing a classroom.

"It's called the Sigillum Dei," she said. "It means 'Seal of God' and it was created by John Dee as a—a *magical* diagram. The names of God and the angels are inscribed on it. The instructions to create it were given to Dee through his scryer, who said he received them from the angels he'd summoned."

"Thank you, Lianna. Would you also tell everyone what it does?"

"Oh, well...when used correctly—read properly through a scryer—John Dee believed that it would imbue him with all the knowledge of God and the cosmos...that he could become the Spirit of God, able to speak with the spirits and the archangels. And control various aspects of light and other people, but that's —that was less clear through his writings."

Marc smiled at her, that disarmingly real grin. "Thanks for

that. You're a very good teacher. Tell us one last thing, though: how does one properly read into the power of the Sigillum?"

Her eyes stayed fixed on Marc Pearson, as though the gravity of what she was saying was sinking in for the first time.

"Someone would have to use the Devil's Eye. You'd have to look through it to read the symbols, to...unlock the seal."

From his pocket, Marc drew out a stone. It looked like a drop of water as big as his palm.

Joe Nassar bent over to see it up close. Prince Albert leaned forward in his chair to peer at the strange object. Effie regarded it, and then her partner. He finally had his prize in hand.

Lexi couldn't believe that something so dull-looking could be the key to anything.

Vicente beckoned Marc Pearson to kneel across the table from him.

"Place it in the center," he said.

Marc put the Devil's Eye on the Sigillum Dei. Vicente placed his fingers atop Marc's, to guide the stone without touching it.

He leaned over and stared into it.

## CHAPTER
# FIFTY-EIGHT

**ABERDEENSHIRE, SCOTLAND**

THE ENTIRE ROOM seemed to hold its breath.

Vicente peered so closely into the Devil's Eye that his eyelids brushed it. He moved it in widening circles on the wax seal, tracking the rings of its design. He began muttering under his breath.

Lexi, clutching her glass with white knuckles, took a slow step forward.

"Semeliel...Nogahel...Corabiel..."

But then Vicente jerked back so suddenly that nearly everyone else jumped. He stared across the table at Marc, stricken.

"It's not for me," he said in a strangled voice. "She wants you."

Marc's eyes went wide. Effie had never seen him hesitate before.

But he leaned forward.

Marc looked down through the Devil's Eye...and his breath caught in his throat.

He whispered one word, "Yes."

Then he rose to his feet as though he was a puppet being pulled. He looked to his left, toward the library. All eyes followed his.

There, emerging from the doorway, was a shadow.

Vicente's jaw went slack. Effie stiffened in her chair. The prince reeled back. Isa looked quickly from the shadow to her boss then back to the shadow. Lianna gaped at it. Dane stared like he could force it back with his gaze.

"What the fuck—" said Joe Nassar, stumbling backward.

Lexi glanced at the door into the hallway. This felt very bad.

The shadow drifted forward, but then it thickened.

It moved toward Marc Pearson.

*What he saw was nothing of darkness, nothing of shadow.*

*Before him stood a young woman so beautiful that the sight made him tremble. She couldn't have been more than sixteen, radiant, with sleek eyes and elegant cheekbones and glossy raven hair. She wore a silky, sheer white gown that flowed as if she was a Greek goddess. And her smile was a temptation all of its own, an invitation on parted lips.*

*She sauntered toward him.*

Every other pair of eyes in that drawing room watched this pillar of darkness. It seemed to *eat* the light. And it was approaching Marc Pearson.

The terrible feeling in Lexi's stomach began to thrash. Everyone else seemed transfixed.

*The woman glided in, closer and closer, until she was only inches away from his face. He had never believed in angels until this moment.*

*Her eyes carried the galaxies in them. She* was *radiance.*

"Who..." *he began, but there was no need to finish.*

*She never spoke. Her lips never moved. Yet she said* "MADIMI."

*Then the angel lifted her hands—*

"Madimi," he said.

—*and placed them on his cheeks.*

Everyone in that room heard Marc Pearson murmur the word "Madimi." Then he was engulfed by the black mass.

*Her face came apart in shreds—as if it was being ripped to pieces by invisible claws. He screamed but no sound came from his throat. He couldn't back away as he watched her flesh stripping off only inches from him.*

*Her jaws seperated, her mouth like an open grave. Her hair incinerated. The bits of flesh became black and floated upward. Every piece of beauty and glory sloughed off. What was left was a creature...mottled ashen limbs...a cratered chest...wrinkled flesh on its wedge of a skull...a flat stump where the nose should have been...thick rows of jagged teeth...and a pair of massive, wide-set eyes that glowed like amber lit from within.*

*The angel touching his face had become a demon clutching his head.*

Ridley, Tavvie, Ocie, and Iain broke from the woods on foot, each wearing a gas mask.

They moved single file along the darkened windows of the ballroom, toward the royal wing. Just as they reached the hall passage that connected the two, Ridley pulled them up short with a raised fist. They were well out of sight of any of the rooms that had thermal images in them.

"Magic Eye," she said quietly into her comms, "drop the beat."

"Copy that," came Eddie's voice.

The drone hovering high over the royal wing nearly dropped out of the sky, but came to a soft landing in the snow of the inner courtyard.

It was a cell signal jammer, so high-powered that it would kill cell phone signals for a hundred yards in all directions.

"We're jammin' now," said Eddie.

"Copy."

No one in this castle would be able to use their mobiles. Though a traditional land line was always kept at Balmoral, it would require knowing where each physical phone was located and standing still in those places long enough to use them.

*And knowing the actual damn number of somebody who could reach this place before we ghost.*

Ridley motioned the go-ahead.

The room watched in dread suspense as the black pillar of shadow disappeared *into* Marc Pearson. He stood crunched up at the shoulders, absolutely still.

For a full four seconds...nobody moved.

And then Pearson shuddered.

He turned around—and his eyes were too bright. He smiled —and his smile was too wide. There was something eerily too much, as if his eyes were lit from behind and his mouth had grown an inch wider.

"Marc..." said Effie, who was on her feet now. "Darling..."

"You all right then?" Prince Albert ventured.

"Immaculate," said Pearson, but his voice was too sonorous.

Joe Nassar gave him a skeptical eye. "Really? You look...you look a little high, man. I dunno what shadow drug you just inhaled, but—"

He lost his sentence when he glimpsed Vicente.

The scryer was still kneeling on the floor before the Sigillum Dei and the Devil's Eye. He was staring at Pearson in abject terror.

Joe looked back up to see the billionaire's eyes fixed on him.

"Double-crosser," came the strange new voice.

"What?" said Joe, a flush of fear rising in his cheeks.

"I know what you did. I know why you haven't agreed to close our deal. I know you, *Judas*."

"I didn't—I haven't signed anything with anybody else!"

Pearson moved too fast. He was in front of Joe Nassar before the man had time to react—snatching the collar of his sweater with both hands.

The sudden violence alarmed everyone, except for Dane. He stood in the corner, coiled tight, watching for the next move from either man.

But he could never have seen it coming.

Pearson's jaws distended—his teeth flashed jagged—and his head shot forward.

He bit Joe Nassar's face off.

From brow to chin, the entire front half of the man's head was gone. His body collapsed, his skull a bloody crater of bone and brain.

Lexi fell backward. Her glass of brandy hit the carpet as screams ripped through the room.

# CHAPTER
# FIFTY-NINE

**ABERDEENSHIRE, SCOTLAND**

The garden entrance door was a simple lock pick.

The tricky part was how it opened into a vestibule, and immediately to the right was the billiards room. That door was ajar.

Ridley crept in, her gas mask firmly affixed. She pulled the pin of a tear gas grenade and rolled it through the cracked doorway.

*Sorry, boys. This one is the devil's smoke.*

She pulled back as the rest of the team—all wearing masks—poured into the vestibule, stacking into position along the wall.

Gas began to stream and billow from the billiards room. The coughs were almost instant, with calls of confusion and alarm.

The optimal window of attack was small. They needed the tear gas to have taken its full, brutal effect, but also needed to retain the element of surprise. Dynamic entry.

Ridley motioned: *GO.*

They swarmed into the room, rifles raised.

The three officers of the Royal Protective Service were doubled over, hacking and coughing, their eyes squinted shut, mucus streaming from their noses. Tavvie, Odie, and Iain each stepped up to a man, drew a syringe from their vests, and popped the cap. They stabbed their needles into the agents' necks.

Each of them slumped to the floor.

It was dangerous. If enough mucus built up while they were unconscious and their reflexes dulled, they could suffocate.

*Better than executing these cops who were only doing their shitty jobs.*

Ridley was just turning to the door that joined the drawing room when she heard the screams.

---

Joe Nassar's body twitched once, blood trickling down from his cratered face toward the carpet.

There was pandemonium.

Albert reeled back in utter horror, clutching at Isa beside him.

"Officers! Officers!" he called to his RPS detail next door.

Effie was frozen, staring at Pearson in shock, as though he was a mythical creature.

Dane recovered from the stun, but he'd been disarmed at the entrance. He grabbed the nearest chair to use as a shield-barrier.

Qualley leapt from the couch toward the door, while Lianna scurried behind it to hide.

Still in front of the coffee table on his knees, Vicente looked up at Pearson like he was a god. He bowed and seemed to be worshipping him.

Lexi bolted for the door.

. . .

Ridley slid into the hallway, her MP9 raised. Behind her, the guys re-stacked into position along the wall. They swept down the wide gallery corridor, closing in on the door to the drawing room, when someone burst out into the hallway.

*Lexi.*

The girl caught sight of the black-clad team gliding down the hallway, guns bristling. Her look of panic became bewilderment. Ridley pulled off her gas mask, lowered the barrel of her rifle, and motioned for Lexi to take cover behind an oversized statue of King Malcolm.

The girl huddled behind it just as Qualley came running out into the corridor.

*Not you, fucker.*

Ridley fired off a triple burst—the suppressed rounds sounding like nothing more than loud snaps—hitting Qualley in the back of his legs.

He spasmed forward with a cry of pain and fell to the floor.

Desperate for his RPS officers, Prince Albert yanked Isa with him toward the door that joined the drawing room to the billiards. Just as he went to rip it open, they noticed a white smoke seeping under the door. Both began to cough, quickly racked with violent hacking and tearing eyes. Albert collapsed on the nearby armchair. Isa slipped into unconsciousness.

Dane realized what was now flowing into the room. He pulled up his shirt to cover his mouth and nose.

Pearson turned to Effie.

"If you could see what I see," he said in his newly rich voice.

"Marc, are you...what was that thing?"

He smiled with those eerie glowing eyes. "An angel who's

been waiting hundreds of years for this. *She* has all the knowledge of good and evil and all of humanity. She is the god I've been waiting for."

As his back was turned, Lianna crept out on all fours from behind the couch. She spotted the Devil's Eye lying on the table. Vicente was still kneeling beside it, but he looked like a man in full hypnosis, oblivious to everything but Pearson.

She leaned in, slid her hand across the Sigillum Dei, and nabbed the stone.

Effie was slack-jawed, looking at Marc, her eyes shining, but it was as much from fright as fascination.

"Is she—possessing you?" she said.

"She's giving me the power of a god."

Dane was overhearing this. He had not signed up for it. He wanted to see his boss satisfied with the delivery, get paid, and get out. He had succeeded. His work was done.

Now he needed to get away from the billiards end of the room where tear gas was trickling in, and past his employer who had just bitten off a man's face.

He set down the small wooden chair he'd been holding and stomped on the legs as hard as he could. They splintered apart. He grabbed the biggest piece, a shard with a knife-like point.

"There's nothing anyone can keep from me anymore," Pearson said to Effie, "and so I know who entered this house tonight to try to stop me."

While the others covered for him, Odie knelt to check the squirming, groaning Qualley for weapons. He had none.

From yards away, Ridley could see Lexi overwhelmed, almost frozen.

"Lexi, we're gonna help you," she said. "What happened in there?"

"There was a shadow thing that went into him, and then he bit off someone's face. His whole face," said Lexi.

*What the shit—*

"He's already used it," said Iain from the rear.

They flanked the drawing room door.

---

Pearson took Effie's hands.

She gasped. She couldn't tell if his touch was burning hot or searing cold.

"Follow me now," he said.

And in his gaze, she was transfixed. She knelt down in front of him, gazing upward.

Out of the corner of her eye, she saw Lianna sneaking out of the drawing room.

Of course, Pearson knew. He swiveled his head—too far, inhumanly far—and saw the professor slipping through the door into the library.

"She has my eye," came his deep grumble.

Pearson crossed the room to the library—

—straight into the line of sight for Ridley, who was crouched in the hallway along the doorframe.

The billionaire stepped right into her sights.

*Boom, motherfu—*

She pulled the trigger. A triple burst exploded from the barrel—

But hit nothing. He was simply not there anymore.

*Not possible...not possible. I have the reflexes of a street cat.*

She heard Tavvie curse incredulously behind her. Then she felt a cold trickle up the back of her scalp. In front of her eyes, the drawing room seemed to flicker with eerie bluish-gray light.

*NO. She's here—Madimi is here.*

"Steel!" she yelled out Iain's codename. "Target's in the library!"

Iain was the closest team member to the hallway's library entrance.

"Moving now!" he called back.

He motioned for Odie to move with him. The former cop nodded—but then his eyes shot up—something down the hallway.

One of the RPS officers had stumbled into the hallway thirty yards away, gagging and spitting. He was clutching a gun, lifting it up—

Odie raised his rifle and unleashed a barrage. The man jerked as the bullets ripped into his torso. He fell dead.

"Shit!" exclaimed Odie. "Are they all awake?!"

They'd drugged the officers to avoid killing them. No longer.

Tavvie stepped into the drawing room, rifle raised, doing a quick read. There was a dead body on the floor. Vicente was climbing up from his knees by the coffee table. The prince was bent over, still coughing. Effie was beginning to gag on the gas trails.

Then from inside the doorframe, a dagger of splintered wood swung around and stabbed deep into Tavvie's bicep.

He grunted in pain, while Dane wrenched the barrel of Tavvie's rifle sideways. As Tavvie stumbled, he tripped over Ridley behind him, knocking her to the ground.

Dane was shockingly quick—ripping the SIG Sauer from Tavvie's holster and barreling out into the hallway—

Ridley scrambled to her feet, her vision narrowing on Dane. A few yards down the hall, Iain and Odie clutched their rifles at their shoulders—but they hesitated.

If they shot, they might hit Ridley. If she shot, she might hit them. She might hit Lexi, still huddled under the statue behind them. Crossfire was deadly.

Dane was surrounded. There was no way to win this shootout, but their second of hesitation was all he needed.

With Tavvie's SIG in hand, he bolted up the staircase across the hall, shooting backward.

Ridley fired at the stairs, but he'd already sprinted around the corner banister.

She leaned over to check on Tavvie, whose upper arm was pouring blood. He was trying to clamp it with his other hand.

*That's too much blood...*

*Dane is getting away—*

*That's an artery, Samaras!*

"Shit," she muttered, yanking a tourniquet from his vest pocket.

"Ah," he mumbled, "my biceps must have got too big."

He started to get to his feet, but Ridley pinned him back. "Hold still."

"Where's Pearson?" said Iain.

"He disappeared!" she shouted back.

The library door burst open, and Lianna Powell stumbled into the hallway.

"Down!" said Odie.

He lunged forward and shoved her down to the floor, despite her stammering protests.

As Ridley affixed the tourniquet as high as she could on Tavvie's arm, she looked back at Lianna with fury.

"Where's the Eye?" she yelled.

"He has it—"

"Who's 'he?'"

"It's Dane," she lied. "Bill Dane's got it."

"Go," said Iain. "We'll get Pearson."

Ridley twisted the tourniquet tight, secured the rod in place, and grabbed her rifle.

She sprinted up the stairs after Dane.

# CHAPTER
# SIXTY

**ABERDEENSHIRE, SCOTLAND**

While Odie kept his post in the hallway, Iain swept into the library.

It was empty. He pushed through the half-open door into the drawing room, the MP9 pulled tight to his shoulder.

There was tear gas still leaking in at the far end. Prince Albert was just starting to recover, though his eyes and nose were still pouring. Vicente was mumbling some kind of prayer, his eyes closed. Effie was trying frantically to make a call on her cell phone.

Rage surged up in Iain's chest. He charged toward her, his rifle bristling.

"Where is he?!" he roared.

She startled. When she met his eyes, he saw nothing of the coy gloating predator he'd encountered at the ball in Vienna. She looked demolished and deeply scared. She also didn't recognize Iain behind the balaclava. Only his eyes burned clear through the face covering.

"I don't know," she whispered. "It's not him anymore. There's something *in* him."

Iain growled at her. He didn't care what was *in* Pearson—the man would pay in the flesh for all he'd done.

But then he spotted Albert behind her, going for the desk.

"Oh, my God," sputtered the prince, trying to clear his eyes. "Where's Terry…"

He was trying to ring for the butler. Iain leveled the rifle at him.

"Don't touch that!"

But the prince didn't seem to hear or understand. He was fumbling toward the call button. Iain lunged forward and cracked him on the head with the butt of his gun. Albert howled and staggered backward.

"Don't touch it!" yelled Iain.

He yanked the cord from the wall.

All that really mattered now was finding Pearson.

He moved toward the billiards room and pulled open the door. The smoke was dissipating, but the two officers inside were still unconscious. They were luckier than the third, who'd woken up to a hail of bullets…

But no Pearson.

Iain swept through the rest of the room and out into the hall.

No Pearson.


Ridley reached the second floor.

There was no sign of Dane. She steadied her breathing, scanning up and down the hallways. There was no way to tell even which way he'd gone.

The way the balaclava pressed against her mouth felt stifling.

*He couldn't have made it up to the third floor without me hearing his steps.*

But choosing which way to go was as good as a coin flip. She picked a direction and padded slowly down the carpet, doing a quick clear of every room along the way.

*This devil's shit-rag likes an ambush...*

Otto's bloody blond hair flashed across her vision.

Ridley clutched the rifle tightly. She prowled forward.

Downstairs in the drawing room, Effie was trembling in frustration. She cursed her phone and hurled it to the ground. It hit the carpet near Joe Nassar's mutilated head, and she clutched at her mouth to fight down nausea.

Then her eyes landed on the Sigillum Dei. It lay on the table like a harmless gob of flattened wax. Except now, she hated it.

She glanced about. Only Vicente and Albert and the unconscious Isa were left in the room with her. The scryer looked like he was in a world of his own hypnotized making. Albert was a scolded, miserable man, trying to recover himself after being cracked in the skull by Iain.

Perhaps if the great wax seal was destroyed, the portal to this "other world" would be destroyed. Whatever was here would be crushed into oblivion. Marc would return to himself. Perhaps.

She picked it up, awkwardly at first. It was heavier than she'd thought, but she carried it to the fireplace.

Hesitating, she looked into the flames. What else could she do?

She tossed the Sigillum Dei onto the fire.

It had just crunched onto the hot coals when she felt a shockwave nearly bowl her over.

Pearson was suddenly beside her. She yelped in surprise.

"What are you doing," he said.

"Marc...you don't need this anymore. We have a good life, don't we? We don't need this trouble—"

She couldn't be sure if she even saw him move, though it would have been one of the last things she ever saw. Suddenly there was a rippling hot coal in each of his palms.

He raised his hands and smashed them into her eyes.

She screamed and screamed.

---

At the sound of bloodcurdling shrieks, Iain rushed back into the drawing room. From the other end, Odie burst in, rifle at the ready.

Effie was alone, crumpled on her knees in front of the fireplace, two coals burning holes in the carpet near her. She was wailing in pain and holding both hands over her face.

The smell of burnt flesh singed their nostrils.

"Did she fuckin' do that to herself?" exclaimed Odie.

Iain whipped about, certain that it had been Pearson, but how the *hell* he was teleporting here and there was maddening.

Odie spotted Albert trying to escape into the billiards room.

"Stop!" he shouted.

The prince only sped up. Odie flew across the room and hurled him to the floor. He yanked out a pair of handcuffs, snapped one onto Albert's wrist and the other around the leg of a desk.

"He's got to be around here somewhere," said Iain. "Come on!"

"I've gotta bind up the rest of the RPS," said Odie, "or we'll have more problems in a minute."

"A'right, go."

As Odie headed into the billiards room, Iain rushed back into the hall, stopping over Tavvie.

The giant of a man was slumped against the doorframe, soaked in his own blood and holding the tourniquet. He'd taken it off somehow, and he was soaked in blood.

"What the hell have you done?" said Iain, kneeling down.

"It was too tight..." he mumbled.

He glanced around. Lexi was behind the statue, her knees drawn up tight, her eyes wide, trying to become invisible. He knew the feeling.

"It's okay, it's gonna be okay," Iain said to her.

She met his pleading look, but couldn't respond.

Then Iain spotted Lianna. She was nearly to the front door.

"Powell!" he thundered. "Stop. Stop or I'll fuckin' shoot you, I swear."

He aimed his rifle at her back. He could have shot her there. He could have. She'd destroyed and double-crossed them. They were only here in this bloodbath because of her betrayal.

But she stopped, raised her hands, and turned to face him.

"Okay, all right," she said softly.

"Come back here!"

She shuffled toward him, looking as meek as a middle-aged professor could. Iain pulled the handcuffs from Tavvie's tactical vest.

"Put these on, you fuckin' Jezebel."

He tossed them at her. She did as told, and looked even more pathetic for it.

"Sit down with your back against this wall and do not fuckin' move!"

Lianna complied.

Iain stood up. Out of the corner of his eye, he saw a light flash. He turned to the window that overlooked the inner courtyard.

The outdoor lights had flooded on, and standing there in

the middle of the snowy yard was Marc Pearson. He wasn't moving. It was as though he was waiting for someone.

"Where's the door outside?" shouted Iain, not taking his eyes off the billionaire. "Where is it?!"

"It's there, I think," said Lexi.

She was pointing down the adjoining hallway.

Iain ran to it.

# CHAPTER
# SIXTY-ONE

**ABERDEENSHIRE, SCOTLAND**

Ridley passed dark bedrooms, closed doors, and empty parlors on her way through the halls of Balmoral Castle.

*Where are you—where are you—*

She padded down the corridor, the carpet muffling her footsteps.

Then she heard a sound a few yards ahead.

It was unmistakably the whine of a floorboard, and it had come from one of the rooms on the left.

She moved down the hallway, her finger resting heavy on the trigger of the MP9. As she slid in front of one of the darkened bedrooms, there was a flash of movement to her right.

Ridley darted into the room for cover as bullets exploded the doorframe around her—

She swiveled around the edge of it and unleashed a barrage toward Dane.

He was hiding around the corner in the next hallway, out of reach. He shot back, forcing her into the room again for cover. A china vase nearby shattered.

*Suppressive fire for himself means he's moving—GO.*

She broke from the bedroom, rushed down the hall, and flattened herself against the L-shape of the wall.

Dodging a look out, she saw Dane backpedaling, his gun raised.

Ridley loosed a triple burst at him—

One of the bullets nicked his upper thigh as he bolted into one of the open rooms.

It was a deadly game to be in the open, chasing after a bunkered opponent, but their time in the castle was running out. There was no other way than to hunt him down.

*All he took was Tavvie's sidearm. He has no extra ammo.*

*No reloads.*

*Only seventeen rounds.*

Dane swung the M17 around the corner and unloaded another two shots.

*He must have realized that, too. He's conserving bullets now.*

She closed in on the room, every muscle coiled, her vision sharpening. The balaclava was stifling her breathing. She tore it off.

Then she realized she had one tear gas grenade left in her tac vest...but she'd left behind her own gas mask.

*Risk it, Samaras. He's in a closed space.*

She crouched down, grabbed the grenade and pulled the pin. She hurled it around the corner, into the room where Dane was taking cover. Then she snatched her rifle up and backed away.

The gagging smoke began to seep out into the hallway... forcing Ridley back even farther. She kept her sights on the doorway, but something was wrong.

*Why isn't he coughing?!*

The door beside her burst open—

*It was an adjoining room—*

She couldn't swing the barrel of the rifle around to get sight on him—it was just inches too long for these close quarters. He wrenched the barrel away, ripping it from her hands.

As he held up the SIG to fire into her chest, she clamped her own hands around his, pushing it aside—

He yanked to pull her off of it—she let go with one hand and pulled out her own M17—

The barrel of his pistol swung wildly. He shot—

Heat seared the edge of her shoulder.

She swiveled her own barrel up to his gut, but he grappled it away—

She smashed her forehead into his nose—

Dane grunted as bone and cartilage crunched and blood spewed from his nostrils. He rammed a knee up into her stomach.

They both stumbled backward—Dane into the room, Ridley down the hall.

The tear gas was blooming toward them.

She reached to find her fallen rifle, but the smoke had clouded over it. She couldn't get to it without incapacitating herself. The chemicals were already starting to sting her eyes and scratch her throat.

Dane couldn't stay where he was either, or the gas would overtake him.

Ridley scrambled back just as he stepped around the corner and fired—she leapt into the open room across the hall—

And heard his slide lock back.

*He's out of ammo.*

*Now he gets desperate-dangerous.*

*The gas will force him this way.*

Lying on her back on the floor, Ridley aimed up at the doorway.

. . .

Iain burst out into the courtyard, his rifle raised.

Pearson stood there, ankle-deep in the snow, expecting him.

"Look at me!" Iain roared. "You coward, pig-fucking scum!"

The billionaire turned. Against the darkness behind him, his strange eyes were glowing even brighter.

"You've been wanting me for a long time," he said.

Iain knew Pearson's voice, and this was not it. This was like the voice of Shere Khan undergoing an exorcism.

But this was still the man he'd been hunting for years, whose trails of human wreckage and anguish he'd tracked with a heartrending fury.

Now face to face, and it was Iain who had the weapon.

He advanced on Pearson, stepping down into the snow. His trigger finger felt almost possessed of its own will, straining for the barrage of murder it could unleash in a second.

"You will transfer a sum fee right now to a bank account I give you. A Christmas gift," he spat, "for Lexi *and* her mother."

"Oh?" Pearson chuckled. "How much do you think a little girlish whoring is worth?"

Iain snapped. He lunged forward—he would have speared the barrel of his rifle into the man's eye and pulled the trigger—

But it was exactly what Pearson was expecting, and he was inhumanly fast.

He sidestepped, clinched the back of Iain's head with one hand and hooked an arm over the barrel of the MP9. He drove a knee up into Iain's solar plexus—knocking the wind out of him—and ripped the rifle away.

Iain staggered, gasping, but was already drawing his SIG M17 sidearm. Without losing a moment, he aimed and—

Pearson shot first with the rifle he now held, hitting Iain's hand on the meaty outer section.

Iain barked in pain, dropping his own gun—catching it underneath with his other hand, and firing.

But Pearson seemed to disappear before the bullet had even left the barrel. He reappeared next to Iain and shot the pistol out of his second hand.

It wasn't possible, but somehow he was doing it.

Iain ripped the Gerber Strongarm blade off his belt and slashed—

Pearson dodged it, smiled and ejected the magazine from the rifle. He tossed it across the courtyard, then fired the last bullet into Ian's shin.

He howled in pain and collapsed into the snow.

Ridley lay on her back, aiming past her own feet, her throat beginning to burn and char...waiting for Dane.

She heard him cough, then cough again.

Then he leapt across the doorway in a flash.

She squeezed off two shots—both missed.

Ridley scrambled to her feet and rushed into the corridor—

Dane was lying on his back, empty SIG still in hand. He kicked out, ramming a heel into her knee, jolting her back.

He hurled the empty M17 at her head—its steel edge striking her brow—

Just as she was recovering her aim, he was on her—rising to his knees, both hands locked around hers, trying to muscle the gun from her.

*A damned pitbull—*

She wrenched the barrel just forward enough—and pulled the trigger.

The bullet tore into his collarbone. His grunt of pain was intense.

But her slide had locked back.

She tried to grab an extra magazine from her vest, but Dane bulled into her, lifting both legs clean off the ground.

She slammed to the floor. He landed on top, nearly knocking the wind out of her.

Ridley rammed the butt of her pistol into his temple. He screamed in pain and cracked an elbow down onto her face.

Her vision exploded white—

As she fought off the stun, he tore the empty gun from her hand, sat up on her stomach and reached for one of the extra magazines in her vest—

She bucked *hard*, throwing him forward over her head—

As he was forced to brace on both hands, she wriggled out beneath his legs and leapt onto his back—snaking an arm around his neck—

Dane pulled at it, writhing, slamming her against the wall—

She held on for her life, trying to tighten it into a strangle—

But he was going berserk for *his* life, and finally bashed her so hard into the edge of a high table that she felt a rib crack.

Her grip slipped...but as she went, she raked a finger into the bullet wound on his collar.

He shrieked and hurled her to the floor.

Ridley scrabbled to her feet, breathing hard. She pushed her hair out of her eyes.

Dane was staggered.

*A wounded animal...*

She yanked the Boker Magnum Spike from her belt.

*You're a fucking wounded animal, too, Samaras.*

She launched forward.

He had no weapons left in his hands—but he had surely seen the knife in hers. Dane blocked with his forearms, taking the first slice, then batted her away.

He grabbed the wrist of her knife hand—she grabbed the

handle with her other hand to reinforce her grip—and carved up into his armpit.

His clothes were soaked with his own blood. Her hands were slick with it.

Dane finally locked on both her wrists, gripping them like a vice, tightening—

They were face to face, breathing ragged—

He lunged his head in toward her neck and *bit down.*

She yelled in pain as his teeth pierced the skin, madly trying to wrest her hands free from him—

With a last wriggle, she got one hand loose—enough to swing the karambit blade around the handle ring on her forefinger—it sliced deep into his wrist, forcing him to break his bite—

And just as he drew back, she lunged—

Ridley stepped one leg between his and dropped to the ground, hooking his ankle as she went—tripping and dragging him down into a bloody tangle.

From the bottom, he slammed another elbow into her jaw, rattling her skull—

He rolled her over to end up on top and pinned the wrist of her knife hand to the floor.

She reached for it with her other hand, peeled his pinkie away and cranked his wrist so violently that his entire arm twisted and he cried out—

And Ridley stabbed the karambit into his jugular.

Blood erupted from his throat, drenching her.

She hooked the curved blade deeper and farther, until it yanked on his jawbone, until his eyes rolled back in his head and blood dribbled from his lips.

"This...for Otto," she hissed.

Dane's full weight collapsed on her.

She rolled him off...drew herself up to her knees...

Ridley stared down at his blood-soaked body and then screamed so hard at it that she bent in two. She rammed the knife into his lifeless chest once more, before finally hauling herself up to stand.

Ridley wiped the sheet of Dane's blood from her face and looked down the hallway, to the stairs.

*Pearson.*

*Iain is going after him.*

# CHAPTER
# SIXTY-TWO

**ABERDEENSHIRE, SCOTLAND**

The snow in the courtyard was spattered with blood.

All of it was Iain's.

Marc Pearson stood over him, empty-handed. He'd tossed away the rifle as a show of total domination. He wouldn't even need it.

Iain was on one knee. His left shin was mangled from the bullet that had blasted through his tibia. His right hand was missing a chunk of flesh and blood dripped down his fingers. His nose was broken and bloody from when Pearson had smashed him in the face with the rifle butt.

And the man standing only a yard away was untouched, radiating an eerie light, with features that were too vivid to be real.

"I thought I could have everything before," said Pearson. "I had no idea how much more there was to have."

"Put her money in the account," muttered Iain.

"Is this how white knights die?"

Iain dropped his head and mumbled something the billionaire couldn't make out, so he took a step closer.

"Did you think if you took these girls away from me that they'd want to sleep with *you?*"

A shudder of rage went through Iain, but he had to keep it under control.

"You may look like the next James Bond, but you lack... everything else," said Pearson. "Mostly, how to get away with it. You *know* deep in your heart that I'll get away with this, right? You know that tonight I'll take Lexi—"

Iain couldn't hear it. He gave the wordless, mad roar of a beast. But then he turned it to a whisper, so weak that the other man couldn't hear what he was saying...

"Speak up."

Pearson took a step closer.

Iain looked up at him.

"I don't lack courage," he said.

He lunged forward and clamped a handcuff around Pearson's wrist. The other end, he slapped onto his own.

The expression of shock on Marc Pearson's face was his reward.

Iain shoved the small set of keys into his mouth and swallowed.

It was the ripple of rage that passed through the possessed man that proved Iain's triumph.

Pearson erupted.

A sound blasted from his lungs, like no earthly noise. His limbs became a frenzy of violence, raining down blows on Iain, thudding against flesh, cracking into bones, battering him down to the ground.

But the more he beat Iain, the more stuck he became, chained to a bloody sack of pulp.

"You'll stop now."

The quiet voice from behind Pearson was so close that at first he thought it was in his own head. He turned.

Into the barrel of a pistol.

Lexi pulled the trigger.

Ridley was limp-racing down the staircase when she heard the crack of a gunshot somewhere outside.

When she reached the first floor, everything became a whirling blur.

She saw Tavvie, slumped against the wall, his skin white, his eyes closed. From the drawing room came the wracking sobs of Effie. Down the hallway, Odie was rushing out of the billiards room, his rifle in one hand as he tore off his balaclava with the other.

"Where are they?" he yelled.

Ridley looked for Lexi where the girl had been sheltering behind the statue of a Scottish king—but she wasn't there.

*Where's Iain—where's Pearson—*

Then she felt a chill draft billow down the corridor, and she remembered the inner courtyard. Ridley ran to the door. It was open.

She burst out into the cold night air.

Lexi stood there over two bodies. The girl was shivering in her Christmas dress. One of their M17s dangled at her side. She was staring down at the red stains in front of her.

*No. No.*

*IAIN.*

Ridley's stomach burned and twisted. She stepped out into the crunching snow.

"Lexi. Lexi!"

*Did she shoot both of them?!*

Lexi turned. If she was horrified at the sight of this woman covered in blood, it didn't show. Still, Ridley tried a soft approach, moving slowly toward the shellshocked girl.

"Lexi...would you give that gun back to me?"

Her voice was hushed but steady. "Yes. I'm sorry."

She held it out to Ridley, who sidestepped the barrel and lifted it from her grasp.

"I stopped him," she said.

"It's okay," said Ridley, putting both hands on Lexi's shoulders and drawing her away from the grisly scene.

"What the hell happ—" exclaimed Odie from the doorway.

"That man's with us," Ridley said to Lexi, desperate to get back to the fallen figures. "He helped us rescue you. His name is Odie. You can go with him and be safe."

Odie beckoned for Lexi, who walked toward him, her gaze still vacant.

Ridley shoved the SIG down into her holster and ran to the bodies.

There was Pearson, near immaculate but for the bullet hole in his forehead and blood spatter on his clothes.

She dropped to her knees in the snow.

*Iain.*

All blood and torn skin and bone sticking out of a crushed leg. Ridley choked back the tide of agony swelling up. She reached for his pulse.

# CHAPTER
# SIXTY-THREE

**ABERDEENSHIRE, SCOTLAND**

It was forty miles from Balmoral Castle to the nearest hospital.

Ridley raced through the snowy hills as fast as the Land Rover could go without spinning off the road. Lexi sat in the front seat, gripping the door handle with white knuckles. Odie sat in the back next to Iain, monitoring his weak vitals, trying to brace his broken body over the bumps.

In the trunk of the SUV, Lianna sat with her hands cuffed. Her mouth was still smeared with dried blood from when Ridley had punched her in the face before shoving her into the stolen vehicle.

They reached the quiet hospital. Ridley and Odie carried the unconscious Iain into the ER, shouting for help.

The orderlies came running. They put him on a gurney and raced off to trauma.

Someone tried to attend to Ridley, whose blood-soaked hair and streaked face looked like the scene of an accident. She shouted at them to get away from her.

She told Odie to go to the vending machine and get water

and snacks and take them out to Lexi. She washed her face in the restroom, then snagged a pencil and a small notepad from the desk when the receptionist had his back turned.

"Iain Carnegie," she wrote. "*36 years old. Gunshot victim with traumatic head injuries and a compound fracture in the tibia. Contact MI5.*"

She slid it across the desk and strode out of the hospital, fighting the urge—the need—to stay with him. The police would doubtless be there soon to investigate the victim of a gunshot.

He had saved Lexi.

Then Lexi had saved herself.

And Marc Pearson would never destroy another life.

---

The officers and medics who arrived at Balmoral Castle that night found a bloodbath. The world would never know of it.

The RPS was dispatched with a commanding officer of the Metropolitan Police's Royalty and Specialist Protection unit. The king received a phone call that night at Sandringham, where he and the rest of his family were expecting his brother Albert the next day.

The Balmoral staff who were in the home that night were gathered for questioning. There was no internal surveillance, so the only clues the police could gather was from one CCTV camera outside. It showed four black-clad figures approaching the house wearing gas masks and carrying rifles.

One of the four was slumped dead in the hallway, having bled out from his brachial artery. He was quickly identified as a member of a well-known criminal organization in Glasgow.

They had shot and killed one of the RPS detail officers outside the billiards room. When the other two revived, they could hardly conceive of what had happened there that night.

An unknown male lay on the floor in the drawing room in a pool of blood, so shockingly mutilated that several of the cops had to turn away to keep from vomiting.

One of the officers recognized the wealthy socialite Ophelia Crowhurst, who was moaning and crying in pain on the floor nearby. Both of her eyeballs had been scalded into her skull.

Prince Albert was blubbering for help in the corner of the room. He was handcuffed to a table leg and his wrists were raw from struggling.

A beautiful young woman with red eyes and a runny nose was huddled on the floor in the corner, rocking back and forth. She had been unconscious, she said. She didn't know what had happened here.

There was another man in the room, almost completely unresponsive. He said a few words in Spanish and then shut down. The only thing remaining was his thousand-yard stare.

The scene on the second floor was something out of a horror film. A geyser of blood had painted the walls and carpet. A man lay there with his throat ripped to pieces, his eyes staring glassy and vacant at the ceiling.

The body in the courtyard was the last to be found. The officer who discovered it called his commander out to see for himself.

It was only when the police commander saw the man's face that he realized how bad this was going to get.

### EDINBURGH, SCOTLAND

Booker arrived in snowy Edinburgh the next day. He met Ridley at a small hotel not far from the university.

He had never seen her so battered. She had bruises on her face, a bandage on her neck, limped slightly, and sucked in sharp jolts of pain every time she moved her torso. She'd bought new clothes for herself and the girl with her, and was now wearing a burgundy sweater over a pair of jeans.

Lexi, in an oversized sweatshirt and woolen socks, was quiet but sharply attentive. She listened to every word between the two, refusing to leave the room without Ridley even to get a snack down the hall.

"Where are the other two team members?" asked Booker, sitting in the desk chair, leaning forward on his knees.

Ridley sat on the edge of the bed across from him. "They left this morning. Got other things to do."

"Untraceable?"

"They'll have nothing to say and nothing on them," she said, her voice hard.

"You saw the news broke an hour ago."

She wiggled her phone and gave a bitter recitation.

"Billionaire financier and tech entrepreneur killed in an electric car crash that resulted in a fire—both were trapped inside and burned to death. They were on their way to Balmoral Castle for a holiday soirée with Prince Albert. He's too upset to speak to the press, of course."

"The Crown takes care of business *quick*," said Booker. "Authorities found the body of a Glaswegian gangster this morning in a snowbank in Aberdeen. Happened to be wearing black tactical gear. Craig McTavish. Known associate?"

Her face tightened but she said nothing.

"Right, I don't want to know," he said.

Ridley glanced at Lexi, who was watching a holiday baking show on the TV, keeping the volume low enough that she could overhear their conversation.

"Her mom is coming today. The only place she wanted to meet her was at the Harry Potter store."

Booker lowered his voice to nearly a whisper. "How is she?"

Ridley cocked her head at her boss with a look, *You should already know the answer. It's unspeakable.*

He gave a heavy nod.

"Have you gotten the hospital to talk to you?"

Her face contorted for only a moment, as though it was about to come undone completely...but she did not let it go.

"His mom and sister and brother got there two hours ago. They're going to hear that he has an epidural hematoma—traumatic brain injury—and that he's in a coma, unresponsive to almost any stimulus. MRIs...are bad."

A tear escaped down her cheek. Booker clamped his hands together as though in silent protest.

"They're gonna move him soon. I've been calling as his cousin," said Ridley, pawing her face dry, "but with his family there now...I'll have to resort to spy stuff."

From across the room, Lexi spoke up. "I don't have my violin. I left it there."

She was looking out the window, to the spires and frosted roofs of Old Town.

"You'll get your violin back," said Booker.

Ridley shot him a look—

"We'll replace that violin," he said.

She didn't respond, but looked back at the TV.

Booker whispered again. "She told you what happened in that room, with the Devil's Eye??"

Ridley nodded.

"And you have it now."

She got up from the edge of the bed, slowing as the pain shot through her, and went to the small closet safe. She punched in the code, opened the door, and pulled out the Devil's Eye.

Booker stared at it. He blew the air out from his cheeks.

"All this...and sometimes it's about nothin' more than a see-through rock," he said.

"I almost smashed it with a hammer."

He gave her a half-amused look of warning.

"I meant I almost wrapped it up in a nice box with a bow on top."

He took it from her, hefting it in his palm. Then he slid it into his deep thigh pocket and zipped it closed.

"What happened to the professor?" he asked.

Ridley glanced at Lexi, then lowered her voice. "I put a gun to her kneecap and made her wire me every last fuckin' cent that Pearson had paid her upfront. And then I dumped her at the train station."

The edge of bitterness in her voice was metallic.

*They said he may never wake up. That even if he did, he might never speak or walk again.*

*If he dies...I'll come back and find her.*

Booker began pulling on his coat.

"Get that girl back to her mother," he said.

"I will."

He palmed a small piece of paper into her hand. "Then come and find me at this address."

# CHAPTER
# SIXTY-FOUR

**EDINBURGH, SCOTLAND**

There was no story Ridley could tell Lexi's mother that would satisfy for long. There was nothing that Lexi could tell her just then that would explain what she'd been through. She couldn't have even if she'd wanted to. Not yet. Not for a while.

But Celia Rapp clutched her daughter in an embrace so desperately tight that it almost seemed like she knew.

Their story—for as long as Lexi needed it to be so—was that Ridley was a second cousin of Marc Pearson's. She'd met Lexi while Pearson and Effie were traveling through London, and agreed to take her Christmas shopping in Edinburgh while the others went to Balmoral Castle.

The bruises on her face? She'd been in a minor skiing accident the week before.

By that time, Celia Rapp had seen the news of the billionaire's death. She had panicked, unable to reach her daughter or Marc Pearson, or his assistant, or Effie Crowhurst. Then Ridley had called her, and her heart could beat again. She could breathe.

They stood on the snowy cobblestone street outside of a shop filled with magical creatures. Ridley watched mother and daughter pull apart from their hug, all weepy smiles of relief.

*It was all about the Devil's Eye for me.*

*For him, this is what it was all about.*

Lexi turned to face Ridley.

It almost hurt to see the openness in those young blue eyes.

"Thank you," said the girl, her voice cracking.

Now it was too much. Lexi threw her arms around Ridley, choking back the tears that were starting to break through.

Ridley felt her eyes begin to sting. She didn't care about the searing pain of her injuries. She wrapped Lexi in a hug so tight that it seemed meant for two.

"I'm so sorry," she whispered.

Lexi whispered, "Thank that other man for me. Please thank him."

## ROXBURGHSHIRE, SCOTLAND

Mother and daughter left Edinburgh on the next flight to the States.

Ridley took a train south. It was getting dark by the time she arrived on the steps of the enormous manor house.

A maid opened the door for her, took her coat, and told her that she was expected.

A fire blazed that evening in the enormous old hearth. The cavernous parlor was decked in garlands and wreaths, candles and baubles and a glittering Christmas tree in the corner.

At the grand piano sat a man in thick-rimmed glasses and a

velvet jacket, his fingers bounding and dancing across the keys. He played to the majestic blonde woman standing by the piano, beaming as she sashayed in place. Diane Bellingsworth looked like the Sugar Plum Fairy in a sparkling white gown, singing and snapping to an upbeat tune of "Have Yourself a Merry Little Christmas."

Her joy was infectious. Half a dozen other guests in fine attire snapped their fingers and moved and sang with her and with each other. There were half-eaten plates of biscuits and petits fours on side tables, glasses of mulled wine and champagne and brandy being lifted.

Ridley, dressed to match the mood in a fresh pair of evergreen slacks and a white cashmere sweater, reclined on an armchair, one leg draped over the other. A champagne flute dangled between her fingers as her gaze roamed about. She didn't know another soul here except for the man on the sofa across from her, his broad shoulders barely constrained by an elegant black jacket.

Booker caught her eyes and smiled. He took a swig of his mulled wine.

*Whatever possessed him to invite me to his friend's manor house for a pre-Christmas Eve party, he was right.*

It was all...perfect. Almost perfect.

For one second—just a flash, her brain playing tricks of the wish on her—she saw Iain Carnegie on the sofa across the room, in a burgundy dinner jacket, grinning and singing that all their troubles would soon be out of sight.

Ridley cracked a smile, raised her glass, and began to sing softly through the pain of her broken rib.

Tomorrow, a new Primavera violin would arrive at the house of Lexi Rapp's aunt, where the family gathered for Christmas. It would have an anonymous note on it, "For Lexi. A replacement."

*Paid for with the blood money of Marc Pearson, courtesy of Lianna Powell's thirty pieces of silver.*

But the first Christmas present Ridley herself got would be a phone call.

## NEW YORK CITY, NEW YORK

From the outside, the four-story brownstone looked like any other on the millionaire's row, but for the initials *MP* cut into the stone beside the front door.

To Odie's great surprise, it was not nearly as secure as it should have been.

Breaching the service entrance had been a simple electronic lock pick. He'd brought the right partner for the job, a mildly autistic systems savant named Will that he'd busted once in London.

They quickly bypassed the alarm that beeped a warning countdown and moved in.

The mansion that loomed before them was extravagant in every way. There was gold and marble and brass and velvet everywhere they looked. Crystal chandeliers sparkled overhead.

The place was ghostly quiet. Marc Pearson had so many houses around the world that he'd leave one for months at a time. Since all this one required was a daily maintenance check, no one lived there during the down time.

Odie and Will went hunting.

It didn't take nearly as long as they'd anticipated. On the second floor at the end of a hall was a plain door.

"Mate," said Odie, nodding to the keypad by the handle.

He held a flashlight on it as Will stepped up, shook out his fingers, and opened his small toolkit. It took him two minutes to hear the door handle click: *unlocked.*

Inside was a wall of little video screens, all a dull powerless gray. The simple console in front of them was a standard security surveillance layout.

In one corner of this room was a stack of computer towers. In the other was a small stack of boxes.

"Get on those," Odie went to the boxes as he motioned Will to go for the computers.

He opened the first one atop the stack. Inside were rows of small hard drives. Holding the flashlight in his mouth, he thumbed through them.

"Ah, yes, you bastard. To hell with your codenames. You *labeled* them."

He pulled one out to hand to Will, who plugged it into his tablet. He drew up the video files and hit *play*.

Odie leaned in closer, wanting to be sure his eyes were really seeing what he thought he was seeing.

"Oh, my God," hissed Will. "Is that—is that..."

Odie began to laugh. "Oh, ho-ho-ho. Oh, my filthy Uncle Scrooge..."

He pulled out his mobile and dialed.

### ROXBURGHSHIRE, SCOTLAND

Ridley excused herself into the foyer as the party behind her was swinging to "The Man with the Bag."

She picked up the incoming call on her cell.

"Are you in?" she said.

"We got it," came Odie's voice over the line. "Got it all. There's loads here. Dozens of people—all code names but they got nothin' to hide behind on these tapes. But most of 'em...I don't wanna watch 'em again, boss."

"I know," she said, her voice hardening. "Put 'em away. Box them up. Soon as I have the drives, I'll wire you the money."

*The rest of Lianna Powell's fee.*

"Yeah, I copy," said Odie. "This everything you wanted, then? 'Cause this place has some pricey *stuff* in it."

"I don't want anything else. Grab yourself something if you want extra compensation, but then get outta there fast."

"A'right then. Merry Christmas, boss."

"Merry Christmas."

Ridley heard Diane Bellingsworth in the parlor begin to sing "O, Holy Night." She hung up and stood in the hall for a moment, alone.

*Otto. Tavvie. Lexi.*

*Iain.*

*For you, I'll destroy them all.*

"Merry Christmas, scumbags of the world," she murmured to herself.

She turned back to the light of the parlor.

# ACKNOWLEDGMENTS

To everyone I've thanked in a previous book, you are all here as well.

To my Savior.
 To my family.
 To Julie, who cared for me as a baby, and thirty-seven years later welcomed me to her home country of Scotland. Thank you for the shortbread, for the baby photos you kept all these years, for a book you knew I'd love, but most of all, for sharing your memories of my loved ones.
 To Kyle, whose friendship has endured such time and distance. Your steady streams of puppy photos were injections of pure joy as I wrote the darkest parts of this book.
 To Salome. It has been a privilege and a delight to share in your faith, wit, and vision for all these years.
 To Mike S. whose passion and thoughtfulness have been the foundation for an unexpected but priceless friendship.
 To Carolina. Who would have thought that an impromptu photoshoot in a dorm stairwell would lead to one of the most wonderful friendships of a lifetime? You are a treasure.
 To my friends and training partners in jiu-jitsu who have seen me through tribulations and triumphs, and heartily celebrated this book thing. You've made my life richer. Nate, Laura, Emily, Ryan, Dave S., Devin, Jeff G., Travis, Dave C., Todd, Jim T., Crystal, Kieran...the list only grows. I admire and appreciate you all.

To Matt D., "the most interesting man in the world," who championed my first book at every opportunity. I hope that Ridley honors the courageous women that you've known in your own life.

To Pete, the best rapper I know. You were there for me every day in a time when I was bleeding grief. I'll never forget it.

To Shannon, whose profound faith brought me to befriend and love the people of Haiti. Your joys have been my joys, and your sorrows have been my sorrows.

Thank you to Christine Reynolds at the Library of Westminster Abbey for indulging the most detailed of questions about the royal burial vaults.

Thank you to T.R. Hendricks, whose tactical insight was earned at a price I'll never understand. Your support and expertise have been a gift.

To the people of Scotland, you are fairly magnificent. Thank you for the hospitality, the castles, my ancestry, and all the drinks.

And for E, who is still — always — alive in everything I write.

www.ingramcontent.com/pod-product-compliance
Ingram Content Group UK Ltd.
Pitfield, Milton Keynes, MK11 3LW, UK
UKHW041830120125
453503UK00004B/56